PRAISE FOR JENNIFER PROBST

"For a sexy, fun-filled, warmhearted read, look no further than Jennifer Probst!"

—Jill Shalvis, *New York Times* bestselling author

"Jennifer Probst is an absolute auto-buy author for me."

—J. Kenner, *New York Times* bestselling author

"Jennifer Probst knows how to bring the swoons and the sexy."

—Amy E. Reichert, author of *The Coincidence of Coconut Cake*

"As always, Jennifer Probst never fails to deliver romance that sizzles and has a way of tugging those emotional heartstrings."

—*Four Chicks Flipping Pages*

"Jennifer Probst's books remind me of delicious chocolate cake. Bursting with flavor, decadently rich . . . very satisfying."

—*Love Affair with an e-Reader*

"There's a reason Probst is the gold standard in contemporary romance."

—Lauren Layne, *New York Times* bestselling author

PRAISE FOR *FOREVER IN CAPE MAY*

"Probst's entertaining take on the friends-to-lovers trope hits all the right beats, enhanced by well-shaded characters readers will immediately love. This irresistible finale does not disappoint."

—*Publishers Weekly*

PRAISE FOR *LOVE ON BEACH AVENUE*

"Probst (*All Roads Lead to You*) opens her Sunshine Sisters series with an effervescent rom-com. The characters leap off the page, the love story is perfectly paced, and an adorable dog named Lucy adds charm. Readers will eagerly await the next in the series."

—*Publishers Weekly*

"The perfect enemies-to-lovers, best-friend's-brother romance! I laughed, smiled, cheered, cried a few tears, and loved Carter and Avery!"

—*Two Book Pushers*

"*Love on Beach Avenue* is a three-layer wedding cake of best-friend's-brother, enemies-to-lovers, and just plain fun. Another yummy confection by Jennifer Probst!"

—Laurelin Paige, *New York Times* bestselling author

"I could feel the ocean breeze on my face as I turned the pages. *Love on Beach Avenue* is chock-full with magic ingredients: a dreamy seaside, a starchy hero with a tiny dog, sparkling wit, and fabulous female friendship—a must-read romance!"

—Evie Dunmore, author of *Bringing Down the Duke*

"*Love on Beach Avenue* is the perfect enemies-to-lovers romance with well-developed characters, sexy banter, and so many swoon-worthy moments! Jennifer Probst knocked it out of the park with this book! Looking forward to the rest of the series!"

—Monica Murphy, *New York Times* bestselling author

"Fantastic start to a brand-new series from Jennifer Probst! *Love on Beach Avenue* is beautifully heartfelt and epically romantic!"

—Emma Chase, *New York Times* bestselling author

PRAISE FOR *ALL ROADS LEAD TO YOU*

"Funny, sexy, emotional, and full of scenes that make your heart swell and the tears drop, *All Roads Lead to You* is a beautiful story set in hometown America and one you will want to read again and again."

—*A Midlife Wife*

"Harper's story was everything I wanted it to be and so much more."

—*Becca the Bibliophile*

"Ms. Probst has a way of writing that I can't help but be 100 percent invested from the first page!"

—*Franci's Fabulous Reads*

"Jennifer Probst expertly blends humor, sexiness, and emotion, keeping the reader delightfully addicted. She entwines these elements, evoking a hope that fate will align and bring love and happiness between two characters that seem to be at once perfect yet ill-fitted for one another. I enjoyed this story; its plot, backdrop, characters, and romance gave me the warm fuzzies."

—*TJ Loves Books*

"Jennifer Probst shines when she talks about her animal rescues in real life, and the saying is true: write what you know, and it will always be the best story. The same goes for this one; it's one of her best stories to date."

—*AJ's Book re-Marks*

"JP writes beautiful words, and I just loved this story. There was enough action, adventure, passion, and swoon factor, not to mention romance."

—*The Guide to Romance Novels*

"A read that will not only fill your emotional romance need but will fill your heart with the fulfilling need to care for a goat that needed to be hugged and be besties with a horse to feel safe."

—*The Book Fairy Reviews*

PRAISE FOR *A BRAND NEW ENDING*

"*A Brand New Ending* was a mega-adorable and moving second-chance romance! I just adored everything about it! Run to your nearest Amazon for your own Kyle—this one is mine!"

—*BJ's Book Blog*

"Don't miss another winner from Jennifer Probst."

—Mary from *USA TODAY*'s *Happy Ever After*

PRAISE FOR
THE START OF SOMETHING GOOD

"The must-have summer romance read of 2018!"

—*Gina's Bookshelf*

"Achingly romantic, touching, realistic, and just plain beautiful, *The Start of Something Good* lingers with you long after you turn the last page."

—Katy Evans, *New York Times* bestselling author

Meant to Be

OTHER BOOKS BY JENNIFER PROBST

The Sunshine Sisters Series

Love on Beach Avenue

Temptation on Ocean Drive

Forever in Cape May

The Stay Series

The Start of Something Good

A Brand New Ending

All Roads Lead to You

Something Just Like This

Begin Again

Nonfiction

Write Naked: A Bestseller's Secrets to Writing Romance &
Navigating the Path to Success

Write True: A Bestseller's Guide to Writing Craft &
Achieving Success in the Romance Industry

Women's Fiction

Our Italian Summer

The Secret Love Letters of Olivia Moretti

The Billionaire Builders Series

Everywhere and Every Way

Any Time, Any Place

Somehow, Some Way

All or Nothing at All

The Searching For . . . Series

Searching for Someday
Searching for Perfect
Searching for Beautiful
Searching for Always
Searching for You
Searching for Mine
Searching for Disaster

The Marriage to a Billionaire Series

The Marriage Bargain
The Marriage Trap
The Marriage Mistake
The Marriage Merger
The Book of Spells
The Marriage Arrangement

The Steele Brothers Series

Catch Me
Play Me
Dare Me
Beg Me
Reveal Me

The Sex on the Beach Series

Beyond Me
Chasing Me

The Hot in the Hamptons Series

Summer Sins

Stand-Alone Novels

Dante's Fire
Executive Seduction
All the Way
The Holiday Hoax
The Grinch of Starlight Bend
The Charm of You

Meant to Be

JENNIFER PROBST

 Montlake

Published by Montlake, Seattle

www.apub.com

Amazon, the Amazon logo, and Montlake are trademarks of Amazon.com, Inc., or its affiliates.

ISBN-13: 9781542034807
ISBN-10: 1542034809

Cover design by Caroline Teagle Johnson

Cover photography by Regina Wamba of MaeIDesign.com

Printed in the United States of America

For Danielle Nelson . . .
It was fate that brought our families together, but it was
friendship that bound us.
Thanks for being such an important part of my life.

Friendship is unnecessary, like philosophy, like art . . . It has no survival value; rather it is one of those things that give value to survival.

—C. S. Lewis, *The Four Loves*

Do not be afraid; our fate

Cannot be taken from us; it is a gift.

—Dante Alighieri, *Inferno*

Accept the things to which fate binds you, and love the people with whom fate brings you together, but do so with all your heart.

—Marcus Aurelius, *Meditations*

Prologue

Chiara Kennedy watched the man cross the room toward her, his gaze full of purpose as he closed the distance between them.

He exuded a sexiness she'd noticed immediately. Thick coal-black hair begged for a woman's fingers. His body was lean and graceful when he moved, muscled without being jacked up. There was an innate confidence that buzzed around him, but Chiara had dismissed him as too arrogant by the crowd of tittering females surrounding him like a thickly coated barrier she had no desire to penetrate. He had seemed to be holding court for his admirers and interested in recruiting new members.

Chiara managed to snag a drink—the bartender was an old friend from high school—then find a spot so she could survey the dance floor and people-watch. Her friends had stood her up due to a work emergency, so she figured she'd finish her drink and amuse herself by watching love connections come, go, or explode on a busy Friday night.

She didn't expect him to chase her.

Breathlessness gripped her as he leaned over, those gunmetal eyes piercing her with a strange intensity. Chiara waited for the big line he hoped to dazzle her with.

He raised a hand with a smile. "Bartender? Can I get three cosmos sent to the table behind me, please?" He threw a few bills on the bar. "Appreciate it."

She blinked, her pride a bit stung. But then she couldn't help the tiny laugh that escaped. Served her right for thinking he was coming to hit on her when he had a full table of women waiting for his return.

Sexy guy cocked his head, turning his attention to her. "What's so funny?"

She tried not to stare at his mouth with those thinly defined lips. "Oh, nothing."

His brow lifted. "Sure? I could use a laugh tonight."

"I thought you were coming over to hit on me."

Delight skated across his features. "Did I have a shot?"

"Depends on what you would've said."

He laughed then, full and deep, like he was a man who did it often. "Can I try?"

This time, she arched a brow. "You're buying drinks for your many admirers. Even you must admit you already have enough women to handle."

Chiara waited for a defense, excuses, or a smooth comeback. Instead, he gave a sigh. "To be honest, they kind of swooped in and I felt pressured to stay. I don't like to hurt anyone's feelings. I'm sending them drinks to lessen the blow."

She considered his statement and wondered why she believed him. "That's your big escape plan?"

"They really like cosmos. They'd had a few rounds before they found me."

Her lip quirked. Damn, she liked him. That rarely happened with men at clubs. "Okay, go ahead. Give me your best try."

Immediately, he turned to face her and stuck out his hand. "Hi, I'm Sebastian Ryder. It's nice to meet you."

Hmm. Maybe he wasn't a player after all. "Hi, I'm Chiara Kennedy." Automatically, she offered her own hand, and his grip was warm and strong, without being overwhelming.

"I'd offer to buy you a drink, but it looks like that's fresh."

"Yeah, it is." She liked his smile. No fake-white teeth gleaming from daily whitening flashed back at her. She noticed his left incisor was chipped. "Come here often?"

This time Sebastian laughed, and she couldn't help joining in. The scent of ocean waves from his cologne teased her nostrils. She fought the urge to move closer and take a big whiff. "Actually, no. I came with some friends from work, but they took off. You?"

"Got stood up. My girlfriends had a work emergency, so I figured I'd grab a drink before I left."

"Then our meeting was meant to be."

She shook her head in mock displeasure. "You were doing so well up to that part."

He threw up his hands. "I promise, no canned lines. You make me want to be a better man."

A chuckle escaped her lips. She studied his face in the flashing lights. He was even more attractive up close. The square jaw, Roman nose, and heavy brows softened the pretty-boy good looks. But it was the easy charm and warmth he exuded that kept her talking. Like he didn't take himself too seriously. Too many men had a goal to win every conversation; they forgot to just enjoy the process. "Hmm, you're funny. Unless that's your big plan—pretend to be understated and genuine to stand out."

Sebastian cocked his head. Surprise danced in his eyes. "You don't trust me not to be one of *those* guys."

"Which ones?"

"The ones who pretend to be everything until you find out too late they're nothing."

A small sigh broke from her lips. "It's hard to separate the truth from the lies lately. All this surface niceness. Getting to know you via a perfect snapshot and blurb written like a marketing hook. I don't know, I just wish . . ."

He leaned in. "What?"

"I wish just once I could meet someone and skip all the bullshit. Just be real and raw." She rolled her eyes. "But that would scare every man off faster than a stage-one clinger."

Something flared to life in that smoky gaze, and for an instant, an electric chemistry shot between them, making her eyes widen. She'd never experienced any type of attraction or pull as fast as this before, and it threw her off-balance. Even more so after he made his announcement.

"Let's do it."

"Do what?"

His grin was slow and sure. "You and me. Let's get real."

A laugh escaped her lips. "Oh, sure. It sounds good, but you'd bail. Or lie. Or pretend you're this deep, artsy type who craves a soul connection when you're really holding back."

His face turned serious, and her heart banged against her chest when he uttered his next words. "I don't lie, Chiara."

Goose bumps broke out on her skin. She was suddenly hot and cold at the same time and wondered what it would be like to press her lips against his, in the shadows, just for a moment. "I don't know you, so how could I tell?"

"We'd both have to take a leap. I'm willing if you are."

It was an insane proposition. She didn't know him. She didn't even know if she wanted to do it. But a force inside her reared up, something bigger than her rational brain—an instinct to allow him to really see her—and she was nodding in agreement. "Okay."

Their gazes locked for a long moment. "How about we go outside? It's quieter."

She followed his lead, exiting the back door where the open patio lured various groups together, smoking, surrounding heaters in the cool late-autumn air. They snagged two chairs on the side, away from the activity, and settled in close, knees touching, the night sky overhead exploding with stars. "How do we start?" Chiara asked.

"Q and A. Have you ever been in love?"

She couldn't help but jerk back at the direct question. "Wow, that's right to the point."

"I'm a dive into the cold water type of guy. Do you like to go in one limb at a time?"

She shook her head. "No, I hate indecision."

"Me, too. Gonna answer the question?"

"No. I mean, I haven't been in love before. You?"

"Yes. Dated her throughout college and figured she was the one. I think I was the girl in the relationship. She broke up with me and I lost time on the couch. Went on a diet of alcohol and ice cream."

She bit her lip to keep from laughing. "Boys eat Ben & Jerry's and drink wine after breakups, too?"

Sebastian shuddered. "God, no. I eat Häagen-Dazs and drink beer."

"You were into her?" Chiara probed his gaze, looking deep. The surprise hit full force when she spotted the sadness.

"I really was. Now I'm thirty years old, but I haven't been in love like that again. I want to find my person. Everyone says I should be enjoying my single life, but I think all these things I'm doing would be better with someone."

Her chest tightened at the honesty laced through his words. "At least you're trying."

"It's weird. A girl wanting to get married everyone understands. But a guy? They call him a loser, a wimp, or even worse? A beta."

She threw her head back and laughed. "I doubt you're a beta, Sebastian."

"Do you relate to any of this?"

"Honestly? I'm focused on work now."

"Cushy corner office with a view?"

She made a noise of disgust. "Being trapped at a desk in an office would kill something in me. I feel like I'm the opposite—every night I dream about flying. I'm over the clouds and looking down at the world, and I'm happy. But then I begin to realize it won't last, so I freak out and have a panic attack."

"Because you're going to fall?"

"No, because I'm afraid I'll get stuck somewhere."

Sebastian inclined his chin, his face thoughtful while he seemed to ponder this. "What will happen if you get stuck?"

"Nothing." The word fell into the space between them, devoid of emotion. It was then she took a step back from this game that felt a bit too real and waved a hand in the air. "It's funny, right? I need to analyze some of these dreams. What's one of your recurring ones?"

He ignored her, leaning in so the space between them shrank. "Don't back off now, Chiara."

She bristled. "I'm not!"

"What will happen if you get stuck?" he asked again.

This time, a shudder racked through her. The knowledge burned the tip of her tongue, but she'd never spoken it aloud before, especially not to someone she'd just met. But his gaze was steady, and calm, and somehow she wanted to tell the truth and be safe with him, this man sitting with her under the stars.

"If I get stuck, I'll never have the life I dreamed of. I'll never have more."

Chiara waited for him to wince at her greed and shallowness, but Sebastian slowly smiled like she'd given him a precious gift. "Makes perfect sense to me."

She smiled back. And knew he was special. And that he could be trusted.

They talked for another hour. It had been a long time since a man seemed to not only listen but hear her.

"Want to get something to eat?" he asked suddenly.

Chiara hesitated. She'd already sensed they wanted different things, and that romantically they'd never work. Yet, a strong connection hummed between them, almost as if they'd met before in another time, another life. She didn't want the evening with him to end. "McDonald's? Burgers, fries, and a shake?"

"Hell yes. Let's go."

They got the food and headed out to June's Bluff, a cliff overlooking the Hudson River with the jagged edges of Hook Mountain sprawled out before them. Chiara loved the quaint upstate town of Nyack and its close location to Manhattan. It was a nice mix of city and small town, and she enjoyed the stunning views as they ate. They talked about everything, sharing secrets and hidden dreams and the monsters in the closet that sprang out only when they thought they were safe. She told him about her distant relationship with her parents. He told her about his asshole father, who'd left when he was young.

Dawn drew near. Light leached away the darkness bit by bit. Her bare feet were propped up on the dashboard of his car. The eighties station blasted rock ballads from the decade they both agreed was the very best. A cool breeze drifted in from the open windows.

"I want to kiss you," Sebastian said suddenly.

Chiara turned, her heart leaping like a Thoroughbred at the gate. God, she wanted it, too. Wanted to feel that mouth on hers, and fall into this connection that had only grown stronger as the hours passed. But the time they'd spent together had given her a startling revelation that couldn't be changed.

They weren't meant to be.

She knew this in her soul, as much as she felt the alluring hum beckoning her to ignore the logic. Sebastian craved love, family, children. Chiara needed the open road and wanderlust in her heart. She had to be free of entanglements and commitments so she could do everything she ever dreamed. Maybe one day she'd change.

But not now. Maybe not ever.

"We can't," she said softly. "It would never work."

He groaned, his head resting back against the leather seat. "I've never felt like this before. It could work."

She smiled because, though he said the words, she sensed he knew the truth, also. "We'd hurt each other, and then we'd never have this. And this night, I'll remember forever."

The sun crept up over the horizon. Blazing yellow and orange and pink hues flooded the sky. Slowly, he moved his hand, and their pinkies brushed together. Peter Gabriel's song "In Your Eyes" belted out from the speakers.

When the sun was fully up, Sebastian drove her back to the club.

She got out of the car, shading her eyes from the sharp beam of light cutting across her vision. "Thanks for everything," she said.

He grinned then, a bit lopsided, that chipped tooth confirming it was all real. And Chiara knew she'd remember this moment forever, this man, who somehow had been meant to come into her life for a little while and allow her to open up.

Even though she'd been the one to make the decision, Chiara dreamed of Sebastian often. She imagined running into him again one day, wondering if their lives might intersect in a different way, and it filled her with excitement.

Until the day her best friend, Rory, introduced him as her boyfriend.

Afterward, she promised herself to never think about that night again.

Chapter One

It was a kick-ass day for a funeral.

The skies wept. Sebastian Ryder stood apart from the group and surveyed the mass of mourners crowded around the grave. The sleet pelted his face with tiny ice balls. God, he wished he were cold. Wished he felt anything other than the numb, empty void in his gut. Like some awful chick flick—*Iron Magnolias* or something—the scene unfolded in perfect movie symmetry, from the storm clouds to the minister's calm voice to the neat line of perfectly pressed black suits and raincoats blocking his view of the elegantly designed coffin. Couples linked hands; women sobbed; men comforted.

He remained alone.

His wife's posse stayed tightly pressed together, hands linked in grief and solidarity, like a barrier blocking the casket from the prying looks of outsiders. Funny, Ryder felt like one right now. An outsider. Even though he'd been married to Rory for three years, it was as if she had always truly belonged to her friends—the three women from her childhood who were more like sisters. Maybe they'd always owned a part of her he'd never been able to claim, and that's why he stood back, allowing them the final goodbye.

He took stock of each of the women through the gaze of an outsider. Malia's long, tight braids spilled down her back, her face tilted upward, refusing to flinch from the sky's outburst. She seemed to be listening intently to the minister's words, maybe trying to find rationalization in the idea of something beyond reality. As Malia was the most logical of the group, Ryder figured she'd struggle the most to understand the sudden loss of one of her best friends.

Tessa held up the end of the line with a fierce frown, obviously pissed off at the whole ceremony. Anger vibrated in waves from her tiny figure, practically sparking off the ends of her wild, tawny curls, now frizzing to epic heights under the sleet. Her volatility was tempered only by her fierce loyalty and love for his wife and the crew she stood with.

Finally, the minister wrapped up his sermon, made the sign of the cross, and nodded to the woman in the middle. With slow, graceful motions, Chiara stepped up behind the casket and looked over the crowd of mourners. She held no umbrella. Vibrant red hair blew and tossed in the wind. Freckled skin. A generous mouth, with lips no Botox needle ever touched because she'd never needed it. And the crescent-shaped beauty mark on her right cheek. She was clad from head to toe in a dark raincoat, leather boots, and gloves, refusing to duck her head against the harsh sleet.

Wide-set eyes the color of warm cognac reflected a raw sadness that punched Ryder straight through the gut. It was the way he should feel right now, in this moment, instead of . . . nothing.

Her voice lifted above the pounding of the rain like an opera singer reaching out to the back row with invitation. "Rory Veronica Ryder was more than my friend. She was a doting daughter to her beloved father. She was a devoted, loving wife. She was the founder of one of the most successful female-run companies in the state. But most of all, she was a woman who loved fiercely—even when it wasn't deserved."

The comment sliced and drew blood, which ran freely. Too bad he still didn't feel the pain.

"Her heart was pure, and her loss is bigger than any of us as individuals. It's a loss to the entire world."

Another wound burst open.

"Heaven is lucky to have you, Rory. You've set an example for all of us left behind. I only hope we can try to live up to it."

A quiet murmur rose from the crowd. Someone sobbed. "We love you."

Chiara put two fingers to her lips and held them out over the coffin. One by one, each person in the crowd duplicated the gesture.

He ached to drop his head and hide, but Ryder was transfixed as Chiara's gaze slowly swept the crowd and caught his. The breath left his lungs like a sharply deflated balloon.

The connection they always fought between them caught, held, and simmered. But there was a new expression marking her elegant features, one he rarely saw and wished he never had to.

Hate.

Her lips tightened and she deliberately turned her back on him, walking away.

Time blurred. The ceremony ended. He shook hands and nodded appropriately to the people who swarmed him with condolences. Finally, the crowd dispersed into smaller, tight groups as people moved toward their cars.

Ryder remained underneath the large oak tree. The ice burned his skin raw, and water dripped over his collar, trickling down his neck and back in freezing rivulets. He stared at his wife's coffin until a hand on his arm jolted him to awareness.

"Son." The voice was gentle, but rough. "We're all going to the café to eat. Talk. Come with us."

He blinked and stared at Rory's father. She'd referred to Mike as a gentle giant, quick of temper, quick to forgive and laugh it off. Obviously uncomfortable in a suit and tie, he had a towering frame and gruff speech that always reminded Ryder of a protective bear, especially with his only daughter. Mike owned the local diner in town, which had served as the center of all their social gatherings for years. Ryder knew he should go, at least to honor Rory's memory, but he couldn't face anyone now.

He knew his limits.

He shook his head, trying to force a smile. "Thanks, Mike, but I can't."

The man frowned, hesitating. "You sure? I don't think you should be alone."

A humorless laugh threatened, but Ryder bit it back. That's exactly what he deserved. "No, I need to be home. Have some time. I hope you understand."

Mike nodded, a deep-seated grief etched in his craggy features. "Yeah, I do. I'll check on you later."

Ryder watched his father-in-law walk away, climb into his car, and drive off.

He remained alone. Like he wanted. Like he deserved.

After all, he had killed his wife. There was nothing left anymore.

It was a long time before he moved.

~

He didn't even have the respect to show up.

Chiara squeezed into the booth and tried to tamp down the bubbling anger ready to boil. It was easier to focus on her resentment toward Sebastian, who not only refused to speak at Rory's funeral but also had the gall to skip out on the funeral meal. Like he was better than all of them, separating himself from even his father-in-law, pretending Rory would have wanted him to hole up alone and ignore the people who loved her.

On cue, Mike dumped a platter of cheese fries and assorted wraps on the table. A dish towel hung from his belt loop, and he'd donned an apron over his funeral suit, not even stopping to change. A piece of her heart broke off as she gazed into his familiar face, finding an emptiness there that would never be filled. "Eat up while it's hot, girls."

"Stop serving and join us," Chiara invited, patting the empty seat where Rory would have been. "There's plenty of help back there."

His smile held no humor. "Like to keep busy, you know that. I can't—" He broke off, choking on the words. "I can't be still right now. Not when there's customers to serve."

Malia shot her a worried look, but Chiara's tone was easy. "Don't blame you, but no need to keep it together. There are no customers here. Only friends."

"Damn right," Tessa said, grabbing a fry and stuffing it in her mouth. "Want some company tonight, Mike? I can camp out on the couch and introduce you to the world of romance series on Netflix. There's a ton to pick from."

He snorted in disgust, but Chiara caught the appreciative light in his pale blue eyes. After his wife died of cancer, Mike threw all his energy into raising Rory and serving his customers. He'd taken the group under his protective wing and become the den father. The girls were just as fiercely protective of Mike and checked on him consistently. "Appreciate it, but I got a date with a bottle of whiskey and my bed. Can I get a rain check?"

"Always," Tessa said, pushing back the wild curls springing around her face.

They watched him head back to the kitchen, where he was most comfortable. Chiara bet the man would stay here most of the night, choosing the comfort of his second home rather than the one where Rory had once slept.

Mike's Place was a cornerstone of Main Street, a cross between a fancy café and a diner, with roomy red booths, an old-fashioned countertop that served ice cream sodas and sundaes, and the familiar black-and-white checkered floor. An antique jukebox still worked, but tonight remained silent. The scents of grease, meat, and coffee drifted in the air, swarming with comfort. It was a place with good food and family connections—the Cheers of Nyack, New York, without the hard-drinking atmosphere, though Mike was known to serve craft beer, local wine, and a mean margarita when tacos were the special of the day.

Malia leaned in. "I'm worried about him but don't want to push. Think he'll be okay?"

"No," Tessa said bluntly. "None of us will. At least, not for a long time."

"I think he needs to be alone more than he needs us for now," Chiara said. "We're gonna have to take this day by day."

They sat in broody silence. She was so tightly wound with emotion, Chiara felt like one wrong word or action and she'd explode. Rory wasn't just the fourth member of their crew. She was the natural leader and driving force behind Quench, the company they'd created. She'd been the one to push them ahead, structuring the business, her creative vision massive with ambition. Sometimes, Chiara wondered if they'd just learned how to go along for the ride when Rory had an idea or a plan.

What would they do without her? She squeezed her eyes shut to fight back tears.

"Don't," Tessa warned, pushing the platter of food her way. "If you lose it now, I won't ever stop. We need to talk and regroup before we collapse. And Mike needs us to be strong in here. Rory would hate the idea of us weeping for her in our sacred booth."

Chiara gave a sharp nod and swallowed back the searing pain, lodging it safely in her gut. Mike's Place was more than a spot to get food or coffee. It was the place they'd grown up in—the safe center in a storm of teen drama, then college stress and boy troubles, and finally, the setting where they created Quench from the ground up. Tessa was right. She would not wail and cry here. "Sorry, you're right. But I can't eat now."

"Take some home for later," Malia said, reaching across the table to squeeze her hand. "I'm not hungry, either."

"Bitches," Tessa murmured good-naturedly. She looked down at her petite frame, ripe with curves that stopped men dead on the street. "Why can't I not be hungry during horrific situations?"

"I'd rather have comfort in carbs right now," Malia said. But she took a fry and chewed halfheartedly, not wanting Tessa to eat alone. "You think we should check on Ryder?"

Chiara couldn't help it. A slight bitterness leaked into her voice. "Obviously, he's fine."

Tessa lifted a generous brow. "Doubt it. He looked like a robot."

"Exactly. Don't you find it weird he didn't want to even speak at the funeral? Or do a quick drop-in here, at Rory's favorite place in the world?"

"What are you saying?" Malia asked. Her brown eyes looked troubled. "That he doesn't care?"

Chiara blew out a breath. "Not really. I mean, I don't know. I feel like since we got the news, we've all been reeling, but he seemed to withdraw from all the things she loved. He's been completely MIA."

Tessa shrugged. "Everyone grieves differently."

"Yeah, but what if he's almost relieved he doesn't have to interact with us anymore? That he can finally hide in his isolated hole and pretend none of us exists?"

Her friends stared at her, shock on their faces. Tessa finally shook her head. "That's a messed-up thing to say."

Oh God, it was. But it came from a deeper place of knowledge, a secret she'd kept from her friends. Still, insulting Sebastian because of her mental crap wasn't fair to any of them. "I know. I didn't mean it. I'm just . . . angry."

"We all are. There's not even someone to blame, or hate, or try to wreak revenge on," Malia said. "The guy had a damn heart attack and crossed into her lane."

Chiara shuddered at the image. Rory driving home late from work, probably blasting pop music and singing off-key. The guy getting chest pains and passing out, careening around the same bend Rory took every day, the route embedded in pure muscle memory. The screeching of metal twisting and melting as it met and erupted.

In one heart-stopping instant, two people were gone.

It was an image she kept replaying even though she hadn't seen it. They were quiet for a moment, listening to the chatter around them, the clink of forks scraping across plates, the hiss of hot coffee and grease from the grill.

Malia rubbed her temple. "I wish I could stop thinking about it."

"Me, too. We need a distraction. Let's talk about work," Tessa said, her voice breaking.

Chiara took a sip of coffee drowned in cream and nodded. Quench was Rory's true passion. Talking about the business they'd created together seemed fitting. She could almost hear her friend's voice whispering in her ear, *"Ladies, get your acts together and make a plan. No plans, no goals, no success."*

"We need to call a meeting first thing Monday morning," Malia said. "Talk to the staff. I know we put out a statement to our subscribers, but we need to do more. Rory was so close to our employees."

"A memorial of some type," Chiara said. "A testament to how Quench was started and everything Rory did to help it succeed. Her vision for how she saw the company growing. It can serve as motivation and a tribute to the company."

"I like it," Tessa said. "We're going to be under intense scrutiny these next months. That's my biggest concern. Losing our CEO and editor in chief will have the sharks circling."

Tessa was right. Profits had risen last year, and they were entering a tricky phase. Too much growth too fast was dangerous without the proper foundation. No one had imagined how Quench would explode within the first three years, forcing them to hire more people and take on more responsibility. Each of them had dug into their main roles, which played to their strengths, but Rory was the critical piece involved in all of them. She'd been able to delegate assignments, organize teams, and oversee the entire organization. Chiara wondered if they could ever fill in the gaps.

"We can always promote from the inside," Malia said, tapping her manicured nail against the edge of the table. "But personally, no one has stood out to me to step into such a big role."

"We can hire from the outside," Chiara suggested. "Companies do that all the time when they're in flux. Get a headhunter to comb through the big names in the beauty industry."

"We're more than beauty, though," Tessa said. "That's been the problem—everyone keeps trying to pigeonhole Quench into one segment of the market, but we're so much more. We believed in our vision, and finally, the world is starting to catch on."

Malia sighed. "Remember that first discussion we had, right here, in this booth?"

The memory cut through, bittersweet with a dash of melancholy. Six years ago. Eating omelets on a Sunday morning, recovering from a drunken night of too much partying. All of them were trapped in jobs going nowhere but paying the bills—editorial assistants, staff writers, and the never-ending sales jobs.

Rory had interrupted the inane chatter. "Aren't you all tired of working for other people who don't appreciate you?"

Tessa had snorted. "Um, yeah. But the job market is pure suckage. I'm stuck."

"What if we opened our own business?"

They'd stared at Rory in surprise. Chiara had figured they were just talking shit. "Sure, that'd be beast. But we'd need a bunch of things— mainly an actual company we want to run."

They all should have realized Rory had been planning her talk for a while. She wasn't one to jump in without having a solid plan and answers to all the questions that would pop up. "We're doing it already. Self-care for women."

Malia cocked her head. "I'm stuck in a corporate finance job. How is that self-care for women?"

"Because you advise female clients all the time about their financial portfolios. You sell products that help families be prepared. That's teaching self-care." Rory jabbed her finger at Tessa. "You do makeovers for women at the department store. You make them all see the beauty inside of them." Finally, she turned to Chiara. "And you're bigger than a staff writer. You research and deliver articles about women's health—physical, emotional, and mental. It's all self-care."

"I never thought of it like that," Chiara murmured.

"Exactly. Now, I propose we pull all of it together and create a company dedicated to women."

"In the beauty industry?" Tessa asked.

"No, so much more. Think bigger. We cater to all the aspects of a woman's life: beauty, fashion, relationships, and creativity. We create a website with specific departments that address things like finances, career, women's rights, sexual health—all the topics that are important and constantly changing. And we stop this wasteful commuting to Manhattan and work from here."

"Work where?" Tessa asked. "On our crappy laptops at Mike's?"

Rory gave a slow grin. "You know that giant Victorian house off Main Street?" They nodded. "It's for sale. That will be our headquarters."

Chiara laughed even as a seed of excitement sprouted inside. Rory had that effect on people—she believed in things so hard, she got other people to as well.

"We can afford it," Rory continued. "Dad will cosign for the house on a thirty-year loan, and the payments will be cheap if we split it four ways. He knows everyone in construction and already reached out to some of his connections. We'd be able to renovate at cost. We'll need a small-business loan, but if we generate most of the content ourselves, we can get away with not hiring many people until we gain our footing."

"This is crazy," Malia murmured, but Chiara noticed she looked intrigued. They'd talked about starting their own business on and off for years but never had a vision.

But Rory did.

They stayed in the booth for three hours. Mike brought out a notebook, and they sketched out figures, creative ideas, and what each of their responsibilities would be. They crafted a mission statement and an overall vision of what they wanted the company to be. Rory suggested the name Quench, and they all heartily agreed. By the time they'd left, all of them were on board to take the greatest risk of their lives.

Chiara shook off the memory. God, they'd been so young and passionate and hungry. Why was life so cruel? All their dreams for Quench were about to come true, but Rory wasn't there to see it happen.

Tessa pushed away the fries and half-eaten wraps. "Rory's position was key to the company, and our next move is critical. We can't trust someone from the outside." She glanced at both of them. "It has to be one of us."

"But who?" Chiara asked. "Anyone want to volunteer?"

Tessa laughed. "Don't look at me. I'd suck at it—I don't have the gift of seeing the big picture, which is critical to Rory's role. I can certainly take on more than the beauty, fashion, and advice features. But you know organization isn't my strong suit."

Unfortunately, Chiara agreed. Tessa was known to show up for the wrong meetings even when they were marked correctly on her calendar. Her assistant deserved every spa gift card she got for trying to keep Tessa on track.

"I can't do it, either," Malia stated, her shoulders set back. "Sure, I can sell anything, and I'm a numbers girl, but leadership over the entire organization isn't my style. I'd choke."

Both of her friends stared at her, and Chiara awkwardly slammed the cup down, splashing liquid over the rim. "Me? You think I can do it?"

"Yes," Tessa and Malia said together.

"I hate endless paperwork! Plus, I despise conflict!"

"Yeah, but you handle it well," Tessa countered. "HR handles the bad stuff; you just need to be the main face of the company, like Rory was. We'll all step it up and help, but if we don't show a united, strong front as the founders, I'm afraid Quench will be affected."

The idea of slipping into her best friend's role invoked a cold rush of fear down Chiara's spine. She had no desire to become the successor. Chiara had branded herself as the navigator of Quench—the one to jump on a plane last minute to attend a big conference, or meet with a beauty brand ambassador, or anything else that needed to be done to keep the company front and center in the public eye. She loved taking on unique challenges and meeting new people, as long as she wasn't tied to the office. Changing her role at this point would severely affect her lifestyle, and right now, she had everything perfectly in place.

A job she adored. Travel and challenges. And no commitments to anything but Quench, her friends, and herself.

But Tessa was right. Quench was at a vulnerable point and needed stability. Recently, there had been a few interested buyers, and if they wanted the option of being able to sell for a lucrative fee and retire rich, she needed to step it up.

Not that they wanted to sell Quench. But they wanted the option to say no.

Even more important, losing their momentum could be detrimental to their audience, and Rory had one strategic theme for all of them to follow, inside and outside the business.

Every decision needed to directly relate to improving women's lives.

It was a path that was hard most of the time but kept them honest and real—different from too many companies that swore to serve women but only wanted them to be a tangled mess in order to sell them something.

Quench's website boasted weekly features on health, love, career, and style. In-depth articles about hot issues such as the #MeToo movement and reproductive rights revolved on the home page. Many went viral, ending up on *Good Morning America* and the *Today* show. But what set Quench apart from other websites with female-centered content was the online classes and lectures from professionals in all fields all over the world. Suze Orman had done a financial class for the young career woman, Lisa Masterson gave a lecture on sexual health and safety, and Theresa May talked about world politics and the economy. With their broad reach, covering topics that touch every aspect of a woman's life, and Quench's increasingly respected brand, professionals and companies paid them to be featured. Finally, Quench was making some serious money, and they didn't want to lose either their vision or profit margin.

Yes, it had to be one of them. And though she didn't want the job, Chiara knew her friends were right. She was the one most apt to step in and step up.

For Rory.

For Quench.

"Okay," she said.

They linked hands and smiled, even as the tears flowed. All of them felt the emptiness of the seat that would never be filled again.

In that moment, Chiara knew their lives would never be the same. And she had no idea what was coming.

Chapter Two

Two Years Later

Ryder drained his Guinness, leaned his hip against the rail, and knew he'd made a huge mistake.

He shouldn't have come. When his friend Ford begged him to be his wingman, he'd told him no, but the guy had seemed desperate. Leaving behind a big night of pizza, beer, and Netflix, he dragged his ass out to be a good buddy, and the asshole had left him. His damn designated driver.

Now he had to take an Uber.

A few years ago, he would've applauded Ford getting any action. The guy was a bit socially awkward, so anytime a woman looked his way, it was a win. But now, Ryder was just bone-tired and felt a decade older than his thirty-five years.

Plus, this place sucked.

The Savior was supposed to be the hottest thing to hit Rockland County, from the new signature cocktails to the fancy dress code and the four-deck dance floor. It was a mix of old and new club style, with enough elegance to court a good after-work crowd yet also attract the hipper, young twentysomethings out to get laid and dance off their angst. He'd already turned down two invitations to dance, and one for sex in the bathroom. No wonder Ford had hit the jackpot—this place was like a rebirth for the tarnished souls of all the other familiar clubs.

Too bad he just longed for Mike's Place, a Coors Light, and a bacon cheeseburger. But he couldn't stroll in there—it would remind him too much of Rory. Mike would try hard to engage him in memories, or even worse, attempt to comfort him. Ryder had been a shit son-in-law, backing away instead of trying to help Mike deal with the loss of his only daughter. He'd abandoned the women who'd been her best friends and built a company by her side. Her second home, Quench, he considered off-limits. He hadn't stepped inside since the funeral.

The image of his late wife burned behind his lids. Rory had now been gone for two years, leaving a hole in the fabric of his life he still hadn't been able to heal. When he tried, the guilt reared up and swallowed him whole like a tsunami. Better to just accept it and take the punishment.

Better to just get drunk tonight and forget for a little while. After all, he wasn't driving anywhere anyway.

He turned and looked for the bartender to order something stronger.

And saw her.

Chiara.

Recognition squeezed him like a merciless boa constrictor.

She was half-perched on the barstool as if ready to exit, head cocked to the side as the guy next to her leaned in close, obviously talking nonstop. One glance showed she was being polite, while the guy was eyeing her like a pimp, sizing up the assets of a prospective mark. She held an empty glass in her hand, and the asshole was waving down the bartender, trying to buy her another drink.

A slight buzz mangled any rational thoughts Ryder may have tried to have as he took in her appearance. She'd cut her hair. The wild red strands were now tamed into a sleek bob, curving underneath her chin. Her wardrobe used to consist of stylish conservative chic. Tonight, she wore a deeply cut black halter top, low-riding jeans, and black leather boots. Those denim-clad legs went on for centuries, and at six feet tall, if she stood up, she'd tower over the pimp guy next to her.

Ryder bet he wouldn't like that.

Rory had affectionately called her an Amazon—a throwback to a mythical time when women ruled wild and free. She always said Chiara was the most mysterious one of her crew and seemed like a chameleon, taking on whatever role a person needed from her and leaving little of her true self.

The observation always fascinated Ryder, and he wondered if it were true. The night they'd met showed him a woman who knew exactly what she wanted, filled with a passion and a purpose. But over the years, he'd glimpsed something else in her gaze and her words. A sense she was getting tired of chasing her life but didn't want to admit it. Ryder knew it wasn't his business, though.

Not since Rory introduced them and Chiara pretended not to know him.

Not since he'd gone along with the lie, burying the memories of that night they'd spent together and allowing himself to fall in love with Rory.

He'd rarely seen Chiara over the past two years. He faded into the background, leaving the women alone to run Quench and follow Rory's vision. Better not to complicate things. He'd made sure to cultivate Chiara's dislike, and it worked best when he stayed away.

But right now? The past seemed to fade as his gaze hungrily drank her in.

What was she doing here? He hadn't spotted Malia or Tessa with her. Unless she was on a date?

Ryder hesitated. Watched as the pimp guy pushed a drink toward her eagerly, salivating over her cleavage. He was positive she could handle herself. There was no need for him to act like some half-assed knight and save her from a loser at a club. She'd probably get pissed to even lay eyes on him.

He was about to turn away when the pimp guy lifted the drink and pushed it into her hand. Even from this distance, something made Ryder uncomfortable; there was a predatory look in the man's eyes that shot straight to his gut. The dude was bad news, and Chiara didn't seem to be pushing him away.

He couldn't leave without knowing she was okay. Even if he was the last person in the world she wanted to see.

Ryder pulled himself up to his full height and started walking over.

~

Oh, she was going to kill Tessa.

Chiara didn't even try to pretend this guy wasn't creeping her out, but he didn't seem to care. He was the exact kind of test subject she was supposed to engage in order to help Tessa with her stupid advice column. She should've been home in her comfy pj's, scrolling through the net and shopping online. Hell, maybe she would've finally pressed the "Buy" button on that pricey Halston gown she'd put in her cart for later. But Tessa had called her, begging Chiara to go to Savior for a few hours and give her feedback about the precise steps to get a guy to leave you without being rude and losing your coveted seat at the bar.

She should've said no. Pulled rank and made her send one of the damn interns who lived for this crap. But when Tessa reminded Chiara that she was alone on a Saturday night and needed some action, she reconsidered.

She was on the verge of her thirtieth birthday and practically had an intimate relationship with the pizza delivery guy. That was all shades of wrong. She figured maybe a hot new club would give her some options and help her realize partying on weekends and meeting new men was fun.

Well, she'd proved one thing.

It wasn't fun.

"Hey, drink up! Then I think we should dance."

She hid a shudder and thought of the last response Tessa had drilled her on: how to extricate yourself after he's bought you a drink, even though you'd politely declined. "Thanks so much, but I think I'm going to hang here for a bit on my own. I have to check in with my girlfriend anyway."

His hair was slicked back like a fifties homage, and his forehead was so big the lights seemed to reflect off it and blind her. "I'll hang with you. Here, take a sip."

The liquid sloshed over the rim and dribbled on her jeans.

Yeah, she was done. Research over. Nothing worked to get rid of a creep in a polite way. End of article.

She was about to open her mouth, give back the drink, and demand he leave her alone when the scent of the ocean suddenly hit her.

"Fancy meeting you here."

Everything inside her tensed. The sound of that gravelly voice skated over her nerve endings, and she froze while her heart pounded in her chest. Slowly, she tilted her head up and crashed into Sebastian's cool, assessing gray gaze. Words failed her for one endless moment. God, it had been so long. Two years with barely a glance as he burrowed into a life that no longer included her.

It felt like only yesterday since the funeral.

He looked good. Lean and fit, his body always seeming to unfold like one of those jungle cats who took their power and predatory skills for granted. She used to watch the way he walked into a room like he claimed it, and tried to pin it on arrogance. It was easier that way to dislike him, but she knew it was an innate confidence that many never achieve.

His face was the same. Thick brows, broad nose, and slashed cheekbones that hardened his features. Thin lips that seemed to hold a hint of dismissal but had the capacity to smile and devastate a woman's heart. Coal-black hair styled away from his forehead with no grease required. He wore jeans and a blue Calvin Klein shirt that molded to his chest and stretched across muscled shoulders. Already, she felt the press of female gazes eating him up.

She discovered her voice and tried to keep her face impassive. "Sebastian. What are you doing here?"

"Came with Ford, but he left me behind. You?"

She shrugged. "Just hanging out on a Saturday night." Why bother telling him Tessa had forced her out of her hidey-hole? Better for him to think she was living her life big and large.

His gaze cut across her and chilled. "Interesting pick."

Creepy Dude did not seem happy. "Hey, man, you're interrupting our conversation."

One brow shot up. "Oh, I figured anyone was able to talk to her."

"I bought her a drink." The slight whiny tone irritated her.

Maybe if she drank the damn thing, he'd finally leave. Even talking to Sebastian for a few minutes would be preferable to this torture.

Chiara lifted the glass and touched her lips to the rim, then immediately lowered it. "Oh, I'm sorry, I asked for vodka and tonic. Not gin."

Creepy Dude looked stricken. "Um, try it anyway! Just a few sips and I can get you a new one."

Sebastian made a slight growl under his breath and plucked the glass from her hand. "I love gin." He drained half the glass, then set it back on the bar. "Thanks, buddy."

Chiara pressed her lips together to keep from laughing. She should have been pissed at him for meddling and being rude, but relief shot through her.

She expected Creepy Dude to get aggressive or push to claim her as his territory, but after his dark, beady eyes widened with shock, he shot up from the stool. "Whatever. Gotta go."

He disappeared.

Chiara shook her head as Sebastian slid onto the empty stool. "I see you're still your regular charming self."

"That guy creeped me out."

She grinned. "Yeah, me too. I just didn't want to give up my seat."

"A woman's cross to bear when you come to these places. Sucks."

The memory of another time, another club, hit her full force. She dropped her gaze in case he could read her thoughts and pushed the gin over to him. "Might as well finish it. I'm done for the night."

"I'm Ubering, so I might as well." He took another sip and shifted his weight. She tried not to notice the hum of energy between them that always seemed to be lurking.

The image of Rory floated in her mind and she stiffened. Last week had been the two-year anniversary of the funeral. She'd gone to the cemetery with Tessa and Malia, laying roses down and taping a picture of all of them with a profit statement to the carved stone. Chiara hoped her friend was proud of how she had stepped into her role, though she knew all the time Rory had done it better.

"How's Quench?" Sebastian asked.

"Great. We had big adjustments the first six months after—well, after Rory passed. But we dug in and worked around the clock. Our profits are steadily rising again, and we just turned down an offer for a buyout."

He nodded, his gaze pinned to her face. She tried not to fidget underneath the intense stare. "Would you ever sell the company?"

Chiara dragged in a breath. "Probably not. But the interest keeps all of us motivated to continue thriving." Her voice lowered. "To be honest, I don't think any of us could do that to Rory."

He winced and looked away. "Of course."

A few beats passed in silence. The sounds of the grinding, sexy music pumped out around them. A group at the bar shrieked with laughter and ordered a round of shots. Chiara wondered if Sebastian missed the club atmosphere—meeting new people, rediscovering the single life. He'd disappeared on all of them, and she refused to think about why. But now, she found herself wanting to ask questions—questions she'd sworn never mattered.

"Why did you give up your control of Quench? It belonged to Rory most of all since it was her brainchild. She would have wanted you to have a say."

Sebastian's lips tightened, and she tried not to stare at his firm mouth. "Because I knew all of you would always be better than me. You knew her vision. You'd protect Quench at all costs."

"So you just walked away?"

His voice hardened. "That's right. It's what I do, Chiara. I walk away."

A strange sense of foreboding swept over her. What did he mean? "I'm not sure it's you walking away as much as you pushing other people away."

He flinched but kept his gaze on the empty glass before him. "It doesn't matter anymore," he finally said. "Things are better this way."

The truth slammed through her and tried to squeeze breath from her lungs. Yes. He was right. It was the exact reason they treated one another like cordial acquaintances even though they'd both loved Rory with no limits. It had taken forever until her friends had finally accepted that Chiara and Sebastian were like liberals and conservatives—they'd never mix.

Suddenly, it was too much. Being close to him with no barriers wasn't safe. It never had been. Chiara grabbed her bag. "I think I better take off."

"Me, too. I'll walk you out and call an Uber."

There was no bill to settle since Creepy Dude had paid, so she quickly donned her short bomber jacket and got off the barstool.

Sebastian stumbled, barely catching himself. Her hand automatically shot out to steady him, squeezing his bicep. "You okay?"

He shook his head, blinking madly. "Yeah. Weird, I only had a Guinness before. Maybe I need some air."

"Sure." She watched him sway back and forth as he lurched forward without any of his usual grace. What was wrong with him? He'd been fine minutes ago. Chiara helped guide him out the door, and the rush of cold air bit into her nostrils. "This should clear your head."

"Yeah, sorry. I'll be fine. You go ahead."

She watched his skin turn an ashy pale and worry nibbled at her. He really didn't look good. "No, let me wait for you until I know you're okay. Here, give me your phone—I'll look for an Uber."

"Thanks." His hand shook as he unlocked the phone and handed it to her.

"Did you eat anything funky?"

"Grabbed a turkey sandwich from the deli before, but that was hours ago. I think—" He broke off and held his head, leaning forward. "Holy shit, everything is spinning. I feel drugged up."

"Did you do anything?" she asked, gripping his arms to help steady him. "Weed? Pills?"

He had enough left in him to shoot her a withering look. "You know I don't do that stuff."

"Sorry, just trying to think of . . . wait." Suddenly, the creepy guy at the bar flashed in her mind. The shocked look when Sebastian had downed the drink. The nervous energy as he took off without even trying to get her number. As if he was fleeing because he knew he'd been caught.

Roofie. That son of a bitch had tried to roofie her, but Sebastian had drunk it instead.

Rage shook through her. She wanted to barge back into the club, track him down, and call the police. But Sebastian was disintegrating right in front of her and needed to get to a safe place fast.

"Sebastian, listen to me. I think that creepy dude tried to drug me but got you instead. I'm going to take you home, okay? Try to follow me."

"Wh-what? Are you kidding me? I'm gonna—" He stumbled forward and she barely caught him.

"Let's go. My car's right over there."

Sebastian mumbled under his breath a long litany of illogical phrases and the occasional curse word. His forehead beaded with sweat, and by the time she half dragged him to the car, he looked ready to pass out. She hurriedly opened the back door and he fell in, collapsing onto the back seat like a rag doll.

"Do you need to throw up?" she asked.

He groaned, and his hand flung out toward her. "Dah no to me."

Oh God, he was so gone. She got a towel from the trunk and laid it on the floor where his head tilted. Maybe that'd pick up most of the sickness if he hurled.

Biting her lip, Chiara debated whether she should take him to the hospital, but her instincts told her Sebastian would hate it. Plus, if the drink was meant for her, and she was half his body weight, he'd probably be okay after he slept it off.

Creepy Dude had wanted her compliant, not dead.

She jumped in the driver's seat. He'd have to come home with her. He couldn't be alone, and she needed to take care of her dog, Dex.

There was no other option, so she headed home.

Chapter Three

"Ugh, no, Dexter! No lick!"

The black lab pushed his nose frantically against Sebastian's face and went into full ecstasy mode, his tongue frantically licking every inch of skin available. The poor thing was probably so happy the stranger wasn't pulling away and was allowing him full access to his face.

But Dex was smarter than Scooby-Doo. The moment Chiara gave the command, he gave her a mournful look and slammed down his backside, then stared at Sebastian like he was a juicy steak he wanted to devour. She would've normally smiled, but sweat clung to her skin from the sheer effort of dragging the man inside. He managed to rouse himself just enough to half help her get him to the door and thankfully stumbled the rest of the way into her living room until he fell on the stylish red sofa. It took her some time to maneuver his legs so he was comfortably stretched out, then she removed his shoes and stepped back.

She patted Dex's head and studied her guest. He seemed to be sleeping deeply with no signs of breathing problems. Tomorrow, when he was back to normal, they'd make a plan to nail Creepy Dude. They both knew what he looked like, and maybe there were cameras at the bar that caught him. The idea he could be doing that to random women pumped fury and fear through her veins.

With a sigh, Chiara grabbed the fluffy leopard-print blanket and tucked it around his body. She grabbed a bottle of water from the kitchen, placed it on the side table, and ripped off the sexy boots that were killing her feet.

Dexter whined.

"Sorry, boy, Mommy sucks. Let's go out."

He bounded up and trotted to the back door, waiting patiently. She still remembered when he was a puppy and how exhausting it got walking him in bad weather, at all hours, so she'd invested in a fence. Dex loved to run and needed to burn up energy while being safe. Now the walks she took with him were pleasurable instead of work.

She'd never planned to be a dog owner, but sometimes, fate had other plans. Dex came into her life when she needed him, and now Chiara couldn't imagine being without the silly giant.

With the dog's immediate needs taken care of, she took a bottle of water for herself, chugged it, wiped her mouth, then stared at the massive figure in her living room.

He shouldn't be here.

The shiver that coursed down her spine contradicted her inner thought. They'd had chemistry since the first time they met, but Chiara had made her choice. She'd moved on, and when he had, too, falling in love with her best friend, she'd buried their connection in ice.

And even though Rory had been gone now for two years, it was still uncomfortable to have Sebastian in her home.

Rory had always wanted to find her soul mate. Her friend dreamed of endless kids, a white picket fence, and being able to work from home to raise her family. Sebastian had checked all her boxes, and if she hadn't died, she probably would've been a mother right now. They'd been trying hard to get pregnant and were beginning a fertility program to help speed things up.

Chiara had always been the opposite. Romantic commitment never interested her. Sure, she'd engaged in some affairs and enjoyed every moment. But it seemed the world judged her for not wanting a husband and kids, claiming she just hadn't found *the one* to make her feel fulfilled. How could she explain that she'd been this way since she was young? One of the reasons she'd been so passionate about Quench was to connect with other women out there like her and begin to change the perception of what women truly want and need. She dreamed of a big, bold, creative life filled with travel and relationships that fulfilled her at the time. The idea of being tied down to a child or man who needed things from her put her in a cold sweat.

She'd personally seen the havoc it wreaked and had sworn years ago she wouldn't contribute. Dexter was more than enough.

She trudged back and let the dog in, spending a bit of time petting him and cooing embarrassing things in his floppy ear. He turned his head and stared at the shelf that held bones and treats.

Chiara sighed. "Nope, it's too late for snacks."

The lab stared back with a long-suffering patience he'd perfected in the two years they'd been together. His big brown eyes turned Puss in Boots sad.

She melted. "Fine, but just this once because Mommy came home late."

The lab bounced up and raced to his special shelf, licking his lips. She pulled out the bacon-and-cheese-flavored biscuits that were worse than crack to her dog. He took it with manners, gently closing his teeth around it, then raced to his doggy bed to savor each crumb. Chiara shook her head and opened up her laptop.

After googling roofies and actions to take, she realized she should've brought Sebastian to the hospital or called 911 immediately. Dammit, she hoped she hadn't made a huge mistake. What if he got sick?

Chiara nibbled at her lip. He seemed to be sleeping it off fine, but she knew she'd better stay up and watch over him the next few hours. Just in case.

Heading to the shower, she washed off the grime of the day while her thoughts lingered on the past.

The night she'd first met Sebastian Ryder.

Chiara had never experienced such a deep need to share her inner soul with a stranger. Like all the secrets and dreams and fears locked inside of her were safe to admit. He listened like he cared, with a razor-like focus that made her giddy. Sebastian had been her special secret, ready to pull out on her darkest days and treasure.

Once Rory introduced him as her new boyfriend, Chiara knew she needed to destroy any lingering connection she felt. She'd vowed not to tell her friends about that night, especially what it had meant to her. It was the only way to protect her best friend and give them a chance, even if it was at Chiara's expense and left her with the haunting question of *what if*.

Chiara turned the water off, wrapped herself in a towel, and stared into the foggy mirror.

The pain of missed opportunity and bad choices slapped her hard, but she took it with a stoic resolution years of practice had taught her, and shoved the memories back down into the locked box where they belonged.

Sebastian may have been on her couch, but she refused to go down memory lane.

Exhausted both physically and emotionally, she donned a robe, said good night to Dex, who was already curled up in his doggy bed, and dropped in the chair across from Sebastian.

His breathing was deep and even. Chiara considered waking him to make him hydrate, but the articles she read said to do that when he woke up. Settling into night watch, she kept busy with her phone for a bit, checking in on Quench's social media accounts and new emails. She tapped out a few notes for Tessa's article that veered from *how to ditch an annoying guy at the bar* to *what you should do if you think you've been roofied*. At least she'd be able to use the experience to benefit their readers. Chiara had gotten lucky tonight. Too many others had not.

Hours later, barely able to keep her eyes open, she did a final check on Sebastian and headed to the bedroom. Dropping the robe, she crawled into bed, pulled the warm comforter up to her chin, and let her head sink deep into the fluffy pillow. It wasn't long before blessed slumber took over.

But she dreamed.

~

Ryder sat up, holding his head, and glanced around in the dark.

Why didn't this look like his living room?

He blinked, trying to make sense of the space around him. Things were hazy, like he was looking through a blurred glass. He'd had some benders before, but this was in another league. What had he drunk?

His memory had gaping holes it in no matter how hard he tried to recall the evening.

He shifted on the couch, a bit dizzy, and spotted a hulking figure before him.

Ryder froze. The monster beast was breathing hard, and terror shot through him. He'd watched horror movies and made fun of the characters acting like total scared idiots, but right now, he was about to run hard and fast and never look back.

After he screamed.

The thing moved closer, and he tried to stumble to his feet, but then two giant paws came at him. Ryder closed his eyes, knowing it was over.

A wet tongue ran down his cheek.

He realized just in time it was only a dog. A very large, very happy dog, who seemed thrilled for some nighttime company.

But, he didn't have a dog.

Yeah, he must be having some sort of deep dream and just needed to get his ass back to bed and sleep it off.

Patting the dog on the head, he struggled to his feet and headed to the left. Good, the hallway was in the right place, and so was the bedroom.

He headed to his king-size bed, stripped off his clothes, and got under the covers. A strange floral scent drifted to his nostrils. The mattress cradled him in a much softer embrace than what he remembered. Ryder pushed the thoughts away. It would all be back to normal in the morning.

He collapsed back into sleep.

But he dreamed.

Chapter Four

The dream took shape with slow images unfolding in his consciousness. Warm, soft lips molded to his, first sweetly hesitant, as if she was intent on learning the texture and taste of him before going further. He remained patient, letting his senses flow with the images of the dream and giving her free rein. Her breath rushed over his mouth as she probed the line of his lips with her tongue. Paused. Then pushed through.

He groaned and opened his mouth for her. He sank into wet female heat and drank deeply, his hands reaching up to bury his fingers in her hair and hold her still for more. He'd never felt so completely aroused by just a kiss, but this fantasy woman made him forget everyone who'd come before her.

God, she was naked. His hands left her hair to caress the sides of her body and sweep around to cup her breasts. Their heavy, solid weight filled his hands, and his thumbs roughly caressed the tips of her nipples until they hardened in response. He heard a throaty gasp and was spurred on.

He massaged the smooth skin of her back and worked his way to her buttocks. Grasped the high curves with both hands and, with one expert motion, forced her legs apart, pulling her up.

He swallowed her cry of pleasure as his heavy erection pressed between her thighs. The damp warmth buried behind tight curls called to him, and he rubbed against her swollen nub, teasing her to let him in. She made husky little groans that drove him to the edge. Fingernails dug into his back, but he rotated her slowly around his shaft, urging her to come, dying to hear her cries in his ear and the shake of her body hitting release.

Instead, she grabbed his ass and bucked upward. With one quick motion, he slipped inside of her.

Home.

Ryder sank deep into female heaven. Tight and slick, she closed around him and squeezed. A strange electric buzz rang in his ears as he joined with her, arching upward and keeping his mouth locked on hers so his tongue surged in and out to mimic his hips. He prayed to the dream gods not to let him wake up, but his eyes unconsciously flew open, and he gazed into gleaming tiger eyes—eyes that had haunted him for years, eyes he swore he'd never forget.

Chiara.

He wasn't surprised. Ryder had never given himself the opportunity to even fantasize about them together. But in a dream, there was no such thing as guilt or betrayal.

He fell into it wholeheartedly.

His hips surged forward at a frantic pace, and exquisite heat gathered tight and low, urging him to let go and explode. She gripped his shoulders while her inner muscles clamped down, massaging his flesh and driving him out of his mind.

She cried out and hung on as the bruising pace pushed both of them to the limit. He alternated between short, shallow thrusts that caused her to squirm, then switched to long, deep pushes he prayed would never end. One hand maneuvered between their bodies, and his thumb found the swollen nub. He massaged it teasingly, once, twice, and—

She came hard, her cries echoing in the room like heaven to his ears. Her features blurred as he tried to drink in her expression, her voice, and the liquid warmth cloaking him like silk. Then he exploded.

The world shattered around him and he rode the wave.

The scent of orange blossoms and sex drifted in the air. He rolled off and collapsed back onto the pillow, one hand still cupping her heavy breast, a dazed grin resting on his lips. Maybe a dream was better than reality after all. He felt . . . complete.

Ryder fell back asleep.

~

Chiara stretched and groaned as her leg muscles quivered. Lord, what a night. She hadn't slept well this past week, so a deep night's sleep was pure heaven. She rubbed her eyes as flickering images of her dream surfaced. Her cheeks reddened even though she was alone.

Damn, that had been erotic. It was almost as if she could still catch the musky smell of him clinging to her sheets. It had also been the most action she'd had in a while, and her fantasy lover had been extremely well equipped.

Dexter bounded into the room, and she braced herself for his affectionate attack. Instead, he shot straight to the other side of the bed, put his paws on the mattress, and began licking . . .

Wait. Who the hell was in her bed?

She snatched up the sheet to cover herself and stared at the half-naked man sprawled on the bed beside her. Thick sable hair. Broad, muscled back. A sharp profile that held a touch of haughtiness even in sleep. Toasty brown skin covered with crisp dark hair.

The realization slammed through her with an icy shock.

Sebastian Ryder was in her bed.

She gave a sharp cry and jumped out of the bed, backing up until she slammed into the wall. With frantic motions, she donned her robe, tied the sash tight, and watched the scene unfold with sheer horror.

He groaned, which caused Dex to shove his nose against Sebastian's bare chest. The man pushed the dog away, murmuring something crude under his breath, and slowly sat up. Cranked his head around to take in the surroundings. Then pinned his metal-gray gaze right on her.

Recognition seemed to hit him like a punch to the gut. His stubbled jaw dropped, and he shook his head, as if she'd disappear like a magician's assistant.

Oh God, this wasn't happening. It hadn't been a dream.

She'd had sex with Sebastian.

"What are you doing here?" he said, a frown burrowing into his thick brows. "And why is a dog in my home?"

In another time and place, Chiara would have been gentle. He'd been roofied and probably didn't remember a thing. But the consequences were too serious, and the anger burning through her was clean and hot and uncomplicated. Better to focus on that. "You're at my house," she said. "You got roofied at the club, so I brought you back here to sleep on the *couch*. But you snuck into my bed last night."

No expression. He just stared back as if she was crazy. "You roofied me?"

Chiara blew out a hard breath. "No, you idiot! Creepy Dude at Savior drugged my drink, but you drank it instead and passed out!"

Dex swiveled his head back and forth between them, tongue lolling out of his mouth. He seemed fascinated with the conversation.

Sebastian ran his fingers through his hair, making the strands stick up. She tried not to focus on his morning sexiness and all that exposed sinewy muscle on display. "I don't remember. My last memory was walking out of the club to get an Uber. Wait, why am I at your house? Why didn't you send me home?"

Now her jaw dropped at his accusation. Like it was her fault he'd jumped in her bed and had sex with her.

No, don't think about that. She couldn't think about that right now.

"Oh, so sorry I was worried you'd stop breathing or something. I had no idea what that guy put in the drink! And I didn't think you'd want me to take you to the hospital, so I put you up here. On my couch. Out there." She stabbed a finger toward the hallway. "Why the hell did you come into my bedroom?"

"I don't remember," he bit out. "This is ridiculous. So I fell asleep in here, big deal." He yanked the sheet off, went to stand up, then quickly sat back down. "I'm naked."

Her cheeks burned. The place between her thighs throbbed. She wanted to throw him out of her house and forget anything happened, but she had a horrible feeling nothing would ever be the same. The memory of that dream would play on endless repeat in her mind.

Instead, she ripped the Band-Aid off and braced for the pain. "We had sex last night."

Shock ravaged Sebastian's features, and though it was silly, the jerk of revulsion he gave sent her ego straight to hell. It was obvious he was repelled by the idea, as she was, but it still would've been nice to think sex with her wasn't a horrifying experience. "Impossible. We would never have . . . never—"

Suddenly, she was desperate to get him out. She could not deal with a morning-after dialogue when it all should've been a dream. Chiara needed silence and space and maybe a hypnotist to wipe it all away. "Well, we did, and all I want right now is for you to leave."

"Do you remember having sex?" he asked, ignoring her request. "I have blank spots I can't fill in. Maybe we didn't."

She wanted to die. D.I.E.

Dex cocked his head, as if trying to decipher her rising stress. He was sensitive to all her emotions and hated when she was upset.

"We did, okay?" she hissed. "Let's forget it and pretend it never happened. We'll go back to the way things were." When they kept their distance and ignored each other.

"Wait, did I force myself on you?" he suddenly asked.

Chiara's cheeks burned brighter. "No. I thought I was having a dream. I was exhausted after staying up most of the night making sure you weren't going to die. And I don't want to talk about this anymore. Get dressed and I'll grab you an Uber. I've got to feed Dex."

Dex heard his name and trotted over happily. Her fuzzy robe trailed on the ground, and she was grateful it was like wearing a winter coat. She didn't want Sebastian to see any naked skin.

Clips of last night flickered through her brain and tried to torture her. The way his mouth had clung to hers. The plunging motion of his tongue. The hot, sweet taste of aroused male. The bite of his fingers on her hips as he held her in place while he—

She shook her head hard and yanked open the back door. Dex bounded out, and she went through the motions to feed him, her numb fingers almost spilling the giant bag of food as she poured the kibble into his bowl.

Rustling movements echoed from the bedroom. Hopefully, he'd get dressed and disappear.

Chiara fired up the Keurig and, in a few minutes, a mug of comfort was in her hand.

"Do I get any of that?"

She stiffened at his growly voice. "There's a great coffee shop on the corner where you can stop in your Uber."

His half laugh held no humor. "For God's sake, Chiara, I really need a damn cup of coffee. To say this morning has been challenging is an understatement."

She bristled but knew she was being bitchy. It wasn't as if he'd done anything on purpose—he'd been drugged. She was the one at fault for not stopping that obscene sex before it was too late.

Oh, and it was obscene. In too good a way.

Don't think about it.

"Fine." She started another cup. "Cream and sugar?"

"Black is fine."

Dex scratched at the door, and she walked over to let him in. Once again he ran straight to Sebastian, probably not understanding what a man was. He'd seen so few of them at her place.

Sebastian knelt down and scratched behind his ears. "I don't remember you ever having a dog."

She handed him a mug and shrugged. "Why would you? We've barely seen each other."

"Rory used to tell me every detail of your life. You two were like sisters. Did you get Dex after Rory died?" Her name exploded through the room like a bullet. But he remained still, drinking his coffee, his gaze locked on her face.

Chiara found herself answering. "Yes. I was in a bad space for a while, like we all were. Getting depressed and just . . . lost. I found Dexter while I was driving home from work. This ball of black fur shot across the road, and I swerved to avoid him. Almost crashed into a tree. When I got out, there he was, all scraggly and whimpering, but he actually let me pick him up instead of running away. It was like he sensed I wouldn't hurt him. I contacted some places, but no one ever claimed him, so I decided to keep him."

"Dex is lucky to have you." His voice scratched. "I love dogs." His face gentled as he murmured to the giant lab.

Her tummy knotted. "Why didn't you get one?"

"We found out Rory was slightly allergic. Wasn't worth it."

She couldn't take this anymore. What were they doing? This was too intimate. Sharing coffee in her kitchen. Hanging with her dog. Especially after last night.

Chiara cleared her throat. "You should probably get going."

He straightened. Usually, most men couldn't meet her gaze because of her freakish height, but Sebastian had a good few inches on her, so she needed to lift her chin slightly. The action made her feel vulnerable. "I'm not leaving until we talk about what happened last night. This is serious."

Her heart beat madly. "Talking about it won't fix anything."

Sebastian frowned. "Of course it will. That dude tried to drug you. We need to make a report."

Relief sagged through her body. She'd rather talk about the roofie issue over the sex anytime. "Oh yes, you're right. I was hoping the club had cameras, but I agree. We should file a report. I wish I'd been able to confront him. Get his license plate or snap his pic. Anything would've helped."

"How bad was I?"

"I barely managed to get you into the house. I should've taken you to the hospital. I'm really sorry I didn't."

One brow lifted. "No need to be sorry. It was only the one drink, and I'm not a light guy. I'm actually surprised it took me out all night."

"Yes, but now I know better. The whole thing makes me sick."

He nodded. "I'll make sure we get him. My friend Keano is a cop. I'll call him and find out what we need to do."

"Good." A shudder worked its way down her spine. "The idea of what could've happened if I'd taken that drink is going to haunt me for a while."

He reached out and touched her hand. The slide of skin on skin made her body jerk in reaction. An instant spark snapped in the air. Her thighs immediately softened, and the memory of last night rushed past her. Being held so tight, being brought to a shattering orgasm under his command, scrambled her brain, and coffee splashed over the rim of her mug to spill on the floor.

Sebastian stepped back. "Sorry." A muscle ticked in his jaw. "I think we need to talk about what happened with us last night, too."

She grabbed a dish towel and mopped up the small spill, keeping her gaze averted. "I don't. Let's just forget about it."

"Like we did before?"

The breath stuck in her lungs. Chiara crossed her arms in front of her chest, needing the comfort. "We did the only thing we could. And it worked out fine."

Sebastian had spent the years he was with Rory treating Chiara with a cool politeness that baffled her friends. Eventually, they'd accepted she and Sebastian would never truly get along, and the two of them settled into a routine that worked for everyone. But this morning, there wasn't an ice cube in sight. His eyes burned like smoke, and having all that focus on her caused an ache deep in her gut. A longing she never wanted to admit, because Chiara hoped it was buried deep enough to die.

Last night proved she'd been lying to herself.

She forced herself to speak. "We had no choice and you know it. Besides, I have no regrets. You and Rory were meant for each other. I wasn't about to seed any doubts or hurt her. We agreed."

His gaze narrowed, and for one endless moment, emotion burned in his eyes. "Funny, I clearly remember you making that decision, not me. But I agree with one thing you said: there are no regrets."

The words slapped back at her, but Chiara made sure not to flinch. "Then I think we have nothing left to say."

"I guess we never did." With those last words lingering in the air, Sebastian turned. Setting his empty mug down on the table, he gave a pat to Dex, then grabbed his coat. "Thanks for the coffee. I'll let you know when I talk to my friend about filing a police report."

She nodded, afraid that if she spoke, her voice would wobble.

When the door slammed, it should've been relief that coursed through her.

Not regret.

Chapter Five

Ryder walked into the silent house, peeled off his coat, and collapsed in the leather chair. His head still throbbed faintly. A stab of loneliness hit him. He should get a dog. He'd thought about it on and off, but time seemed to slip away quickly. Now, two years later, he felt stuck in the same damn place.

He looked around, noticing how much he'd never bothered to change. It had always been Rory's house, decorated with her style and taste. Sure, he'd packed up her personal items eventually, but the heart of the house still belonged to her. Maybe he refused to make it more his own as another punishment. Ryder was good at that. Punishing himself for things he felt responsible for.

He was beginning to tire of it.

His phone pinged and he hit the answer button. "You finally get lucky?"

Ford's hesitation spoke volumes. "Not really."

"Dude, you walked out with her and ditched me. What the hell happened?"

"We got a cab, went back to her place, and I started getting this weird feeling that she lived with someone."

"Hmm. What tipped you off?"

"Men's clothes littered all over the place. The king-size bed. The sports memorabilia on the walls."

"Ah, shit."

"Exactly. I asked her, but she was kissing me and dragging me into the bedroom, and before I could get a fix on things, the dude comes home and finds us."

Ryder shook his head, unable to express words. Ford seemed to sense the male support and continued.

"He starts going apeshit and they get into this screaming match, and when he's distracted, I get the hell out of there. Thank God I wasn't naked. I ran a few solid blocks before I called an Uber."

"I'm sorry, man."

"Me, too. Should've known I was being used."

Sympathy flared. Ford was the nicest, funniest guy he knew, but his insistence on looking for *the one* at endless bars wasn't the greatest plan. He also had a tendency to seek out women who were beautiful on the outside but innately selfish. His last girlfriend had wrung him dry, squeezing out expensive dinners and lavish weekends without seeming to give any type of softer emotion back to the poor dude. It had ended when she cheated on him with a slick Wall Street stockbroker who had more money and time and harder abs.

Ryder hated the way his friend had been treated, yet Ford kept making the same bad picks. He needed a woman who'd appreciate everything he could give. So far, no one had come close.

"Dude, listen up. That crap has happened to me before, so don't get in your head about it. Okay?"

"Sure. Anyway, sorry I left you. How was the rest of your night?"

The ridiculous question made him snort. "I got yours beat. I ran into Chiara and got roofied."

"By Chiara?"

"No, by this pimp-like guy who bought her a drink. I ended up drinking it instead and passed out. She dragged my ass back to her place to sleep it off. Now, I gotta call Keano and track this guy down and try to bust him. It could've been bad."

Ryder left out the rest of the night, keeping one more secret locked up. He still didn't remember much. Maybe that was better.

"I can't believe Chiara was almost date-raped. That's messed up. How's she doing? Been a damn long time since I've seen the crew."

Ryder thought of their night together and choked back the memory. "Fine. Quench is doing well, of course."

"Not surprised. They're a bunch of smart women. Plus, they're looking out for Rory's legacy."

The bruise in his chest had eventually lessened at the sound of her name. The guilt still throbbed, but more like a splinter than an open wound. "Yeah."

Silence settled over the line. His friend cleared his throat. "It's time, dude."

"For what?"

"To begin moving on. You can't keep yourself locked up in that house all alone. It's been two years. Go on a damn date."

A humorless laugh escaped. "Sure, I'll just swipe on Tinder and get back in the game."

"Yes! Man, that's exactly what you need to do. You need to get over this guilt that you shouldn't have a life."

The accusation hit too close to the truth. "I went to the club last night and got roofied. Maybe it was a sign."

Ford groaned. "It was a sign not to be an idiot and take someone's drink! Clubbing 101. I'm disappointed in you."

A flash of humor cut through him. "And you're the expert in Clubbing 101, huh? You ended your night jumping out of a woman's bedroom window. Naked."

"I told you I had my clothes! There should be a quick questionnaire both parties are required to answer before they go home together."

This time, it was a real laugh. "Yeah, like yes or no, 'I have a boyfriend waiting at home' and 'I am a serial killer.'"

"Exactly."

"Dude, you shouldn't be looking every weekend for hookups. They rarely lead to more."

"Says the guy who's been celibate for so long, you'll probably need to blow the dust off it when you finally get some action. Hey, how about I set you up? Or help you with a dating app?"

"I'm hanging up now, before you set up my secret dating profile so I can meet someone who's meant for me."

"I knew you watched those crappy Hallmark movies. I'm worried, man."

"Bye, Ford. Check in with you later."

He hung up and shook his head. Ford was wrong. He'd watched a ton of Hallmark movies and none of them were crappy. He always looked forward to the Christmas in July marathon.

Groaning, Ryder got his ass off the chair and headed for the shower. He needed to do some work, head to the gym, and food shop. Maybe even begin to take down some feminine accents in the living room. Parts of what Ford had said struck him, and maybe he needed to begin leaving some of the past behind.

He stripped, turned on the water, and froze.

"Feels good." The throaty, feminine catch in her breath drove him to take her lips with the need to possess her whole. His tongue sank deep, thrusting against hers, drowning in the sweet taste of her. Orange blossoms swarmed his senses. Drunkenly, he opened his eyes and captured the whiskey-gold gaze of the woman who'd always haunted him with what-ifs. The woman now naked and needy beneath him. For one soul-crushing moment, he thought about pulling back, stopping the dream from going forth in case of the temptations it brought, but it was already too late. He watched her face with satisfaction as she exploded beneath him.

Ryder shot his hand out to lean against the shower door as memories of last night suddenly assaulted him. Oh God, he remembered. The arch of her hips as he pleasured her; the wet, hot heat surrounding him; the drugged look of satisfaction in her eyes when he was buried deep inside. Not only had it happened, but it was better than anything he could have imagined.

And now that he remembered, the images were scorched into his brain forever. He'd finally tasted her.

He'd never forget.

He stumbled into the shower and soaped off her scent, trying to scrub away the guilt. Yes, it had been two years since Rory died, but he still felt he'd betrayed her with her best friend.

Fate had a sick sense of humor.

Ryder got out of the shower, dressed, and headed to the kitchen to make a pot of strong coffee. Grabbing a notepad from his counter, he scribbled down a task list, which always helped him focus. The kids he worked with as a high school guidance counselor liked to make fun of him and his organizational habits. His office was filled with checklists, calendars, whiteboards, and planners along with color-coded Post-its.

Sipping his coffee, he texted Keano, who quickly gave him the info on what police station to call and the name of a guy to contact. Chiara would have to be with him when they filed a report, but after, he'd avoid her. It had worked for them before, and it'd work again. He'd begin to reset his life and try to be more open to other possibilities. Living like a monk had affected him, forcing him to linger on a past that he couldn't change.

Ryder thought of the way Chiara had tried to freeze him out, the regret plain to see on her face, and he was sure she'd be happy to avoid him, too. It was for the best.

A secret one-night stand didn't have to blow up either of their lives.

Satisfied, he headed back out the door, not realizing until he started the ignition that he might be in bigger trouble than he thought. Because Ryder had just remembered one very important detail.

He hadn't worn a condom.

Chapter Six

"We need to talk."

Chiara's first response was to shut the door in his face. Her insides rattled as she stared at Sebastian on her porch, hunched over slightly from the bitter February wind. Every winter, she wondered why she had to love the East Coast so much. She did better in southern sun. Instead, she clenched her teeth and hissed, "What are you doing here?"

"Freezing my ass off. Gonna let me in?"

Trying not to scream with irritation, Chiara motioned him in and slammed the door a bit harder than normal.

Dex had no such problems with his company, bounding over in three giant leaps to say hello. Sebastian's face lit up. "Dex! At least you wouldn't let me become a permanent snowman out there. Why is Mom so mean?"

Chiara rolled her eyes. "I'm really busy. Whatever you need to say, you could have texted or called."

"I tried calling. I figured you were deliberately ignoring me."

Chiara glanced behind her, where the toppling work space of her dining room table exploded into chaos. She'd been writing for the past two hours, caught up in the new article she wanted to highlight on the web page. She always turned her phone off while writing or nothing got done. "Didn't have my phone close—I was working."

He strolled over and winced. "That's how you work?" He pointed to the teetering piles of folders, colored sticky notes covering every inch of space, and two computers squeezed into the mess.

She bristled. "Yes. Organized doesn't necessarily mean productive. A too-clean desk freaks me out. I thrive in the mess."

A touch of a smile hit his lips. "And I'm used to the motto 'A clear desk equals a clear mind.'"

"Well, my mind is dirty." Her eyes widened, and damn if she didn't feel the blush in her cheeks. With another guy, she would've laughed it off. But Sebastian narrowed his gaze on her lips, and a blast of heat shot through her. She didn't want to remember that mouth over hers, hungry and demanding, coaxing a response from her she hadn't felt in years. "I have to get back to work. What do you need?"

He seemed to sense the energy shift and that they were back to business. "Got in touch with my cop buddy. We need to report the crime to the precinct by the club. Both of us need to go tomorrow—that's when my friend's contact is on duty."

Her Monday was packed, but this was more important. "Of course. I have a morning meeting, and then I can shift the rest around."

"I'll take half a day off so we can leave right after."

"Great." The clean scent of snow and ocean clung to him, tickling her nostrils. She took a safe step back. "Well, thanks for setting that up." Chiara still wasn't sure why he'd needed to drive over when a text would have accomplished the goal.

"I remembered last night." He pinned those smoky eyes on her and cut right through the inane, polite chatter.

She jerked as the scene hit her full force: the scorching intimacy of naked limbs tangled together, mouths clinging, the sheer hunger clawing at her to be satisfied by only him. "It's better if you forget," she managed to choke out. "I thought we agreed we'd pretend it didn't happen."

"No, you did. Not me. I have a bigger problem."

Irritation ruffled her nerve endings. Why couldn't he just go away and let her be? He wasn't safe for her. Never had been. For years, she'd had to focus on balancing her friendship with Rory with trying to avoid situations around Sebastian. After the funeral he kept his distance, which allowed her to sink into a comfort zone, and though she'd been a bit lonely, her life was finally clutter-free. Work, friends, travel, rest. A few attempts at dating thrown in along the way. Rinse and repeat.

Now he was rattling Pandora's box, and she desperately needed it to stay closed for her sanity. "Sebastian, I don't think we need to—"

"I didn't wear a condom."

The words shot through the air like bullets. A shattered silence hung over them. It took Chiara a few moments to understand his words, the meaning still foggy amid her need to get him out of her space. She blinked, retrieving the scene, that heart-stopping moment when he'd slipped inside her and her entire body had sighed with pleasure, a word echoing in her mind like a mantra.

Home.

But she didn't remember a condom. She'd believed it was a dream, so there was no need for sexual responsibility.

He hadn't used a condom.

Not once had she thought of the consequences physically—she'd been caught up with the emotional complexity of sleeping with her best friend's husband.

The panic spiraled from her gut and coursed outward. She choked on it, backing up and falling into the dining room chair, her gaze wildly clinging to his. "I'm not on birth control," she finally said. There'd been no reason. She'd been on it for years but had begun having side effects, so she decided to switch to condoms for the rare times she did have sex. Chiara figured if she ever got into a relationship, she'd revisit getting on something more permanent.

Sebastian gave a nod. Walked slowly over, pulled out the chair next to her, and sat. "I wondered about that."

Her hands shook as she pushed her hair back from her face. "It was just one time."

"It only takes once."

"I don't need a guidance counselor now! I know it only takes once, but the odds are extremely low. Plus, you had drugs in your system. I'm sure that affected your . . . potency."

"You may be right. But there's still a possibility."

Her hands came up automatically and lay across her stomach. Pregnant. Dear God, was it possible she was pregnant?

Her head spun, and she tried desperately to grab on to something solid. "Wait—when is a woman most fertile?"

"Approximately five days before ovulation. Do you have regular periods?"

She tried to pretend this was a normal conversation and not shockingly personal. "For the most part, yeah. I just finished my period a few days ago."

"How many days?"

She quickly counted. "Four."

He nodded. "It depends, but you're probably right on the edge. Most charts would say 'relatively infertile.'"

She clung to the term *infertile* and ignored *relatively*. She couldn't deal with even the hint of a possibility or she'd lose her mind.

Chiara didn't need to ask how he knew so much about a woman's cycle. Rory had told her they'd become experts at narrowing down the perfect window for getting pregnant. The thought of her friend made her slightly nauseous. "Then it's fine."

"Maybe, but Chiara, what if it's not? You still may have time for the morning-after pill."

The breath left her lungs in one swoosh. She didn't want kids. Never had. For a while she couldn't answer. All she could think of was her conversation with Rory, who couldn't get pregnant because of a cystic issue with her ovaries. Her friend had confessed she'd been starting treatments because they'd both wanted a family desperately. If by some monumental chance Chiara was pregnant with Sebastian's baby, there was no way she could get rid of something Rory wanted more than anything. The decision would haunt her forever.

She lifted her head and felt a calmness wash over her. Something like that wouldn't happen to her. It would be too cruel of fate. "No, I don't need it. There's no way I'm pregnant."

"You're probably right. But I counsel my kids to plan for the worst. If you are, we can't deal with this type of a challenge the way our relationship is."

"We don't have a relationship!"

"Exactly." His jaw clenched with pure stubbornness. Chiara felt the waves of determination radiate around his figure. Is that why he was so good at his job as a high school counselor? His entire will and focus on another person seemed to sweep you away, and troubled teens desperately needed that attention. "We have about three to four weeks until you can take an early-detection pregnancy test, which means we should use the next month to get to know one another again. This cold war between us isn't good. We've avoided each other to a point where it affects everyone around us. It's one of the reasons why I've kept my distance from Mike and Quench."

Chiara's jaw dropped. "I never told you to separate yourself from us. In fact, I'm still pissed you didn't come to the diner after Rory's funeral. It was like you just disappeared from Mike's and our lives. Like we weren't important anymore."

She was stunned to see the ravaged pain in his eyes. He tunneled his fingers through his hair and murmured a curse. "I was messed up for a while after Rory died. Distancing myself was the best thing to do."

Something else flickered over his features, a sharp regret she didn't understand. Her tone softened. "We all were messed up. But you left this gaping hole, and we all needed to scramble to fill it. Losing Rory was bad enough, but Mike needed you."

"I have a lot of regrets, Chiara. Too many to list. That's another reason why I think it's important we spend some time together. If you are pregnant, we need to move forward as a team."

Suddenly, the situation seemed overwhelming. She needed distance, and space. He was too . . . close. "I'm not pregnant—it's pretty much impossible, so there's no reason to even go there. Can you leave now? Please?"

Afraid he wouldn't understand she was near the breaking point, she felt relief flood through her when he nodded and stood. "Yeah. I know it's a lot. I'll pick you up after your meeting tomorrow."

Her chin jerked up. She'd already forgotten about going to the police. Her head felt like it was about to explode. "I can drive myself."

"No need. We're going to the same place, and it will give us an opportunity to talk more."

"I don't think—"

His tone turned firm and implacable. "I do."

She watched in astonishment as Sebastian patted Dex goodbye and disappeared, his demand lingering in the air.

Asshole. If she wanted to take her own damn car, she would and he couldn't stop her.

Chiara went back to her work, but there was no way she could concentrate. All she could think of was the possibility of carrying a baby. Sweat broke out over her skin at the terrifying thought.

She could never be a mother. What would her friends say? Mike? The entire world would judge and point fingers and accuse her of being a husband stealer.

When she'd left him after seeing the sunrise together, Chiara knew she was giving up Sebastian and the possibilities of them for good.

But had she been daring fate instead, pushing it to play a mean game of chicken?

Chiara had assumed she'd find another man who she'd connect with as powerfully as she had with Sebastian. She never did. No one came close to making her feel so alive and seen for who she truly was. It was as if there were a screen separating her from other men. Eventually, Chiara figured she'd run into Sebastian again, which would prove they were meant to be.

Oh, they'd run into one another. With Rory practically glowing, already madly in love. There had been those few precious seconds when Chiara knew she had options. She could tell her best friend the truth immediately and deal with the uncomfortable fallout. She could pretend their time together meant nothing. After all, they'd never even kissed.

Instead, one look into his stunned eyes confirmed the truth: there was still a connection that burned between them, forged from one brief night, a night she'd never forget.

But Chiara knew Rory was perfect for him, wanting everything he did and everything Chiara didn't. So she hadn't given Sebastian a choice. She'd stuck out her hand, pasted on a bright smile, and said, "So nice to meet you."

He'd followed suit, and from there, nothing was ever the same. They never spoke about the past. They kept their distance, even through wedding planning, late nights together with their friends, and crowded booths at Mike's. It had worked for over two years, but Rory was supposed to be here right now, pregnant with Sebastian's child, living the life she was promised.

The sob fell from Chiara's lips. Immediately, Dex trotted over, laying his massive head carefully over her knees. The rush of love from her dog filled her up, and she hugged his neck, taking the comfort, and finally, letting herself cry.

Chapter Seven

Chiara walked into the Monday morning meeting laser focused and ready to tackle the week. After her good cry, she'd spent most of last night getting her mindset recalibrated. She wasn't pregnant. She wouldn't let Sebastian boss her around. And she'd take her own damn car to the police station.

"Morning, sunshine," Malia chirped, coming out of her office. She'd pinned her long, dark braids up around her head like a sexy Princess Leia. Her polished red suit and Louboutin heels hinted at a big advertising pitch. It was her power suit, screaming presence and *don't fuck with me* in boardrooms that were mostly filled with men. "How was your weekend?"

Chiara hesitated. She needed to tell them the truth, but now wasn't the time. "Chaotic," she said.

Malia rolled her eyes and fell into step with her. "Tell me about it. I had the worst date Saturday night. I swear, I'm never ever doing another blind date. All the people I trust suddenly throw away my standards and think I won't care so long as he's got a pretty face."

"Who was it this time?"

"My cousin Helen. Who's a doctor. And usually smart."

"How bad was it?"

"Let's just say he called his mother twice during dinner."

"Was she sick?"

"No, just likes to check in, he said. And he still lives with her! No way am I going down that road. Can you imagine fooling around in his mama's house? When I yelled at Helen, she told me he had a good job, never been married, and that I was being unreasonable. I'm not talking to her for a while."

Chiara snorted, nodding automatically to various team members. "I never failed you on a setup," she pointed out.

"Because you never tried, babe. You're worse than me. I've never seen anyone pickier about men."

"Better for us to have high standards than be trapped and miserable."

Malia shot her a big grin and a thumbs-up. "Toasting to that! How was Savior? Did you get Tessa's article done?"

"Actually, I want to talk to you guys about that after our normal business."

"Ooh, interesting." They all sat down and Malia snapped open her laptop while their team began to stream in.

When Quench launched, it had been just the three of them and Rory in an old purple Victorian house with bad heat. They'd worn winter jackets, more concerned with paying for good Wi-Fi than warmth, and crammed into this exact room to build an empire. Now the place was renovated into fifteen offices. All the dusty antiques had been taken away and replaced with modern furniture and office equipment, but accents retained the Victorian charm.

Gorgeous Oriental throw rugs. Gleaming beaded and crystal chandeliers. Polished mahogany floors. The bathroom was a female haven, decorated in pale pinks and cool snow whites, with giant gilded mirrors, a makeup center, and a counter filled with every luxury imaginable.

All the product samples Quench received were first distributed to the team to try out and eventually claim—creams, fragrances, fashion, and cosmetics. One of their rooms was stuffed with endless boxes of products sent from all over the world by brands desperate to be featured on the website. Quench was careful about who they collaborated with, choosing a small number of Instagram influencers to create a bigger demand for the products instead of using endless accounts, and it paid off. Their brand ambassadors had a voracious following, so when a new product or pic dropped, the audience went crazy.

And no, they'd never even considered asking the Kardashians.

Chiara chatted with her assistant, Kelsey, a young, dynamic graduate student from NYU who'd transitioned from intern to full-time. Her purple hair, various piercings, and punk-meets-flower-child plus-size wardrobe was half the fun of Chiara's day. "Where did you get this treasure?" she asked.

Kelsey did a quick spin. "Salvation Army and the Odds n Ends store downtown." A short floral skirt flounced just above her knees, paired with an oversize fluffy white sweater. The black tights with delicate daisy stitching set off buckled ankle boots. Endless bangs and sparkly hoop earrings kept the focus on her style. Kelsey was a size eighteen and loved her curves.

"Let Magda take your picture, okay? You're beginning to cultivate a following."

The girl looked delighted. "No. Way."

"Way. Readers like the way you mix and match styles, but more importantly, you own your space. That's what Quench is trying to sell. Female confidence."

Quench had built a reputation early on for offering diverse sizes and fashion for all types of women and never sold anything that was made only in sizes under six. Their "Fashion and Culture" page, which featured cultural fashion in fresh ways, had millions of views daily. For the company-sponsored Fashion Week, one of the top designers for plus-size women was doing a private sneak-peek show and offering a few samples to the audience.

Chiara was afraid they'd end up crashing the site due to the heavy traffic, so their tech guru was already working on optimizing their content delivery systems.

"Thanks," Kelsey chirped, settling in next to her. Her fingers flew across the keyboard. "Good weekend?"

"Chaotic," she repeated, sticking to the only word that was truthful but didn't invite follow-up questions.

Tessa came storming in, a cloud of feminine energy and power. Her wild corkscrew curls were pinned up high on her head, and her heart-shaped face was set in determined lines. She wore a sleek apple-green wrap dress from a brand-new designer Quench was featuring. Tessa made sure to wear all the products they were selling and guaranteed everyone knew the names. Mondays were her favorite because she was pumped with adrenaline. Malia shot Chiara a look, and they shared a smile. Their friend was a thing to behold in Monday morning meetings, full of ideas from her weekend and pumped to be back at the office.

Rory had been a proud workaholic, but Tessa had always come in a close second. It was another reason Chiara wondered if she'd been the right choice to replace Rory as editor in chief. Tessa maintained she could do more keeping to her assigned roles, and so far it had worked out, but there was always a lingering doubt.

Chiara had just learned to live with it over the past two years.

Tessa dumped a box on the conference room table. "New samples from California Kool Denim and Coach for the summer line."

Everyone grabbed for the items and Tessa stepped back, letting the team fight it out. It always ended up even—they made sure each person on staff got something they wanted—but a good battle on a Monday got them all energized. Chiara watched Kelsey practically leap across the table and score a cute pink crossbody bag. The rest of the staff streamed in, pissed they lost out on first dibs because they were a few minutes late.

Once they were finally settled, Tessa crossed her legs, took a sip of her coffee, and nodded to Chiara. It was her sign to begin the meeting, since Tessa was always the last of the partners to file in.

Chiara studied the team with a warm smile. "Weekend roundup? Kelsey, you start."

Each of the dozen team members got to rattle off a short summary of their weekend highlights. Kelsey gave a bright smile. "Jessica and I had a romantic dinner at the Bistro and made it official. We are now a couple."

Everyone clapped. Chiara regarded her assistant with curiosity. "I thought you already were a couple?"

"We were, but she didn't want to admit it. So now, it's super official."

"Oh, cool." They went around the table, where Chiara heard about Glen's car accident with a deer, Sara's fight with her sister, and a bunch of other details that were important to her, Malia, and Tessa because it bonded them with their team.

A flashback attacked her vision, and suddenly she saw Rory across from her, huddled in her winter coat, dark eyes gleaming with excitement.

"Quench is going to be more than a company made for women. I want all of our employees to feel a part of our mission, and not just in writing. That means we listen to them—their personal lives, their weekend details, who they're dating. All of it. If we don't see our own team as individual people, how can we serve an entire world of unnamed, unseen women?"

Slowly, the image shimmered away, leaving a longing in Chiara's gut. God, she missed her friend. Missed her laugh and spirit and the fierce way she loved everyone in her path. She'd been the heart of Quench, and still was. They made sure of it.

Chiara shook herself out of the memory and refocused.

Tessa waved her hand in the air. "You're up next, Chiara. How was your weekend?"

"Chaotic," she said. Everyone nodded in support when she didn't expand. This was a safe place to say anything. Or nothing. "Anyone need to talk anything out at the table?"

If something was bothering the team and they wanted to share an opinion or advice or have an old-fashioned bitch session, there was a time allotment for three people. This morning, no one raised their hand.

Chiara nodded. "Okay, let's dive in. Tessa, give us an update on Fashion Week."

Tessa jumped in with enthusiasm. "I'm still working on the material for the special edition feature. Magda, I need all the shots by tomorrow. That'll give us a whole day to edit."

Magda stuck her thumb up. "Covered."

"Hunter? Sasha? Where are we with the 'Female Power' and 'Fun' sections?" Chiara asked, making her way down the list.

The staff writers flipped through their notes. "A piece on the Obama girls would fit in nicely."

Chiara's brow shot up. "They're always good material, but I'd rather do an unknown up-and-comer. Anything there?"

"I wanted to begin tapping some volunteer organizations and find a fresh face. Wasn't sure if I had the time, though," Hunter said.

"Do it. I'd rather have something better for next week and take the hit this week. We can make up for it in the other sections—the algorithms will keep us afloat."

Sasha tapped her lip. "I wanted to pitch a piece on the dog clothing market. It's booming, and there's a new designer who uses recycled materials to create lines for specific breeds. Think cool T-shirts with slogans. Lots of bling. A percentage goes to rescue animal organizations."

Chiara leaned forward. "I've heard of her! Jersey Sanderson—I was checking out her online store for Dexter. The lab stuff is great."

"Love it. Magda, can you get me some shots with some cute dogs?"

Magda rolled her eyes and stretched her legs in front of her. She always dressed in the same uniform—black leggings, black T-shirt, black boots even in summer. Her long black hair framed her face like a waterfall of black silk. "I don't like to work with animals."

Sasha shot her a pleading look. "I'll help you. Willow can be your model, and Jersey can send me some samples overnight. I already contacted her."

Magda grumbled. "Your dog is a Chihuahua. They bite."

Sasha gasped. "Willow is the sweetest! She'd never bite."

"You said she attacked that boyfriend of yours and that's why he broke up with you."

Sasha's pale skin turned red. "Willow sensed he was a liar and a cheat, so she ran him off. She picks up on bad juju. If you're a good person, you're fine."

"I am not a good person," Magda announced. "Everyone knows I'm a bitch."

Malia waved her hand in the air. "Stop bickering. Who loves dogs at the table?"

A few raised their hand, including Chiara.

"One of you come up with a dog model that Magda doesn't hate and let's move on. Women love their dogs. It's an important piece, and I can sell the crap out of some dog advertising. Shoot me Jersey's email, Sasha."

"Got it." Sasha aimed a suffering look at the photographer, but Magda was inspecting her nails. The woman was a challenge, moody as hell, but one of the best photographers in the business. Other companies had been trying to poach her for the last year, but she told them she'd never leave Quench and to leave her the hell alone. Magda may have been eccentric, but she was loyal to the core.

They went around the table, confirming upcoming feature articles, classes, product highlights, and the various other components that went into a successful website updating daily. When they'd finished up, the team slowly dispersed, leaving Chiara, Malia, and Tessa alone.

Tessa moved to the chair closest to them and grinned. "Hi, chickies."

They laughed. "Why am I not surprised Magda doesn't like dogs?" Malia asked.

Tessa shrugged. "Magda doesn't like anyone or anything easy to love. She thrives on challenges. I bet she'd prefer a snarky, independent cat who only wants to use her for food."

"True. She once told me she dumped her boyfriend because she made him cry. I'm glad she's on our team," Malia said.

"Speaking of teamwork, Chiara, my love, you never answered my texts. Did you bring me my juicy article on disengaging from unwanted men at clubs?" Tessa asked.

Chiara's heart pounded. She wiped her sweaty palms on her black pants. How was she going to tell them the truth? That she betrayed Rory and may be pregnant with Sebastian's baby?

She must've looked a bit pale because Tessa's brows snapped in a frown. "You okay?"

"Something happened at the club that I need to tell you both. It's private. And it's . . . hard to share."

Malia immediately took her sweaty hand. "Better to rip off the Band-Aid. We'll help you heal it."

"Or kill the person who put it there," Tessa added.

Chiara gave a strangled laugh. "Wait until you hear my story first. While I was at Savior, this creepy dude was coming on to me. It was exactly what you needed for the article, Tessa, so I started doing everything we talked about. He was perfect—even bought me a drink."

"Sounds good so far," Malia encouraged.

"And then I ran into Sebastian."

"Rory's husband?" Tessa asked, obviously surprised. "God, I haven't seen him in ages. It's like he disappeared."

"He had." She told them what had happened with the roofied drink and how Sebastian ended up drinking it instead of her.

Malia's hands shook. "God, you could've gotten hurt. Raped. I'm freaking out here."

Tessa groaned. "This is my fault. You haven't been to a club in a long time, and I forgot to remind you to watch your drinks. Dammit—I should've known better."

Chiara shot her a warning look. "Don't you dare! That's just as bad as me blaming myself for not checking. It's not us, it's the asshole who did it. Don't get me mad, Tessa."

Her friend immediately snapped her mouth closed. "Sorry, you're right. Why is it so easy to take the blame for something that's not our fault?"

"We've been fighting these battles too long," Malia said quietly. Her dark eyes filled with pain. "It almost happened to me at a college party. Bunch of guys wanted us girls to do shots in their bedroom and I bailed. Found out much, much later there was a girl who'd gotten assaulted. Never reported it." She swallowed. "I still think about her and what could've happened if I had stayed."

Chiara squeezed Malia's hand, and Tessa reached out to do the same. Chiara thought about all the women who hadn't been able to get home safely. "Sebastian and I are going to the police this morning. Hopefully, the club has a camera; otherwise we have no proof that the drugs were in his system—I never brought him to the hospital. It may be our word against his, if we can even find the guy. Don't even know his name."

"I'm so sorry, Chiara, that must've been scary. How's Ryder? Did he get really sick?" Tessa asked.

"No, he ended up sleeping most of the night." She hesitated, forcing herself to say the rest. "There's more. Something bad happened, guys."

"Worse than the drugs?" Malia asked. "Oh, girl, you're killing me. Just say it."

Chiara held her breath and glanced back and forth between her friends. Once she said the words aloud, everything would change.

Whether she was pregnant or not, they'd both know she slept with Rory's husband. Could they ever look at her the same way?

She half closed her eyes and vomited the words. "I slept with Sebastian."

No one said a thing. Her friends stared at her, obviously in complete shock from their dropped jaws and wide eyes. She waited it out, licking her lips.

"Details, please," Tessa said quietly. "Not the sex. Tell us how it happened."

Chiara jumped from the chair, unable to sit still. She paced back and forth, fingers pressed to her temple. "I don't know! I stayed up half the night watching him because I was afraid he might have had trouble breathing. I finally stumbled back into my bed and had this crazy dream I was having sex. I swear, I thought it was a dream—I don't even remember waking up. In the morning, Sebastian was in my bed, and we were both naked."

"Holy. Shit," Malia breathed, her hand clasped over her mouth. "This is like a bad soap opera. You never even liked him!"

"Wait—he didn't force you, did he?" Tessa asked in a high voice.

Chiara shook her head. "No. It was a good dream." Her cheeks burned. "Ah, hell, I didn't think it was real, guys! I was in such a deep sleep, and I guess the drugs were still in his system because he said he didn't remember anything. He thought he was in his own bed."

"What did you do when he realized what happened?" Malia asked.

Chiara crossed the room repeatedly, needing the movement. "He was shocked. Wanted to talk about it. I freaked and threw him out, telling him we needed to just pretend it never happened."

"Don't blame you," Tessa said. "I would've done the same thing. The land of denial is my favorite place to stay. Plus, the two of you never really clicked anyway. Talk about awkward."

"There's more. Last night, he showed up at my door and said he finally remembered . . . stuff."

Malia seemed to ponder the statement. "That means it was good. Bad sex is easy to forget and move on. Good sex? Good luck."

Heat flushed Chiara's skin. "Yeah, it was good. But that's not what he wanted to talk about." She stopped walking and faced her friends. "He wanted to remind me we didn't use protection and that I may be pregnant with his baby."

The crash shattered the sudden silence. Chiara blinked, taking in the sight of Malia sprawled out on the floor, legs splayed, head tilted upward with her guppy mouth open.

Tessa reached out, yanked her up, and held her firmly. "Steady, girl. Do you need a paper bag to breathe into?"

Malia shook her head, struck dumb.

Tessa guided her back gently to the chair. "Crap, this is bad." Her friend seemed to realize that wasn't the best thing to lead with and immediately changed her tune. "Okay, no worries. Chiara, the odds against pregnancy are high. Did you think about the morning-after pill or an IUD? Maybe there's still time."

Her voice broke. "I can't. I keep thinking about how bad Rory wanted a baby and the lengths she went to. I feel that if I did something specific to stop it, I couldn't live with myself."

Sympathy flickered over Tessa's face. Her tone gentled. "I get it. Then you're not pregnant."

"It only takes once," she said in a high voice, repeating Sebastian's words from last night. "What if I am?"

"You're not."

"If I am?"

"We'll deal with it all together," Tessa stated firmly.

Chiara looked at her other friend, who still looked like she'd been electrocuted. "I feel so bad. The last time Malia went into shock like this was when she found out Aunt Becky got arrested."

"She really loved *Full House*," Tessa whispered.

A sharp knock sounded and the door opened. "Chiara? Sebastian Ryder's out front waiting for you."

Son of a bitch. She'd sent him a text reminding him she'd meet him there and not to pick her up. But now it'd look weird if she tried to take her own car, since he'd actually come into Quench.

Malia raised her hand and opened her mouth, but nothing came out.

Tessa sighed. "Listen, we got your back. We'll work this whole thing out, and it will all be okay. You understand?"

Unbelievably, her friend's determination soothed her nerves. Tessa was the perfect person to step up in an emergency. She'd been the one to save them when they got caught sneaking into the high school to try and change their failing math test grades. Malia had fallen mute, Chiara had burst into tears, and Rory had tried to run. But Tessa talked her way out of the entire thing, spinning a tale of confused teenage drama about how they were only trying to get an incriminating letter a boy left in his desk. By the time they were escorted out of the school, the police were actually on their side, lecturing them about getting involved with boys who may ruin their lives. It helped they both had daughters.

Chiara nodded. "Understood. I gotta go—I'll text you when I'm back." She hesitated and bit her lip. "You're not disgusted with me?"

Malia tried to speak again but fell short.

"Don't be an idiot. It wasn't your fault—neither of you went looking for that situation," Tessa said with a huff.

Relief poured through her. "Thanks."

Then she went out to face Sebastian.

$\sim$

Ryder stood in the lobby of Quench headquarters as the memories rushed past him.

How many hundreds of times had he walked through those doors to see his wife? Even now, he imagined the tap of her heels on the wooden floors as she rushed to meet him, the faint scent of sandalwood drifting from her skin, the husky laugh against his ear as she embraced him.

Ryder blinked and watched as another woman headed toward him. Chiara marched with purpose, a fierce frown creasing her brow. Amber eyes snapped with irritation and something else, something he wasn't ready to probe.

She reached him, and he breathed in the floral scent of orange blossoms. Her lips were formed in a tight smile, but her teeth clenched. "I told you I'd meet you there," she hissed under her breath.

"And I said I'd pick you up," he said easily. "Let's go."

She followed him out with stiff shoulders and didn't talk as she got in his car, buckled up, and stared straight ahead.

Humor snuck at him in a surprise attack. He never figured her for a temper, but that red hair should have warned him. Mostly, since he began seeing Rory, Chiara had kept a cool, polite distance. He figured the wall of ice was permanent.

But it was a lie. Saturday night proved it. Something had formed that night together—beyond the physical. Beyond their shared past. It had always simmered but had now sprung to a full-fledged forest fire.

He wasn't sure what he was going to do about it.

He drove in silence for a while. "The place looks good," he finally commented.

She gave a sharp nod. "We're thinking of putting in an addition for three more offices. Most of the staff like working from home, but we've found having a center for everyone keeps us connected and on point with Quench's goal."

"Which is?"

She cocked her head. "Every action is to empower, help, or inspire women. When we're working on various content, it's easy to lose the focus when we're in our individual places. Everyone needs a reminder this is a group effort."

"Seems like an impossible task. Eventually, greed or ambition takes over even the best of people."

"It can. But if you don't set lofty goals, you'll never know what can be achieved."

He smiled. "That's what I tell my kids."

She seemed to relax a bit in the seat. "Are you still working at Stony Heights High?"

"Yep."

"And you still like it?"

He tapped his finger against the steering wheel. "Some days are a challenge and some are a joy. Some are boring as hell. But when I get up in the morning, I have purpose. That's all I've ever wanted."

He found it odd he was being so truthful. There'd been a barrier up for so long between them—for their own safety—he figured it'd be impossible to tear it down. But already he felt comfortable in his own skin with her. Like that first night. The night he locked away and tried never to think about since he fell in love with Rory.

"How are the kids?"

He laughed at the question. "No simple answer for that one. They're teenagers on the brink of adulthood. They're fucked up, and brilliant, and confused. They're real, or at least trying to be real, and looking for someone who doesn't give them bullshit. It's the same at the youth center."

Ryder sensed her gaze on him. "I didn't know you had another job. Where?"

"The Dream On Youth Center. I volunteer there on weekends."

"What do you do?"

"Different things. I work with the teen council. Hang with the kids who show up. Spearhead sports and activities. Every other Saturday we put on a breakfast social. Depends on what's needed."

"Doesn't sound like you have a lot of free time."

He shrugged. "Work keeps me busy and satisfied."

Chiara jerked. "Me, too. I'm living my dream. I've gotten everything I always wanted."

He knew she was lying. It was in the defensive tone threaded within her voice. Ryder wondered what was missing. So far, she hadn't settled into any type of steady relationship since he'd been with Rory. It was as if she was this beautiful butterfly, looking for a place to land, but afraid once she did, she'd lose her wings. He shook the ridiculous imagery off and decided to probe. "So this is it for you? Run Quench, keep growing, and make more money?"

"Is something wrong with that? This isn't a normal job I log in and out of. Quench takes up all of my time and is a constant challenge. There are people who are dependent on the success of this company, and I don't take that lightly."

"I'd never question that. I know what Quench means to all of you. But is that it? Are you saving any room for a relationship?"

She blinked. "That's never been my focus. Not like Rory."

Her name hung heavy in the air between them. It always would, so Ryder figured they'd better get comfortable. "You're right. She wanted Quench to succeed, but she wanted kids, too. Had her sights set on four." Grief pounded through him, but he battled back the familiar waves. "I regret that the most for her—that she didn't get to be a mom."

Chiara's voice shook. "I know. We used to talk about it all the time. How she wanted two boys and two girls. How hard she prayed for the fertility treatments to work. I remember thinking I was glad I'd never wanted something so fiercely that not getting it tears you apart. But Rory wasn't afraid of anything." She paused for a heart-stopping second. "Not like me."

His ears roared from the words that were more like a confession. The car was warm and squeezed around them like a bubble where any secrets could be told and held. This time, Rory's name didn't make him feel like he wanted to run from Chiara. Only his late wife's best friend could understand his pain. He'd been unable to share his grief with anyone, choosing to suffer for what he'd done. But for a little time, on this ride together, his soul was soothed. "We're all afraid of something, Chiara. Even Rory was, and we both know it."

She swiveled her head around to stare at him. "What do you think it was?"

He answered because she hadn't asked the question as a challenge. She seemed honestly to want to know. "Not being seen. She once told me being invisible in the world was her greatest fear."

He heard the tiny catch of her breath and fought the urge to reach over and touch her. He wanted to ask what her fear was. Or more specifically, if it had changed from years ago, from that one night they shared all their secrets. But things were different now. There was no reason for her to ever confide in him again, and the thought made his gut clench. "Did you tell Malia and Tessa about us?"

Tension snapped from her aura. "I had to."

"How'd they take it?"

"Malia's in shock. Tessa wants to nail Creepy Dude's ass to the wall. We're dealing more with the whole pregnancy scare later."

Ryder tightened his fingers around the steering wheel. "Chiara, I need to know. Do you blame me?"

The question haunted him. He prepped himself to deal with whatever answer she gave, but Chiara whipped around and shook her head. "No. I know in my heart you had no idea what was happening. If I hadn't been so exhausted and felt it was a dream, I could have stopped you at any time."

Relief softened his shoulders. His breath came a bit easier. "Thank you for that."

"It's just the truth."

"I know how important your friends are in your life. But when you're dealing with the fallout, don't leave me out. I'm part of it."

She bristled again, and they were back to square one. "*If* I'm pregnant, of course you'll be involved. But Malia and Tessa have always been my safe places. Don't ask me to automatically add you to the group because of one night we barely remember."

The words singed. Ryder wondered what it would be like to be Chiara's safe place. To have earned the right to hear her troubles, soothe her, or be a support system. To see her smile, hear her laugh, and dry her tears. An odd longing swept through him that he didn't want to linger on. It was too dangerous. Too confusing. And it had no place here.

So Ryder didn't respond. They reached the station, and he found a parking space close to the entrance.

He turned. "Ready for this?"

Without waiting for him, Chiara got out of the car and slammed the door.

Chapter Eight

"I'm not going to college."

Ryder regarded the boy in front of him. He kept his posture relaxed, like Kristofer's announcement meant nothing. He'd been worried about this but hadn't truly known how he'd handle it until faced with the stubborn teen. Now it was go time. He hoped he could find the crack.

There was always a way in. Sometimes, it wasn't enough and an excavation was the only hope. It was so much bigger than the kids. It was their environment, parents, friends, and personality that had developed over the years. Sure, Ryder was no clinical psychologist, but listening without judgment and understanding the kid's life as a whole were critical to this job.

Good thing he was still motivated to dig.

"You scored a whopping 1550 on the SATs," Ryder said, not bothering to look in his file. He'd already memorized it.

"My grades suck. Plus, I'm not spending my money on more school. I can get a job with my dad working cable. He told me he can line it up."

Ryder nodded. "Definitely. Your dad's been at TV & Cable Works a long time, right? How many years?"

Kristofer narrowed his gaze with suspicion. Acne dotted his chin, his dark hair was sticking straight up in somewhat of a Mohawk, and his jeans barely clung to his ass they were so large (Ryder couldn't believe that was still "in"), but the boy had extraordinary blue-green eyes filled with sharp intelligence. Of course, Kris tried to hide it, especially around his buddies. Most of the smart ones did. At least, the ones who were in his office all the time.

The school didn't have enough funding for its own mental health professional, so the kids shared one with the district. Ryder became the stand-in substitute and guardian of the gate—he referred them to Danielle, the district psychologist, if the problems were bigger than he could handle. He tried to stick to grades, advising, and college, but he also ended up handling friend problems, anger management, sex talks, and a hodgepodge of other teen issues in the cauldron.

"Twenty years," Kris said.

"Right. Damn, that's a long time. If that's what you'd like to do, I say you're right. Skip college. You'll get good pay and a steady job. Get yourself a place, a partner, and settle in." Immediately, the boy's eyes flickered with distaste.

Kris didn't study or do the work in most of his classes. Except English. The kid was an innate writer. The exact opposite of his dad. Ryder respected the hell out of the man who'd raised Kris, but the boy in front of him would wither in that type of environment. Unfortunately, money was a problem, but it usually was at Stony Heights. Most kids came from working-class families and were grateful to go to community college.

Ryder scratched his head and tossed Kris a pamphlet. "I contacted the dean over at Harrisburg. They have an interesting creative writing program, but the admissions process works a bit differently than other colleges. Grades aren't the primary element. You need to submit writing samples."

Kris leaned forward. His scowl contradicted his body movement. "Writing?"

"Yeah, writing. Mr. Kempsey said yours is exceptional. Harrisburg still makes you take the core requirements—which you need to pass—but their program has first-year students in writing classes. You don't have to wait two years to dig into the meat."

Kris picked up the pamphlet.

"There's a crapload of scholarship money available for this school. They have an actual grant department, so we could work on it. No guarantees, but personally? I think I'd try. Oh, I printed out the application, and they waived the admission fee for you."

Kris took the paperwork. The stubborn curl to his lip had softened. He was intrigued.

Yeah, Ryder had used contacts at the prestigious school to get the admission fee waived. Yeah, he'd gone way over the limits of his job to personally talk to the dean to give Kris a chance, including asking for an extension on the application deadline, which had already expired.

Ryder didn't care. He had a burning need inside to make sure Kris didn't get left behind. It was rare for Pete Kempsey to come across such raw natural talent, and the English teacher had been haunting his office about doing something for Kris.

Ryder would lead the kid to water, but Kris would have to drink.

And yeah, Pete would kill him for even thinking of that boring cliché about his favorite student.

"Look it over. Come see me if you decide to pursue it so I can tell the dean your application is on the way. Mr. Kempsey will write your recommendation."

"And I gotta write a story?"

"Two to three. Probably a lot to take on just for an application." Kris remained quiet, but it was obvious the challenge had already lit him up. Ryder rocked back in his chair. "I think that's it. I'm here if you have any questions."

Kris nodded and stood up.

"Kris?"

He paused at the doorway. "Yeah?"

"Sometimes, you gotta make decisions not everyone likes. Just for you. It's a bitch, but it's necessary."

The boy didn't answer or turn around. Just left.

Ryder took off his black-framed glasses and rubbed his nose. He'd done his best. Hopefully, it would be enough to interest the kid in trying. The chances of getting through to teens bent on not hearing was low—and Kris was stubborn. But Ryder wouldn't be able to sleep at night if he didn't try. Many subscribed to the theory to concentrate on the ones you could help.

But Ryder had bigger goals.

His motto was "No kid left behind." And he refused to think about failure.

The image of Carl floated in his mind. It was easy for people to lecture about not getting attached to the ones you lost. Ryder felt differently. He thought about Carl all the time and questioned every move he'd made. Could he have saved Carl if he'd done anything more? The gutting loss of the kid he'd gotten attached to at Dream On haunted him, and he let it.

Because maybe he'd learn from those mistakes and do better next time.

Ryder deliberately pushed the thought from his mind and refocused. He grabbed his lunch bag and munched on his turkey sandwich at his desk. There was too much to do now that they were in the most important season for school—third-quarter grades, extensions on college admissions, and coming up on graduation. Spring fever hadn't hit yet, but when it did, the hallways would be overrun by hormones and wanderlust.

He scrolled through his computer, answering a few emails as he ate. His phone buzzed, and he glanced at the message notification. Ryder swiped up and saw Chiara's text.

Police called. Bartender didn't remember. No camera shot. No evidence. Not much else they can do.

He paused with his finger on the screen. Since the police station, he'd kept his distance, respecting her space. She'd been so angry, she hadn't said much on the drive back to Quench, and Ryder figured she needed time to process. But maybe this was an opportunity to connect and discuss their options.

He quickly dialed, and she picked up immediately. "I don't think they'll get him, Sebastian. We didn't get to the hospital for you to take a drug test, and no one remembers him. Bastard is out there, ready to do it again."

She was right. The cops had a million cases like this, and with no hard evidence, it was impossible to prosecute. Frustration shot through him in waves. "We can't let him get away with this. There must be something we can do."

"I've been thinking about it nonstop but can't come up with anything. And then I spiral out at the idea he'll do it to another woman."

He let out a hard breath. "Let's go over what we do know."

"That he's an evil asshole?"

"Yes. We also know what he looks like."

"Yeah, but how is that going to help?"

The idea slowly formed. "What if we do our own recon? If the guy is confident and has an ego, maybe he isn't worried about getting caught."

A short silence fell over the line. "What are you proposing?"

"Me and you hit Savior Friday and Saturday night. Keep our eyes open. If we see him, we can take his picture, track his license plate, or even catch him in the act again."

Her laugh was sharp and humorless. "We're not detectives. Plus, the odds are low he'd show up there again, and we can't be stopping at every packed club in Rockland County. I think it's too much."

It probably was, but the idea he might be able to help was too much to ignore. "I think we owe it to the community to try. You're the head of

Quench. You could do a spotlight feature on this. You have the power of something bigger than the law, Chiara. You're the press."

Silence hummed. He wondered if he was pushing too hard. God knows, they were already entangled awaiting news of a pregnancy, and he only wanted a route back into her life. But tracking down Pimp Guy meant spending more time together as partners. She might want to run far away from anything that put her in his vicinity.

The emotions swirled inside of him in discomfort. Yet, he felt in his bones this was a good plan.

"I'll think about it," Chiara eventually said. "I don't know."

"Fair enough. I don't mean to pressure you. Last thing you want to do is keep thinking about what could have happened. And you're right—we're not cops or detectives."

"Are you now backing off from your suggestion?"

He laughed. "No, just don't want you to feel guilty if you want to move on. Nothing wrong with that."

"I'll think about it," she said again. "I gotta go."

The phone clicked. Her husky voice still echoed in his ear. He used to compare it to Scarlett Johansson, the gravel wrapped in silk that ruffled his nerve endings. Odd how a few hours with a person could change everything. When Chiara had left him behind that first night, Ryder couldn't stop thinking about her. How many times had he visited the club, hoping to see her again? She'd visited his dreams every night. Ryder became tortured by the fact he'd met his soul mate and she'd run away, convinced they were too opposite in their dreams and goals to be together.

All Ryder knew was she filled up a missing piece in his chest that had been there his whole damn life.

Until he met Rory.

Ryder shook his head and cleared away the memory. The past and present seemed to hang in balance with no easy answers. The only thread that held them together was a possible pregnancy. Until he knew, Ryder had a responsibility to reconnect.

He refused to be an absent father like his own, a deadbeat drunk who had run off. No, his child would be loved and cared for. His child would never know what it's like to grow up without a father.

He imagined his baby growing in Chiara's belly, and longing hit him like a sucker punch.

He'd dreamed of having a child for so long. Seeing Rory struggle with her own need and frustration tore him up. But now she was gone, and the possibilities reared up before him with another woman.

The voice slithered and whispered in his ear. *You killed your wife. You don't deserve happiness with anyone.*

The guilt rose up until he squeezed his eyes shut. No one knew the real reason behind the accident. It was his dirty secret—one he couldn't bear to tell anyone, especially Chiara.

After Rory, he'd blocked himself off from so much, numbness was his only solution. He allowed himself to open up only with the kids—they deserved that from him. Except for his friendship with Ford, he'd been lonely but hadn't realized it until he began talking to Chiara. He didn't want to push her away any longer. She touched something inside of him he'd imagined dead and gave him hope.

But he didn't deserve hope. That was his punishment.

Heart heavy, he finished his lunch and got back to work.

～

"You're going to be bait?" Malia asked in a high-pitched squeal. "Have you lost your mind, girl?"

Tessa grinned. "Glad to see you recovered your voice."

Malia glared. "Sorry if shocking events make me mute, but it's how I deal."

They were settled in their booth at Mike's Place. Mike had Jerry, the cook, make their favorite salads—chicken Caesar for Malia, goat cheese and walnut for Tessa, and grilled shrimp and avocado for Chiara. Mike always knew when they needed comfort food, a cocktail, or to go the healthy route the moment he looked at them.

Watching Mike battle through the loss of his daughter tore them apart. For the past two years, they'd made sure to gather regularly at Mike's café, the empty space within their booth simply part of who they now were. They kept Mike busy and an active part of their lives, from bad dates, work mishaps, and Sunday Scrabble tournaments, so he always felt a piece of Rory was with him.

Chiara stared at her best friends and her heart squeezed with love. She wouldn't have gotten through such a loss without them. As a group, there'd been some shifts and growing pains. Rory had always been the leader, so it was hard to change up roles when the core was suddenly ripped away. But they stuck together and had finally gotten to a place of acceptance.

"I'm not going to be bait," Chiara corrected, sipping at her seltzer with lime. "Sebastian mentioned hanging at the club to see if we spot Creepy Dude. We're the only ones who know what he looks like."

"If you see him, what's the plan?" Tessa asked.

"Not sure. Take his picture. Follow him to the car and get his license plate. Spy on him to make sure he doesn't try to drug another girl."

Malia shook her head. "You're not a cop and can't arrest him. You also don't know how dangerous he is. I'd let it go."

"But what about the other women?" Chiara asked. "In a way, I feel responsible since I know he's out there and got away with it. If a few nights out can help my conscience, I think it's worth it."

Tessa tapped her fuchsia nail against the chipped laminate table. "It could be a feature on Quench. A lot of our readership could relate to this type of story. We could take an investigative angle."

Malia frowned. "Feels a bit like exploitive storytelling. Will women be better off after this kind of article?"

Chiara sifted through her friend's question. It was the backbone of Quench and needed to be answered honestly. "Well, it's definitely sensational. But that doesn't mean it's not important."

"May depend on how we write it," Tessa said. "We can't glamorize trying to track down your attacker."

Chiara rested her chin on her palm. "No, that won't work. Our original intent focused on trying to get away from unwanted attention. Too many of us are polite—we're stymied by what we think we should do. Same thing with taking a drink from someone. We can combine both angles into one, then dive deeper into the culture of drugging women and what we should know about it. We don't concentrate the story on fear. We push self-awareness surrounding society's expectations of how women should act."

"A self-reflection of what you went through, Chiara. You could've been any woman in that bar who experienced that predator. It needs a personal view to resonate," Malia said.

"Agreed," Tessa said. "Whether or not this guy is found isn't the story. When can you get it written?"

"Spring break is coming up—it would fit nicely for the website that week," Malia said. "I could probably get a huge ad boost with some of our clients when it comes out. It has the potential to go viral."

Chiara mentally ran through her cramped schedule but knew this was a priority. "I'll get it done. Let's have Jeanette get us some hard numbers and research on arrests, prosecution, and reports."

"Texting her now," Tessa announced, her fingers flying over the screen.

Mike's voice interrupted. "Girls, I see a lot of working and not a lot of eating. And don't tell me you're too full for the lemon meringue pie."

Chiara grinned and picked up her fork. "Sorry, Mike. We're eating."

He winked and moved past them to serve one of his regulars—retired high school English teacher Ms. Primm. She had her usual book propped up in front of her, probably another highbrow classic she loved to teach. The woman always wore a hat to match her outfit. Today, it was basket-weave brown, tied with a red slash of color to accent her blouse. She dressed neatly and had never worn a pair of jeans or a T-shirt in all the years Chiara had seen her. At least pantsuits were back in thanks to Hillary Clinton.

All of them turned around to spy as they watched Mike put down her plate of pancakes and Earl Grey tea, noticing the way the older woman stared at him like he was a hamburger and she had been starved for too long. He never spoke much to her—just a few words, which she returned in a stilted, polite manner.

"Why can't he see she has a crush?" Malia whispered.

"He's stubborn. And clueless," Chiara said. "He comes up with an excuse for every woman we've tried to set him up with."

"Well, he better not say anything about her fashion style. He's no beauty prize, either," Tessa stated.

Chiara tamped down a giggle. "That's mean. Mike's a sweetheart. He's just lost interest in keeping up his appearance."

Tessa rolled her eyes. "Rory always said he ignored the females who liked him and focused on the ones who never gave him a second glance. That's Bad Male Behavior 101."

"Or self-sabotaging behavior so he never had to replace Rory's mom," Malia countered.

They watched as Mike walked away and Ms. Primm's shoulders dropped with what looked like a long sigh. Yeah, she was definitely into him. Too bad the woman hadn't changed her appearance since the early nineties. Her hair was like a smooth brown helmet stuck together with hairspray Chiara imagined was Aqua Net. Her glasses were plain gold-rimmed spectacles that gave her a bit of a bug-eyed appearance. She had a full mouth that was currently smeared with an orange color too bright and garish for her face. Unfortunately, that was the only makeup she wore. Some foundation or blush would soften the sharp angles of her face that sloped into a pointy chin. It was as if she'd become old before her time, and she was still alone.

Chiara's heart panged. "I feel bad for her. She was the one who actually made me like Shakespeare."

Tessa had a thoughtful gleam in her eye. "Maybe Mike needs to see her outside of this diner. Give them an opportunity to actually converse."

"You think so?" Chiara asked doubtfully. "She seems pretty rigid. I'm not sure if they'd be a good match."

"She could be shy or socially awkward. I think it's time I do some research on Ms. Primm. Help her out."

"Like a makeover?" Malia wrinkled her nose. "Helping her not smear the wrong color lipstick on her face won't change who she is. If a physical transformation is required to make Mike finally notice her, we're not helping anyone."

"I'm not talking about a *My Fair Lady* montage! I'd focus on her as an individual, then tweak the energy that's stuck between her and Mike to give them a chance."

They stared at Tessa. "You never spoke about energy before," Chiara said.

Tessa shrugged. "I'm leaning into metaphysical data to back up my matches and serve our readers better. It's fascinating stuff."

"And one of the most highly clicked segments on Quench," Malia said. "I say go for it."

Chiara agreed.

Tessa grinned. "Project Primm shall commence. I'll let you know what I find going through her social media and digital imprint."

Chiara laughed. Tessa was a magician with figuring out what women needed to boost their confidence. Readers loved her sassy wit, straight talk, and willingness to tell the truth about how crappy women were with self-talk and what they think they deserved. A therapist regularly contributed Q and As, but she never resonated like Tessa did.

With that settled, Malia turned toward Chiara. "How are you feeling?" she asked, her voice hushed.

On cue her stomach twisted, but it was all mental. She tried not to think of the possibility that a new life could be growing inside her, choosing to concentrate on getting to the four-week mark, when she'd either get her period or take a pregnancy test. The day was circled on her calendar in red. "Fine. I try not to think about it."

"I noticed you said no to a cocktail," Tessa pointed out.

"I have three more weeks until I find out. For now, I'm being careful."

"How's Ryder with this whole thing? He seems to be reaching out and not trying to pretend nothing happened," Malia said.

Reaching out indeed. He'd managed to set off her temper in the car. Besides bullying her into riding with him, he was insisting on being a part of her life, which brought up feelings she didn't want to think about. After all this time cultivating distance, how was she supposed to calmly accept his continued presence? It had been easier to storm off and not talk to him.

Now the image of Sebastian seared her vision. The easy strength of his hands clutching the wheel. The clean scent of man and soap with just a hint of spice. The low rasp of his voice. The piercing heat of those charcoal eyes as he looked into her soul . . . stayed . . . lingered.

A shiver raced down her spine. She had to stop thinking of him like this. It was wrecking her concentration and playing havoc with her usual calm focus at work. "He's intent on sticking close just in case." A lump settled in her throat. "You know how bad he and Rory wanted a baby."

Malia nodded. "Yeah, I think about it a lot. But you never planned for this, Chiara. I know you, and I'm afraid you're torturing yourself with guilt."

She stared down at her half-eaten salad. "It's hard not to. God, guys, if I am pregnant, it's like I'm stealing her life."

"You are not pregnant," Tessa stated with a conviction that would've convinced a jury. "Plus, you and Ryder never even liked each other. It's not as if you had a secret crush or affair with the guy! Don't worry, everything will be fine."

Her friend's words hit her like a missile, ripping her apart with guilt. She'd lied to them, and so had Sebastian. Somewhere, Rory now knew the truth—Chiara had met him first. Would she be forgiven? They hadn't kissed. Hadn't been physically intimate. But the emotional affair somehow felt worse. If only she could go back to that one moment Rory had introduced them and not pretend she was meeting Sebastian for the first time. But she'd panicked, and then it had been too late.

Chiara should have known better. Secrets always sprang to the surface and destroyed everyone in their path.

She forced a smile and took a sip of her seltzer, but the words still stuck like peanut butter in her throat. "You're right. Everything will be fine."

She only wished she believed it.

Chapter Nine

"I cannot believe we're doing this."

Ryder glanced over at Chiara and tried not to laugh. "I can't believe you made yourself a blonde. It's definitely a showstopper."

She pursed her lips and shot him a glare, which only made him want to laugh harder. The wig was long and wavy, with bangs that were swept to the side. She'd paired it with heavy makeup and loud lipstick, and with the black fake-leather belted jacket and red boots she wore, it gave her a rocker-like look that was completely different from her natural beauty. "My damn red hair makes it easy to recognize me," she said, leaning against the back wall. Savior was packed, but they found an empty corner with a good view of the bar. "Why don't you look different? I thought that was the plan."

He cocked a brow. "What am I supposed to do? Add a fake mustache? I changed my clothes from my usual club outfit."

She squinted in the flashing lights. "You'd definitely look like a porn star with facial hair."

"Thought women dubbed mustaches sexy."

"Only on a chosen few. Think vintage Tom Selleck. You know, from *Friends*? Plus, you were wearing jeans the last time. What changed about your outfit?"

"My jeans are a darker color. I'm also wearing a jacket, even though it's hotter than hell in here."

"I know, ugh. I can't believe I liked doing this every weekend." She unbuttoned her coat and wriggled it open. "Think he'll be here?"

"Not sure. He may feel safe enough—it's been a whole week and nothing's happened, plus it's Saturday night. I'll watch the bar, and you can watch the dance floor."

"This undercover stuff is kind of boring."

"We won't stay too late." Someone bumped into him, forcing Ryder to step closer to Chiara. "Umph, sorry." His thigh brushed hers and he winced, hoping to God he didn't embarrass himself. The scent of her surrounded him, a light citrus that made him want to bury his nose into her neck and take a deeper whiff.

She didn't seem as affected. "It's okay. How many people do you think come here to try and hook up?"

"A lot."

"I wonder how many actually fall in love."

"Not many."

She gave him an amused smile. "Better or worse than dating apps?"

"Probably worse."

"Why?"

He studied her expression. Her gaze narrowed intensely, those golden eyes flickering with the possibilities of his answer, as if she was getting ready to challenge him. He remembered the night they'd first met, and how deeply they fell into a dialogue that stripped away the surface niceties. He remembered thinking he'd never get bored of this woman, because she had too much to think, to say, to fight for. But he'd never gotten to test the theory. Perhaps they would've ended up tearing each other apart instead. "Because nothing's planned here. Alcohol impedes judgment. Music encourages loss of inhibitions. Darkness masks ugliness in all forms. All of it leads up to falsities, until one night is all anyone wants."

She froze. He wondered if his words were too intimate, dragging them both back to that night in his car, heads together, breath intermingling, while a ripe full moon slowly descended and a raging disk of fire took its place. The music deafened, but he was able to hear her voice, even as a whisper. "Do you believe it was real, that night between us? Or were we both caught up in our own ideas of what it could be?"

The question stunned him. After she had pretended not to know him, Ryder figured that night hadn't affected her as much, that he was the only one who'd fallen so hard.

He'd asked that same question of himself many times, until he'd made a decision to shut down the voice and lock it away. There was no room for both Rory and Chiara, so he'd chosen and never had a regret. But now, staring into Chiara's eyes, for this moment, he only had the truth. "I know it was real."

Her lips parted into a little O. Their gazes locked, and heat raged between them like a wave, catching him off guard. He reached out, palm up, to cup her cheek, or touch her hair—anything to feel closer.

A group of girls, one of them wearing a bridal tiara, suddenly surrounded them. Giggling in a throng, they began to shout to the DJ to play something for the bride-to-be until the crowd roared in approval and the music cranked to Billy Idol's "White Wedding." People flooded the dance floor and threw up their hands, rocking out to the classic, and the moment between them was gone.

Ryder wasn't sure if he was relieved or disappointed.

Three weeks to go. She'd confirmed the date her period was due. For now, he'd make sure he saw her enough to break down that icy distance between them, in case she was late and the pregnancy test was positive.

And if she wasn't pregnant?

He'd go away again. There was no need for their lives to intersect.

"Sebastian, I think that's him." She motioned toward the dance floor, where a guy was putting major moves on a petite brunette who seemed more interested in Billy Idol. He looked about the same build and height as Pimp Guy, but Ryder wasn't sure it was him from this distance.

He grabbed her hand. "Let's get closer, I can't tell from here."

She followed him onto the dance floor, and they stayed on the edge surrounded by writhing bodies enjoying the vintage tune. He kept trying to grab a better look, but it was like chaos exploding around them, and the dude kept his head ducked toward the girl, who didn't seem to notice or care who her partner was. He noticed the glass she held in her hand, half-drunk, and a sliver of alarm cut through him.

The pulsing rhythm ground to a halt, and a sexy, slow song came on—something from the Weeknd. Everyone paired up and began swaying, pressing together, girls and boys, girls and girls, and even tight threesome groups.

Automatically, he pulled Chiara in against his chest, buried his face in her hair, and kept his gaze tight on his target. "Move with me," he commanded. "I'm going to ease closer."

"She has a drink," Chiara said, voice trembling. "What if—"

"We'll find out and stop it."

She relaxed a bit, and he shifted to cradle her closer, arms resting against the small of her back. Moving in circles, he managed to get past a few couples and grab a clearer view.

The dude was trying to grind against the girl, who seemed to finally realize she wasn't interested. She pulled back, said something to him, and began walking away. The guy turned, giving Ryder a straight shot of his face. His features were twisted in a bit of anger and disappointment, but there was no malice in his beady eyes. He gave a sigh and watched her go, then spun around and headed in the opposite direction.

Not Pimp Guy.

"It isn't him," he said in Chiara's ear, half relieved and half let down. The adrenaline came in choppy waves, and he calmed his breath.

Her feet stumbled, and he adjusted her so his thighs bracketed hers, moving automatically to the throbbing pulses of sound.

"Damn, that was close," she said. "I was getting all pumped up."

"Me, too. Just another disappointed dude on the dance floor."

"And another girl who escaped to her friends. I must be old. This scene is exhausting."

He chuckled. "Then I'm a dinosaur since I'm ahead of you."

"Yeah, but you were always interesting. I knew that the moment we met."

The words popped out and seemed to hit them at once. She stilled in his arms, and suddenly, Ryder realized they were clasped together like an intimate couple.

His hands pressed lightly just above the tight curve of her buttocks. Her hips cradled his, and he felt the long, lean line of her legs entangled with his. His little brain realized what was happening and immediately swelled to life. The hair from her wig scratched slightly across his jaw, so he turned his lips near her cheek. The feminine scent of her enveloped him, causing his blood to heat, and she immediately softened, as if responding to his sudden need to sink into her.

A small gasp emitted from her mouth. She tilted her head slightly, and their gazes clashed, pinned, flared. Recognition shuddered through him, and those pale pink lips parted with invitation. The Weeknd growled about feeling good and letting go. The darkness cloaked them amid the press of anonymous bodies who didn't know their past or struggles or secrets.

The flash of memory nearly dropped him to his knees.

His hot mouth glided across her silky skin as he pushed her thighs apart and slid into her wet, tight center. "Oh yes." The tug of his hair as she arched violently underneath him. "More."

Time paused.

He lowered his mouth and took hers.

Her lips melted under his and she opened for him. His tongue speared inside, gathering her taste, while his palms slid lower to cup her ass, lifting her harder against him. His brain fogged, and everything around him misted like a dream. The taste and scent of her invaded him, touched deep, and exploded the lockbox deep inside, letting the demons rush out in a frenzy.

Chiara seemed just as frantic to be as close as possible. Her arms clenched around his neck, kissing him back with a wild hunger, her tongue meeting his to spar and match and surrender, her muscles like liquid until he didn't know where he ended and she began. It was a kiss that lasted seconds but felt like a lifetime.

It was a kiss that completed him.

The music changed, and the lights blasted out a rainbow of colors. They both stepped back at once, staring at each other, jolted out of the moment.

Her fingers came up and touched her swollen mouth. His gaze burned with the need to continue the kiss, to step forward and claim her as his. Her amber eyes filled with a crazed rush of emotion, and he opened his mouth to say her name, but she'd already turned and left him on the dance floor.

Ryder sucked in a breath and followed. "Chiara—"

"I think we should go home. It's been a long night," she said calmly. Hitching her purse higher on her shoulder, she looked at him like the stranger she'd been the past few years. Irritation ruffled his nerves, but he gave a sharp nod and followed her lead. Now wasn't the time. But he knew something too important that wouldn't be caged in secret any longer.

That kiss had changed everything.

She was quiet on the drive back, and he didn't push. He turned on music to keep them company and left her in the shadows to her own thoughts.

When he pulled up to her house, Chiara unbuckled her seat belt, opened the car door, and stepped out. The wig was tilted on her head from the trip. Her red lipstick was slightly smeared. But her voice never wavered. "I don't think we should see each other again."

Ryder wondered why his stomach dropped. After all, he hadn't planned to see her once he knew she wasn't pregnant. He kept his question neutral. "You don't want to go back to the club?"

She hesitated. He tried to probe her gaze, but the walls were completely reassembled and impenetrable. "We can't let that . . . happen. It was a mistake."

His chest tightened. He tried to form the right words but none came.

She dragged in a breath and stared into the distance. "Don't contact me this week. Okay?"

His instincts roared to life. Ryder ached to push, to question, to convince her they needed the time together in case they had to raise a child, but even then, he knew it was so much more than that. It had moved from the possible pregnancy to the need to be in her company. To understand this woman on a deeper level because he'd never gotten over that one damn night. Because she was slowly tearing him apart, and he didn't know what to do with his emotions anymore.

"Okay."

The car door slammed. He drove home and walked into the loneliness, trying to convince himself it was for the best.

Chapter Ten

Kelsey popped her head into the office. "Don't forget Career Day is at three p.m."

Chiara blinked and stared at her assistant. "Malia had that covered, remember?"

"She was supposed to but called earlier to say she's stuck in Manhattan. Some problem with the trains. Said she texted you."

Chiara groaned and reached for her phone under a stack of papers. It was off, and the stream of messages began buzzing in. "I can't, Kels. I've got a million deadlines to hit and no time. Can anyone else here do it? They can talk about photography or social media or whatever else we do."

"Hardly anyone's here. It's Friday, and most are working from home or on assignment." She paused, and Chiara immediately sensed the younger woman's discomfort. "It's only half an hour. In and out. I'll take the weekly numbers and chart them for you."

Chiara shot her a suspicious look. "You hate charts. Why do you want me to go to this? I doubt the kids will care if I'm there."

"Because it made a difference to me once," Kelsey said. "A fashion designer came in to speak when I was a junior and had no frikkin' clue what I wanted to do. She had curves and style, and said she'd started her own clothing business from her house while taking business classes on the side. It was a light-bulb moment that I didn't have to follow the normal pattern everyone else was."

A smile curved her lips. Kelsey was a great reminder not to forget where they'd all started—in a diner booth with a dream. Kids needed to know it could be done. "Okay, you win," she said with a sigh, grabbing her phone. "I'll go. But you need to do the math."

Kelsey wrinkled her nose. "Send it over and I'll get it done."

Chiara shot her the email, cleaned up a few odds and ends, and headed out. Pulling into the high school parking lot brought back a ton of memories. The four of them had been super tight, growing up together with all the ups and downs of adolescence, heartbreak, and challenges. For Chiara, high school had been a place to be with her friends. She hadn't begun chasing boys until after graduation—most of the ones in school were so immature and kind of icky. At least it helped keep her grades up, though heading to the community college for two years while the others moved into dorms had been hard.

There just hadn't been enough money for her, and her parents had never cared what she decided to do with her life. Once she turned eighteen, they'd officially announced they were done. For Chiara, there'd been no mentoring, counseling, or support other than from her friends and Mike. She'd been lucky to have them as her makeshift family. Too many kids weren't so lucky.

Kelsey was right. These presentations were important and could positively impact teens who had no one.

She reached the front door, showed her ID through the window, and was buzzed in.

"Career Day?" the woman at the front desk chirped.

Chiara nodded.

"Fill this out and take your name badge. Then head to the auditorium—down the hall and to the right."

The ripe scent of puberty and unicorn dreams filled the air as she took the familiar route. The institutional blue lockers squashed together, the chatter of voices in the halls, and the endless posters taped along the badly painted walls made her shake her head. She nodded to a few others streaming down the hall, some clutching props and impressive posterboards, and hoped she'd be able to pull this off. Maybe she should've come up with a presentation on the car ride over.

But this was only thirty minutes in front of high schoolers. She pitched to successful companies with boardrooms filled with executive staff. Hell, she'd been on television once, a feature about female leaders. Career Day was nothing she couldn't handle.

The auditorium door squeaked and crashed behind her. Chiara looked up as rows of kids crowded in their seats, staring at her with slightly judgy expressions. In a few seconds, she felt ripped apart and ranked in the way only teens could accomplish. Swallowing hard, she made her way up to the stage, where a woman in a black business suit and pinned-up dark hair waved her frantically over.

"And now we're proud to introduce Malia Evergreen, one of the owners of Quench, a website catering to women's self-care. Let's all give her a big hand."

A halfhearted clapping filled the air and quickly died down before she could reach the microphone. As she glanced nervously around, her gaze snagged on a familiar figure sitting on the side of the stage in the shadows. Long, lean limbs crossed at the ankles. Jeans and a sports jacket hugging broad shoulders and slim hips. Thick black hair combed neatly back, and a pair of black-framed glasses perched on the end of his nose.

Sebastian.

She'd forgotten he'd be here as the guidance counselor. He'd probably set up this entire event, expecting a polished presentation from Malia.

He nodded encouragingly at her, seeming to sense her panic. She froze for a few seconds, caught up in the rush of heat that exploded inside her body and weakened her muscles. Oh Lord, he was hot. He had that academic, buttoned-up sexiness radiating from his figure, and Chiara wondered how many teenage crushes this man dealt with on a daily basis.

They hadn't spoken since they'd kissed nearly a week ago. He'd given in to her wishes and hadn't texted or checked in. Every day she held her breath, wondering if he'd show up at the office for a casual lunch or try to phone her to engage in a dialogue about what had happened. But there was only respectful silence, just as she'd asked.

It was driving her crazy.

A snicker rose from the audience, and she realized she'd been staring for a while. Chiara pasted on a big grin and dove in, trying to emit a positive energy so the kids would like her. "Hi, everyone! Sorry, my name is Chiara—my coworker Malia wasn't able to make it today. She got stuck in the city. But I'm also an owner of Quench and would love to tell you all the juicy details about running your own business!"

No reaction.

She ramped up her enthusiasm. "What's really cool about the company is that I started it with three of my best friends a few years after college. We decided our goal was to create content for women, and we worked hard to make it a reality. It took sacrifice, perseverance, and big dreams, but I'm happy to say, years later, we're one of the most profitable companies in women's self-care!"

All Chiara saw was a mass of heads turned down. Were they on their phones? Why weren't they excited? She certainly wasn't boring like a banker or accountant.

She began to ramble faster. "Quench has a website that serves over a million readers daily. We offer specialized classes, featured columns, research, and in-depth articles on subjects affecting women everywhere in the world. Fashion, beauty, health, fitness, entertainment, career, and of course—the hottest places to go and meet men!"

The joke fell flat. No one laughed. Phones buzzed and a few ringers went off.

Sebastian's gravelly voice came over the microphone. "Attention on the stage, please, people. In two minutes I'll begin confiscating phones for fun. You all know how that goes."

She blinked in astonishment when most of the students looked up, their bored gazes slicing right through her. Ouch. She'd die if she had to deal with these kids all day long. Why did they all seem so surly?

Chiara managed to speak for a few more minutes, heaping more accolades and motivation on them before finally falling into silence. She'd failed Kelsey. No one was inspired. She sent a desperate look over to Sebastian, who was watching her with a narrowed gaze, as if trying to pick her speech apart. Her cheeks reddened.

Slowly, he leaned into the microphone. "Why don't we open it up to questions?"

No hands were raised.

She hadn't failed this spectacularly since her oral book report in Ms. Primm's class.

"You've got the ear of a CEO who created a profitable empire from a diner booth with her childhood best friends. Don't even tell me you have no questions."

Another shiver shook through her. His teacher voice was so sexy and commanding. Chiara squirmed under the rush of heat between her thighs. How. Embarrassing.

A hand shot up, and she practically jumped up and down. "Yes?"

"Are you one of those places that exploit women's bodies by showing them in expensive clothes, with perfect hair, and no stomach or ass? 'Cause I know those women don't eat chocolate chip cookies, and that's all shades of wrong."

A murmur rose in agreement. She waited to see if *ass* was a curse word Sebastian would discipline, but he seemed just as interested in her answer as the student. "Actually, if you go to our website, you'll see Quench shows a diverse range of sizes, clothes, and ethnicities. We're interested in real bodies—and we're proud that our photographer does minimal edits. That means no polish on the skin, no rubbing out curves, and keeping each model's imperfections part of their story."

Another hand rose. "What about your staff? Is everyone white?"

She jerked back in surprise, then realized it was a fair question. "No, our team is pretty diverse. Malia, the co-owner and co-founder who was supposed to be here today, is half Black. Our photographer is Asian. We need all women's perspectives—not just one type."

"How do you decide what new content to post and how often?"

Relief cut through her. Thank God, they were beginning to engage. "Daily content is essential to keep refreshing the site and gaining clicks, but that's usually because of social media feeds. If there's a hot topic or story, we try to share it with our readers once the research is vetted. Variation is key so the consumer keeps checking back. We do weekly in-depth articles and thought pieces that really dig into making women's lives better. For instance, we've covered the effects of meditation and self-affirmations on success, how to be more powerful in saying no, how to communicate more easily with the people in your life, and thousands of other themes."

"Do you do quizzes like *Cosmo*?"

She grinned. "No. Answers to short, gimmicky quizzes that pigeon-hole people into rigid categories really don't help in the long run. But we offer some in-depth classes from industry leaders and professionals who provide evidence-based content to help women learn about themselves better."

The questions kept coming, and the more she delved into Quench and what they were doing on a daily basis, the easier it became to engage. Soon, she was joking with the girls and bantering a bit with the boys, who took the whole thing good-naturedly. She loved one of the boy's ideas that they needed to hire more men to provide their perspective on communication mishaps with the opposite sex. Chiara told him to drop his contact info off and she'd think about hiring him as an intern this summer.

And then everyone applauded for real.

By the time she walked offstage, she was sweaty, tired, and happy. Funny, she felt more energized talking to these high schoolers than doing a keynote for a roomful of excited women. Maybe because the students made her work for it without her usual sales pitch. She made a mental note to dig deeper at her next event. Enthusiasm was good but sometimes brought out an overly salesy approach.

"Chiara!"

She stopped and turned. Sebastian made his way toward her, his loose-hipped, long-legged stride closing the distance quickly. Up close, the rugged lines of his features hit her full force. The broad slope of his nose, the thin line of his lips, the intense gleam in his gray eyes behind the glasses. Why hadn't she seen him wearing them before? Maybe they were just for work? Either way, they were sexy as hell. Her palms grew damp, and she inwardly cursed this awful chemistry between them that just wouldn't go away. "Hi."

"You pulled it off. They're a tough crowd."

She laughed. "I'm not used to dealing with kids like Malia is. She actually likes them."

His lip quirked. "I compare some teens to cats. It's better off being standoffish and letting them come to you. They respect truth more than anything."

"You seem really good with them. They listen to you."

He shrugged. "Been doing it a long time, and it's still a crapshoot." They fell quiet, and she shifted her weight. "You feeling okay?"

Her hands went to her belly, then froze. Her tone came out a bit shrill. "Yeah, I feel great. One hundred percent. There's nothing to worry about."

He tipped his chin. "You're probably right. I'm heading back to the club this weekend. Did you want to join me?"

Chiara hesitated. She wanted to nail Creepy Dude, but the kiss was too fresh in her mind. She desperately needed distance from Sebastian. "I'm slammed with work this weekend. Maybe it's best you go alone."

His gaze drilled into hers. "Okay."

She hugged herself and fought off goose bumps. What were they doing? There was no baby. No future. No reason to be standing in a high school hallway, twisted up inside, while she stared at a man who was never meant for her. "Text me if anything happens at the club."

"I will."

"See you."

She walked out on shaky legs and didn't relax until she got in her car. Soon, this would all be over. There'd been no signs of pregnancy. Tessa and Malia drilled her every morning like clockwork.

Any exhaustion or tiredness?

Sore or swollen boobs?

Nausea? Upset stomach?

Crying jags? Mood swings?

In ten days she'd take the test and prove she wasn't pregnant, and they'd never see each other again.

All she wanted was to go back to the life she knew well. Work, travel, friends, and Dex. Fulfilling and free of drama. Exactly the way she liked it.

Chapter Eleven

"That guy looks like a deranged leprechaun," Sebastian muttered.

Chiara followed Sebastian's gaze to the five-foot stocky guy with a green hat and long-sleeved jersey. Bright green sneakers glowed from his feet. He was carrying a green beer and yelling random Irish-sounding things that didn't make any sense, but the crowd seemed to forgive easily. Anything went on Saint Paddy's Day.

After two weekends of turning down Sebastian's invitations, Chiara had decided to join him, sensing the big Irish party night could bring Creepy Dude out again. Sebastian had gone with his friend Ford to a few clubs the past two Saturday nights but told her the only thing he came home with was a slight headache. Chiara figured with the two of them on spy patrol, and the big holiday party Savior had been touting, they had a good shot. She'd also have the opportunity to dig deeper into the feature article she was writing on sexual predators.

She hadn't talked to Sebastian since that day in the high school. Chiara couldn't stop thinking about the way they'd lingered in the hallway, staring at one another like lust-struck teens while electricity crackled around them. She desperately needed distance to reset and remind herself why they shouldn't be together.

Chiara planned to take the pregnancy test over the weekend and finally put this chapter behind her, so tonight would probably be the last time they needed to be together. She'd spoken to Malia and Tessa, who agreed to help her keep watch for Creepy Dude on the occasional weekend out. If Sebastian wanted to keep looking, he could go out on his own with Ford. After tonight, it was time to part ways.

"Why didn't you wear green?" she asked him. They were settled in a dark corner at the far left of the bar, where it was almost impossible to get served. It gave them a good view of the entrance.

He made a face. "I work at a high school. I was forced to wear a ridiculous shamrock hat and take crap from the kids during my shift in the cafeteria, where I was stuck eating green cookies and breaking up an argument about to turn physical. The last thing I want to do is revisit the holiday trappings."

"Grumpy," she said, trying not to grin.

For the occasion, she'd worn a green sweater with jeans. Her disguise was a black wig with green streaks in it, which Tessa had happily lent her. He'd gone with the casual look most of the men sported—khakis with a black button-down shirt and rolled cuffs. The sinewy muscles of his forearms were sprinkled with dark hair. She'd wondered many times if his whole chest was covered with hair and how it would feel against the tips of her fingers.

Now she knew.

His body was like a beautiful canvas painting—all bumps and smooth textures, with glorious colors and wild, free strokes. That's exactly how her body felt under his, no matter how hard she wanted to forget.

She hoped he didn't see her red cheeks in the dim, flashing lights.

"I noticed you haven't traveled much lately," he said, obviously blind to her peaking hormones. "I remember you used to go on business trips at least once a month."

"When I stepped into Rory's position, I had to cut back. As the editor in chief, I need to stick closer to home and keep an eye on operations. We hired a PR specialist to take over most of the events."

He lasered in with that intense focus, making the rest of the room drop away under his gaze. "Do you like your new job? Or do you feel trapped?"

She tilted her head. "It took some adjusting. Why would you think I felt trapped?"

"You once told me being locked in an office all day would kill you."

Shock hit her in waves. The conversation they'd shared so many years ago suddenly fell between them, adding a layer of intimacy they'd been able to fight before. Rory had helped keep the barrier strong because they both loved her. But now she was gone, and the memories resurfaced with a new intensity.

Her voice came out husky. "Yes, I meant it at the time. But I was young and didn't realize life throws curveballs, and sometimes we need to compromise. Quench is worth it."

"Would you want to do something different?"

She looked away, needing safety from his gaze. He'd always seen too much. "I don't know. That's the beauty of things—I'm accepting my role for now, but anything can change."

"Even if that change is something you never wanted?"

She knew what he was aiming at and refused to go there. Her gut and her soul knew she wasn't pregnant. There was no sense of sharing her body with another. There were no strange emotions or side effects or anything that hinted at a big change. Soon, the test would prove it, and this chapter would be closed for good.

"I'm not worried," she said. He frowned at her answer but didn't challenge it. "What about you? Any big changes in your future? Or do you want to stay at the high school forever?"

He gave a lopsided smile. "Maybe. The pension is good. But work was never everything for me."

She hated the question that shot from her lips but couldn't stop it. "Have you dated anyone yet?"

His whole body stiffened. "Not yet. Not ready."

"I get it."

"And you? Anyone worth sacrificing time from Quench?"

She took a mental step and refused to engage. "No. Dex is enough."

He muttered under his breath.

"What did you say?"

"I said it must be difficult to think of juggling a serious relationship with Quench. It's been number one in your heart for a long time."

He was right. But it was also her choice, and not a fallback because she was scared of love. Screw that. "Rory managed."

"You've never been like Rory." The words were like ice pellets, and she struggled to mask her reaction. She must've failed because he frowned, taking in her expression. "I meant, you and Rory wanted different things."

Yes. Rory had been the grounded one. The caretaker. The leader.

Chiara needed constant challenge and change—to know what was around the next corner. Losing Rory had forced them all into different roles they'd never sought out. Malia and Tessa had also been affected as they closed ranks on a missing, vital piece of themselves.

Yet, Sebastian's words only poked at an issue that had risen within her before. One she always promptly buried.

Would she ever be as good as Rory?

Chiara knew she'd been a solid replacement as editor in chief and did her job well. She'd learned and adjusted to expand in her new role. Still, Rory had been born to run Quench, and Chiara sometimes felt as if she were consistently chasing behind her friend, trying to catch up.

"That's him."

Sebastian's face was impassive as he studied the couple a few feet from the door. The woman was giggling, and the man held her tightly against him, grinning and leading her toward the exit. She stumbled a bit but went happily, seeming like a hookup that both parties approved of.

Chiara caught his face full-on when the door opened and he turned. Beady, dark eyes. High forehead. Slicked-back hair. Short stature. The features were all on target, but it was the look on his face that sealed it. *Predator.*

"Let's go." Sebastian grabbed her hand and zigzagged in and out of the crowd, keeping his eye on the couple.

"Should we call 911?"

"Eventually. Right now, I don't want him out of my sight until we know that woman is safe."

Chiara agreed. They tore out the exit and looked around the empty parking lot. She caught a glimpse of Creepy Dude's black jacket and the way he glanced around, as if making sure no one saw him. Bastard. Rage curled within her, but she knew it was important to be clearheaded. "He's heading to the back lot."

"Chiara, listen to me. I need you to go back inside the club and flag down the bartender. Ask him to get security out here and call the police. Let him know we suspect someone's getting assaulted."

"What are you going to do?"

His eyes grew ice cold. "Stop him."

She didn't bother to question him further.

Chiara raced back to the club.

~

The son of a bitch was putting her in his truck.

The door was ajar on his black Ford pickup, and he was trying to jolly her in. The drug must've just started to hit her, because she swayed back and forth with her hands in front of her, as if making one last attempt to reject his advances.

"Come on, bitch, just get in," Pimp Guy growled, grabbing her roughly. He spun around, then froze as Ryder came into his vision. His eyes bugged out, immediately recognizing him, before turning snake mean. "Wanna be a hero the second time, asshole?" he asked.

Ryder eased steadily closer. "Nope. Just wanna rearrange your face so it's part of your ass."

He knew Chiara would have someone out here soon and didn't want to lose focus. But Pimp Guy must've sensed his time was limited and he was smarter than Ryder thought.

With one quick lunge, the guy shoved the girl at him. She shrieked, stumbled backward, and crashed toward the pavement. Automatically, Ryder caught her, allowing the asshole to jump into his truck and lock the passenger door before crawling frantically toward the driver's seat.

Quickly maneuvering her to the ground, Ryder shot to the driver's side. Flinging the door open, he grabbed the guy by his coat collar, and they both crashed down in a tangle of limbs. Ryder fell into adrenaline mode and let his fists fly, but the guy got up and began kicking him in the ribs. Ryder rolled to protect himself, ready to jump to his feet, when a warrior yell reached his ears. Chiara sailed through the air and landed on the guy's back, yanking madly at his greasy hair while he began to twist and buck her off, a mad gleam in his eyes.

Holy shit, the woman was out of control.

Ryder gave his own roar and grabbed him before he could hurt Chiara, but she was already being pulled off by a burly dude with a security jacket on. Within seconds, Pimp Guy was on the pavement with his arms twisted behind him. Another security employee quickly joined them, and the blare of a police siren screeched into the lot, the cruiser's lights flashing.

He flew toward Chiara, who was bent over slightly, sweaty and breathing hard. "Are you okay? Did you get hurt? Are you insane?"

His heart pounded in a panic, and he reached out to draw her into his arms, ready to comfort and soothe. Then paused.

A big-ass grin spread across her face. Those golden eyes glinted with a fierce satisfaction that reminded him of a lioness who'd just made a big meal out of her prey. "We got him," she spit out in triumph. "We got him, Sebastian."

He couldn't help it. He laughed, cupping her cheek with his palm, desperate to touch her. "You scared the living hell out of me," he said. "What were you thinking?"

"He was hurting you," she said simply.

Pride and respect hit him full force. This was a woman who had no fear to go after what she wanted. That type of ferocity was scary as hell, and also turned him on like nothing else had. Chiara Kennedy took no prisoners and hadn't thought twice to fight.

For him. She'd been protecting him.

He didn't know what to do with that fact. It aroused a primitive stirring in his gut that ached to be released, and there was nothing he wanted more than to grab her, kiss her, and stake his claim of her.

The police officer stepped beside them. "Folks, I have some questions for you."

Ryder bet they did. He was grateful they'd filed a report, even though nothing had originally come out of it. Now, at least, with this other girl as a witness who could get a drug test, they might be able to get this guy behind bars.

"We're ready, Officer," Chiara said.

It was going to be a long night.

Chapter Twelve

Chiara attacked the keyboard and tried to keep up with her spiraling thoughts. She was so close to finishing her feature article and chased the end like a demon, reliving the entire experience in her mind.

The last few days were a blur. After the long night at the police station, Sebastian had dropped her off and she'd collapsed into sleep for endless hours, mentally and physically exhausted. When she woke, she immediately called Malia and Tessa, and they'd shown up for an emergency session at which she told them all the details.

The girl, Sydney Lassiter, had gone to the hospital and the drug results came back positive. Chiara and Sebastian shared witness accounts, and Creepy Dude was arrested.

Chiara paused to breathe, repeating his name in her mind.

Ronald Daley. A simple name, but one that would forever haunt her. He'd come so close to attacking another woman. God knows how many he'd assaulted in the past, but she was hopeful she could use Quench's platform for healing.

Dex whined, and she looked down where he was sprawled out over her bare feet. "Sorry, love. Give me two more minutes and we'll go for a walk."

His tail thumped, and he laid his head back down, practicing patience. She grinned, got back to work, and finally finished up.

Slumping back in the chair, she stretched and considered the in-depth article she'd rewritten four times.

It was good. Combined with the stats and prior research Chiara had been sent, Quench would begin an open forum of communication with women who'd suffered experiences with a date-rape drug. The police had agreed to issue a short statement, and the article would run this upcoming week, linked with phone numbers for crisis counselors ready to give support and hear women's stories. It was a piece she was proud to run and have her name on, and the thrill of a good writing high reminded her she still gained satisfaction from work that grounded her.

Over the past two years, there hadn't been much time to do the soul work that really drove her. The daily grind of Quench and taking over Rory's responsibilities had been key, but lately, Chiara had tried to include more writing and work she was passionate about. Perhaps it was time she started to ease back into some of her original duties and delegate others.

Another whine had her pushing back her chair. "Okay, Dex, let's go for a run."

He exploded from the floor in doggy excitement and raced over to his leash hook. Chiara laughed, clipped it on, shoved her hair into a short ponytail, and hit the street. They did an easy jog—she was no experienced runner—and her muscles began to stretch and uncramp from the long hours spent hunched over her computer. The morning was crisp and full of potential. Finally, the snow had melted away, and green buds popped up on the trees lining the sidewalk.

Chiara headed down to Memorial Park, keeping a steady pace. Nyack was an eclectic mix of city and quaint small town, and she loved exploring all the hidden treasures popular in the Hudson Valley. Besides the festivals and street fairs, Main Street bustled with various craft shops, cafés, wine bars, and fine restaurants. Alongside sprawling modern brick buildings, large old homes boasting vintage Victorian and Gothic architecture sat beneath gnarled oak trees, delighting onlookers. There was easy access to the Hudson River, so residents regularly gathered on the pier overlooking the mighty Mario Cuomo Bridge for picnics, jet skiing, and fishing. The stretch of mountains dazzled, dominating the skyline and soothing her soul. She'd thought of moving south for the warmer weather, but her travel lust cooled when she thought of leaving Quench or her best friends.

Her sneakers pounded in time to her heartbeat. She kept repeating scenes from the club in her mind. When she'd spotted Sebastian on the ground getting pummeled, something snapped inside her. She'd raced ahead of the security guys and leapt on instinct, not planning what would happen next.

He'd called her insane, but the tender urgency in Sebastian's eyes as he stared at her, mixed with the primitive flare of hunger, had Chiara craving him with every cell in her being. Thank God the police officer had interrupted.

Adrenaline rush. She'd read multiple times that during moments of extreme fear and stress, the body kicked in hormones that made one want sex. It was strictly a biological reaction in response to danger. No need to dig further.

Chiara finished her run past the gazebo, where ducks squawked from the water and young mothers watched their screaming kids on the playground. She slowed to a walk and decided to head to Main Street. "Want to stop at the bakery?" she asked Dex, who immediately barked, recognizing the word. "Good. I think we both deserve a treat."

She chatted with Mandy, who owned the local pastry shop and always had hand-baked doggie treats for the canines. After Dex lapped up a bowl of water and happily munched his treat, they headed next door to the candle shop.

Ebony rushed from behind the counter with a squeal. "I was hoping you'd stop in!" she said, giving her a quick hug. "I have a whole new batch of candles ready to ship out. We can't seem to keep them in stock on our website, especially after Oprah put them on her faves list."

Chiara beamed at her. Quench was big on using local, organic products and pushed to feature female-run companies that gave back to the community. Ebony's soy candles were made with fragrant oils and fresh herbs, and she had a small team of specialized chemists that consistently tested new products. "How's the lotions coming along? Do you think you'll have something to sell by end of year?"

Ebony nodded, dropping to her knees to give Dex some love. "Hopefully. We're on schedule to launch beginning of next year, but you know how life gets in the way."

Chiara laughed. "I do."

Her friend straightened up and studied her face. "Girl, what have you been doing lately? You're glowing."

"It's the sweat from my run," Chiara joked. "Trust me, I think stress has been my own special scent lately, and no one would buy it."

Ebony laughed. "Our stress relief candle is a top seller, but yeah, I'm gonna pass on that one. Work crazy? How's Tessa and Malia?"

"We're all good. Been working on some big feature pieces, the women's conference, and of course, Fashion Week."

Ebony rubbed her hands together. "I cannot wait to see all the pics. But my favorite is when you take all the looks and refashion them for real women like me." She cocked a hip out like she was posing. Ebony was all ripe curves and adored fashion. Her Afro was big and bold like her, and the outfits she picked were unapologetic about who she was. Her spiritual practices of meditation and yoga gave her the vibe of a modern, bold yogi.

"Tessa is the master of it all. I let her work the magic." Chiara glanced at her watch and sighed. "Better get going. Let's get together for drinks?"

"Definitely. I'll send over the new inventory order so you can restock on the site."

Chiara blew kisses. "Sounds fab. See you!"

Dex barked goodbye on cue, and they strolled at a more leisurely pace back to her house. Things were good. A predator had been caught, and justice would be served. She'd connected back with her love for writing a meaty article and figured it may be time to pull back from the endless management at Quench and do more hands-on work. The company was back on an upswing and solidified to a point where she felt comfortable taking some chances. She'd talk to Tessa and Malia later about it.

Whistling, she led Dex inside, figuring she'd pop into the office for a bit and get ahead on paperwork. She grabbed a change of clothes and went into the bathroom to wash up. It wasn't until she caught sight of the box of tampons in the cabinet that a slow realization began to roll through her.

Her period had been due yesterday. With the week's excitement and stress, she'd completely forgotten.

She usually experienced a low pressure in her abdomen and a slight cramping right before she got it. Chiara concentrated on the sensation and tried to laser in.

Nothing.

Her heartbeat began to ramp up, but she tried to remain calm. It meant nothing. She'd probably get it tomorrow, especially now that she was more relaxed and had done some exercise.

Just take the test, the inner voice whispered. *Prove it's nothing to worry about and get back to your life.*

With trembling fingers, she reached into the cabinet and pulled out the kit. She ripped open the box and took out the stick. It was an early pregnancy one, and results were statistically high that the hormone could be traced and detected after four weeks.

Chiara sat down on the toilet and peed on the stick.

A hysterical laugh bubbled up as she laid it on the edge of the sink. She washed her hands, set the timer on her watch for three minutes, and waited. She felt like she was trapped in a bad romantic comedy, where the results were known to every viewer, prepped for the zany but happily ever after journey about to unfold in the safety of their own living room.

Chiara stared at the Tuscan tiles. She hadn't scrubbed them in a while. Maybe she'd take an hour later today and go through the house to freshen things up. A good dusting and clean floors always gave her satisfaction. It was a good thing she'd taken the time to notice how neglected her home had been. Maybe she'd even clean the stove.

One minute.

They needed to spend an evening with Mike, outside the diner. It was too easy to get wrapped up in their lives and forget Rory's dad needed quality time with them. They would talk about Rory and the good times, play Scrabble, and eat pizza. Chiara always felt like he looked lighter after they left. She'd talk to the girls and set something up.

Two minutes.

Should she pack up most of her winter clothes and drag out some spring outfits? With daylight saving time behind her and the weather getting warmer, she craved lighter colors and footwear. She was done with boots—most of them had been ruined by salt. Not that she was ready for sandals full-time, but things were closer. And that also meant a pedicure. Maybe she'd see if Ebony wanted to do a beauty day rather than drinks.

Three minutes.

Her watch buzzed.

Chiara wiped her sweaty palms on her jeans. She needed to look now. Of course, it would be fine, but she recognized this was a moment in her life she'd never forget—a fork in the road where each path was so significantly different, it was like splitting up into two people. Like that movie *Sliding Doors*, she bet she'd keep coming back to right now and wonder if another timeline was playing out somewhere else.

Her stomach rolled. She lifted her gaze and slowly picked up the stick.

Seconds turned into minutes. Maybe hours. Or maybe it just felt like that inside because everything froze and an eerie silence took over. Like she was trapped in space but there were no stars, just darkness and a quiet that resonated through her, disturbing in its totality.

Positive. The plus sign was a light pink but obviously there.

Chiara sank to the floor, her knees pressing against the hard tile. Her fingers clutched the stick in a death grip.

It wasn't possible, yet the evidence stared right back at her like a cocky, mocking grin.

She was pregnant with Sebastian's baby. Her best friend's husband. The man she'd once walked away from in order to save them both from a future she just couldn't envision.

She did the only thing left to do.

She got up from the floor. Grabbed her coat and keys. And headed to the drugstore to get more tests.

It was wrong. It had to be.

Because if it was true, she had no idea what happened next.

Chapter Thirteen

Ryder stared at the group of kids in front of him and sensed it'd be a rough afternoon.

He worked at the Dream On Youth Center on weekends and never questioned what he was giving up—he got it all back and more. The nonprofit was housed in a former church that had been renovated to serve the teen community. The building was old and drafty and desperately needed updating, from Wi-Fi to space, but they made do with what they had.

Ryder knew there were bigger, fancier places that offered a menu of goodies for children to pick from, but Dream On focused on teens, especially the after-school and weekend programs meant to keep kids busy, engaged, and hopefully out of trouble. The center was on the outskirts of town and served a different high school than where he taught. A high school with a hell of a lot less money than his.

The kids rotated depending on who wanted or could show up, but he had a core group that had bonded. The wisdom, drama, and laughs from his time spent with them were better than binging a Netflix series or falling into a video game pit.

Except today.

A droopy energy rippled through the group and set Ryder on edge. There were only five today, but the mood seemed unusually somber, especially when spring break was so close. He hoped to God no one had gotten hurt or killed this past week. Many of their lives stretched beyond the usual teen hurdles, and he never knew what they'd be dealing with on a daily basis.

When Ryder began volunteering at the center, the director had been consistent and clear: Ryder's main job wasn't to fix any of them. Just show up. Build trust by keeping his word. Be truthful when he didn't know shit. And try to have some fun. So far, it had worked.

"Manny, what's with the face?" he asked. "Anything happen?"

Manny was built like a linebacker. He was tough on the outside and a teddy bear on the inside, which made things difficult for him at home. He'd begun coming to the center to get out of the house whenever his older brother got drunk and violent. Eventually, Manny made a makeshift family here. He was hoping for a football scholarship in two years if things kept going well.

The kid rubbed his buzzed blond hair. "Yeah, something happened. I trusted the wrong people and now I'm gonna pay."

A chill worked its way down Ryder's spine. Manny's brother had been trying to drag him into his world, and while the kid had managed to keep himself out of trouble so far, Ryder knew the odds were stacked against him. "Someone coming after you?" he asked calmly.

"Hell yes. My bookie. I lost big in the game and shot my load. Now I got nothing until I grab another shift at the store."

It took a few seconds before the relief hit. He had to tamp down a smile. "March Madness, huh?"

Manny let out some curse words, which Ryder allowed. He didn't care how they expressed themselves as long as they weren't disrespectful. "The point spread was ridiculous, but I had a tip. Was supposed to be set! It was a solid fix!"

Jeremiah let out a hyena-type laugh, which got him a dirty glare. "Man, are you stupid? How much did you lose?"

Manny grumbled. "Enough. What are you laughing about? Heard you got dumped this weekend."

Jeremiah's face was wiped free of his grin. His long string-bean body stiffened. "Who told you that? I broke up with her. She was kinking my style."

"She was kinkin' all right," Manny said. "With someone else."

"Least I got money in my pocket and a stack of numbers to call. You haven't moved on since Tracey."

Ryder straightened up in the chair. He'd have to work a bit harder today to focus them. Manny and Jeremiah hadn't gotten along at first but had slowly formed a friendship. Didn't mean they didn't insult and prod each other to get reactions. What was it about guys that they showed affection by ripping each other down?

"The cardinal rule of gambling is to make sure to only bet what you're willing to lose," Ryder said mildly.

Pru rolled her eyes. Her long hair was in a ponytail, and she wore her usual outfit: jeans, sneakers, and a denim jacket. She was a bit of a math genius, and her parents were strict, giving her two options for her future: physician or lawyer. Her older siblings had followed the plan, but she came here on weekends to rebel in a safe place away from their protective bubble. At first, the kids were standoffish since Pru's family was financially well-off. They warmed up when they figured out her parents treated her like a scientific experiment rather than an actual kid with feelings. "Well, fuckity fuck, Manny, what'd you expect? Suck it up and just eat ramen noodles this week until you get another shift. I'm not in the mood to be sympathetic today. I'm over the rain, I'm dreading spring break since I'll be stuck with my parents, and I need a distraction. What are we doing today, Ryder? And where's Ford?"

Hearing Pru curse like a trucker always gave him a jerk of surprise, but he liked that she felt comfortable enough to show her true personality. "He's running late again. And I have an activity planned for today that we haven't done yet."

"Can we play poker so I can win some of my money back?" Manny asked.

Maria grinned. "How about Jenga?"

The kids all groaned, because she was a champion at knowing exactly what piece to pull or avoid. Maria was in foster care and spent almost two years not speaking due to a traumatic event Ryder would never know about. She bopped around for a while until a nice couple took her in, the mother a local artist. One day she put Maria in front of a canvas, and in the next few hours, Maria completed five canvases and then spoke at dinner. She was hoping for an art scholarship, and though Ryder knew nothing about art, he felt something when he looked at her work. Uncomfortable things. He read up on art therapy with children and began incorporating art here and there, amid protests from the guys. But they did it for Maria because she'd become one of them.

Ryder looked outside, where the rain was picking up. The Dream On Youth Center wasn't the most booming or well known in the district, but that's what he liked about it. They may not have had a ton of volunteers or charity drives, and he'd never been able to take them on some fancy field trip, but Ryder knew good people showed up and cared. Ford was a regular, and they recruited coworkers to come and give classes or talk about interesting topics. Of course, there was more demand for Ford's guests since he worked in sports radio. Way more impressive to teens than a high school.

He directed a curious gaze at the final member of the group, who'd been mostly quiet. "Derek, what about you? How was your week?"

The kid smiled, but it didn't seem to reach his eyes. "Good. Saw my dad."

Ryder nodded. "Anything worth reporting?"

Derek shrugged. Picked at his nails. "Not really. Went to the diner. Tried to see a movie but there was nothing good out. Then he said he had to stop at a bathroom, and I ended up waiting in the car for a while, so I just left."

His throat tightened with his own memory. He knew that drill well. "Did he decide to stop at a bar?"

"Yep. Whatever. He's an asshole. I wasn't about to go in there to pull him out."

The kids murmured in support, using various profanities. Derek's shoulder-length rock-star hair fell over his face and hid his expression. Ryder didn't need to see it to know how he felt.

"How'd you get home?" Ryder asked. Derek had lost his driver's license after he got busted for drugs, went to rehab, and ended up on probation. Ryder had watched him pull his shit together and show up regularly at the youth center, wanting to be clean for both himself and his mother. But it was a rough road with an alcoholic father.

"Walked."

"You could've called me, man," Jeremiah said.

"Yeah, I know. But I needed to blow off some steam. I'm okay." He looked up, and Ryder watched the tight lines of his face ease. Derek's features were strong, but those blue eyes were killer, along with a wicked sense of humor that put people at ease. "Better than getting dumped or losing all my money. I got a good burger out of it."

Everyone laughed, and Ryder relaxed. He was ruthlessly fair with all the kids he encountered in his life but had to admit a soft spot for Derek. The kid had a light inside of him that seemed to shine no matter what the obstacles. He'd dropped out of school but was now taking classes at night, trying to get his GED. Derek kept getting knocked down, but he always got back up.

The boy reminded Ryder so much of his own experiences with his father. The emotional abuse and distance. The ugly need inside to still want approval from a dad who didn't care. The difficulty of having a single mom who still, somehow, missed what she shouldn't. It was an entangled, poisoned mess that lurked, waiting for weakness to spring.

Ryder had made it his job to help. After all, he understood. He'd slowly built trust with the boy, and now Derek sought him out often to talk, bitch, or just ask for advice. It was like the relationship he'd built with Carl, another troubled teen with a similar background and demons. But Ryder couldn't fail Derek like he had Carl. It was as if he'd gotten another chance, and this time, he'd make a difference.

The door burst open and Ford walked in. He shook out his wet, shaggy hair and lumbered over, calling out greetings to each of the kids. "Did I miss anything good?"

Ryder kept a straight face. "Hell yes. Maria got an art scholarship, Manny won bucks off March Madness, and Derek just came back from a Hawaii trip he'd won in a sweepstakes."

Ford grunted, peeled off his wet coat, and fell into the metal chair. "Cool. So there was nothing good."

The kids smiled and gave him some heat for being late, but it was all part of the routine. Ryder was the serious one, and Ford gave the comic relief and relaxed-dude vibes. Together, they made an unbeatable team. "We were talking about everyone's crappy week. Care to share?"

"Hmm, Gonzaga broke my damn heart and my wallet when they lost to the Bears. I got stood up on a date. And I made some poor decisions afterward I'm still paying for."

Ryder tamped down a grin, knowing the bad decision was too much IPA. "Good thing I have the perfect antidote to bad weather, bad moods, and bad decisions." He reached down and took one of the bags from under his seat, then slid out a board. "Figured I'd teach everyone how to play chess!"

Yeah, that didn't go over so well. All of them stared back looking disgusted, including Ford.

"Chess?" Manny asked. "That's for boring, rich assholes."

Pru propped her feet up on the empty chair next to her. The neon pink and yellow lines on her sneakers seemed to be the only bright light in the room. "Chess isn't bad."

"You play?" Ryder asked her.

She shook her head. "Nah, my dad's been trying to teach me forever, but I don't want one more thing on my schedule. I just pretended to be stupid about the moves until he got mad and gave up."

"Well, maybe you want to learn on your terms," he pointed out. "Guys, I'm telling you, chess is for master manipulators. It's trying to outmaneuver the other player by looking into the future."

"Is it like that *Queen's Gambit* series," Maria asked, "where the girl plays the game in her head while she's high on drugs?"

Ryder winced. Not the point he wanted to focus on. "Well, yeah, but that was a show. Made up."

Ford stared at the board with obvious distaste. "How about we play Jenga instead?"

"Yeah!" Maria shouted.

"No!" the rest of the group howled in unison.

Ryder let out a short breath. "Look, it's a crappy day out. Let me teach you, and if you hate it after you try a few games, I won't push anymore." Ryder knew anything he suggested was a simple exchange between him and the kids. He offered something to do or talk about. They decided if it would fly. If not, Ryder usually let his idea go and moved on. Sometimes, it was timing. Some suggestions were wildly popular and others tanked. He just wanted to bring fresh things to the table, but unfortunately, even Ford was bucking him on this.

"What if we're bored?" Manny asked. "Maybe I'll fly."

"Cheap shot," Ryder said easily. "You know how I feel about taking off just because you don't get your way."

"I'll give it a shot," Derek finally said. "Nothing much else to do today."

Ryder noticed the glint of interest in the kid's eyes. Something told him Derek would like the challenge, which was one of the reasons why he'd brought the board today. Good thing he had a second half to his plan to tempt the naysayers. Ryder yanked out the other bag and opened up the ties. The kids sprang to attention.

"You brought candy?" Maria asked, her voice vibrating with interest. "To bribe us to learn chess?"

"It's not a bribe," Ryder said, even though it clearly was.

"Is there enough Sour Patch Kids in there?" Manny asked with a slight whine. "'Cause I don't like peanut butter cups. They are overrated."

Pru held up her middle finger.

Ford grabbed the bag and pawed through the contents. "He got pretzel M&Ms! They're always sold out when I try to buy them."

Ryder pressed his lips together. "Let's get started."

"I need music," Manny said. "Helps me concentrate better."

"Fine, put it on. Just don't crank it too loud." Ryder clapped his hands together and headed over to the long, battered table in the center of the room. The rain beat against the windows, and water trickled through some of the seals, leaking slowly onto the floor. A slight musty smell lingered in the air—the same smell he'd gotten used to for the past two years. But right now, they had music, and candy, and chess, and each other.

Afterward, as the kids filed out, Derek stopped in front of him. Shifting his weight, he ducked his head, obviously uncomfortable. "Hey, Ryder. Can I talk to you for a minute?"

"Of course." He motioned him over to the corner while Ford said goodbye to the others. "Hey, I was impressed with your skill today. You picked it up quick."

Derek swiped his hair back. Pleasure reflected on his face. "Thanks—it was kind of cool. I like that the queen has the power and not the king. And the medieval-looking piece . . ."

"The rook."

"Yeah, the rook is my fave. I think it's underrated."

Ryder grinned. "Agreed."

"So I wanted to tell you that I got a job working at the Mobil as a cashier."

"That's great news! I know you were having some trouble finding something."

"Yeah, I'm happy, but my mom can't drive me because she's working two jobs, and an Uber is expensive, so I'm running into some issues with my shifts. Wondered if you knew anyone from the school who'd want to drive me back and forth for cheap or if you have any other ideas."

His brain calculated and dismissed most options. Having a car was important where they lived—it wasn't like Manhattan. The buses were limited, and there were no subways as alternates. Most took taxis or Ubered. "Tell you what, let me look into that. In the meantime, I have no problems taking you."

His head jerked back. "No! I'm sorry, I wasn't trying to get you to do it for me. I—"

"Derek, I know that. I'm saying I get out early and I stay up late, so until we figure something else out, if you need a ride, text me. This job is important for you."

He began picking at his nails again, obviously uncomfortable. "I don't know."

"I do. I wouldn't offer if it was a problem. Now, stop being a pain in the ass and get out of here. Make sure you text."

He nodded, then looked up. "Thanks. That . . . means a lot."

Ryder's chest tightened. It felt good to help. There were too many kids who just needed a chance in life. It also gave Ryder hope he wouldn't end up a loser like his father. He'd make a positive difference in a kid's life.

It was a good day.

~

Tessa picked up one of the many sticks littered across the bathroom countertop. "You took eight tests?"

Chiara sat on the toilet seat cover, still in semishock. "Yeah. I tried to buy more, but they ran out of inventory."

Malia stared at her with sharp concern, then knelt beside her. "Babe, I know you're freaking out right now. But you have options here. We can go through every single one when you're ready, and we'll help in any way you need."

"How am I going to tell Sebastian?" she murmured. Every time she imagined telling him, her mind rebelled. "I was just getting ready to have the kiss-off convo. You know, *'Hey, Sebastian, we did good by nailing that scum bucket, and we've mended some bad blood, but it's time to move on with our separate lives. See you around.'*"

Tessa winced. "Yeah, you won't be having that convo." Malia shot her a glare. "Oops, sorry. I mean, I wanted to repeat what Malia said. We got your back and we'll work through this. Together."

"Rory wanted a baby for so long. She tried in every way possible and felt positive she'd be a mother. Now she's gone." Pain and guilt tore through her. "How is that fair?"

"Life isn't fair," Malia said. "But torturing yourself over this helps no one. You didn't go looking for this, Chiara. It happened, and as I like to say—"

"Don't," Tessa said.

"Everything happens for a reason. It's fated," Malia finished.

Chiara let out a strangled laugh. "Then she is one twisted bitch."

Tessa laughed and joined them on the bathroom floor. Dex sensed there was a party going on without him. He stared from the doorway, delighted that his favorite people were gathered at his level, then squished his way in to happily plop between them. Tessa scratched him behind the ears. "You should get to the doctor to be sure—even with that many tests done. I know you didn't want to take the morning-after pill, but now this is reality. Assuming the results will be the same, are you sure about what you want to do?"

With each happy pink plus that emerged on the sticks, Chiara confirmed her initial decision. Even now, imagining a tiny life inside of her gave her a strange yet terrifying thrill. The night with Ryder may have been a mistake, but she didn't want a baby brought into this world believing they weren't wanted.

"I'm going to keep the baby." Not only for herself, and Ryder. But for Rory.

"Not gonna lie and say I'm not excited. We're having a baby! Can I be godmother?" Tessa asked.

Malia shook her head. "You are a piece of work. I bet next you'll wish for a girl."

Tessa looked affronted. "I do want a girl. Not gonna apologize for that."

This time, the laugh came from Chiara's belly. God, it was good to know she had them by her side. She'd need all the help imaginable. "Let's not get ahead of ourselves here. First, I have to tell Sebastian."

"Say you want to talk to him and meet for coffee," Malia said. "A public place may keep emotions from spiraling out of control."

Tessa lifted a brow. "I'm impressed, Mal. Good thinking."

"Do you know what type of role you want him to play in your life?" Malia asked.

The past spun with the present in a dizzying whirl. Her friends had no idea she'd met Sebastian before Rory. She opened her mouth to spill her last secret, but fear of their disgust held her back. No, it was better to move forward. She had no idea how Sebastian would fit into this new life, but he was the father, so she knew there was some type of bridge they needed to build for the baby's sake.

If only she weren't still haunted by her feelings. By that intense connection that buzzed between them when they were in the same room together. It had been easier when she could step back and keep space between them. But now?

They'd be linked together forever.

A shiver of fear went through her. "No, I don't," she finally answered. "We'll need to talk about it." Her numbed mind began working again. Unfortunately. "Oh my God, what am I going to tell Mike?"

Malia nibbled on her lip. "We'll tell him the truth together. He'll understand."

Distress rose. "What if he doesn't? What if he can't forgive me for stealing Rory's life?"

Tessa snapped her voice like a whip. "Don't go down this road, Chiara. Mike loves you, and this wasn't planned. It's going to be all right."

"But this isn't a normal situation. The Quench team will have a million questions, and when they find out Sebastian's the father? They know him as Rory's husband, even though he wasn't actively involved in the company."

Malia squeezed her hand hard. "We'll deal with that when we get there. There are a million single moms who make this decision and thrive. Yes, it will be hard. Yes, you're going to have times you'll freak out. But you are an amazing person with a big damned heart, and this baby is so lucky to have you."

"And us," Tessa said.

Chiara held back a sob, and suddenly, they were hugging her tight, with Dex's wet nose pressed against her cheek.

She only hoped they were right.

Chapter Fourteen

Ryder stared at her from across the booth. It was strange not being at Mike's, but he figured she didn't want Rory's dad overhearing anything. This coffee shop was located downtown and offered an array of trendy organic, vegan, and gluten-free options. He'd settled on a chocolate chip muffin he was sure had no real chocolate in it and an espresso. The place was mostly empty due to the strange twilight hour after lunch and before dinner. Chiara stirred her chai latte but hadn't taken a sip yet.

"Are you sure?" he asked.

She nodded. "I waited to confirm with my doctor. I'm due around Thanksgiving."

A shudder worked its way through his body. He hadn't heard from her since her period due date, so he'd finally convinced himself there was no way she'd be pregnant. The raw flash of disappointment caught him off guard. But when he'd begun to realize there'd be no further excuses to see Chiara, he'd battled an even stronger reaction.

But now? Their lives would be forever entwined. "How are you feeling?"

She cupped the mug and stared down at her brew. "Fine. I have absolutely no symptoms. That's another reason I was in shock when I saw the results. Plus, it's still early. I'm not even six weeks along."

"Did you tell Tessa and Malia?" He knew they were like sisters and figured they'd be the first to be told.

"Yeah, I called them after I took a few home tests last weekend."

"How did they react?" He wondered if they judged him, thinking he had taken advantage of her. Even though he didn't remember much except for flashes of their night together, it was possible her friends blamed him. Ryder tunneled his fingers through his hair. "Are they pissed at me?"

She looked up, her amber eyes widening. He got caught in their depths and the swirls of caramel, pulling him in. Immediately, his body responded by hardening, the scent of her reaching his nostrils, reminding him of that last kiss they shared on the dance floor, when they'd both been stone-cold sober. "No, Sebastian. It wasn't either of our faults. It was just . . ."

"Fate?"

A mixture of emotions flickered over her face but cleared before he could figure them out. "It just is," she finally said. "We need to move forward with a plan. I'm going to call Mike so I can tell him privately. I'm not sure how he's going to take it."

Immediately, his guard flew up. "No. We'll go and tell him together. This shouldn't fall on you."

She waved a hand in the air and continued. "No need, I'll handle it. I'll send you a list of appointments for the doctor, so if you'd like, you can join me. I'm going to keep things quiet at Quench for now, until after my first trimester. Then I'll hold a meeting when I've gotten a better handle on how this is going to affect my life."

"Our lives."

"Of course." She seemed to warm up to the subject. "I've got some travel coming up for conferences you can add to your calendar, too, just so you know when I won't be in the area."

Ryder wondered if she thought she was being generous, allowing him a peek into her calendar as his baby grew in her belly. A slow irritation began to boil up, along with sheer frustration. He'd waited for a child so long, and now she seemed to think he'd be a sideline dad, happy to step back and let her run the show.

It was time she knew his own plan.

He let her ramble on. When she finished, she smiled at him, as if waiting for him to thank her. Ryder knew she was going through a big change and needed plenty of time to sift through the consequences. Chiara had never wanted children—she'd told him clearly that night it was a path she preferred not to walk. Now that she'd been forced on it by him, he intended to be by her side the entire way.

He placed his palms on the table and leaned in. Her head tilted slightly while she waited for him to speak.

"I appreciate the information about your plans. The problem is, you haven't heard any of mine yet."

She blinked. "What are you talking about?"

"You're carrying my child. I can't imagine that type of burden on your body, and your lifestyle, especially when this happened without planning for it. But now that we're here, there's no longer a you, Chiara. There's an us. I'm not about to step aside while you make all the decisions, because we'll be making them together once the baby is born."

Red flushed her cheeks. "Excuse me? You're not giving birth—I am!"

"Absolutely, I'm not denying that. But I want more than to attend a few doctor appointments. I want to be involved in every aspect of our baby's life. If we start out from the beginning with you believing you're a single mother, it'll be that much harder for you to understand later that we're a team."

"I *am* a single mother."

"Not in my book." His gaze narrowed. A surge of raw emotion caught him by surprise, the waves choppy and sharp. "I watched my father leave me and my mother without a look back. I watched her struggle to be both parents to me, trying to erase the sick feeling in my gut that told me I wasn't good enough because my father didn't want me. I waited every holiday and birthday and prayed to God he'd call or show up at the door and tell me he made a terrible mistake—that he loved me. I craved it, even though he was a drunk asshole who scared the shit out of me. But that day never came." His voice turned cold. "I promised myself my child would never grow up like that. I intend to be there every day, every moment, through this pregnancy and the birth and beyond. You will never feel alone, or struggle, or wish for help. We are going to do this together, whether you like it or not."

Her chin jerked up, and Ryder wondered if he'd sounded too harsh. Maybe he shouldn't have added that last part? She'd never been a woman to take orders, and she could be feeling trapped. But he thought it was best to lay the groundwork now, before further complications could occur. She needed to know he wanted one hundred percent involvement.

"I'm perfectly capable of taking care of myself and the baby, Sebastian. You can't just expect I'll simply drop into line and happily share my life with you."

His tone softened. "I don't. Of course you need time—we both do. I just want us to be comfortable with each other, Chiara. I don't want to show up after the baby's born and feel like I stepped into an unknown world. I want us to learn how to do this together."

She groaned and half closed her eyes. "This is so crazy. We spent all those years making sure we kept apart, and suddenly, you're back in my life permanently. It's too much."

He couldn't help it. He slid his hand across the table and clasped her fingers. They were warm, and slender, and instantly closed around his, as if she couldn't help her response to him, either. "We'll figure it out. I want to get to know who you are again. I only know the girl who dreamed big and bold and shared every thought with me all those years ago. But we're different people now. I think we both owe our child this, don't we?"

She didn't pull away, and suddenly, the low hum between them flared to a full buzz, an electric connection he'd never known with anyone but Chiara. Their gazes met and locked, and Ryder glimpsed a softening that gave him hope.

"I can try," she said. "But I'm warning you, I suck at this stuff."

"What stuff?"

She shrugged. "Relationships. Sharing. Probably motherhood. I'm scared."

He ached to pull her into his arms, but she wouldn't welcome that type of intimacy. Not from him.

Not yet.

"I'm scared, too. And no one bad at relationships can have such a tight-knit circle. There are a lot of lonely people out there. You happen to be loved by some of the best."

A breath shuddered out of her. Slowly, she pulled her hands back, and he knew she was thinking about Rory. "Okay. I want to wait until I'm at least twelve weeks before we tell Mike."

"Makes sense. In the meantime, can I take you to dinner one night?"

"That's weird."

He laughed. "It's not a date. It's a casual meeting to get food and talk."

Worry flickered over her face. "Sebastian, it's really important we don't give off the wrong impression. I don't want people thinking we're romantically involved and judging us." She hesitated. "There can't be any more slipups."

She was talking about the kiss. The hot, mind-searing, heart-pounding kiss. His body may rebel against being denied such a strong physical connection, but he understood. Romance and sex had no place in the new relationship they were trying to build. But Chiara had never been the type to shrink from public opinion or question what she wanted. Was she protecting her role at Quench, or something more? "Do you really care what people think?" he asked quietly.

"No, but I care what they'd say about Rory and her relationship with you. I care that as the owner of Quench, any negative press can affect more than my hurt feelings—it affects the entire company. And I care about blurring lines that need to be crystal clear. Do you understand?"

He did. And Ryder didn't like it. But he certainly didn't want to make this situation more stressful for her—not now. He gave a sharp nod. "Yeah, I get it. We'll keep a low profile. I'll take you to McDonald's."

She laughed, and satisfaction rolled through him. She had an easy sense of humor he rarely got to indulge in. Maybe he'd get to see more of it now. "As long as we go Dutch. I can pay my own way."

He grinned back at her, the pressing seriousness of their conversation a bit lighter. They could make this work. If they looked at each other as partners and began to build trust, the foundation would be strong enough to offer stability to his child.

Lao-tzu had said, "Every journey begins with a single step."

Ryder's journey would begin with fast food.

~

"Chiara, we're not going to make deadline. I'm still waiting for Brianna's piece for the Fashion Week think tank. I've got the designer outfits from the Gucci, Kenneth Ize, and Anna Scholz collections mocked up, but I need the damn comparison."

Chiara looked up from her desk, which had grown by monstrous proportions, with piles stacked so high, she could barely see Kelsey over them. "Can't we push it to the next day and put in one of our backups?"

"We're all out of backups. If this story doesn't go, I'll need to grab a fluff piece from somewhere on the net."

Her jaw dropped. "You're telling me we have no alternate pieces in the tank? I'm supposed to know when we get low so I can get out some extra assignments!"

"I know, but we've all been busy with the politics and more royals blowouts and Fashion Week. I'm overloaded, Chiara. I'm doing my best."

She took a deep breath and tried to settle. Kelsey was right. They were all doing their best, but her workdays now stretched into such crazy hours, she'd occasionally brought Dex to the office. Normally it wouldn't be a problem, but Hunter was allergic and had to work from home when Dex was there. "I'm sorry, I know. Did you text Brianna?"

"Yes, no answer yet."

Her mind clamored for a quick solution. "Give me half an hour, okay? If she doesn't appear with the goods, we'll switch it out with an opinion piece."

"Whose opinion? Someone good?"

"Yeah, me." Chiara smiled cheekily. "Don't worry, it's been knocking around my head for a while, so I'll get it done ASAP. Good?"

Kelsey blew her kisses. "Better than good—you're a rock star. Oh, did you check out Tessa's piece on Fabiola Manirakiza? She made a splash last year with her Botticelli-inspired African pieces, and we're reaching out for a collaboration with Quench."

"I didn't know about that. Sounds perfect. Who's handling it?"

"Tessa."

"Good, one less thing I need to worry about. Now get out of here so I can write."

Kelsey waved and disappeared. Chiara looked at the full in-box she'd just emptied of tasks and brought up a document. An opinion piece was a bit easier for her to write because she had such passionate viewpoints, but as editor in chief, she also needed to be careful. Opinion pieces were delicate in this current volatile social environment, so she had to show some restraint when making her case.

She took a second to light one of Ebony's key lime pie candles and took a huge sniff. God, she was hungry, but the scent would have to do for now. Tonight was supposed to be her dinner with Ryder, so she quickly texted to let him know she was stuck at the office and had to reschedule.

Would this still be her life when she was a mother, or would she leave Quench and be stuck at home for endless periods of time with no intellectual stimulation? Would she hate it or embrace a new type of lifestyle? Who would she be as a mom?

The questions had been roaring through her brain that week, attacking any quiet moments in between work. She remembered asking Rory if she'd pull back from Quench after she had a baby and being surprised at how easily Rory said yes. Quench had been everything to her, but she said her real dream was to raise a family. It always puzzled Chiara to hear her best friend talk about relinquishing her main leadership role and intense work schedule to work from home. Not that she judged—she was happy Rory knew what she wanted. It was yet another reminder that Chiara would never be as good as Rory. Not at work. Not at relationships. Not at raising children.

Chiara groaned and rubbed her temples. She needed to refocus and get this piece written, then head home to Dex. Maybe she had some Chef Boyardee left in her cabinets. It was her secret guilty pleasure, taking her back to when her mother had forgotten to give her dinner and the Chef had saved her from hunger on too many occasions.

The next half hour slipped by, and suddenly Kelsey was at her door. "Got it! Brianna came through. Did you finish your piece?"

Chiara laughed and fell back into the chair. "Yes."

Kelsey's face pulled into a frown. "I'm so sorry, Chiara. I shouldn't have bothered you—now you're way behind schedule."

"Don't be silly, now we have something in the bucket. I'll send it over—have Michelle copyedit it for me first."

"Michelle left, but she'll get it done in the morning. Everyone's gone home, so be sure to lock up and don't stay much later."

"Yes, Mom."

Kelsey wagged her finger in the air in warning, then left. Chiara would do one last thing and call it a night. It'd all be waiting for her tomorrow.

On cue, her stomach growled.

"Sounds serious." She jumped at the deep voice, then saw Sebastian framed in the doorway. "Good thing I'm here with reinforcements."

She took in the two bags he held with surprise. "I thought I canceled our dinner."

He moved toward her, those long, muscled legs giving him a graceful prowl. So much sexier than a regular walk. Placing the bags on the table, he crossed his arms in front of his chest and regarded her. "You did. But I remember how easy it is to get lost at Quench headquarters. People fall in and are rarely seen again. Figured some food would be welcome."

A rush of vulnerability hit her. She stared at him, then the food. "This is really nice, but I planned to eat at home."

"You cook this late?"

She bit her lip. "No. Pantry stuff."

That lower lip quirked. "Ramen noodles?"

"Chef Boyardee."

"Nice. Spaghetti and meatballs?"

She rolled her eyes. "Ravioli."

"Well, how about Panera instead?"

Her mouth instantly went into Pavlov's dog mode. "Yes, please."

The quirk turned into a full-fledged grin, and his face softened. "Good. Let's eat."

In companiable silence, he unpacked the bags, laying out sandwiches and fries. He handed her an iced tea and she sucked it down gratefully, reminding herself to eat like a civilized human in front of him. After one bite, that resolution was shattered.

"Mmm, so good," she muttered. "Why can't I be the girl who loves salads?"

"No one loves salads. Unless there's good stuff on it, which mutes the purpose. Is anyone else here?"

"Kelsey's finishing up, but I'm the last one to go tonight. I had to squeeze in an extra piece before deadline, so it put me behind."

Sebastian seemed just as hungry, happily scooping up his fries after loading them up with ketchup. "What do you do about Dex on late nights? Dog walker?"

"My neighbor will pop in if I'm desperate, but I usually end up just driving home to let him out, then coming back here. Sometimes I bring him to the office."

"Bet he loves it."

"Oh, he does. I had to have a strict talk with the staff, though, after the first day. He threw up on the way home. They all fed him parts of their lunch. Poor thing ended up with a terrible stomachache."

He laughed. "Can't say I blame him. Met him twice and I'm already charmed."

"You'll get to know him well." She paused, realizing what she'd said. Yes, he'd get to know her dog, but also her, in a more intimate way than even her friends. Uneasiness stirred, so she slowed down, taking a break. "You really didn't have to come by. I don't want you to think I need babysitting."

"Chiara, that never even crossed my mind. I was home early enough, and it didn't bother me to stop by with some food. I'd hope in the future we'd back each other up if one gets stuck."

"You mean after the baby comes?"

He nodded. "Figured it'd be good practice. Besides, I enjoy talking to you now."

"You didn't before?"

He pulled his face into a wince. "No. It was too stressful. There was a wall between us that made conversation awkward. It was better to just step back and keep our contact to a minimum."

His words hurt, but she agreed. After all, Chiara had made the choice for both of them. Their love for Rory had always kept them safely apart. But now there were no barriers, and it gave her a strange mix of excitement and dread. "It was like we had this dirty secret, but we never even kissed."

"Physical intimacy is easier to explain than emotional. It was hard to describe what we'd shared."

His soft voice evoked a shudder. The memory pressed in. Her bare feet propped up on the dashboard, elbow hanging out the open window. An old eighties station on XM playing in the background. The smell of grease from the fries drifting in the air. Their tight connection obvious to both of them as they spoke about things without fear, safe within the shelter of the car.

Their gazes met and held, and the sweet images of that night shimmered between them, driving away her breath. His pupils darkened, and for a moment, they were back there, completely bonded with each other.

Sebastian cleared his throat. "Did you tell your parents about the pregnancy?" he finally asked.

The dull throb of the wound took center stage. "Not yet. It won't matter. We barely talk."

"It never got better with them, huh? I remember you mentioning you had a difficult relationship."

She tried to give him a tight smile but failed. "They were terrible parents and would have no interest in being grandparents. I'm in no rush to share the news." It was hard to keep her voice from turning bitter. Knowing she'd never been wanted was bad enough. Living with the fact while she watched her parents ignore her and tear each other apart almost made her go under.

"I feel really bad for them," Sebastian said slowly.

"Trust me, they're fine. Living their life without limits now."

"No, you misunderstood. They had the opportunity to have you in their life, and they chose not to. They're the ones who missed out, Chiara. You thrived without them. I wonder if you'd be as strong if you'd had the perfect upbringing."

His words startled her but rang with truth. The toxicity of her childhood still haunted her, though she'd tried to make peace with it. Even thought of therapy. But her friends had been her support group, and Mike had been there as a substitute dad. Chiara decided she'd been luckier than most, and focused on her successes in life. Hearing Sebastian explain it like that soothed an angry part of her that still existed. "Thanks." She fiddled with the wrapper and stuck it in the bag. "I'm sorry about your dad."

His chin jerked in a nod. "Me, too."

"How's your mom?"

His face smoothed out, and those cool gray eyes softened. "Good. Got remarried to a great guy and moved to Australia. I don't see her much, but she's happy, and that's what matters."

"We're both orphans by choice," she joked. "Not the best models for perfect parents, are we?"

He didn't laugh. Just stared at her with a seriousness that threw her off-balance. "We'll be ahead of the game because we'll love the baby and do our best."

The room thickened with tension. She felt the inevitable pull again—the same one from years ago. The same one from that night on the dance floor when they kissed.

She cleared her throat, wiped her mouth with a napkin, and faced him. "Thanks for dinner."

"Do you need to stay longer? You still have that alarm system, right?"

"Yes, it's state of the art. But I think I'll finish up at home. Dex has been alone for too long."

Sebastian nodded, grabbing the empty bags and taking them to the trash. "I'll walk you out."

He waited while she grabbed folders and shut down her computer. Chiara trailed behind him, her body stiff. She had to get these physical sensations under control. She couldn't afford any distractions. Her life had just been blown up in a thousand directions. She needed to deal with her treacherous body getting all weak and needy when she was around him.

An awkward silence surrounded them as Sebastian escorted her to the car. All of a sudden, she wondered if this could work. The rising sexual tension brought back old memories of trying to deal with him as Rory's husband, yet maintaining a safe distance. Would their encounters be strained? Would he push to deepen their relationship for the sake of the baby but end up destroying both of them? Would—

"Chiara?"

Her heart pounded. She couldn't do this with him. It wasn't going to work. She needed to say something. "Yeah?"

He reached into his pocket and pulled out a crumpled receipt. "You owe me twelve dollars and fifty-eight cents."

She blinked, staring at the paper. "Huh?"

"Your half of dinner. It's okay if you don't have cash now. I'll get it next time."

The implication of his statement slammed through her. And then she was laughing, relief pouring through her. She immediately withdrew a ten-dollar bill from her handbag. "Take this for now. It was well worth it. Thanks for bringing it."

He grinned. "Anytime. Say hi to Dex." He strolled away, disappearing into the shadows.

Shaking her head, she got in her car and drove home.

Maybe things would be okay after all.

Chapter Fifteen

"I invited a guest over."

Chiara stared suspiciously at Tessa. Her friend had whispered the words, which was a harbinger for trouble, as they were walking into Mike's house to meet for pizza and Scrabble—a monthly Sunday tradition they'd continued after Rory passed away. It was the only time he left the café at high noon and allowed himself half a day off.

Malia gave Tessa the same stare. "Who?"

She preened. "Ms. Primm."

Chiara gasped. "Get out!"

Malia's dark eyes bugged out. Her braids swung past her shoulders as she shook her head wildly. "Have you lost brain cells, girlfriend? Mike is going to be pissed!"

Tessa shrugged. "No, he won't. He's too polite. She should be here soon."

"What did you tell her?" Chiara asked, half-impressed by her friend's ballsy move.

"I did some digging and found out Ms. Primm—Emma—attends Scrabble tournaments! So I reached out and told her we get together at Mike's house some Sundays to play, and that we'd love another player. She agreed. End of story."

Malia snorted. "You mean the beginning of a horror story. She'll be all moony, Mike will be uncomfortable, and the whole thing will be awkward."

"Why do you have to be such a Debbie Downer? This will be good for both of them. Mike needs to see her in a new light. Appreciate her intelligence. We get his interest piqued and then *bam*. They fall in love and live happily ever after."

Chiara laughed. "You sound like a romance writer. Why don't I think this is a good idea?"

"Because you're paranoid. Come on, Mike's waiting."

Tessa rapped sharply on the door and walked in. The small, green ranch-style home was basic but held the element of warmth and family Chiara always craved. There were thick piled rugs, rich wood, and an open-style kitchen with an oversize table that accommodated the crew. She thought back to their regular Sundays together, with Rory in charge of board games and the menu, as Mike grilled them for updates on their lives. He never judged them and never yelled, except for the time Rory came home and threw up all over the place after they'd snuck gin to her boyfriend's house and drank all of it with fruit punch.

Chiara still couldn't drink gin.

Mike came to greet them dressed in jeans, a loose navy-blue T-shirt, and dirt-old sneakers that were his favorite. The hair he had left stuck up in the back. Chiara wished she could tame it before Ms. Primm came, but then he'd be suspicious. "Girls, how are you? Pizza's on the way, and the game is set up." He rubbed his hands together. "I'm feeling good about tonight. Hope you have money to lose."

They dropped their purses and jackets and got comfortable. "Sorry, Mike, I've been reading the Scrabble dictionary in my spare time. I hope you emptied the register at the café, 'cause I'm taking it all," Tessa said, already in the kitchen and taking out the wine.

Malia got the glasses lined up and grabbed Mike a Coors Light. "We're not going over ten bucks," she warned. "It ruins the pureness of the game."

Mike winked at Chiara. "Says the one who's lost the past three tournaments."

Chiara giggled at Malia's glare. "My letters have sucked. Not my fault—I'm definitely the smartest in the group."

Tessa made a gagging sound. "No, you're not. I got higher scores on the SATs."

"I had the best GPA," Chiara cut in. "Plus, I made honor society."

"Oh, please. Everything's not all academics. I got the medal for fastest time on the 5K and was president of the debate club," Malia said.

Tessa handed out glasses of wine and Chiara's lime seltzer, cocking a brow. "Debate, huh? Is that why you go mute at the most crucial of times?"

Chiara almost spit out her first sip with laughter.

Mike shook his head, used to their banter. "Chiara, are you feeling okay? I got your favorite wine."

Chiara stared at him, blinking furiously. "Um, yeah, I'm fine. I . . . I tied one on the other night, so figure I'd stick to seltzer."

Mike grinned. "Those hangovers are wicked. Let me know if you need some aspirin. But don't think I'm going to take it easy on you. I intend to win all the money tonight."

Disaster averted. For now.

Guilt and fear mixed together, clenching her gut and making her slightly nauseous. She hated lying to him, but it was still early in her pregnancy. Besides, she wasn't ready for such a serious, life-altering conversation. What if Mike shut her out? He was a crucial part of her life, and she'd rather die than hurt him. Would he distance himself from her? Refuse to see her? Their tight-knit group would break apart, and it'd be all her fault. The thoughts spun wildly in her mind until the sound of the doorbell broke her rising panic.

"Pizza's here. A little grease will do you good, sweetheart." His grin froze when he confronted the guest at the door. "What are you doing here?"

Uh-oh. This evening was beginning to fall apart.

Tessa jumped into action. "Oh, Mike, I forgot to tell you I invited Emma to join us tonight. Come on in, we're so happy you're here. Aren't we?" she added between gritted teeth, shooting Mike a warning glance.

The man jerked back and stared at the retired schoolteacher like she was a naked stripper. Chiara wanted to close her eyes to the imminent disaster, but she couldn't. Tessa needed help.

She raced forward. "Hi, Ms. Primm! Wow, this is great, we'll finally have another player. It gets dull with only four people."

"I don't think it's boring," Mike muttered, glancing back and forth between them.

Emma stepped over the threshold, and Tessa slammed the door behind her. She startled, her hand going up to check her hat. It was a brown felt suede with a hunter-green ribbon. A matching cable-knit sweater hung from her open coat, so thick the fabric seemed to swallow her thin frame whole. The pants were also green, and dear God, were they polyester? She wasn't that old! "If it's a problem, I can leave," she said stiffly.

"Of course not—we invited you!" Malia said in a chirpy tone that she never used. Mike stared at her with suspicion, but her friends were masters at this game. All they had to do was pass the conversation torch until Mike understood Emma was staying. "Would you like some wine? It's a buttery chardonnay, or there's beer or seltzer."

"Tea?" she asked, taking off her coat and neatly folding it in half. "I'm driving, and with my body weight, even one glass would place me in the danger zone."

Mike pointedly looked at Malia and Tessa, who had full goblets of wine. Malia winced.

Chiara hoped underneath the shy exterior, Emma had a backbone. She certainly had shown it in English class. Mike needed a woman to stand up to him or he got too bossy. He was used to being in control—at the restaurant and at home. Rory had regularly challenged him, and with both of their Irish tempers, some of their fights were legendary. Chiara knew they had enjoyed testing their skills against each other. It was another thing that made her feel she was with a real family. Grudges were never held, so a healthy argument cleared the air.

"How's Lipton?" Chiara asked.

"Perfect."

Chiara made the tea, and Malia took her coat. Tessa kept up an easy chatter to ease the tension, and then the pizza arrived. They gathered around the table with their dinner, and the gilded Scrabble board was the centerpiece.

"What a lovely set," Emma said. "I have one similar, but I don't get to use it much."

"Why not?" Tessa asked.

"Can't play Scrabble with one person," she said. "That's why I began attending tournaments."

"That's so cool—I bet you're an amazing player."

"I manage to hold my own." She reached out and patted Tessa's hand. "You shouldn't use *cool* and *amazing* in the same sentence, dear. You're better than that."

Chiara swallowed a laugh as her friend gaped at the teacher, properly schooled. Mike stared at her almost in fascination.

Emma went back to eating her pizza. The woman made quite a production getting ready to eat. First, she patted off the extra oil, then methodically removed loose strands of cheese. She used a fork and knife to cut off the very tip of the slice, then continued to eat tiny, perfectly squared-off pieces that fit politely in her mouth.

Mike shook his head, then dug into his pizza with his normal gusto. He liked extra cheese and ate sloppily, believing food should be eaten with enthusiasm. Chiara noticed Emma's frown as Mike inhaled his slice and ignored the napkin until most of his pizza was gone.

"You eat very fast," Emma said. Her tone was as pleasant as if she'd uttered *"Have a nice day."*

"You eat very slow."

Emma blinked. "Digestion is aided by taking your time and indulging in smaller bites."

"You're probably right." He grabbed a second slice, grinned, and shoved it in his mouth.

Emma made a distressed noise but didn't say anything else.

Mike finished quickly, wiped his hands, and distributed the trays. "Let's play. Everyone put your ten bucks in."

Emma stared in astonishment. "You gamble at Scrabble?"

"Of course. Keeps things interesting. You have ten bucks, right?"

Her mouth made a prim circle. The gesture struck Chiara as more stuffy than sexy. "Well, yes, but I don't feel right about turning an educated game into some type of dirty money grab."

Mike's gaze narrowed. "Those fancy competitions you play in, is there prize money for the winner?"

Emma's cheeks flushed. "Well, yes, but that's different."

"No, it's not. The winner at those tournaments gets a lot more than fifty bucks."

Malia laughed, but it seemed forced. "We don't have to play for money this round, Mike! Let's just have some fun. Keep it easy—after all, this is the first time Emma's playing with us."

Tessa was less graceful, glaring at Mike with a fierce warning. He caught it and jerked, finally realizing he was being rude to a guest. Chiara had never seen him like this before. Usually, he loved company and treated people like he did in his café—with warm joviality and an ease that made him everyone's friend. Why was he acting so odd?

"Sorry. It's fine, we'll play for fun," he said gruffly, backing off.

Emma adjusted her hat. "Thank you."

Tessa took a tile from the bag and passed it around. Malia and Emma both pulled an A, but Malia got to go first when her second letter was a C. It took a while to get everyone settled, since Emma picked the rest of her letters the same way she ate her pizza. Methodically. She looked and thought about each letter before slowly reaching back into the bag for the next one. When she was finished, Mike grabbed the bag and took a handful, muttering something under his breath about waiting to die.

The first round went easy enough. Chiara had been playing with her friends and Mike for a long time now. They weren't professionals by any means, and their copy of *The Official Scrabble Players Dictionary* was dog-eared, but everyone knew their two-letter words, how to get rid of a Q without holding a U, and how to exploit their letters for maximum points.

The second round, Emma made the word A-L-E-R-I-O-N.

"Wow, you got rid of all your letters already! Great job," Tessa said, beaming.

Chiara and Malia also congratulated her. Emma looked pleased and a bit shy. Chiara wondered how often the woman was able to enjoy some praise. When Tessa did her research, she'd told them Emma lived alone with a cat, attended a local book club, and tutored a few children. She'd never been married, never had children, and seemed to live a reclusive lifestyle. Was she lonely, or satisfied with her choices?

"Wait, that word has a double L in it," Mike piped up.

The pleasure from her face drained away. "It can be spelled with one L or two."

"I challenge."

Chiara stared at him. "What? Mike, I'm sure she knows how to spell the word."

Emma flushed hot. "I certainly do."

"I just think she made a mistake. I've seen that word before. Maybe she's bluffing."

Their guest resembled her last name as she screwed her face up with disdain. "Scrabble is not a game where you bluff. You must've mixed that up with poker."

Malia glanced back and forth between the two of them. "Um, Mike, I'd rethink that challenge if I were you. Losing a turn now would be critical."

"I stand by my decision. Look it up."

Emma's lips tightened into a thin line. "Very well."

Tessa looked it up. "*Allerion* can be spelled with one or two Ls," she said. "Sorry, Mike. You have to skip your next turn."

This time Mike flushed, but he gave a jerky nod.

The tension notched a bit tighter, so Malia began idle chatter as they resumed the game, and Chiara refilled wine glasses between turns. If only Emma drank, maybe she'd be a bit less uptight and talk more. Maybe she'd even laugh. The skin around her mouth and eyes was smooth and free of small wrinkles or creases. Could it be from lack of smiling?

Chiara admired the woman's command of Scrabble and had to admit the extra competition leveled up the interest of the game, but Mike barely glanced at her. It was obvious Emma had a crush. She kept staring at Mike, fiddling with her tiles in a slightly nervous manner.

Tessa shot Chiara a knowing glance, as if she noticed the same thing, and brought out the big guns. "Okay, guys, I have this great story to tell you. I was doing this feature on first date mishaps, where women reached out about wanting a second shot at a date with a guy they'd initially liked but disaster happened. I got all kinds of responses—some tragic, some funny, but the one that stayed with me always makes me crack up."

"Oh, I love this story!" Malia shrieked, taking another sip of wine. "Go ahead, tell them."

"This woman, we'll call her Amy, had a first date with this guy six months ago. They went to South Street Seaport in New York, had drinks, got to know one another, and were having a great time. She excuses herself to go to the bathroom, and there's this spiral staircase. Her heel gets caught and she tumbles down the stairs, ripping open her skirt and basically lying there, spread-eagled, with all the goods on full display."

"Was she hurt?" Emma asked, eyes wide behind her spectacles.

"That's what makes the story funny and not tragic—she didn't have a scratch. Said she did daily yoga, and she just bounced along and only had a few bruises. So this guy rushes down, sees it all, and asks if she's okay or if she needs an ambulance. Amy jumps up and starts laughing hysterically, tells him she's fine, then rushes into the bathroom."

"One of the most awkward first dates I've ever heard," Mike said, shaking his head. "What happened?"

Tessa propped her elbows on the table. "Amy left. Watched from the bathroom until he wasn't looking, then took off. Got an Uber back home and never responded to his texts."

"Poor woman probably figured she'd shown her main course before the appetizers came out," Malia said, giggling.

They all burst into laughter except Emma. She stared at them in confusion. "Well, I think that's an awful story. Events like that can damage a woman mentally. It could ruin her entire life!"

The laughter died down. Tessa looked properly chastised. "Um, yes, but that didn't happen. Amy couldn't stop thinking about the guy, but she was afraid to reach out directly. She asked Quench to help get back in touch with him and make sure he wasn't involved in another relationship. I called him, put them back in touch for another date on Quench, and I heard they're talking about moving in together."

"That's something," Mike said. "Rory would have liked that story."

A wave of longing passed over Chiara as she stared at him. She wished Rory were there, sitting in her place, ready to spring the news about a baby with Sebastian. But that wasn't possible any longer. And soon, she'd have to tell Mike the truth and pray he'd be able not only to forgive her but be a part of this baby's life.

Emma regarded them. Chiara waited for her to say something about the loss of Rory, something comforting to win Mike over. Maybe that would open up the channels of communication a bit, and they'd find some common ground. She was staring at Mike, as if trying to find the right words, her face a mixture of emotion.

Finally, she seemed to break out of her trance.

One by one, she slipped a letter tile into its place, adding to the word Malia had just put down.

O-R-G-A-S-M-S

A shocked silence fell over the table. Emma began counting points, her pencil scratching against the pad. "Eighty-eight points plus the fifty bonus for using my seven letters is 138. There are no letters left, so I gain all of your points, too."

"You had two Ss all this time?" Mike asked in astonishment.

She looked up, surprised. "Of course. I save those in order to maximize points toward the end of the game, unless there's a bigger opportunity earlier. I think I won."

"Oh, you won, all right," Tessa said with a defeated sigh. "Fascinating word choice."

"Mostly lower-point letters, but Malia left herself open for a plural. That was fun. Shall we play another?"

Mike got up from the table. "Actually, I think we need to call it an early night. I got a headache."

"What a shame. I have aspirin in my purse," Emma said, her hands clasped neatly in her lap.

"No, thanks. I think I really need sleep."

Chiara jumped up. "I'm exhausted, too. What a week, right, girls?"

"Sure," Tessa said, a trace of disappointment in her voice.

"Well, I understand. It was a lovely evening. Thank you for inviting me. Perhaps we'll do it again?"

Malia gave a sick laugh. "Um, sure! Yes—we'll call you!"

Emma got her coat, slowly put it on, removed her keys from her purse, and rearranged the hat brim. "Goodbye, Michael. Thank you for inviting me to your home."

He stood a safe distance away from her, as if she'd try to hug him goodbye. "It's Mike. Yeah, sure. Drive safe."

"See you Monday morning at the café!"

And then she was gone.

Chiara braced herself for the fallout. Mike gave them each a hard look—the same exact one he'd bestow after they got caught doing something bad. "You will not invite that woman back, do you understand?"

Tessa was the only brave one. "But Mike, she likes you! And she's very nice, once you, um, get to know her. It just takes a bit of time to get used to her personality."

"There's not enough time in the world for that, Tessa. I mean it— no more crazy setups. She's alone for a reason."

"That's mean. Sometimes people close themselves off. Look at you! You're not old enough to shut yourself away in your home and restaurant for the rest of your life. Maybe this is an opportunity for you to get back in the game."

Mike gave an incredulous laugh. "I'm not interested in getting back in any game, especially with Ms. Primm, who couldn't even giggle over winning with the word *orgasms*. We come from two different worlds and could never relate to the other's."

Chiara frowned. "What do you mean?"

He cut his hand in the air and dismissed the question. "Never mind. Now, girls, I appreciate your concern, but the matter is closed. I'm happy being by myself, running the restaurant, and having you over for Scrabble and pizza. Alone. Agreed?"

Chiara and her friends nodded.

"Good. I'll see you at the café. Be good."

They packed up and left. Outside, they stopped at Tessa's car. "That went well, genius," Malia said.

"Fine, it was a bit strained," Tessa said with a toss of her head. "It will be better next time."

"Next time?" Chiara repeated. "Didn't you just hear what Mike said?"

"Of course. That was only the beginning. It's obvious they got their signals crossed, but I can do some work with her. She's a bit socially awkward and happened to say the wrong things. But I'm sure it's because she was very nervous."

"Mike didn't seem thrilled with her company," Malia pointed out. "What are you going to do about him?"

"There's something else going on there. I think he's afraid of opening the door to caring about anyone, and it was easier to cast her in a bad light."

Malia sighed. "You're so damn stubborn."

"Where's your sense of hope?" Tessa asked.

Malia swung her braids and grunted. "It's gone, okay? I'm starting to realize it's almost impossible to find that special connection to another person. Maybe the bulk of the population never finds it, so they just settle in order to have a shot at a traditional family life."

Chiara and Tessa stared at her. "Another bad date?" Tessa asked.

"The worst. It started out so well. Good conversation. Decently attractive. Cracked a joke or two. Even paid the bill! And then it happened."

They leaned forward, waiting.

"He asked if I was okay with threesomes."

Chiara's eyes widened. "Excuse me?"

"Yep. He announced that he wanted to be up front about his needs and asked if I was sexually adventurous."

"That's ballsy for a first date," Tessa finally said.

"Oh, it gets worse! He said my photo gave him the impression I'd be open to 'nontraditional ways of love and commitment.' What the hell, man? Does my cute photo at the park give off ménage vibes?"

Chiara offered her a hug. "I'm so sorry, sweetie. Where are you finding these guys?"

"All over. This one worked at a bookstore, so I thought I was safe." Malia schooled her features into her kick-ass mode. "Maybe I need to look at alternate routes to have kids. My parents will disown me, my relatives will write me off, but at least I won't have to meet awful men."

"Not all men are awful. Maybe I could try and set you up with—" Tessa began.

"No! Please, Lord, no more setups. Stick to Mike and Emma, even though I'm against that, too. He doesn't like her and never will. You should give up."

"I just need to practice some easy dialogue with her and suggest fun things to talk about with him," Tessa said. "Come on, guys, she really likes him. It's just hard for her."

Chiara softened as she watched her friend's enthusiasm. Tessa had such a passion for helping women break out of their molds and build confidence, and all of them had been worried over Mike the past two years. Other than the diner and their monthly Sunday Scrabble dates, he stayed home and kept to himself. He was a man who knew everybody but spent quality time with no one.

"Okay, I'm in," Chiara said.

Malia shook her head. "Not me. I'm getting off the crazy train. See you guys later."

After Malia took off, Tessa grinned and squeezed Chiara's hand. "Don't worry, I'll get her back on board soon. I'm so excited. Project Primm take two!"

Chiara laughed, and suddenly she was hugging her friend super tight. "I love you, Tessa. You have the best heart."

Tessa made a snort of self-derision but hugged her back, reminding Chiara that with her friends at her side, she could get through anything.

Chapter Sixteen

The next few weeks rolled by, and Ryder sensed he and Chiara had begun to create a tentative routine. They ate dinner together one night a week, usually at an out-of-the-way pub where no one knew them. Conversation flowed, and slowly, they began to learn about each other again.

The bill was always split evenly.

As the weather warmed, Ryder learned she liked to take Dex for a run on Saturdays, so he began coincidentally meeting them at the park. At first she balked and tried to ditch him, but Dex had taken a shine to him. Ryder brought him treats, and soon the canine was solidly on his side. Chiara finally softened, and he got his first hint of how she'd be as a mom.

Her dog was well disciplined and well loved. Ryder liked to watch her eyes grow warm when she glanced at Dex and hear her throaty laugh when the lab completed one of his antics. She kept a close watch when he was in the dog park, over both his behavior and any other dog who might be trouble. Ryder realized he craved more time with her. Time to become comfortable in her world and vice versa.

So when he discovered she was speaking at a popular health center regarding happiness in the here and now, Ryder was curious. He'd seen her talk to the high school students, but that had been on short notice. He wanted to see Chiara in her element. He also wondered how she'd address the topic, since stress seemed to be climbing to an all-time high for everyone. Ryder had found out she wrote a lot, that she was excited about diving into features to bring to the Quench audience. The article she'd published on date-rape culture impressed the hell out of him, and it had been picked up by social media outlets and blew up, citing her as a new leader among women. She had a way with words that served her audience well—simple, clean, and raw.

He was looking forward to seeing her in action.

Thankfully, there were still tickets available, so he donned a Mets baseball cap, jeans and a T-shirt, and his favorite Jordan sneakers and headed out to the Hilton. He made his way to the Grand Ballroom, stopping by to check out the displays for Wellness Weekend. It was packed with women, but organized, so he didn't feel like he was bumping or squeezing his way through. Ryder nodded to the men accompanying their partners, grabbed an agenda, and seated himself in the back.

Chiara was one of the keynote speakers, and the space held a good one thousand people. The lights dimmed in warning, and soon the place was jammed. Her intro was packed with all the accolades audiences expect from a keynote. He'd watched Rory many times easily command a room, the fire of her personality a natural motivator to the crowds. When Chiara came to the stage, he was hit by a completely different sort of energy.

Quiet. Capable.

Her sky-blue business suit was clean-cut and had no designer labels. The color emphasized the fiery red of her hair, which had been left loose to swing sleekly under her chin. She smiled at the crowd, and a murmur of anticipation settled over the room.

"As you've just heard, my bio is full of impressive credentials and potential social media hashtags to lure in a huge number of likes. I'm sure you're expecting me to stand in front of you today to share the steps I took to make myself into a successful entrepreneur with a million-dollar company. But I'm not."

She walked slowly back and forth, maintaining eye contact with the crowd. "Since this is a wellness convention, I'm sure you'd at least expect me to talk about finding easy ways to de-stress when you're hit with a client phone call, crying baby, and your family asking when dinner will be ready." Low laughs rippled. "But I'm not."

"Instead, I'm here to tell you something else. A truth about myself I don't tout on social media or put in my impressive bio. You see, my parents never wanted me. I was born a mistake. And that never changed—I never became the miracle or joy baby or feel-good story that other people tell. Nope. I was an inconvenience. I was told every day to be grateful my parents were taking care of me, and when I turned eighteen, they said they were done. When I was of legal age, they patted themselves on the back, cut me loose, and went on with their lives, happier that they were alone again."

Stunned, he stared at her vibrant figure. The huskiness of her voice brought a hushed intimacy to the room. No one moved.

"I've had to carry that truth throughout my whole life—that I'd never been wanted. It played out in various ways, through relationships and choices. Let me ask you all a question. Who's had a challenge you needed to overcome, about an opinion or so-called truth about yourself from someone else? Raise your hand."

Every hand went up.

"Every woman I've ever talked to carries this around in her heart and soul. If someone says you've gained weight or look tired. If a colleague or boss mentions you're not good at your job or failed in some way. If a spouse or partner belittles you in a joking manner and calls you too sensitive. If a parent judges the choices you make with your own children, ready to 'help you.' That is what bonds us in this room. Our struggles as women and humans to figure out our worth and our voice."

She stood in the center of the stage, palms raised in the air. "It's time we own who we are, not what others want us to be. It's time self-care becomes something more than getting a massage or lighting a candle. It should transform us into making bold choices about our happiness, so we finally have something to give others. It's about saying no, in order to say yes later, to a bigger, better opportunity. It's about changing those so-called truths that are all false, because they live in our mind from the past."

Ryder's throat felt thick. She seemed both vulnerable and fierce in the spotlight, connecting with these strangers in the dark.

"My parents didn't want me. But that wasn't because I was unlovable. I sat in a café booth with my three best friends and dreamed about a business for women, by women, who actually gave a shit. Not to sell stuff, or be popular on social media, or pretend we're some kind of gurus who can help everyone solve all their problems. Every day, we want to show up, like all of you do. We want to be kinder to ourselves and stop chasing the same old story that plays in our minds that we're not worthy. That we're not loved. That we're not enough."

She raised her hands higher along with her voice. "We. Are. Enough."

Clapping broke out.

"*You* are enough."

The applause rose to a deafening sound.

"My parents didn't want me. Yes, it will always be part of my identity. I believe in therapy, and meditation, and exercise. I believe in friends, and opening your heart to love, and allowing grief to become part of our landscape rather than running from it. Take what you need for yourself, even if it's in tiny increments, because you're important. That's what today is about. A reminder. A restart. A reckoning. Every morning we wake up, we get a do-over. Isn't that the greatest gift we can ever ask for?"

Her arms fell back to her sides. Her smile was full of warmth and hope and dazzled every onlooker in the room. And then she did something that Ryder would never forget.

Slowly, her hands lifted and rested on her belly.

It was as if within those seconds, everything changed. Somehow, she sensed the baby growing inside of her—that subtle, unconscious movement so many women completed a hundred times per day. An acknowledgment of a new life inside of her.

His baby.

Raw emotion tore through him. He sat, slightly stunned, not able to move as he took in the thunderous applause rising in the air, knowing a part of him would forever belong to her and vice versa.

But the triumphant moment passed way too suddenly, taking everyone by surprise.

In one swift movement, Chiara bent over and vomited all over the stage.

~

"I'm fine. My damn pride hurts more than my stomach."

Ryder shot her a worried glance. After the shocking scene, she'd been whisked offstage while a team had gone to work cleaning up the mess. He hadn't liked the way a particular woman jumped in front and began taking pictures of the incident, then faded into the crowd. A quick announcement followed that Chiara wouldn't be able to chat with attendees because of a stomach virus but that she was fine and heading home to rest. He insisted on driving her.

"Do you think it's morning sickness?" he asked.

"I have no clue. I haven't had any symptoms yet. Maybe it's something I ate?"

"Did you eat sushi?" He'd read a list of potentially toxic foods women shouldn't eat when Rory had been trying. "Maybe we should call the doctor."

Chiara shot him a look, but it softened when she seemed to realize he was clueless. "I ate a grilled chicken salad with veggies for lunch, and a yogurt for breakfast with some granola. Don't worry, I already downloaded the list of foods to avoid, so I won't be eating sushi."

He let out a breath. "Sorry."

He relished her warm smile. "No, it's okay," she said. "We're both learning this together. I think—"

"Yeah?"

She turned a shade green. "I think you need to pull over."

He did. Afterward, she collapsed against the seat, and he drove as fast as possible to her house. Dex bounced around when they got through the door but seemed to immediately sense his owner's distress. He calmed down, pushed his wet nose against her side, and whined.

She rubbed behind his ears. "Baby, Mommy's gonna lie down. Sebastian will let you out, okay?"

The lab turned mournful eyes toward him, as if worried to leave her. "Don't worry, buddy, you can take a pee break."

Ryder helped settle Chiara on the couch with a blanket, then took care of Dex. "Can I get you some tea?" he called.

"Yes, please. Ginger is in the top right cabinet. I bought it last week, thank goodness."

He filled the teapot and brewed himself a cup of coffee. Her kitchen was roomy, warm, and casually messy. Yellow accents offset the dark wood cabinets and floors. Her home reflected the interesting balance of her personality. A pop of bright, sunny colors mixed with classic wood. Stylish but comfy furniture mingled with crochet blankets, fuzzy pillows, and fun knickknacks. The dining room table was used as her office. He peeked down the hall and wondered how many bedrooms she had. She'd need room for a nursery.

So would he.

Pushing the uneasy thought aside, he retrieved Dex and rummaged in the pantry for some saltine crackers.

"You're spoiling me," she said when he brought the crackers and her tea out on a tray. "Do you make chicken soup, too?"

"When warranted. Rory was always the expert on cooking, though." He inwardly cursed mentioning Rory right now, but Chiara just nodded.

"Yeah, she was good at anything she put her mind to."

"She only liked cooking when inspiration hit. Daily meals and survival didn't interest her."

A smile curved her lips. "Sounds about right. I'm not the best cook, but I learned to do basics."

"Like ravioli?"

He loved the sound of her laugh. "Exactly. I hope you don't judge my pantry. There's like thirty cans in there just in case they ever stop making them."

"You'll be ready for the zombie apocalypse." Ryder settled in the chair next to her and sipped his coffee. She nibbled at the crackers, and Dex laid his massive head on her thigh, squeezing himself next to her. The quick bite of jealousy surprised him. In that moment, Ryder wished he could lie next to her, arms wrapped in a tight embrace, offering comfort.

"Hey, why were you at the conference today?" Her question came quick and sharp. "I was surprised to see you there, but I got distracted by all the chaos."

"I wanted to see you speak," he said simply.

Chiara blinked, those extraordinary eyes filled with uncertainty. "But why? It had nothing to do with you."

The comment cut, but he understood. They'd spent years learning how to avoid each other, and suddenly the rules had changed. "Quench is a huge part of your life, Chiara. You're passionate about it, and I wanted to watch you talk about something you love. Maybe it was a way to feel closer to you."

Her jaw dropped. He didn't blame her. This was a hell of a lot of truth so early in the game. But his baby was growing inside of her, and every day, he moved closer to the realization he wanted more than a casual relationship with her. He just didn't know how to navigate or even approach her with how he wanted to go about it. Also, Ryder wasn't ready to be rejected if she didn't feel the same.

"Why?" she asked again, rubbing her eyes. "I'm not going to cut you out of the baby's life; we've already established that. You didn't have to sit through a woman's seminar to prove anything."

A simmer of anger danced along his nerve endings. He allowed the bite to seep into his voice. "This isn't a tit-for-tat game. Years ago, I saw a glimmer of who you were, and I wanted more. Fate chose differently, and I embraced all of it with no regrets. But you're back in my life again, and we're having a baby. We get a second chance to see this through, Chiara. Do you understand what I'm saying?"

Shock flickered over her face. "No."

"I think you do." He dragged in a breath, cursing himself for pushing. "But now's not the time. You need to rest."

Her lower lip jutted out in stubbornness. "I'm not tired."

He tried not to smile at her obvious lie. "Okay, then can we talk about your speech?"

"You're not going to give me criticism and feedback, are you?"

"Hell no. You nailed it. The crowd was hanging on every word. You managed to take a rah-rah keynote and turn it into something deeply personal. I had no idea you were such a great speaker."

He liked the flush of red on her cheeks and was glad her color was back. "Thanks. It took some practice, but I finally learned the only way to really connect with people authentically is to share some of your truth. Women are constantly surrounded by people but feel alone most of the time. We build these communities, but it's all surface and gloss—we need real connections. That's what I'm trying to do at Quench."

Ryder studied her. Her face wasn't classic or lushly beautiful. It was a face with great character and depth, from her pointy chin, angular cheekbones, and too-wide golden eyes. The freckles sprinkled over her nose and the small crescent mole on her cheek only added to his fascination. But it was her heart that kept leading him deeper. Chiara was quiet, focused on the people trapped in groups who rarely heard their voice, the leftovers on the edge of cool crowds. She had a unique ability to rouse a bigger response because of that quality.

It was something he recognized well, because he felt similar. Ryder never dreamed of being a CEO or charity president or holding any other leadership position. He wanted to help kids on a day-to-day basis and get dirty. He liked to see not only the individual potential of his students but the unique way they carved out their path. Being a small part of their choices and offsetting some of their parental angst satisfied him and kept him challenged. Yeah, a guidance counselor may not win big awards or stand out, but if he did his job right and cared enough, he could make a small difference.

That was enough for him.

Chiara finished her tea and curled her elbow under her cheek. Her energy seemed to settle into a lazy drowsiness.

"Can I ask you a question?" he asked.

"Only if it won't piss me off. I lied. I'm a bit tired. I guess throwing up does that to you."

"That stuff about your parents. I remember you saying you felt disconnected from them, and that you weren't close, but I never heard the full story. Do you really feel they didn't want you?"

She didn't startle or avoid his gaze. Her voice held steady. "I meant every word. My mother told me that often. I spent most of my life wondering why she just didn't have an abortion or give me up, but it was like this code of honor for her. She was proud of herself that she hadn't taken 'the easy way,' as she termed it. She did her duty and raised me, and when I turned eighteen, she got her life back."

Pain snaked through him, dull and achy. "That's fucked up."

Chiara grinned. "Yep. That's why Mike and the girls were so import-ant. They helped me realize it didn't matter—my parents didn't have to define my story. I mean, it wasn't always easy, and I still struggle, but I think it's important women get that no one's alone, not like they think."

"It was a powerful moment in your speech." He paused, letting his thoughts sift to settle on the question he really wanted to ask. "Is that why you told me before you didn't want children? Because of your experience with your parents?"

She wrinkled her nose and seemed to consider the question. "I don't know. I grew up fiercely independent, so the idea of being responsible for others was never appealing. Taking on Dex was a big deal. Still, when people hear I'm not looking for marriage and a family, they either think I'm lying or call me selfish. Maybe I am." She stared into the distance, caught in her own memories. "Maybe I don't want to bring more pain to any kids in this world."

His throat tightened. The loneliness in her voice made him ache to touch her. "You're one of the most unselfish people I know."

A wobbly smile curved her lips. "Doubt it. I just know who I am and don't want to apologize."

"No, you had the guts to think about the consequences, which is a great gift to the world."

Her gaze snared his. Connection hummed between them. They sat with it for a while before she spoke. "What about you? That stuff with your dad was rough. Didn't that affect your view on kids?"

"It's the reason I wanted a job helping kids. I knew I wasn't cut out for the hard stuff like social work, but I was always drawn to teens. I had a great guidance counselor in school who'd just talk to me about shit. Tried to get me to focus on stuff I liked and gave me permission to dream. He made a mark without even knowing it, so yeah, that's what I felt drawn to.

"As for children? I always craved a big family. A therapist would probably term it my 'do-over.' You know, be the best dad ever to make up for my own scars?" He grinned to soften his words, but she didn't let him get away with it.

"I remember we talked about that years ago. How badly you wanted to show you'd be different."

He thought about that night and how she left, leaving him with a hole inside. "Funny, isn't it? Because that was the main reason you left. We were too different."

She stroked her belly, and again, the gesture blasted through him. "Yeah," she said softly. "It felt like the right move at the time."

He nodded and got up with his coffee mug, needing some space. "Let me put this in the sink."

She yawned. He liked that it was big and loud and not dainty at all. "Don't bother. I'm gonna take a nap after all. You can get out of here."

Ryder realized he didn't want to. He wanted to stay and take care of her. Walk Dex. Make her dinner. What the hell was happening? She was still early in her pregnancy and already he was experiencing signs of attachment. Was it some weird nesting stage? Didn't that happen to the woman later on? He'd need to look it up. "Sure. I'll check on you later. Do you promise to text if you get sick again?"

Her eyes were already closed. Dex snuggled against her bare feet like a warm rug. "Hmm, I will. Thanks for taking care of me."

He did the few dishes, dried his hands, and grabbed his keys.

She was already asleep.

He watched her for a while, dog and owner squeezed together, her hand still lying half on her belly. A fierce sense of possession roared through him, and one word echoed over and over in his head.

Home.

Ryder cursed under his breath and turned away. He wanted Chiara Kennedy to belong to him. But she didn't know the truth about the night Rory died. What he'd done. Eventually, he needed to tell her, knowing full well it may destroy the fragile bond they'd finally built.

Ignoring the slice of regret at the thought, he closed the door behind him and refused to look back.

Chapter Seventeen

The next few weeks drifted by in a flurry of activity. The school year was wrapping up and kept Ryder busy. Chiara fought the dreaded morning sickness on and off, and he made sure to be on hand with tea, crackers, and help with Dex. Of course, as soon as her stomach settled, she was scurrying back to work in a frenzy and seemed to be brimming with creative ideas for new articles.

He realized he liked taking care of her as much as he enjoyed watching her thrive at Quench. A fierce protective instinct had flared to life, and it wasn't all about the baby. He wanted Chiara to be happy.

But there was one important step still hanging over them that needed to be addressed, and the day had finally arrived.

As they approached Mike's house, Ryder glanced at Chiara, who swallowed hard as she stared up at the door, fingers trembling slightly. He reached out and squeezed her hand on instinct. He needed to be the strong one even if his own stomach was tied in knots.

At least she had kept her relationship with Mike strong. Ryder was the asshole who'd dropped his father-in-law and disappeared after his daughter's death. Sometimes, he woke up in the middle of the night thinking about it, the guilt practically strangling his breath.

When Chiara phoned Mike to ask if they could both come over, he almost expected the man to tell her no. Ryder certainly hadn't done anything to deserve his kindness. Instead, Chiara said he was excited to see him, noting it had been a long time.

Mike opened the door and waved them in. "Hey, it's so good to see the both of you! Not gonna lie, though, you sounded mighty mysterious why you wanted to meet me at the house instead of the café. You guys want something to drink? Eat? I have leftovers and can fix you a mean turkey club."

Shame assaulted him at the man's easy warmth. He was the type of father Ryder always aspired to be. When he'd married Rory, Mike had treated him more like a son than an in-law. Ryder felt comfortable to be himself around Mike, who created a space of safety, where everyone could tell him things without worry he'd judge. Ryder hoped today would prove the same and he'd understand the circumstances around Chiara's pregnancy.

"No, thanks, we're good," Chiara answered, shedding her coat. She squeezed herself around the middle, as if protecting the baby, and took a seat at the dining room table.

Ryder was struck by how many meals he and Rory had shared here, confessing their hopes about having a family of their own. Mike had always been supportive and believed one day they'd be pregnant.

Now Ryder would be making the announcement.

But it wasn't with Rory.

He dropped in the chair beside Chiara and dragged in a deep breath. "Mike, we want to tell you something that will be a big shock to you. And we're just asking you to give us time to explain the circumstances."

Fear shot from the man's blue eyes. "Someone's sick."

"Oh, no!" Chiara said quickly. "I promise, we're all fine."

His shoulders slumped and he joined them at the table. "Thank God! You had me worried it was something bad."

"It's not bad. At least, we hope you see it that way," Chiara rambled. "It's an odd story to tell."

"And we just hope by the end of it, you'll understand," Ryder continued.

Mike put up his hand. "Guys, you're killing me. Stop chasing your tails and just spit it out."

"I'm pregnant," Chiara said.

"With my baby," Ryder added.

The shock in the man's face was expected. Ryder was hoping to avoid the disgust, anger, or hate that may come later. "Wh-what are you talking about? Pregnant?" Mike smoothed a hand down his head. "I don't understand what's going on."

"Can we tell you how it happened?" Chiara begged. "I promise it's not what you think."

Chiara took the lead, sharing most of the story, and Ryder fleshed out other details.

Mike shook his head as if trying to clear it. "So, that night, drugs were involved?"

Chiara's cheeks turned bright red. "Yes. Neither one of us knew what was happening. And afterward, we were both sure there'd be no pregnancy. But when I missed my period, I took a test, and it was positive."

"I know this must be hard," Ryder said. "We've been twisted up about this ourselves, thinking of Rory and . . . well, how badly she wanted this. But we both want this baby, Mike. We want to give it a loving home, with both parents. And a grandfather who means the world to both of us."

"We never meant to hurt you," Chiara whispered.

Mike stared at both of them for a long time. His body trembled like he was in the grip of a fever, and he closed his eyes, as if fighting for the right words.

Ryder clutched Chiara's shoulder in comfort. No matter what the reaction, they needed to weather it together. And Ryder swore he'd do anything in his power to get Mike to eventually accept the baby.

"How would you ever believe this would hurt me?" he finally muttered. His eyes flew open, shiny with dampness. "Both of you are like family to me, and this baby is part of all of us. Even Rory. To know I'll be involved in this, well, it gives me a purpose I haven't had in a long time."

Chiara gave a small cry and went to him, and they hugged hard. "I'm so relieved. I thought you'd be upset or feel betrayed—"

"Never. I lost my daughter and barely survived. I know neither of you would do anything on purpose to hurt me or Rory." He let out a strangled laugh. "In fact, it was hard for me to accept when you stopped coming around to see me, Ryder. I never blamed you—I knew you were in your grief—but having you back, and happy? Well, it means a lot."

Guilt slammed him. Ryder's heart, which had been filled with hope a few seconds ago, slowly deflated. Because he knew he was still living with a lie, and he needed to tell both of them in this moment, before it poisoned his very soul.

Even if he couldn't be forgiven.

"Mike, there's something else I need to tell you. Chiara, you too."

They looked at him with curiosity, still wrapped up in the emotion of the moment.

Ryder laid his palms faceup in his lap and finally confessed. "The night that Rory died? I was the cause. I got her killed."

Shocked silence filled the room. He forced himself to look at them and accept the revulsion on their faces, but there was only a deep confusion.

"What are you talking about?" Chiara asked, her voice hitting a high note. "You're scaring me, Sebastian. Tell me what's going on."

He took a deep breath. "We'd had a huge fight. The fertility drugs were causing some friction between us, and I felt like she was using work and her friends to avoid me. As if she blamed me for not being able to give her what she needed." The shame rushed in, but he pushed on, refusing to stop. "I was trying to persuade her to come to bed early. To talk and watch a movie and have some downtime together, but she wanted to work. I got mad and snapped, blowing up at her. She packed up her stuff and said she was going to Quench because she couldn't be in the house with me anymore. She stalked out and I went to bed."

The result of that decision haunted him every hour of every day. What type of husband had he been not to go after the woman he loved? He'd known she was upset, but he allowed her to get in the car and drive away.

"I woke up when the police knocked on our door. I never even knew. I never texted to check on her. Never apologized or told her I was being an asshole. I went to fucking bed and slept and figured we'd work it out in the morning. But for her, morning never came." He stared sightlessly at the wall. "Rory died because of me."

Emptied, his insides felt hollow. He knew what was coming. Knew Mike would make him leave. Chiara would blame him for what happened. Ryder not only deserved it, maybe he was wishing for it—for someone to finally know and force him to be accountable.

Mike regarded him with careful precision. "You kept this to yourself for two years?" he asked.

"Yeah. I'm a selfish prick. And I'm sorry—I'm so sorry every damn day. It's the real reason I stayed away from you after the funeral, Mike. I felt like I was the reason why your daughter was taken away, and I pray for her forgiveness all the time. I know it's too much to ask from you now." His voice broke. "But I don't want to be cut out of your lives."

Mike got up and walked over, and Ryder stood up so the man could face him head-on. Ryder would take whatever anger he deserved and not try to excuse himself. He'd abandoned his father-in-law in his time of need and would have to live with the consequences.

Mike gripped both of his shoulders, then shook him. "Son, I need you to listen to me. Hear me. Can you do that?"

Ryder nodded numbly.

"You had nothing to do with Rory's death. It's not your fault. She was hit by a driver who had a heart attack at the wheel. And that wasn't his fault. It was a messed-up, tragic accident that was nobody's fault."

He tried to focus his gaze on Mike, beyond the pain tearing him up. "But I made her leave."

"No. She left because that was how Rory dealt with things. When we'd fight, she would always stalk off. Rory needed space to think before she was ready to come back. It was how she processed stuff, and you know this—you were married to her. I guarantee there was nothing you could have said or done to make her stay that night. Do you hear me?"

Suddenly, Chiara was beside Mike, and her beautiful amber eyes glowed with a fierce, simmering anger that was glorious to see, even if it was directed at him. "Mike is right; she was always one to storm off. And no one thought to chase her down, because she always came back."

A deep trembling gripped his body. Why was he shaking? He felt as if he were half here and half somewhere else, but Chiara was forcing him to focus. He stared at her face and listened hard. She was telling him something important. Something, he believed, that might change his life.

"Sebastian?"

"Yes?" Was she crying? He didn't want her to cry.

"It wasn't your fault. It was never your fault."

The words struck clear and true. Mike nodded, and suddenly, the icy barrier that had been protecting Ryder finally crumbled, leaving a rush of relief so pure, it was like a burst of light and oxygen in a dark, suffocating room.

"Do you hear us, son?" Mike asked. "Rory would have never wanted your guilt. She loved you, and you were a damn good husband. Okay?"

He managed a nod. "Yeah." A sense of peace and acceptance settled over him. If they could forgive him, he could try to forgive himself. "Okay."

Mike glanced at both of them. "Well, I'll be honest. I've never wanted a shot of whiskey so badly in my life. Well, except the time Rory announced she was getting engaged to that biker guy her senior year."

"I remember him!" Chiara said with a laugh. "I think he ended up doing time."

"Great. Now I feel like Father of the Year."

Ryder grinned. "Is that what I'll be in for?"

"No reason to scare you both off this early in the game. That's what Pop Pops is here for."

His throat tightened.

"Peanut will be very lucky," Chiara said, patting her belly.

The nickname hit him full force, along with the tenderness in her voice. "Peanut?"

She laughed. "Well, he or she needs to go by something, and 'baby' seems impersonal."

Mike grinned. "Seems appropriate to me."

Ryder stared at her, caught up in a rush of emotion. "I love it," he said softly.

They stood in the center of the room, gazes connected, and for a strange moment, the air shimmered with energy, as if a presence had settled upon them, bonding them even closer.

It was probably just his imagination.

Right now, Ryder concentrated on the gratitude sweeping through him, allowing him his second chance. For not only a family, but the possibility of much more.

~

Ryder had just thrown on sweatpants to chill on the sofa that evening when the text came in.

Can you pick me up?

He texted Derek back immediately. Be right there.

It didn't take him long to drive to the convenience store. He knew the boy hated to ask for help, but Ryder was grateful he trusted him enough to do it anyway.

He'd noticed Derek pulling back a bit at the center. He wasn't as quick to engage with the others, giving off a moody silence that concerned Ryder. The kid was probably slammed with work, studies, and home stuff, but he thought it might be a good time to check in.

He pulled into the parking lot where Derek waited. The kid climbed in the car and shut the door. "Thanks, man. I'm sorry to ask last minute. Mom got a flat tire, so the car's been stuck in the driveway. I gotta fix it for her."

"No problem. I was just watching some reruns on TV. How was your shift?"

Derek shrugged. "Same. The work's boring, but I need the money." The scent of smoke clung to him, but Ryder couldn't discern any weed.

"How's your mom?"

"Okay. She'd been fighting a cold or something, which makes her tired."

"Those colds can knock you out. Maybe bring her some chicken soup from the lunch special." Derek gave a small smile. "How about your GED? Classes going okay?"

"I'm falling behind a bit. With all the shifts I'm taking at work, I missed two classes, and helping out my mom, there's not enough time to study. I'll catch up, though. The stuff is easy—I'm actually pretty good at every subject but English. I hate writing."

Ryder grinned. "You're a numbers guy. Maybe after your GED, you can take some business classes at the community center. Accountants and finance folks make good money."

"Maybe. Not sure I'm the college type."

"What, smart?" he asked. That got him a grin so he pushed a bit more. "College gets you a better job with higher pay. Plus, more job satisfaction. I can help if you need it. With applications or questions or stuff. I happen to be a guidance counselor."

The boy shrugged, but Ryder caught the quick look of hope on his face. Ryder's heart squeezed as he realized Derek was half man, half kid, on the verge of a future he was scared shitless of. "I'll think about it."

"Good enough."

Derek fell into a silence that spoke of deeper things. His fingers beat a restless rhythm on his leg, matching one shaking leg.

"Anything else you want to talk about?" Ryder asked neutrally.

He didn't answer for a while. Ryder waited. Shadows leapt and played across the boy's stoic profile before his hair swung forward and masked his face. "Can I ask you a question?"

"Anything."

"Did you ever get tired of it all? Like, you were on this hamster wheel, and no matter how fast you ran, you'd always end up in the same place anyway?"

A chill skated down his spine. Derek's question wasn't laced with the usual sarcastic humor he was known for, but held a darker tone. Ryder didn't like where the signs were pointing. Between the boy's withdrawal at the center and current stress load, Ryder wanted to be careful about how he answered.

He pulled onto Derek's block and cut the engine. He turned toward him and gave him his truth. "Yeah, I got tired of it. Tired of my father drinking and beating on my mom. Tired of hating him after he ran out and didn't care how we ate or lived. Tired that I didn't get to go to one of those fancy colleges with a fat scholarship and play on the lacrosse team. But it didn't matter. It got better, and it will for you, too. I promise."

Doubt gleamed in Derek's piercing blue eyes, along with something deeper, something that made Ryder pause. "You can't promise me that."

"Yeah, I can. Because you're a smart kid. Focus on the GED, then take the next step. Nothing changes overnight, but when you look back later, you'll see how far you made it. You gotta just keep moving forward."

Derek opened his mouth to say something, then shut it. He nodded. "Thanks."

Something still didn't feel right. Ryder shifted in the seat. "Derek, do you want to talk to a mental health counselor? I can get you a direct contact with someone I work with. No questions asked."

"No, Ryder, I'm fine. Appreciate it."

He studied Derek's face. He remembered how Carl had begun to change, and Ryder had never directed him toward help. He'd mistakenly believed he was the only person Carl needed to talk to. "What about your sponsor? I don't like the vibe I'm getting."

"I'm all right, I swear. I go to my regular meeting tomorrow night, but if I start feeling worse, I'll text my sponsor."

Ryder had to accept it. It was important Derek learned to navigate the ups and downs of being an addict. Once again, he was reminded he couldn't do the work for any kid—no matter how bad he wanted to. He could only support and direct them toward help. "I'm around night or day, so you can call or text me, too. Anytime."

A real smile curved his lips, and Ryder relaxed. "No worries. I'm not planning to do anything, I promise. I'm gonna fix the tire, eat some of Mom's lasagna, and crash. I'll see you at the center."

"Need help with the tire?"

"I got it." Derek got out and shut the door, giving him a quick wave. Ryder watched him enter the house before pulling away.

He needed to keep a closer eye on him. Ryder was glad they'd been able to chat tonight—he felt as if Derek had righted himself after a bad night. Ryder would just keep showing up for the kid and help him any way he could.

The memory of Carl made his fingers clench around the wheel. This time felt the same, but he had to believe it would be different. He was able to reach Derek—Carl had been too embroiled in the crap around him to see a way out.

Ryder just couldn't slip up this time.

Chapter Eighteen

Chiara trudged into the kitchen to make her one precious cup of coffee. After reading a variety of articles and research, she'd decided one cup of caffeine was fine for the baby. Dex trotted back inside and attacked his breakfast while she stared longingly at the coffee dripping into her mug.

Thank God it was Saturday. Sure, she needed to work—there was always work—but even this early the sun was out, and she sensed it'd be a beautiful day. Maybe she'd check the weather and see if she could squeeze in some running time.

She was just reaching for her phone when it began shrieking. Hitting the speaker button, she spoke loudly. "Are you calling to tell me about another disastrous date?"

Malia's voice held no sign of humor. "Did you see the post?"

"Which one?" Chiara asked, already opening up her laptop. "Did someone big die and we're the last to know?"

"Yeah, I wish it were that simple. Wait, Tessa's calling me. I'm going to patch her in."

Oh no. This must be bad. She breathed and tried not to panic, scrolling through the major news outlets. "I can't seem to find anything. Give me a link."

Tessa came on the line. "You can start with BuzzFeed, but it's pretty much everywhere. I'm afraid it's catching on fast, those bastards. You didn't tell me a reporter was spying on you at the Hilton."

Chiara shook her head and tried to keep up. "What reporter? Are you . . ." She trailed off as the headline suddenly hit her.

New Queen of Quench Spills All Her Truth and It's Not
Pretty!

There she was, tossing her cookies for the public's amusement. The bitch had managed to catch her at the most unflattering angle, with her face all squished up and ugly. Chiara skimmed through the brief article, which touched on how she was speaking at a wellness convention, talking about her "horrific" childhood, when she got sick onstage. The hook and picture were true clickbait.

And the subject was her.

Malia began babbling. "I can't believe they did this at a self-care convention! What's wrong with her? Do you know this Wynter Davis?"

"Never heard of her," she said. God, she craved wine even more than coffee right now. This not drinking thing was a bigger sacrifice than she thought. She hoped Peanut appreciated it.

Tessa huffed out a breath. "It's disgusting and cheap. There's not even a story, just poor Chiara getting sick onstage where she had everyone inspired."

"We're one of the top female-run companies and just got featured in *O* magazine. People are paying attention to us, especially after we lost Rory," Malia said. "But it's no excuse for making a beautiful keynote ugly."

It was true. Owners of companies other than the big ones—Apple or Amazon or Facebook—were mostly swept over and rarely made the news unless there was a scandal. She felt horribly exposed in a way she never had before. "I'm sure she was there for a fluff piece and took advantage," Chiara said calmly. "It'll pass. I mean, honestly, guys, it's not that interesting. Except I hate she called me the queen."

"Yeah, the *new* queen. Tasteless," Tessa said.

They agreed to get their PR person on it. Probably not engaging would be the best move to make it disappear. By the time they'd hung up, Chiara was sipping her coffee and trying not to let the piece bother her. Too much good had happened in the past few days to ruin it.

Telling Mike about the baby had been a turning point. Knowing he accepted the circumstances and actually embraced them allowed Chiara to finally feel free to begin moving toward her new future. But it was Sebastian's confession that had truly shaken her to the core.

The idea he'd carried such guilt with him all this time made her heart ache. How could he have blamed himself for something he couldn't control? She could only imagine how it'd affected him. When they'd left Mike's house, he'd kept holding her hand, and Chiara hadn't broken from his grip. She wanted to be the one he turned to for support. The ferocious need to be there for him, to ease his hurt, had startled her in that moment.

And now, something had changed. She just didn't know what to do with it yet.

On cue, her phone buzzed again and she immediately picked up. "Hey."

"Hey. What are you doing?" Sebastian asked.

"Finishing my one and only precious cup of coffee."

"Good. Make sure you eat, too. I don't want you to get nauseous."

She decided to let him get away with his bossiness, though he had a tendency to be a bit high-handed when it came to her health. The knowledge he was also concerned about Peanut softened her answer. "I will."

"Then get dressed. You're playing hooky."

She craned her head and peeked through the back window. "It's Saturday. You can't play hooky on a weekend."

"You can. It's going to be seventy degrees and no rain in sight. I refuse to let you do paperwork all day or get trapped in the office. We need to seize the day."

Lightness spread within her. The idea of spending time with him made her a tiny bit giddy. She'd finally stopped worrying about who saw them together. It was as if Mike's approval had been needed for them to move forward, into whatever type of relationship they were trying to build.

If only the damn man wasn't so hot.

Even now, his voice practically smoked with intimacy over the phone. When they were together, his gaze seemed to penetrate all her hidden corners inside. Worse? She was genuinely in like with him. He'd always been so distant after he married Rory, as if trying to keep them in their own bubble. Now she realized his actions over the years had one goal: keep the barrier firmly erected between them. Chiara finally understood, and new feelings seemed to blossom daily the more time they spent together.

"What did you have in mind?" she asked.

"A little outdoor activity. You've been cooped up at the office a lot lately with deadlines. How about some bike riding?"

She laughed. "I haven't done that since I was twelve."

"That's criminal. I'll come pick you up in an hour."

"Should we bring Dex?"

"Absolutely. He'll love it and can run behind us."

His words poked at her heart. There was something about the way he loved Dex that got her mushy inside. "But what if I can't? I told you, I haven't ridden in years."

"Guess what?"

"What?"

"It's just like riding a bike—you never forget. See ya soon." He hung up.

Chiara laughed. Dex cocked his head and wagged his tail, sensing he was about to accompany her on a new adventure. When was the last time she'd blown off work for a fun activity?

She couldn't remember. Maybe because work had always been her fun place.

She showered and took her time getting ready, then headed outside to wait on the porch. Her jeans were getting a tad tight, and she wondered when it would be time to embrace the yoga pants. Chiara shuddered. She always equated yoga pants with minivans.

Yet, here she was. Who knew what would happen next?

Sebastian pulled up, and Dex danced with delight. Chiara was amused as he greeted the lab first, then stood and turned to her with a grin. "Hope you can ride a super-speeder with twenty-four gears."

Her jaw dropped. "What? I can't ride something like that—I told you!"

"Just messing with you—they don't make anything like that."

She rolled her eyes and got in the passenger seat. "You trying out for a part-time job as a comedian?"

"Nope, just a bit blissed to see the sun. The kids were out of control this week."

"What were they doing?"

He pulled out of the lot and headed toward the park. "Let's just say teen hormones are insane. Besides making out in the hallways and a few fights over girls breaking out, the custodian found a couple half-clothed in his damn broom closet. Even worse? It was during bio class and not even on their break."

She laughed at his disgust. "I almost forgot what that was like."

"I feel like I'm corralling a bunch of rabid animals wanting to mate. It's the final push to the quarter, and I hate to see them lose focus, especially my sophomores and juniors. And of course, my seniors are obsessed with prom, which thankfully is next weekend."

Chiara sighed. "Wow, talk about a blast from the past. Rory and Tessa scored dates for prom, but Malia and I stayed home. We pretended we were cool but admitted later we felt like losers."

"You didn't go to prom?"

She lifted a brow. "Um, you don't have to make it sound like I committed a crime! No one asked me, okay? My boyfriend had just broken up with me, and everyone else already had dates."

"Those boys must've been blind not to ask you."

Girlish pleasure washed over her. "Thanks. It's only when I see those teen movies that I get a bite of regret. Mostly, it was about the dress."

Sebastian laughed. "It's always about the dress. Well, I get stuck chaperoning every year, so it's a different experience for me now."

She glanced at him, studying his carved profile. He needed a haircut, but she loved the way the thick ebony strands curled a bit wildly around his ears and neck. His bright blue T-shirt hugged his shoulders and chest. The scent of ocean and soap filled the car, and she fought the impulse to bury her face into the curve of his neck and breathe deep.

Thankfully, she remained still. But the urge remained.

They arrived at the park and unloaded the bikes hooked to the back. Chiara was relieved to find that hers was a simple beach rider with a generous seat, wire basket, and no fancy gears to intimidate her. She put on her helmet and swung one leg over the frame, happy that her toes touched the ground.

"Want to take a few spins around and get used to it?" he asked.

She nodded, pushed off with her foot, and began to ride. Immediately, her instinct took over and she was off in a blur, easing into the turns and enjoying the tug of wind against her hair. She came to a stop and gave him a thumbs-up. "You're right. It's like riding a bike."

He grinned and hooked Dex's leash to the frame of his bike. "We'll take it slow. Follow my lead."

"Yes, sir."

She fell into line behind him, and Dex took a steady pace, ears pinned back in ecstasy. The day fell around her in springlike glory, and she basked in the heat of the sun, the sway of the trees, and the bustle of activity around her. Kids screamed with glee from the playground, the bright red slide a beacon for fun. Bees buzzed and drank from fat, colorful blooms. Birds swept low and cackled in conversation. Squirrels played tag back and forth on the pathway before careening up oak tree trunks. Chiara let her worries slide away and enjoyed the ride.

Her feet pedaled faster until she cut in front of Sebastian, showing off with some figure eights and taking her hands from the bars to wave them in the air. She giggled at his stern warnings to watch herself, standing up fully on the pedals and letting the natural speed of the hill whip her away, hearing Dex's barks in the background.

God, when was the last time she felt like a kid?

Never. Growing up, she didn't have a dad who taught her how to ride a bike, or a mom who took her clothes shopping. She'd always been on her own to figure things out. Sure, they kept a roof over her head and food in her belly—mostly Chef Boyardee since her mother barely cooked. Chiara hated complaining when so many others had it worse.

But she rarely fell into impulse and allowed herself to open up and just be . . . silly. Sebastian had made her laugh the past few weeks more than any other man she'd been with.

But he's not yours, the inner voice whispered. *He'll always belong to Rory. Don't forget.*

She wouldn't. Today, he was on borrow, and she didn't want to think about anything else.

"You're a regular daredevil," Sebastian said when he caught up. "You gave Dex a heart attack. Thank God you're wearing a helmet."

She rolled her eyes at his teasing. "You won't be cracking jokes when I start taking skateboarding lessons. It's been on my bucket list."

Those gray eyes warmed. "I'd never stop you from doing anything you truly want," he said softly. "I hope you know that."

She stopped the bike next to him. The space between them tightened with awareness, crackling with energy, and her heart sped to a gallop as warmth turned to heat. His words pulsed with hidden meaning, and she was suddenly off-balance, not knowing how to respond. He kept his gaze tight on hers. And waited.

Finally, she spoke past the strange lump in her throat. "Good to know. Maybe after Peanut is safely sprung."

He shifted closer. "I like that you call our baby Peanut."

Shivers raced down her spine. "Yeah?"

"Yeah. Makes me feel like you claimed our baby."

The word *claimed* did something to her insides, and she was unable to answer.

His voice dropped to an intimate pitch. The wind caught his scent and cloaked her in it. His jaw held a bit of stubble, giving him a sexy scruffiness. "Chiara?"

Sweat broke out on her overheated skin. She moistened her dry lips with her tongue. "Yeah?"

"There's a Mr. Frosty truck behind you."

She blinked. The spell broke, and she glanced back. "Is this a life-changing moment?"

His grin lit up his face and stopped her heart. "Yes. I love Mr. Frosty—it's the best. Let's go get some ice cream."

She smiled back. "I think that's a great idea."

After a long time perusing the menu, she went with a classic twist cone and rainbow sprinkles, and he went with a hot fudge sundae. They ordered a baby cup of vanilla for Dex, which was topped with a dog biscuit. Sebastian staked out a good bench for people-watching, and they sat together enjoying their ice cream.

"Do you want a boy or a girl?" he asked casually.

She paused in licking her cone. "If I'm honest, a girl. But only because I don't understand boys or the penis."

He chuckled, eyes twinkling. "Can't blame you for that. But boys and their moms? Heard that was an intense relationship. Same thing with daughters and their dads. An opposite sex thing, I guess."

"My parents were so hands-off, I can't imagine what that would be like."

"Yes, you can."

She cocked her head.

"Rory and Mike."

Chiara nodded. "You're right." They'd seemed to have an intimate relationship no one else was invited into—an understanding and fierce devotion to the other, especially after Rory's mom passed. She thought of the way Mike's face lit up when he spotted his daughter, and how Rory called her dad to discuss so many aspects of her life and get advice. Instead of jealousy, Chiara embraced the hope that sprang from within. She could have that with her own child. She didn't have to be anything like her parents.

"When do we find out?" Sebastian asked. "Or do you want it to be a surprise?"

"I'd like to know. My ultrasound is scheduled for week nineteen, so they'll be able to tell us then. If you want to come, of course."

"I want to come." His voice vibrated with intensity. "I hope that's okay."

Weeks ago, she would've been uncomfortable at his hovering, afraid he threatened her independence. Now she viewed it differently. Sebastian had a generous heart and a nurturing warmth that touched her. He automatically cared about her as the mother of his child and wanted to be involved because he was a hands-on man. He'd been like that in his marriage to Rory, and made his desire clearly known about Peanut.

What concerned her was how much she was starting to depend on him herself. She had to be careful not to assume his interest, affection, or warmth was for her alone. It was strictly because she was the carrier of Peanut. Forgetting the real reason even temporarily could be dangerous. She'd fallen hard for him once after an evening in his company. Now, under his full attention, it was crucial she didn't fall for him again.

She finished her cone and tried to sound casual. "Of course. You're free to attend anything you want."

Sebastian's gaze felt hot, but Chiara didn't want to look. Already, her tummy was jumping, and she knew it wasn't Peanut. The pregnancy books she'd read talked about a butterfly sensation when the baby moved, but there'd been nothing so far. No, this was due to the man sitting beside her and his intense energy that was all physical.

If only he didn't belong to Rory.

He seemed to sense her discomfort and refocused on attacking his massive sundae. "I have to head to the youth group later on. Interested in coming with me?"

Surprised he'd asked, she searched for an excuse. It seemed like such a personal part of his life, and Chiara worried she might begin to become more entangled with him. "I have Dex."

"The kids love dogs. He'd make their day."

She shifted on the bench. "I'm not good around kids." He lifted a brow. "I mean, teens. They scare me."

"Like babies?"

His mouth quirked into a half smile, and she couldn't help but laugh. "Yeah, exactly."

"Then I'm not worried. I don't want to push. I just think you assume these things about yourself because you've never really had exposure to them. They're all awesome. Tough, sometimes, but real. Better company than too many adults I know."

Fascinated, she studied the light in his eyes and the animation on his features. These kids were important to him. The need stirred within to see him in his element. After all, he was Peanut's father. It would be more like research than spending intimate time with him. Perfectly acceptable. "Okay. I'll give it a shot."

He grinned. "Great. Let's finish our ride and we'll head over."

She began to rise, but he grasped her hand, stilling her. Her heart pounded in anticipation, and suddenly, her body was on lockdown, watching him draw nearer, helpless to move, aching for him to put her out of her misery and just kiss her. She half closed her eyes and swayed toward him.

A napkin gently swiped the edge of her lips. "You missed a spot."

Was it her imagination or did he sound breathless? Embarrassed, she straightened up and took a step back. "Oh. Yeah. Thanks."

He cleared his throat. "No problem."

Dex rolled over on his back, paws stuck straight in the air, and let out a big fart. A couple walking past burst into laughter, and the weird spell between them was officially broken. "Gross, Dex! I told you about manners!" she scolded.

Sebastian grinned. "No napping, buddy. We're hitting the road again."

The lab jumped back up and trotted near the bike, waiting for takeoff.

As they climbed back on for their final loop around the park, Chiara was struck by the image they already seemed to make together.

A family.

Chapter Nineteen

Chiara got out of the car and stared up at the Dream On Youth Center.

The building was a squat, square structure that looked a bit rundown but seemed abuzz with activity. A group of boys engaged in a fierce game of basketball, showing off some stellar moves. Some younger kids screeched and ran around the playground, which was a bit bare and consisted only of three swings, a simple slide, and a teeter-totter that had seen better days. There was a decent field behind the building, but it was covered with weeds and brush. She imagined it would have made a great baseball or soccer field.

"I don't know much about this place," she admitted, glancing around.

"Most don't," Sebastian said. "There's a larger community center that caters to all ages and brings in some heavy donations. They're able to offer more classes and performance arts. Then there's a few ministries and Catholic centers spread around. But for Dream On, it's more of a ragtag group. Most staff are volunteers, and we don't have a lot of funding." He handed over Dex's leash as they began heading toward the doors.

"Why not?" she asked curiously.

Sebastian shrugged. "This area is a bit underserved, and most kids don't want to take a bus or drive out so far to hang for a few hours. Our groups are smaller, which usually means less public attention and fewer donations. The director is great, but it's hard to get local businesses to come in for lectures or classes. Competition is hard nowadays. So many places to give your time and money. Dream On just doesn't have that wow factor people look for."

She frowned, not liking the way he put it. "You mean the better spin, website, and big-name interest equal supposed value?"

He nodded. "Most of the time."

"It shouldn't be like that."

Sebastian lifted a brow. "It's still a business, Chiara, even if it's not for profit. Sure, I'd love to see more done here—these kids deserve it— but we do the best we can, and I have to believe it's worth the effort."

The quiet intensity of his voice settled her. It reminded her of the sense of purpose and ferocity when they'd created Quench—the need to help others. Sebastian believed in these kids and didn't care where the interactions took place. It was another part of him that called to her on a deeper level. He was a man who cared for others and did something about it. Too many were all talk and no action, as she'd learned over the years.

When they got inside, he took her down the hall and into a larger room like an auditorium. Metal folding chairs were set in a circle in front of a small stage, and colorful signs and banners filled the walls. There were graffiti murals, canvases, and sketch art in various formats. A giant vintage boom box was set up on a table.

Kids were scattered in small groups. A larger man turned and grinned, waving at them. She recognized Sebastian's best friend, Ford, and smiled easily back as he came over and gave her a big hug. She'd always enjoyed his warmth and hearty humor. Ford was the typical nice guy who was too easily overlooked. He had an average body type—not too bulky, and not too tall. His hooded, sleepy-type eyes were a beautiful shade of hazel and were his best feature. His jawline was strong, with full lips, but it was mostly hidden by a scruffy goatee. Chiara always found his booming laugh, easy personality, and quick wit attractive, but

Sebastian mentioned a few times that Ford had trouble finding a long-term relationship. He had a killer voice, though, rich and husky like he was confiding secrets. Probably what helped him carve out a successful career in sports radio.

"Chiara! It's so good to see you. Is this Dex? I love labs—he's a beauty." Dex agreed, because Ford was treated to extra doggy licks as the lab basked in the compliment, along with the scratches. "Congrats are in order, I heard. How's the little one?"

She liked the way he didn't seem awkward about her pregnancy or mention how the whole thing went down. She smiled back. "We're both doing good. I didn't know you worked here."

"Volunteer, just like Ryder." He uncurled to his full height and winked. "I lead a glamorous life at the sports station. Need the kids to set me back to reality."

Sebastian snorted. "Sure, your digs reflect a real Hollywood story."

"I like my place. It's cozy."

Sebastian turned to her. "Ford's apartment is like Men Gone Wild without the college experience."

His friend didn't seem fazed. "I have the biggest TV and best sound system. Who cares about the rest?"

Chiara shook her head. Their ease and affection with one another told a story of old friends who'd been through it all together. Suddenly, the image of Rory flashed before her, followed by the familiar pain. They'd been inseparable for so long, losing her was like losing a limb. She still woke up sometimes feeling an empty ache and knew it was the loss of her bestie.

Yet, here she was with Rory's husband. Pregnant. At the youth center. Hanging with Ford. Like Chiara had stepped into an alternate life that had never been meant for her.

Like she'd stolen it.

"Let's meet the kids," Sebastian said, interrupting her spinout. She shook off her thoughts and followed him over.

He greeted all of them with a genuine enthusiasm and fell into some banter with Ford and two boys who seemed completely different from one another. Dex sat quietly at her side, sensing this was a work setting and that he needed to wait for further instructions.

"Listen up, crew. I brought a guest to hang with us today. This is Chiara. She's a friend of mine," Sebastian said.

Chiara smiled and opened her mouth to speak.

Then got bum-rushed.

The kids raced over and crowded around Dex. Immediately, the canine relaxed into doggy play mode and rolled over for belly scratches. Even the guys grinned and called him cool.

Sebastian laughed. "And this is her sidekick, Dexter. I'm disappointed you didn't ask permission first to pet him."

A girl in a denim jacket groaned. "Come on, Ryder, it was obvious he doesn't have issues or you wouldn't have brought him."

"As usual, Pru, you're right. Go ahead and do your worst. He loves the attention," Sebastian said.

"Can everyone at least introduce yourself while you ignore Chiara and smother her dog?" Ford asked with amusement.

One by one, they recited their names, and she quickly memorized the info to match with faces. Sensing that everyone was comfortable around Dex, she unclipped his leash, stepped back, and let him be the focus of attention. "Does anyone here have a pet?" she asked curiously.

Manny spoke up. "I have a Komodo dragon. My mom's allergic to dogs, but she allows reptiles."

"Oh, cool, what do those eat?" Chiara asked.

"Skinks and rodents. It's intense."

She shuddered. "I'll stick with dog food cans, thank you very much."

Maria laughed. "Me, too. I have a dog. He's a stray. I fed him on the sly and snuck him into my room at night."

"Oh, did your parents not want to take on a dog?" Chiara asked.

Maria shrugged. "I'm a foster kid, so they don't want to care for anything additional. We agreed I'd pay for the food and do all the work. It's a good deal."

Her tone struck Chiara in the chest. The girl seemed matter-of-fact about her circumstances, which only made it more poignant. "What's the dog's name?"

"Sparky."

Jeremiah groaned. "That's the dumbest name I ever heard. I'd remain a stray rather than get stuck with being called Sparky."

"Hey, I had a parakeet named Sparky when I was young," Ford said. "Stop throwing shade."

Manny began cracking up. "Dude, that's so flawed. I agree with Jeremiah."

"It's like putting those fancy dog clothes on Chihuahuas and making TikTok videos. *Painful*," Derek said.

Pru cocked her head. "I do that with our cat."

"That's cruel, Pru. I hope you didn't name it Sparky, too," Manny joked.

Her cheeks flushed red. "Cat."

The group stared at her. "You're kidding," Jeremiah said. "You didn't even give it a name?"

Pru shrugged. "It seemed unique at the time." Suddenly, her gaze sharpened like a predator. "Don't know why you're acting holier than thou, Jeremiah. Want to share what your ferret's name was?"

The kid stiffened and mumbled something.

Pru put her hand to her ear. "What was that?"

"Earl Sweatshirt."

Everyone cracked up. Jeremiah glared. "That's one of the best rappers, okay? It's fresh."

"It's awful," Maria snorted. "No wonder your ferret was so angry all the time."

Chiara laughed, enjoying the mixed energy and general snark layered in affection.

"Well, this was an educational chat," Ford said. "How about we head out into some sunshine? Throw around a Frisbee?"

Chiara waited for a general groan and backlash, but everyone agreed. They gathered on the back lawn, spread out, and began the simple passing game that she hadn't played in years.

"Can Dex play?" Manny asked.

"Sure, he's used to balls, but he can catch anything. It's giving it back we're still working on."

Sebastian volunteered to hang with Dex as a partner.

"Are you Ryder's girlfriend?" Maria asked, expertly tossing the disc across the circle.

She cursed the brief hesitation but tried to bluster through. Thank goodness she wasn't showing yet. That could be awkward. "Nope," she said.

"She rejected me a few times already," Sebastian said with a grin.

"Smart woman," Ford said.

The kids laughed. "So why'd you come hang?" Manny asked.

"Because Sebastian's a friend of mine and invited me."

"What do you do?" Pru asked.

Chiara jumped to catch the high toss and managed to snag it. "I work at a company called Quench."

"Chiara is one of the founders," Sebastian added. "Now it's a multimillion-dollar company."

"I know the Quench website," Pru finally said. "From what I've seen it's cool."

Pride filled Chiara. "Thanks, that means a lot. Anyone else check us out?"

Jeremiah caught the Frisbee and flicked off a toss toward Dex. "No, but I like that you built it yourself. Maybe one day I'll launch an app and make a killing."

Maria raised a brow. "What do you do with all your money?"

Chiara blinked. "What do you mean?"

"If you're such a profitable company, do you give it to stockholders? Do you reinvest? Do you give back?"

A tingle ran down her spine. It was a question she was rarely asked, especially by a teenager. "Um, we do all three. Except, we don't have shareholders. I own the company with my two other friends."

She risked a glance at Sebastian, but he was letting it go, allowing the questions to be asked. Dex stayed by his side, snatching the Frisbee when it was their turn, then releasing it gently back to Sebastian to throw. Ford was also quiet and seemed interested in her answers.

"So how does that work when you make millions?" Derek asked. "What'd you do? Build a giant home? Get a cool car? Go on vacays?"

She shifted her weight and thought about the question. "Well, I reinvested a lot of it in the company to make improvements. I bought my own house, but it's definitely not a mansion. My travel is business-based trips. And my car is a Jeep because Dex likes the wind blowing in his hair."

Sebastian stepped in. "What's the real issue here, guys? I feel like there's concern about Chiara's job."

"Yeah, the concern is how I get a job that will set *me* up for life," Jeremiah said with a grin. "And how is it so many people can get on camera and do nothing and get rich and famous? It's such a sellout."

Manny puffed up. "I'm gonna get rich playing football—that's my path. Ain't that right, Ford?"

Ford smiled. "Maybe. You got the talent, but there's also some luck needed for it to all work out. Make sure you have a backup plan. Too many stars I've spoken to said they put everything into an athletic career, and it wasn't enough. An injury can take anyone out, at any time."

"Then I better not get hurt!" Manny said with a grin.

"Well, we didn't start Quench to be rich," Chiara said. "We wanted a place to make real things happen for women, without harming them in order to sell a product. That it became successful and makes us money is something we're always grateful for."

She caught Sebastian's gaze. Charcoal eyes held a light of appreciation and respect. She was glad to be real with these kids. How easy it would be to talk down to teens who had their own visions of how they saw their lives, citing experiences they'd never had. It took a strong person to hold the space and listen rather than consistently talk and advise. Sebastian had that skill. So did Ford.

Chiara wanted it, too.

"Game time. Pick a career where you'll make a million dollars. What are you doing with it?" Sebastian asked the group.

The topic spun out as everyone took their turns. Chiara loved hearing each of their dreams described in detail, especially the careers they chose to get them there. Manny wanted to be a star running back, and Pru was a math whiz who only wanted to be around kids instead of locked up in research. Jeremiah dreamed of building his own business via a new social app that could take on Facebook, and Maria was a talented artist. Derek was quieter than the others, as if something was bothering him, but finally shared he wouldn't mind being a stockbroker like Will Smith in the movie *The Pursuit of Happyness*.

"We didn't say what we'd do with the money," Jeremiah said.

Maria didn't hesitate. "I'd give it all away."

The cackle of unbelieving laughter echoed in the spring breeze. "Right," Manny scoffed. "Sure you would."

"Do you mean you'd give it to family or friends?" Sebastian asked.

Maria shook her head. "No. Money makes things . . . complicated. It turns people bad. I wouldn't want to take that chance."

Pru tapped her lip. "How will you live?"

"As simple as possible. A small place in the woods. I'll paint, live off the land, have animals." Shadows crossed her face, and Chiara realized something had happened to the girl. Something dark that had changed her. Within her expression was a fierce will to thrive on her terms. Chiara wondered what circumstances had brought her to such a goal.

"Maria's right," Ford said quietly. "The more you have, the harder it is to figure out what really makes you happy. I think if you pursue something you love, other than the goal of money, you have a better chance of being okay."

"Some of us don't get that opp," Derek said. He glanced at the others, and something passed between them, a type of understanding Chiara knew she'd never be part of. "Money is sometimes the only way out."

As she stared at Derek and heard the slight murmuring of agreement from the group, Chiara was reminded no one got to judge another's life. Each of them faced unique challenges and did their best.

Sebastian respected their silence, lending a perfect balance of understanding but not allowing them to sink too deep into negativity. The warmth and obvious care he showed were special. But it was the kids' reaction to Sebastian that really got her. They stared at him with respect and a tad of hero worship that charmed her.

And as Sebastian laughed and played Frisbee and listened to each of them, Chiara realized he was going to be the perfect father for Peanut. The thought brought a rush of goose bumps and an aching need that took her off guard.

As if knowing things were getting too heavy, Dex broke the circle, grabbed the Frisbee from Ford's hand, and took off across the yard.

Everyone burst into laughter and settled into the chase.

Chiara was happy she came. An idea brewed in the back of her mind, one she wanted to work through for a while. The kids had inspired her to make a change. So had Sebastian. It seemed every step forward she became more wrapped up in his life, which was exactly what she had wanted to avoid.

The real problem was simple.

She liked being part of his life. She just needed to figure out what to do about it.

~

"Derek, can I talk to you a sec?"

Chiara was chatting with Ford, and the rest of the kids had taken off. The day had gone well, and watching the kids bloom under some simple play and Chiara's attention filled him up. But there was a nagging doubt in Ryder's gut that kept growing stronger regarding Derek.

He studied the kid, looking for signs that could guide him. His face was thinning out, the sharp lines more prominent, especially with his hair tied back. The light in his blue eyes didn't hold the usual enthusiasm. Today, he'd been eerily quiet and unengaged.

Ryder had been driving him back and forth to work regularly, and after their past talk, Derek had seemed a bit better, though he was still struggling. He wasn't crazy about his job and odd shifts, but he was showing up and doing his best. Ryder had hoped things would get better, but Derek's mom was still sick and refused to go to the doctor. Between worry about her and his asshole father stirring things up, he sensed the kid needed some extra care.

"How's your mom feeling?" Ryder asked.

Derek shrugged. "Not great. She missed a few shifts at the bank, and they're threatening to fire her. The electric bill is due and we can't get it paid."

"I'm sorry, that sucks."

The kid kicked some pebbles around the ground. "Yeah. I just feel like such a loser, you know? I've been trying to save, but scoring shifts is hard, and if they turn out the lights? I don't think my mom can handle it. She's proud. Doesn't like taking money from people."

"Is your father helping out with child support?"

Anger blasted from him in ragged waves. "Nope. He says we got the house and that's enough. Mom tried to take him to court, but he just disappears and works places he can get cash. He hasn't paid us a dime, and last week when I told him about the electricity, he laughed and said it's not his responsibility. I think he was actually happy to hear we were struggling." The kid began to shake. "I don't want to see that bastard again."

"What about an advance on your paycheck? Would they consider it?"

"Nah, I asked. I gotta wait for next Friday, and even then I won't have enough. Guess I'll invest in some flashlights and hope we'll be okay."

Ryder already knew the drill. Derek didn't have anyone to go to and would never consider a shelter. There were a few organizations they could apply to, but that would take time, and the kid didn't have any left. The burning need to help Derek shook through him like a fever. He couldn't let down another kid on his watch. "What if I lent you the money to get the bill paid?"

The kid's eyes widened in shock. "I couldn't ask you to do that. It's too much."

Ryder's decision had already been made. "How much would you need?"

"One hundred fifty. It's for the month we missed before, too. But, Ryder, I'll figure it out. Not your responsibility, man."

"I know, Derek, but sometimes, it's okay to get a helping hand when things get tough. You can pay me back in installments as you get paid. Soon your mom will get back on her feet, and this will all be behind you."

A trickle of unease hit him. Volunteers at the youth center were required to abide by strict rules. The cardinal one? Never give a kid money. It was to protect both of them, and Ryder knew he was going outside the box big-time by doing this. But his soul cried out that Derek needed a break. God knows his father, or the system, wasn't giving it to him.

Ryder could make a difference.

He quickly reached in his pocket, pulled the money from his wallet, and shoved it into Derek's palm. "It's between me and you, okay? But I need you to do something important."

"What?"

"You need to talk to someone. Stress like this makes you susceptible. Okay?"

Derek pocketed the money with shaky hands. He kept blinking wildly, as if unsure how to respond. "Yeah. I'll call my sponsor." He paused. "I just . . . I just don't know what to say. No one's ever stepped up for me like this."

Ryder jerked back when he finally met Derek's gaze and found tears burning in his eyes. His chest squeezed painfully. As a kid, he'd wanted the same thing. Some type of male mentor to give a shit. It was a reason why his high school guidance counselor had made such an impression on him. "It'll work out. Do you understand, Derek? It's all going to work out."

The kid gave a sharp nod. His name echoed through the air. "Thanks. Better get going."

He ran off, and Ryder watched him with a sense of rightness. He may have broken the rules, but sometimes, in certain circumstances, a person had no other choice.

Heading over to Ford and Chiara, he grinned broadly. "Are we ready to head out? You want to join us for dinner, Ford?"

His friend's face was suddenly set in stone. A jagged, hostile energy emanated from his figure. "Sorry, I've got plans, but hopefully next time. Can I have a quick word with you, Ryder? Chiara, it was lovely to see you. Don't be a stranger, okay?"

"I promise." She gave Ford a quick hug and turned to Ryder. "I'll wait in the car. Let's go, Dex."

She left them, and Ryder frowned. "What's the matter?"

"I saw you give money to Derek. What the hell, dude? What's wrong with you?"

His lips tightened. "Just drop it."

"I can't! Did he give you a sob story about why he needed money? Ryder, the kid was in rehab. Why would you do something so stupid?"

Irritation skated over Ryder's nerve endings. He lowered his voice. "He didn't come to me, Ford, I was the one who offered. And to answer your question, I did it because the kid needed some help and had no one else to turn to. It's to pay a bill. His mom's sick."

Ford shook his head. "Is it the truth or a setup to score some drugs?"

"The kid's clean. For God's sake, I know it was against the rules, but I'm not going to stand around and watch him drown when I can help! He's got a job. He's staying clean. He's showing up here."

"I heard you're also driving him back and forth to work."

He stiffened. "Just a few times so he doesn't have to get an Uber. It's hard without a license."

"You're getting in too deep again. Same thing happened with Carl. How'd that turn out for you?"

Ryder stared at his friend. A sense of betrayal washed over him at the memory. "That was different."

"No. It was a boy with a crap father who you tried to help. But he wasn't ready for your help, dude. And you still haven't gotten over it. You're still trying to save everyone."

He refused to go down that road again. Losing Carl to the streets was a wound that still rubbed him raw. He'd slapped a Band-Aid on it, but the loss of a smart, kind kid trying to battle his way out of his environment haunted him. He kept thinking he hadn't done enough.

This time, he wouldn't lose Derek.

"He's not you," Ford said quietly, his gaze cutting right through the shit. "I know you think you can save him, but you can't. Not unless he wants it."

White-hot anger raced through his bloodstream. How would Ford know? He'd never had to deal with the feelings of being rejected by a parent, or what it was like to get a fist to the face. "You don't understand," Ryder retorted. "You've got the unicorn life of love, security, and a happy home. You can show up and pretend to know what Derek is going through, but I'd advise you to back off until you've walked the walk."

Ford shook his head. Ryder hated the quick flash of pain in his friend's eyes. "Yeah, sorry, I forgot I led a charmed life, so I have no skin in this game. But I'll tell you what I do know. I'm tired of watching you replay your past. No matter how many kids you save or don't, you'll never change what happened with your father. Maybe it's time you begin to accept it and be in the real world, because you're just fooling yourself by thinking your effort alone will save a kid like Derek from using again." He threw up his hands and backed off. "But what do I know, right?"

He stalked off, leaving Ryder staring after him.

Crap. Ford meant well, but there was no way he could understand. Derek needed someone to take a risk on him, which had nothing to do with Ryder's past. He had a gut instinct about Derek that he knew wasn't wrong. Eventually, when it worked out, Ford would see he'd done the right thing.

The only thing.

Right now, he wanted to focus on other things. Like the surprise he'd been working on for Chiara. They'd only grown closer after telling Mike the truth, and Ryder's confession had finally set something inside of him free. He wanted to concentrate on their connection. Riding bikes with Dex and eating ice cream in the park had fulfilled him more than anything else had in the past two years. For the first time, he felt there was a real shot for them to become more than just good parents, or friends.

There was a chance for love.

Chapter Twenty

Was that a knock?

Chiara picked her head up, blinking away the writing fog. Dex trotted to the door and whined, sticking his nose in the crack under the door. *No one comes over without texting,* she thought. *It could be a salesperson.*

She kept still, but another knock pounded, and Dex barked. She headed over and peeked through the peephole. Sebastian stood in the doorway with a bag in his hand, staring at the door like he could see her through it.

Chiara noticed two things. One, her heart leapt at the idea of being fed, since she hadn't stopped to prepare a meal in the last few hours. Second, her belly clenched at the sight of his hot male body and intense stare. The cravings were getting worse—both for food and sex. She had to button it down or she'd be a three-hundred-pound horndog.

Chiara threw open the door. "What are you doing here?"

"Am I interrupting? I'm sorry—I just wanted to drop this off. For dinner. Or a snack. Or lunch tomorrow. Hi, Dex."

She squinted at him suspiciously. He was acting weird. A bit jumpy. "Are you okay?"

He bent down to pet Dex and avoided her gaze. "Yeah, I'm great. How are you and Peanut?"

She rubbed her belly automatically, which was still a soft swell and easy to conceal. Not for long, though. "Good. A bit gassy. Maybe it was the spinach. You didn't have to stop for me."

Sebastian stepped in, now familiar with her home and routine, which usually consisted of work, walks with Dex, and hanging with the girls at Mike's. "It's always good to have Chinese food on hand. You working?"

She sighed and trudged toward the kitchen. "Always. This time it's a proposal for Quench. A new direction for the company."

"Sounds intense."

"It's a good thing. I'm going to run it by Malia and Tessa this week, and then I'll let you know."

"Good. I'm here if you want to discuss anything. Or just listen."

She liked the way he never pushed for information, respecting her privacy. Too many men she'd previously dated loved to spout opinions and direction, not realizing it made her hot. And not in a good way. "Thanks. Hey, do you mind if I put the food aside for later? I just want to finish up some things."

"Of course. Um, but I have something you'll definitely want to open now."

She cocked her head. "What?"

Sebastian reached in his pocket and took out a wrapped fortune cookie. "Here you go. You can read your fortune." He was staring at her like he'd handed her a diamond ring and was expecting a bigger reaction.

"Oh, cool. I'm actually one of the rare people who eat those. I'll tear into it after I'm done."

Was he sweating? He began to pace in short bursts in front of her. "How about you eat it later but open it now? I'd love to see your fortune!"

"Wow, I've never seen anyone so excited to crack open a cookie."

He seemed to ponder this. "I need your lucky numbers."

"Huh?"

He gave an impatient shake of his head. "Your lucky numbers. They print it on the bottom of the fortune. I'm, um, making a bet on something and need direction."

She tried to hand him the cookie. "Oh, then you can just have it."

"No! It needs to be you. It's better luck if it's someone else's numbers."

Chiara frowned and crossed her arms in front of her chest. "Are you going to harass me until I open this thing?"

"Yes."

"Fine." She ripped open the cellophane wrapper and split the cookie in one neat crack, then pulled out the crisp piece of paper. "Lucky numbers are 2, 7, 12—"

"What are you doing?"

"Reading you the numbers. Are you okay?"

A muscle ticked in his jaw. He got eerily quiet, and tension ratcheted the air. "Can you just read the fortune, Chiara?"

She bit back her annoyance and the impulse to throw it at him. Why was he being so stubborn? Her gaze dropped to the words printed in blue.

Will you go to prom with me?

Huh?

She blinked, read it again, then looked up. "It's not a fortune, it's a question. Do you still want the numbers?"

Sebastian stared at her in slight shock, then slowly walked over to the chair and dropped in it. He rubbed his temples. Raven hair slid through his fingers and fell messily over his brow. She itched to repeat the same movements with her own fingers. To press her lips against the temple that hurt. To wrap her arms around him and—

"Chiara, I'm asking if you want to go to prom."

It took a while for her to process the words. She went over and sat in the chair opposite him. "I don't get it."

"I know. I asked my damn students, and they said it needed to be epic, that no one just asks in a normal way. You need to do the big thing—the gesture! Skywriting, or a billboard, or a sign with a boom box in front of the window. I thought of the fortune cookie, but of course, you didn't get it. Can we just forget the whole thing?"

"Wait a minute. You're asking me to the high school prom?" The realization hit her in one hard swoop.

He nodded, misery etched in his features. "That was the plan. I heard what you said when we were bike riding, about regretting not going. And I have to chaperone, so I thought it would be an opportunity to give you an experience you never had. Now I see it was stupid. I'm sorry, I'm going to go solo. Forget it."

"No!" She flew out of her seat. "I want to go to prom!"

He looked at her with suspicion. "You do?"

"Yeah. I just didn't understand about the prom ask."

"It's called a promposal, and the only reason I know is I deal with it every damn year with my kids."

His grumpiness was hiding a sweet spot that made her tummy tumble. Her fingers curled around the paper, protecting it. "I love it, Sebastian. Thank you."

His lips relaxed into a smile. "Yeah? I swear it won't be too torturous. They're holding it at a nice venue—Althea's. There'll be a DJ, and decent food, and we can spike the punch." He jerked back. "Sorry, no spiked punch for you. I'll make sure they have sparkling seltzer with lime."

Yeah. He was adorable.

"Thank you," she said again. Her voice came out husky. His gaze lifted and locked with hers, and then there was a brand-new tension in the air, one filled with a rising sexual awareness. She swallowed and stepped back but knew she wasn't out of danger.

"I better get going. You need to work. Oh, Ford's having a birthday party in early June. He'd like to hold it at Mike's and invite some friends. Specifically, Malia, you, and Tessa. Would you come?"

"Of course! That's so nice! We haven't all been together in so long. Not since . . ." She trailed off, but the unspoken name hung in the air, heavy between them.

He stared at her. She licked her lips.

"Chiara?" Sebastian gave a slow, almost sad smile. "I'm glad I get to take you to prom." Then he turned and headed to the door.

On impulse, she opened her mouth to call his name, wanting him to come back. Needing to say that she was glad, too, and that there wasn't another man she'd want to go with. But it was too late.

He left.

It was probably a good thing.

~

"He invited me to prom."

Tessa dropped her fork and stared. This time, she was the one who went mute.

Malia gasped and slammed her water glass down. "Are you kidding me? When? How? Do you have a dress? I'm so jealous!"

"No, I need to go shopping. He stopped by with Chinese food and forced me to open a fortune cookie that said 'Will you go to prom with me?'"

Malia gave a dreamy sigh. "That is so sweet. These prom asks are bigger than the actual prom! So much competition. I still wish we'd gone together instead of staying home, eating bad pizza."

Chiara stabbed her fork into her grilled chicken salad. "Yeah, I told Sebastian about getting dumped right before senior prom, so I guess he was trying to be nice and give me that experience."

Tessa finally found her voice. Loudly. "Are you both high? You're a grown-ass pregnant woman going to prom as a chaperone! Why did he go to all the trouble stuffing it in a fortune cookie?"

Malia tossed her a look. "Why are you being so mean? I think it was a nice gesture." She looked at Chiara and clapped her hands. "You guys need a limo. Want me to text him?"

Tessa groaned and pushed her plate aside. "This isn't about Ryder trying to be nice. He asked Chiara to prom because he's falling for her."

Chiara took a slug of sparkling seltzer, then coughed. Malia's eyes widened as she glanced back and forth between them. "Oh. My. God. I think you're right."

"What? No. He has to go anyway, and I'm his baby mama. It's the only reason," Chiara said.

"No, that's how it started. But this is bigger, and it's been escalating for a while now. He brings you meals all the time. Checks up on you. Meets you at the park and takes care of Dex."

"He also invited you to the youth center," Malia continued, getting into the discussion. "If it was just about the baby and being friendly, he wouldn't be bringing you to his places of work."

"He wants you for himself," Tessa finished. "I think he's falling in love with you, Chiara."

The stark words hit her ears and her heart. An ache emerged, but it was the fierce wanting that shamed her the most. Things were getting real, and the baby hadn't even been born. What type of attachment would spring up once they held Peanut?

He belongs to Rory.

She shook her head hard to stop the voice. "We're becoming parents. We went from barely able to talk to each other to drugged sex to friends. He just wants to keep building on that so we're strong when the baby comes."

"That's what I used to think," Tessa said. "Not anymore. But the real question isn't about his feelings. It's about yours."

Pain splintered inside her. "I would never betray Rory," she whispered. "Sebastian and I can't be anything other than friends."

Malia and Tessa shared a glance. "Why not?" Malia asked.

Chiara stared at them with shock. "Because he's Rory's husband. The only reason we're spending time together is the baby."

"I've seen you guys at the office. There's a connection that goes deeper," Malia said simply.

Her hands shook so badly she hid them in her lap, twisting her fingers. "We're just friends. I'm excited about going to prom for *me*. That's it. Nothing else is going on."

"I disagree," Tessa said. "And if you do have feelings for him, I think it's wrong to cut yourself off from feeling them. And as much as we love and miss Rory, she's gone. You both need to move on."

A wild laugh burst from her throat. "Oh, sure, easy peasy. People will completely accept that I stepped into the late editor in chief's role and got pregnant by her husband. The press would have a field day."

"No one would care," Malia said.

"Yes, they would. Quench is big enough that a juicy story like that would go viral."

Malia sighed. "Babe, this is important. If you're falling for Ryder, you owe it to both of you to explore it a bit. This is your life, not the world's. Tessa and I will have your back to the end. So will the staff. And Mike."

"Why are you both trying to push me toward Sebastian? It's just . . . wrong."

"Wrong is pretending you don't feel things. Wrong is choosing a life the world approves of but makes you feel empty inside. Wrong is being too scared to try."

She stared at Tessa, her long speech roiling through her mind. She was emotionally ravaged and not up to testing limits. "I can't deal with this right now," Chiara said softly. "Is that okay?"

They both smiled back at her. "Totally okay," Malia said. "We just love you, babe."

"Then stop busting my balls," she muttered, picking up her fork to dive into her salad again. "Pregnancy should come with some free passes."

"It does. You gain weight and no one cares. In fact, it's celebrated. Any cravings?" Tessa asked.

"Ice cream. Ben & Jerry's specifically."

"I'd pick Häagen-Dazs," Tessa said.

Malia grinned. "It's not your pregnancy."

Tessa stuck out her tongue.

"Guys, I actually got us together so we can talk business," Chiara said. Immediately, her friends straightened up and got into work mode. "I've been thinking a lot about where Quench is as a company. I know we give back to various charities, mostly female-based, but I was wondering if we could discuss doing something bigger. Our profits are healthy, our expansion has been solid, and no one seems ready to sell to the highest bidder." She regarded them both with a questioning gaze. "Are we?"

"Hell no," Tessa muttered. Malia agreed.

"Great. What if we began directing more of our profits into local communities? There are so many worthy causes that don't get noticed because they're small and have no marketing budget."

Malia jumped in quickly. "I love that idea. I just read that there are more homeless kids and families needing to rely on food pantries than ever before."

"Agreed. When Sebastian took me to the youth center, I was able to see things differently. Those kids were amazing—and he wasn't doing anything extraordinary. He was just showing up. Hanging out. Listening. Making them feel important. If there were more funding, it could serve a larger population," Chiara said.

Tessa tapped her French-manicured nail against the counter. "I've been wanting to offer career and educational opportunities through internships. Maybe even recruit at the high schools and colleges. It's an ambitious program but something I've been excited to do."

Chiara nodded. "You talked about that before, but we were always so overworked. It's taken this long to get to the next level to do bigger things with Quench. But I feel now that the company's stabilized and profit is steadily growing, we can take some risks. Maybe shift our responsibilities around a bit."

"You're right," Malia said. "It's time we use what we built for an even greater good. What if we reach out to our contacts and investors to see if they'd be interested in sponsoring? It doesn't have to be only Quench. I can bring it to the advertisers. Imagine the brand recognition they'd receive for a piece of the pie."

"That's brilliant," Tessa said.

Malia preened, looking extra smart in her hot-pink business suit. "Thanks."

Excitement fluttered in her belly. Chiara's mind buzzed with ideas and ways to make Quench better for everyone—especially the communities it served. "I love it, too. Are we all agreed we begin researching this new endeavor?"

"Agreed," her friends said together.

"What are we doing now, ladies? Taking over the world?" Mike asked, eyes filled with humor. "Need another seltzer, Chiara?"

"No, thanks, I'm good. But I think you'd love to know we have a new plan for Quench."

"Would Rory like it?"

She swallowed, choking back the lump in her throat. "She'd love it."

"Need a pen and paper?" His grin was wide and warm.

She looked at her friends. The memory of that first meetup in this exact booth sprang to the forefront. The way Rory drove her vision home until they could all see it as possible. How Mike sat with them, sketching out plans and budgeting, and his offer to help. It seemed like both a lifetime ago and just yesterday that they'd all been together at the beginning of this journey.

"Yeah. Do you have a minute to sit with us and hear the idea?" Malia asked.

Mike blinked, then quickly turned. "Sure. Be right back."

It felt right he'd take Rory's place today. To be part of what they were beginning. The idea phase was the most exciting to dive into.

Chiara snapped her fingers. "Oh, I forgot—Ford's having a party here first week in June. He wants you guys to come."

Tessa's face turned surly. "Do I have to?"

Malia slapped her arm. "Don't be rude. Ford is lovely!"

"He is, he is," Tessa groaned. "It's just he has no clue. Like an overgrown friendly bear who wanders into a socialite's tea party and expects everyone to welcome him."

"Doesn't that make you want to help him, though?" Chiara asked curiously. "He's got a great heart."

"Sure. But all I remember when we get together is his obsessive talk about sports."

"He works in sports radio," Malia said.

Tessa waved her hand in dismissal. "So? I don't talk about women's self-care all day, do I? Plus, he's scruffy looking and awkward. He spilled his entire plate of food all over my dress at the Quench event, remember? And when I told him it was designer, he said I was stupid to spend that amount of money on something I'd only wear once."

Chiara tried not to laugh. "It was an accident. And he's kind of right."

Tessa glared. "Forget it. I'll go."

"I'm sure Ford will be thrilled. Definitely wear the Tom Ford dress from the new spring collection," Malia said.

Tessa threw her napkin at Malia, and they burst into giggles.

Mike came back and filled the empty place in the booth, sliding a yellow legal pad and pen over to Chiara. Her hand touched her belly, and bittersweet nostalgia filled her as she remembered her best friend.

Slowly, Chiara took the pen and stared at her friends, who all nodded.

And they began.

Chapter Twenty-One

Ryder escorted Chiara through the doors of Althea's and wondered why he felt like a kid again.

Unlike her, he'd gone to his senior prom. Been decently popular at school and hung out with a good crowd and never worried about bullying or loneliness. He'd taken his date to a hotel afterward, and they'd consummated their relationship. Still one of his fondest memories.

Rory had never joined him as a prom chaperone. He'd never asked, since it was more of a job than an event, and she'd always been focused on work. But with Chiara by his side, his gut was churned up, and his nerves were jagged. Like he had an intense crush and wanted to impress her.

He was losing his damn mind.

But his body didn't care. When he first caught sight of her, his palms literally sweat. She was stunning in a long, draping gold dress that caught the light and sparkled when she moved. The generous V in the front showed off her burgeoning breasts and smooth, pale skin. Her hair was pulled up into a tight chignon, exposing the graceful curve of her neck. It had taken all his strength not to pull her into his arms and kiss her the way he had that night at the club. Claim her mouth and her body until they both had no guilt and no other thoughts but each other.

Of course, he didn't. He stood stock still, complimented her on the dress, and tried to keep his sweaty hands to himself.

It was getting harder and harder the more time they spent together.

"This is beautiful," Chiara said, glancing around. The waterdrop crystal chandeliers shimmered, and the red carpet was plush under their feet. Music pounded in the air from an enthusiastic DJ, and a lavish buffet was set up along the wall, with an old-fashioned punch bowl manned by tuxedo-clad waiters.

"Yeah, they go all out for prom and cut back on some other activities," Ryder said, leading her through the massive room. They passed various groups sitting at tables and standing tightly together. He nodded and high-fived a few kids, admiring the way they cleaned up and took the event seriously. Teen boys looked gangly and grown-up in their tuxedos, hair slicked back and tamed, shoes shined, boutonnieres in lapels. The girls dazzled in long and short dresses in poppy colors, hair elaborately styled on top of their heads, heels so tall a quarter of them had already kicked them off.

He called out greetings to various teachers and stopped at a table toward the back that gave a decent view of the room.

"What do we have to do?" Chiara asked.

"Try to make sure they're not drinking alcohol or doing drugs. Watch out for fighting. Make sure no one gets naked."

She laughed, her golden eyes shining up at him. Her lips had been painted a dark bronze with a touch of gloss. He realized now what men would give up for a kiss. Right now, he'd bargain with his very soul. "I'm sure that's one thing we won't need to worry about."

Ryder cleared his throat. "Are you kidding? Prom brings out all the hormones. They practically do it on the dance floor, but I try to give them slack. After all, this is their last goodbye to a life they've known forever."

"I like the way you talk about them," Chiara said, gaze trained on his. "Like you remember. Not many of us do anymore. We tuck the past and who we were away and pretend it never mattered."

He thought of his asshole father and the way school had been his outlet and savior. The tight closeness of friends like Ford, drinking at football games, making love after prom. The pain and beauty of that time had never left him, and he was glad he got to see it every day and be reminded. "Yeah. Times change, technology advances, fashions ebb and flow. But the emotions are the same. That's not something that will ever change."

"I'm sorry, Sebastian."

He blinked and stared at her. "For what?"

Regret shone in her eyes. "I never gave you a choice. When I first saw you with Rory, I forced myself to shut down any emotions and pretended I didn't care."

The truth of her words slammed through him and opened up a portal inside, an opening he could finally work with. He took the chance and took her hand, tangling her fingers within his, in the darkness where no one could see. "You weren't wrong. It was the best thing for both of us." He paused and made sure he emphasized his next words. "Then. Not now."

The connection surged between them. His breath hurt in his chest as he fell to temptation and stepped closer, not caring where they were or who watched. He bent forward.

"Ryder! Made it to another prom, man! Agh, saw you brought a date."

Trying not to curse, he turned toward Pete. "And I see you still didn't rent a tux," Ryder said with a quick grin. The English teacher was beloved and feared by students. With his staggering height, bright red hair, and matching beard, he was a cornerstone of the high school. Ryder had always considered him a friend. There was so much politics and bullshit in academia, it was nice to hang with faculty who didn't play the games and kept it real.

Pete gestured to the same tweed suit and red shoes he wore to prom every year. "I'm a classic and will never go out of style."

Ryder introduced them. "This is my partner in crime tonight. She's a prom virgin."

Pete laughed. "Good, we need a fresh pair of eyes to see all the things we miss."

Chiara laughed and pointed to a couple making out on the dance floor. "Like that?"

"Nah, Lucretia and Joe have been dating for two years. They're both going to the same college and can't keep their tongues out of each other's mouth." Pete sighed. "Good times, man."

Ryder shook his head. "Gwen took pity on you. That woman is a saint."

Pete turned toward Chiara to explain. "My wife and I met in senior year. Still married with four kids. We were that couple."

"That's the sweetest thing I ever heard." She blinked, staring off into space. "You know, that would make such a great feature article: 'The Pros and Cons of Marrying Your High School Sweetheart.' Would it be okay if I interviewed you both?"

Pete puffed up. "Sure thing. You're a writer? That's cool. Anything published?"

"Oh, I work at Quench," she said. "I've only published online articles."

Ryder laughed at her modesty. "She's editor in chief and one of the company's founders."

Pete blinked in surprise. "Like Rory?"

The energy suddenly deflated. Ryder noticed the way Chiara shifted her weight, nibbling at her lower lip, obviously uncomfortable. It would always come back to Rory. If they continued on this path, they'd need to talk about it head-on.

But now wasn't the place.

"Yeah, like Rory. Listen, Pete, we're gonna grab some food. If you run into Kristofer, tell him I want to talk to him."

"Of course." Pete stroked his red beard. "You did good with him, man. Kris is one of the most talented writers I've seen in a while, and if you hadn't pushed, he wouldn't have tried college. That scholarship was a game changer. I was a bit surprised you got him an extension for his application, though. That was way above what most of us could pull off." He turned to Chiara. "I'm telling you, we've never had a counselor in this high school who cares half as much as Ryder does. It's like he has a need to save the kids from themselves."

Ryder shrugged, but the words sounded faintly like Ford's. "I only led Kris there. His talent got him in. See you later."

He took Chiara over to the buffet. She was quiet as she began loading her plate.

"Chiara?"

"Yeah?"

"It's okay, you know. That you're here with me."

She jerked but didn't look up. "I know."

He wasn't convinced. He was going to commit to making sure she had a great time at her first prom. "Were you impressed with the limo?"

She smiled. "Yeah. And it was white. I always wanted white. The sparkling apple cider was a nice touch, too."

"Gotta ply you with the stuff so I can get to third base. That's the real goal of prom."

He loved the way she laughed, full and loud and true. "You're so bad. Besides, you already got lucky." She patted the small swell of her tummy, and a fierce possessiveness roared through him, knowing she carried his baby. "Too bad you didn't remember much of it."

This time, it was him who laughed. God, he was crazy about this woman.

What the hell was he going to do?

～

She was having the time of her life.

They got to break up a potential fight with two boys arguing over the same girl, who seemed delighted rather than upset that she was the center of attention. Sebastian was firm yet relatable as he got them away from each other, and Chiara jumped in to talk to the girl, who gave her a blow-by-blow account of all the drama. Seems she was torn between them and couldn't make a decision. It was better than a Netflix series.

She met some of Sebastian's students, who seemed to both like and respect him. Pride filled her as she watched him converse, praising their decisions on the future or just falling into casual chatter to keep it light. He posed for pictures and took the good-natured gibes at his attempts at counseling with a chuckle.

She watched the prom queen and king crowning, finding herself caught up in the moment, clapping and cheering as hard as the kids.

But the best part?

Dancing with Sebastian.

He only joined her for two fast dances, obviously a bit awkward in front of the kids and because of his older dance skills. But when a slow song unfolded—a classic John Legend ballad—he wordlessly led her onto the floor and took her into his arms.

Time stood still as she leaned against his muscled body and wound her arms around his shoulders. She breathed in the clean ocean scent of him and stared into his hooded, intense charcoal eyes that blazed with things they shouldn't want. His lips firmed into a thin line, but she remembered how soft they had felt on hers. She burned, and ached, and craved. He seemed to be fighting the same battle.

Afterward, they broke apart slowly and walked back to the group at their table. Pretending the awful, glorious energy of attraction would finally go away. Knowing it wouldn't.

Sebastian took her home in the limo. They were silent in the back seat, lost in their own thoughts. When he walked her to the door, she hesitated. "I had a great night. I'll never be able to thank you enough for giving me my prom."

His smile seemed forced. "You're welcome. I had fun. Everyone loved you."

"Not like the way they love you. You're a special man, Sebastian."

He closed his eyes and muttered a curse. His body tightened, as if he was holding himself back by a thin line of control. "Can I come in and say hello to Dex?"

The request thrummed with danger. She opened her mouth to turn him away and be safe, but found herself saying, "Sure."

He was in the house before she could take it back, and like a sexy vampire from the novels she read, he prowled inside with grace and a touch of entitlement.

Heart racing, Chiara greeted her dog, then went to check on his water bowl and flip on more lights. Sebastian spoke in affectionate murmurs, sending Dex to doggy heaven, until his need to pee overturned his need for attention. She opened the back door, and he bounded out into the night.

"Want something to drink?" she asked.

"I like that lime seltzer," he responded. Behind her, his footsteps prowled around her living room. She got the can of seltzer, filled a glass with ice, poured his drink, and turned.

Her mouth dried up. Sebastian leaned against the wall of the kitchen, ankles crossed, blocking any sort of exit. He'd ripped off his tie and shed his jacket. The top three buttons on his crisp white shirt were undone, showing a peek at his muscled chest. His male presence filled up the room, and that sexy gaze focused straight on her mouth. Her hand shook as she offered the glass to him.

"Thanks." He drank, the long column of his throat working as he swallowed. She watched him, entranced, unable to move.

What was she doing? What was he doing?

What were *they* doing?

"Aren't you thirsty?"

She shook her head numbly. "No."

"You tired? Proms are exhausting, and it's been a long day." Did he take a step closer, or was it her imagination?

His scent rose in the air and surrounded her. "No."

He tapped his lip. "Good."

"What are you doing?" Her question came out softly, but a storm brewed inside her. She felt raw and on the edge of an explosion.

Dex's scratch at the back door interrupted. Sebastian walked past her, placing his glass on the table, and let the dog in, then locked up.

Dex bounded to the shelf and gave Chiara the face.

"What does he want?"

"Treats. That's his shelf."

"Can I give one to him?"

She nodded.

Sebastian took a meaty chew from the bag. "Should I make him do a trick?"

A smile ghosted her lips. "It's late. He doesn't have to perform."

Sebastian gave it to him, and Dex took it gently between his teeth, then hauled ass to his bed to enjoy.

"I want to talk about us."

The breath rushed out of her lungs at his stark declaration. She stared, unable to put together a response. "Huh?"

"You asked what I was doing." He crossed his arms in front of his chest. "I think we owe each other a conversation, don't you?"

She lifted a brow, attempting a lighter tone to put a damper on the raging physical attraction between them. "You don't expect me to put out just because you took me to prom, do you?"

His lip quirked. "No."

"Good, because it's late and I think you should go."

"Why?"

"Because it's safer."

He sucked in a breath. Dammit, why did she always blurt out the truth with him? It was a terrible habit.

She turned sharply away, ready to show him to the door, but he moved quickly and was suddenly in front of her. His fingers were gentle as he gripped her shoulders. "I have to say some things you deserve to hear. Feelings I'm having for you that go beyond friendship." She looked up into his face and met twin coals of smoke piercing straight through her defenses. "Dreams I've been experiencing that leave me sleepless and aching."

Goose bumps broke out over her skin. A sinking pit tumbled in her stomach. "Maybe you need to take a Tylenol PM."

A low laugh rumbled from his chest. His hands began to move, rubbing up and down her arms, touching her waist, slowly sliding around to cup her ass through the silky material of her dress. She gasped. He kept her gaze, waiting for her to stop him.

She didn't.

"It's already complicated," she whispered. The ache between her thighs matched the one in her heart. No matter what happened between them, he'd always belong to Rory. She'd always be second, with no hope of moving upward. Could she live with it? Could she bear the burden of guilt for stealing her best friend's husband? For taking over the life Rory should have been living? Her mind screamed no, but her body didn't care as she leaned in, desperate for connection and touch.

"Sometimes it's not. Right now, it's just us, and this need I have for you seems to be taking over my life."

"You're just having emotions for me that are really for the baby." Her voice was desperate in her last attempt to step back. "Everything's getting mixed up."

She tried to turn, but his hands lifted to cup the back of her head and force her to meet his gaze. A shudder racked her at the fierce heat she saw, the raw hunger that called to her to slake it and demand her own.

"Not for me." Sebastian's breath whispered over his lips, gentle and soft. "Maybe I need another memory to keep me warm at night. I can't stop thinking about you, Chiara. Not just having you in my bed. You're becoming my best friend and I don't know what to do about it."

If he'd said anything else, she could have been strong. Walked him to the door and been safe. But the raw emotion in his voice, the naked longing in his gaze, touched the inner parts of her she'd never gifted to anyone. She only knew she needed to steep herself in him, to claim him completely for one perfect night. Maybe then she'd be able to get things back to the way they were, as partners and friends in raising their baby. But now, she needed so much more.

Wordlessly, she went up on her tiptoes and pressed her mouth to his.

Warm, soft lips moved over hers, as if treasuring her surrender with a pure humbleness and care. He sipped at her, over and over, until her knees grew weak and her body softened.

And then he claimed her full force.

His tongue speared into her mouth and plundered, the raging need from both of them too much to handle. His fingers tightened in her hair, holding her still while he kissed her long and deep and hard, slanting his mouth to dive back in, his teeth scraping against her sensitive lower lip.

Her body exploded, and she pulled desperately at his clothes, ripping open buttons and pushing down his pants. The dress slid off and fell into a pile of gold silk around her heels. He groaned and cupped her breasts, encased in nude lace, doubly sensitive from her pregnancy. Without missing a beat, he moved his hands to cup her ass, lifted her up, walked into the bedroom, and kicked the door closed behind him.

Darkness shrouded them. He slid the straps down and captured one hard nipple in his mouth, sucking with the perfect pressure until she was squirming helplessly against him. His fingers worked her underwear down until she was naked, and then she was being pushed gently back on the bed.

He stared down at her. Breath ragged, his gaze roved over her like a conquering warrior. She bloomed under the attention, loving the new ripeness and curves of her body, the driving need to have him inside her and ease the growing pressure. "You're so damn beautiful, it hurts to look at you."

A pleased smile curved her lips. "You're overdressed." She urged him close, tugging at the briefs that covered him.

"I'm trying to go slow. I don't want to forget a single second of this."

Her throat tightened. "You can go slow after you get naked."

Grinning, Sebastian shed the briefs and pressed his hard body over hers. Slowly, he used his foot to drag her legs apart, propping himself up so he could stare down at her with obvious appreciation. Then he ducked his head.

He licked every inch of her, moving downward, pressing kisses over her swelling belly. She twisted under his hot tongue and demanding hands, and then his mouth hovered over the center of her. His breath teased, and her hips jerked in need.

She cried out his name as he lowered his head and tasted her, gently rubbing the tight bud to keep her arousal to the highest level. Every stroke rippled pleasure through her body. She shook and let him take her where he wanted to go, and then his lips gently sucked, his fingers moving in perfect rhythm, and she fell into her orgasm.

Every cell inside of her splintered. A scream ripped from her lips. She'd barely come down when he pushed her thighs wider apart and surged inside her, hot and thick, filling her completely. Her hands twisted in the sheets, and she reached for more, wanting to be carried away, needing him to wring every thought from her mind and satisfy the awful empty ache inside.

He did. Gaze pinned to her face, he took her back up with slow, steady movements. She arched into every delicious thrust, heels digging into his hips, loving the fierce expression on his face as he climbed higher and higher.

"Come for me, Chiara," he commanded, his voice rumbling in her ear. "I want to see you."

The sexy words pushed her right over into another orgasm. She gave herself up to it, letting her body convulse into the pleasure, and heard his shout as he joined her.

Afterward, she waited for the assault of guilt and regret, but there was only a pleasant exhaustion and need to cuddle close.

Sebastian wrapped her in his arms, easing her to the side, and kissed the top of her head. "Sleep, baby. We'll talk in the morning."

She closed her eyes. The warmth and strength of his body made her feel safe.

Made her feel like she was finally home.

Chapter Twenty-Two

Chiara woke up and, this time, knew exactly what they'd done.

Worse? She didn't regret it.

Sebastian snored softly beside her. His leg was thrown over hers, one arm holding her close as if afraid she'd try to sneak away in the middle of the night. He'd reached for her two more times during the night, making love to her as the sun struggled over the skyline. Thank God it was Sunday and there was nowhere she needed to be.

A whine hit her ears, and she turned her head.

Uh-oh. She was such a bad doggy mom. "I'm sorry, sweetheart," she whispered at the lab's shaking body. He wanted to jump on the bed so bad and lick Sebastian awake but sensed he'd get disciplined. "You must have to go potty—you let Mommy sleep in."

His tail thumped in canine pride.

Slowly, she disengaged from Sebastian's warm embrace and grabbed a robe. She winced at the soreness in her legs as she hobbled out of the bedroom to let Dex out and feed him. Damn, it had been a long time since she'd engaged in such mind-blowing sex. As she put on coffee, Chiara realized last night hadn't quenched her desire. Her body had gotten a taste of excruciating pleasure and wasn't about to let her mind toss the source out the door.

"Hey."

She turned and stared. Sebastian was wearing his briefs and nothing else. He stretched and yawned sleepily, and Chiara couldn't look away. Every carved muscle was on shameless display, and she drank him in, her body instantly responding.

"Morning." She sounded ridiculously breathless. Thankfully, she had a job to do getting the beverages in two mugs, dumping creamer in hers, and handing him his own cup of the steaming brew.

"Thanks." He sipped, staring at her over the edge of the mug, as if curious about her reaction the morning after.

Dex scratched at the door. Sebastian carried his mug, still steadily sipping, and let the dog in. Dex glanced at him in delight, not used to overnight visitors. "How about some bacon, Dex?" Sebastian asked. "Do you like it crispy or fatty?"

"He likes it crispy," she answered, smiling at the way Sebastian looked at her dog with open adoration. "I can make it. Eggs?"

"Scrambled?"

"Sure. Breakfast is my super meal. I'm practically a gourmet chef."

He laughed. "Can I help?"

"Nope." Chiara paused, hand on her belly as strange bubbles floated inside. How could she have gas after a few sips of coffee?

"You okay?"

She nodded. "I've had this weird gassy thing lately that seems to be getting worse. The thing is, it doesn't hurt; it kind of tickles. I don't know."

"Did you talk to the doctor about it? Want me to look it up?"

She waved her hand in the air and began pulling eggs and bacon out of the fridge. "We have the ultrasound next week. Plus, it's not painful, just strange."

A frown furrowed Sebastian's brow. She had to stop herself from going over and running her fingers through his hair, which stuck up in delightful ways. "Let's just make sure it doesn't get worse." She gave a mock salute and he grinned. "Do you have anything planned for today? Going into the office?"

"No. I need to finish an article, make some calls, clean the house." She wrinkled her nose and whipped up the eggs, dropping oil in the skillet. "Boring Sunday stuff."

"Me, too."

"No youth center?"

"Not today."

They fell into silence. She wondered when he was going to bring up the sex. Wondered what her plan of action should be. Tell him it could never happen again? Turn off the burner and drag him back to the bedroom? Don't mention anything and pretend nothing had changed?

He left her alone with her thoughts while he sipped his coffee and murmured to Dex. It didn't take long to slide breakfast on the plate.

"This is delicious," he said. "You are a great breakfast chef."

"The secret is milk and cheese in the eggs."

Dex barked. They laughed.

"Okay, boy, here's your slice." Sebastian handed him the biggest one, and Dex raced to his bed to eat in peace.

Chiara drew in a breath, trying to broach the subject of their relationship when he was sitting across from her in droolworthy form.

He propped his elbow on the table, finishing his second cup of coffee, and pinned her with his gaze. "Wanna talk?"

Her tummy leapt again. A wayward curl fell over his brow. The rough stubble clinging to his chin gave her all sorts of naughty fantasies. Chiara swallowed. "You mean, now that we don't have an audience?" she asked, gesturing to Dex.

The grin was fully self-satisfied and masculine. "Yeah. I'll go first. Last night was incredible."

A strangled laugh escaped her lips. "Not going to argue about that. But I think it was a mistake."

He arched a brow. "Why?"

She ticked off the reasons. "We should be focused on Peanut, not us. You're my best friend's husband, and we'll always be judged by others. If things blow up, we still need to parent together. One of us can be hurt. Isn't that enough?"

Sebastian nodded, seemingly accepting her reasons. Her shoulders sagged in half relief, half disappointment, but he wasn't done. He lifted his hand. "We are focused on Peanut, whether or not we decide to take our relationship to the next level. And if you're feeling half of what I am, it could make things better. It could make us a family." She jerked in surprise, but he kept speaking. "We both loved Rory, and yes, I was married to her. But Rory's been gone for two years. We never created this situation between us, it just happened. Call it fate. What we do with it, though, is a different thing. I believe she'd want us to explore our relationship if we're both happy and emotionally connected. I believe she'd want us to be together. And what the world thinks of our decision isn't any of our business."

"But—"

"Chiara, you know that judgments are made without knowing the real story. You said exactly that in your speech at the conference. Anyone else's opinion of what we choose is none of our business," he repeated. A shiver worked down her spine as the words caught and held her in a trance. "Finally, you're concerned one of us can be hurt." A gentle smile curved his lips and his eyes warmed. "Baby, every time you decide to love, you risk hurt. It's part of the package. Would you rather we didn't have Peanut so we can guarantee we'll never experience that hurt?"

The idea of not bringing Peanut into the world shattered her. She shook her head hard. "No."

"Same with me. I feel things for you. And yeah, last night the sex blew me away, but it's so much more than that. I want to try and see what this is without trying to label it. We have time before the baby comes. And if we swear to be honest with one another about our needs, we'll be okay."

A tangle of emotions knotted within her. He wasn't proposing marriage or happily ever after. He wasn't pretending it wouldn't be hard as more people found out. But he was being honest about wanting to try. He believed, somehow, that Rory would understand.

Would she ever accept it? Or would she be slowly torn up by guilt and regret until it destroyed them? She'd hated the way Sebastian's coworker had looked surprised when he'd found out she worked at Quench like Rory. She could be setting herself up for a lifetime of comparisons.

"I don't know."

He grinned, surprising her again. "Fair enough. I'd like to spend the day with you, if that's okay. I know you're working, and I have some stuff to accomplish, also. I'll run home and grab my laptop, and we can hang out."

She blinked. "Hang out? I've never worked at home with someone else here."

"I'm quiet. And since Peanut will be here in a few months, maybe you should get used to working with company."

That coaxed a smile from her. "Good point." She thought about it, then nodded. "Okay. We'll spend the day together. But I don't want to have sex."

His face filled with sorrow. "Well, that sucks."

A laugh burst from her, deep and full. "If we're going to do this, I need to take the sex portion out of it. For now."

A long sigh broke from him. "I understand. Can I try and seduce you?"

"No."

"Fine."

Damn, why does he have to be so adorable? It took everything not to crawl onto his lap and kiss him, voiding her declaration within seconds. Instead, she remained in her chair. "We better get to work. We already slept in."

"I'll clean up, you cooked." Sebastian stood and began clearing the table when she suddenly jumped, her hand pressing against her belly. "What? Are you okay?"

"The bubbles. It's almost like . . ." She trailed off. "Oh my God."

He dropped the plate on the table and ran over. "You need a doctor?"

A light burst within her and she laughed, grabbing his palm and placing it over her stomach. "Sebastian, I'm so stupid. It's not gas. It's the baby moving!"

His face looked dumbstruck. "You can feel Peanut?"

"I think so. Get the book! It's on the table."

He raced over and began flipping through *What to Expect When You're Expecting*. "Here! It says early movement can feel like gas to new mothers." He read the passage aloud, and then their gazes met. "Peanut's moving!"

She tipped her head back and closed her eyes, enjoying the sensation, feeling filled up with so much joy it was going to burst from her. Now that she recognized what the bubbles were, it made total sense.

Sebastian's hands were warm as he cupped her belly, sharing in the experience, and when she opened her eyes and met his gaze, she realized how much she'd been lying to herself.

She wanted Sebastian Ryder—body, heart, and soul.

She just didn't know if it was possible without ruining everything.

~

"A toast! To Ford, for making it another year to official old-man status!"

A whoop rose from the café at Sebastian's declaration, which emitted an eye roll from the birthday boy. Chiara laughed, settled in her booth with Malia.

The place held a nice crowd with a mix of Ford's work buddies and other friends. Jeremiah, Manny, Pru, and Maria from Dream On had stopped by briefly, and Mike had made them his famous root beer floats. Chiara loved seeing the way the kids went from awkward and shy to relaxed under Ford and Sebastian's care as they were introduced and welcomed with enthusiasm.

Malia's voice shifted her attention back to the booth. "I think it's so great you brought up using more of our profits toward giving back to the community. I needed a new direction to focus on."

Chiara studied her friend in surprise. "You never told me you were getting burned out on sales. Are things okay with you?"

Malia sighed and propped her chin in her hand. "Yeah, I guess I've just been in a funk lately."

A flash of guilt pierced her. "Malia, I'm sorry. I feel like this thing with Sebastian and the baby has taken up all of our conversations lately. Tell me what's going on."

"Don't be sorry—it's just a bunch of silly things that are adding up. I went on another date last night."

"Damn, I forgot." Chiara gave her a sympathetic look. "I'm assuming it didn't go well."

"You assumed correct. I wish I could squeeze a funny story out of it, but he didn't even show. I sat in that damn restaurant, drinking a glass of expensive wine all alone."

She stared at her friend in frustrated puzzlement. Malia wasn't only gorgeous, with her dusty brown skin, glamorous braided hair, and lean body that she took good care of, but her intelligence was off the hook. Her personality may not have been as strong as Tessa's, but she was the consummate business professional, able to command a room with a look. Could that be the problem? Were these idiot guys intimidated by such a perfect package? "Malia, I swear I don't know what to say anymore. You know how I feel about these guys—it's truly their loss. But I really hate seeing you drive yourself crazy."

"Yeah, I know. Maybe I need to refocus on my career and stop obsessing about my personal life. I've been a bit restless. Dealing with bigwig corporate America to convince them to advertise with Quench used to be a challenge. But lately, I want a more passionate goal, and I really think it's this new program. I'd like to be more heavily involved. I'm beginning to reach out to some key players, and I'm excited."

"Of course! I think all of us are shifting our focus. We've been in the same roles for a while and need a change. I know Tessa can't wait to start the new internship program."

"What about you and editor in chief? I know you didn't want the job. Is it working out?"

Chiara sighed. "To be honest? I'd rather do more writing and get back to some travel, but it depends on Peanut. I think I'm looking for more flexibility in my job rather than being chained to endless paperwork."

Malia shook her head and grinned. "Girl, you have changed! You used to swear you hated kids and animals and relationships. Anything that tied you down made you break out in hives."

She smiled back. "I know. I didn't see this coming, but the more I lean in, the more comfortable I feel, though I'm still terrified of being a mom. I mean, there's no manual that comes with a baby. I'm going to make a ton of mistakes."

"You're supposed to. But you'll give your attention, support, and love. That's the difference between you and your parents. I'm glad you're finally opening up to bigger things in life." A touch of sadness gleamed in her friend's dark eyes.

"You want them, too?" Chiara asked softly. But it wasn't a question. Malia had always been vocal about wanting to find a man to love and settle in with. Her parents and sisters were happily married and were constantly pushing Malia to find a husband. But love came when it came, and watching her friend force herself out on endless bad dates hurt her heart.

"Yeah, I do. I guess it's just not my time yet. Maybe trying to sell with a different direction in mind will spark some new creativity. Hell, maybe it'll lead me to Mr. Right," she said jokingly.

"I bet it will. Hey, where's Tessa? She's late."

Malia shook her head. "I hope she didn't try to bail. She promised to be here."

On cue, the last of their crew came through the door, wild curls bouncing, dressed in a vibrant red shirt and dark-wash jeans, looking her usual fashionable self. And it seemed she brought a date.

Emma Primm.

The older woman wore a burgundy pantsuit with a matching hat, the brim so wide she could have been at the Kentucky Derby. Thank goodness her lipstick was dimmed a bit, but it was still a garish melon color. Emma looked around like a nervous bird, pulling at her black leather purse.

"Oh boy," Malia murmured. "Mike's not gonna be thrilled."

"Hi, guys," Tessa chirped. "Sorry we're late."

"No problem. Nice to see you, Emma. How are you?"

The woman smiled, but Chiara caught the look of unease on her face. She did another look around, obviously searching for Mike. "Fine, thank you. How's the baby? Are you feeling well?"

Chiara patted her swelling stomach. "Yes, we have the ultrasound scheduled soon, so I'll be able to find out if it's a girl or a boy."

"How exciting!" Emma's lips curved in a genuine smile. "I'm sure your parents can't wait."

She ignored the tiny pang of pain by sheer habit. "Unfortunately, they're not really involved."

"Shame on them." Emma's tone was stern. "They're missing out. What I wouldn't have given to have children of my own. But at least you have Michael. He's been like your dad anyway, hasn't he?"

Her throat closed up with emotion. "Yeah."

"Then that's even better, because you both chose each other."

Stunned, Chiara realized there was a lot more depth to Emma than she realized. Maybe Tessa was right—with patience and some time she may open up. "Come sit with us."

"I will, but I want to say hello to Ford first and thank him for inviting me." She pushed her awful glasses up on her nose, took a breath, and headed over to the guest of honor.

Tessa sank into the booth next to them.

Chiara tamped down a laugh. "Um, she wasn't invited, though."

Tessa waved a hand in the air. "Like Ford will care. He's a nice guy—he'll smile warmly and pretend they know each other."

"You're so bad," Malia said, but she was grinning.

"Did I miss any gossip?"

"Didn't realize you and Emma had gotten so close," Chiara said.

Tessa reached over and began eating the rest of Malia's cake. "I didn't realize I'd get attached. She's lonely, so I invited her out to coffee last week and spent some time one-on-one. She's absolutely lovely."

"Too bad Mike doesn't feel the same way," Malia said.

"Well, we can't force him. Fate will step in when the time is right," Tessa said confidently.

Chiara and Malia shared a look. "Um, who stole our friend? Is this an *Invasion of the Body Snatchers* thing?" Chiara asked.

"Where's the anger and *fuck that*?" Malia asked.

Tessa laughed. "Stop! I'm not that bad. Ah, here comes the birthday boy."

Ford reached their table and placed his palms flat on the surface, leaning in. "Ladies! Thanks so much for coming. Do you like the cake?"

"It's delicious. This place is popping. Your friends seem really nice, Ford," Chiara commented.

"Thanks. They are." His gaze skittered to the right and focused on a beautiful woman with honey-blonde hair. She was in a circle of a few guys, holding court, her tinkling laugh rising above the chatter. But it was the look on Ford's face that had Chiara doing a second glance. He had puppy dog eyes and a yearning that was carved into his features. The man had a crush.

Unfortunately, Tessa lasered in on the look, too, and came to the same conclusion. "Who's that?" she asked in demand, pointing to the woman.

Chiara winced. Oh Lord. This might be bad.

"Oh, that's Patricia. She works with me at the station."

"You like her."

Ford stumbled back as if it were an accusation. "Huh? Of course I like her. She's very nice."

Tessa snorted. "You know what I mean. You find her attractive. Did you ask her out?"

Poor Ford. His cheeks grew ruddy, and those hooded eyes narrowed on Tessa. "No."

Tessa pounced. "You're lying. What'd she say?"

"Um, Tessa? Maybe this isn't a great time to talk about this," Chiara prodded.

Ford shifted his weight. Irritation radiated from his figure, but he answered. "She said we were friends and didn't want to cross the line and ruin it."

Tessa nodded. "Friend zoned."

"I'm not worried. She just needs time."

Chiara glanced again at the woman. She was a swanlike creature and seemed to love attention. Her clothes were designer. Her hair was sleek and glossy. Chiara bet the idea of dating Ford would seem like a step down. Which was screwed up and oh so wrong, but reality.

"I don't think so," Tessa said. "Do you just talk about sports, or have you tried to get to know her personally?"

Malia cleared her throat. "Um—"

"Man, you're just as rude as I remember." Ford glared down at Tessa, fists on his hips. "It's my birthday. We're having a party. Are you still mad about that ridiculous dress? It wasn't that nice anyway."

Tessa's jaw dropped. "I'm rude? I'm trying to help you!"

"Yeah, like Mo Vaughn tried to help the Mets in 2003. No, thank you."

"I have no idea what that means."

He exuded satisfaction. "Exactly. I think I'll go get more cake and try to have some fun." Ford stalked away without a look back.

Tessa exploded. "I knew it! He has no manners. There's no way in hell he's going to get Patricia to look at him twice with that type of attitude."

"Why did you have to push like that?" Chiara hissed. "Ford can figure things out on his own."

"You, too? Fine. Next time, I'll just make sure we avoid each other. It was easy enough with you and Ryder when he was with Rory."

The words fell into a sharp silence. Tessa clamped a hand over her mouth.

Chiara caught the look of horror on her friend's face and interrupted her apology. "No, it's okay, I know what you meant. I don't want either of you to feel weird about bringing up Rory and Sebastian."

"Ugh, I'm so stupid sometimes."

"Yeah, you are," Malia sang cheerfully. "I can't wait to see the man who tames you."

"That is so archaic and chauvinistic."

Malia puffed up in pride. "I know. But it's what you need. You just don't like to admit it."

"I can't help it if men are scared of me," Tessa mumbled.

Chiara patted her hand. "It's their loss, babe. You couldn't scare away Malia and me, even when we were young and you tried to bully us at lunch."

Tessa laughed and the tension defused.

Emma came over with a plate of cake and took her seat in the booth. "It's cannoli. Just delicious," she said, eating with extremely small, precise bites.

A shadow fell over the table. Chiara tilted her head up to smile at Mike, but he was staring at Emma. "Hi. Does anyone need anything?"

Emma stared back, cake forgotten. "No."

"Do you like the cake?"

She blinked. "Of course."

"Oh. 'Cause you're eating it real slow like you hate it but are trying to be polite."

"Did you make it?"

He blinked. "No."

"Then it shouldn't matter." She stumbled and backed up. "I mean, it's delicious. Much better than anything I've had here before. I mean—"

"Never mind."

"No, I just happen to eat slow and mind my manners."

Mike winced. "I understand. I'm sure you think a man like me doesn't have any manners. After all, I have no college degree and just sling burgers at a café for a living."

Emma looked at him with shock, along with all of them.

"Is there a full moon or something?" Malia asked aloud. "Because people around here are going nuts!"

Tessa opened her mouth to rescue Emma, but the schoolteacher was already rising to her own defense. Her lips pursed in disapproval, and the tense stiffness was back full force. "Michael, you're being ridiculous. But the rude way you're speaking to me makes me begin to doubt my original assumption. Now, I'd like to get back to my dessert. Did you need anything else?"

Everyone stared at Mike. His cheeks reddened, and he stared back at Emma with a strange mix of emotion. Then he cleared his throat and stomped away.

"Well, that was fun," Tessa said.

Emma's hand shook slightly around the fork. "He just doesn't like me."

"I don't know. That was pretty strange and very unlike him." Chiara tapped her lip. There had been something in Mike's expression that puzzled her. It was as if he was drawn to Emma and deliberately tried to rattle her. Make sure she didn't like him. What was going on?

"I don't even want to come back here for my pancakes," Emma said sadly, continuing to cut her cake in perfect pieces and place them slowly in her mouth. "Maybe I need to find a new place."

"Don't you dare let him run you out of here," Tessa said.

"Tessa's right. Just ignore him. You'll find someone better, Emma. Someone who will really appreciate you," Malia said.

Tessa bumped Emma's shoulder. "You just need to build some confidence and be comfortable around men. I think we need to branch you out of Scrabble tournaments. There's a few local groups that meet to do nature walks, and a senior club that takes trips."

"That sounds like fun," Chiara said encouragingly.

Emma looked at the girls with a helpless expression on her face. "Yes, maybe. I guess I just wish . . ."

"What?" Malia asked.

"That I felt better about myself." She sighed with defeat. "I don't know how to make myself look nice. I've never been to a spa, or gotten my nails done. I've gone to the same hairdresser the past thirty years and she died. The woman who took over barely glances at me. Just trims it and charges me forty dollars."

"Ouch," Chiara said. "That's highway robbery for a simple cut. And a woman's hair is sacred."

Tessa snapped her fingers. "What if we all get together and have a girls' day? Get our hair and nails done. Maybe a facial. That always makes me feel good."

"That's a great idea," Chiara said.

"I'm in," Malia said.

"Oh, you girls don't want to be stuck with me. I'm old."

"Well, I guess our secret is out. We're being nice to you for one reason only," Tessa said seriously.

Emma frowned, looking nervous.

"We want you to change our English grade and give us that damn A on our Shakespeare project."

Emma's lips quirked. "It was a solid B, girls. That's all you deserved."

They all chuckled. Soon, Emma was engaged with them in girl talk, and by the end of the party, Chiara was happy she'd joined them. She also liked the way Tessa watched out for her. Tessa was the helper in the group; she just hated anyone to know.

A tingle on the back of Chiara's neck made her turn. Her gaze collided with Sebastian's. Slowly, he smiled at her, and in those charcoal eyes flickered the memories of their night together. Even across the room, a connection burned hot and bright, no longer able to be denied or hidden.

Damn the man. He was so . . . virile.

Not that she'd be testing out that part for a while. They'd spent last Sunday in a comfortable cocoon. After a while of being distracted by him muttering and frowning at his laptop, chewing on a pencil, and pushing those sexy black glasses back up his nose, she'd forgotten his presence and immersed herself in writing. They had a break to walk Dex, he helped clean her house, and they ended up cooking dinner, sharing space in the kitchen like they'd done it before. Then he'd kissed her gently and left.

She hadn't slept well that night, even though she was exhausted. It was as if now that she'd tasted him, her body craved a regular hit.

But as the days passed, and they fell deeper into their relationship, Chiara knew it was only a matter of time before something tipped the scale. Soon, a decision would need to be made. She just wasn't sure she was ready.

If she'd ever be ready.

For now, she enjoyed his presence, bloomed as Peanut grew, and tried to focus on the work that drove her. The work Rory had given all of them.

"More cake?" Malia asked, interrupting her thoughts.

Chiara refocused on her friends. "Yes. I think I'll have more cake."

"And eat it, too?"

It was so corny she found herself laughing hysterically, and she pushed Sebastian and their relationship from her mind.

Chapter Twenty-Three

The moment Ryder walked in to Dream On, he knew there was a problem.

The kids were talking in a tight circle, obviously in a deep discussion. Knowing he needed to respect their privacy, he pretended to be doing something on his phone to give them more time. When they seemed to realize he was waiting, they broke apart.

"Hey, everyone. Something going on I can help with?"

He took in all the kids' expressions, noticing Derek was the only one missing. Again. It was his third session in a row, which he'd never done before. Maybe he had to work extra shifts?

Manny was the one to answer after a brief silence. "Nah, everything's good."

"Sure?"

He hoped they trusted him enough to help. But Ryder felt he'd missed a critical moment, because all of them shook their heads in unison.

Jeremiah spoke up. "I think we're all beat today. Manny suffered through a sick weight lifting workout, and I had a fight with Tracey."

"You back together?" Ryder asked.

Jeremiah shrugged. "We were. Now, not so sure. But she always comes back. She loves me."

Manny grunted but didn't say anything. Pru nudged his shoulder, as if to warn him in case he decided against silence.

"Okay, then let's get this party started. Ford can't be here today—he had a big guest on his show—but he mentioned an opportunity to visit his station. Anyone want to go?"

They all jumped on it, so Ryder made a note to confirm with Ford and get it on the schedule. They spent the next hour doing a bunch of miscellaneous things—Pru helped Manny with the algebraic equations he was struggling with, and Ryder got on the ancient, battered laptop to research some colleges Jeremiah might be interested in. Maria sat with some paper and pencils and sketched them, as they agreed to be unagreeable models. Conversation seemed a bit stilted at first, but finally eased to gossip and light chatter.

At the end of the session, Ryder sought Manny out. "Hey, have you talked to Derek recently? Haven't seen him in a while. Want to make sure he's okay."

It was the look Manny gave that made his heart sink faster than the *Titanic*. Manny rubbed his buzzed blond hair and regarded him with a guarded expression. "Sorry, Ryder. Haven't seen him."

He knew he shouldn't push. Knew it wasn't his place, but he was worried. "Is he okay?"

The kid shrugged. "Not sure. I think he may be in a bad place."

Everything inside of Ryder stilled. "Using?"

"Maybe. Haven't heard anything. All I know is he hasn't asked me for a ride in a while—not to work or here or to one of his girlfriends. Hasn't answered my last text. He just disappeared."

It was a sign. And Ryder knew what his job was—what he promised when he began working at Dream On so many years ago.

Let it go. Be there when Derek came back—if he ever did.

There was nothing to report at this point, and he wasn't Derek's therapist, sponsor, or teacher. He was just a guy who spent time with the kids and hoped he made a small difference. Most of the time, Ryder accepted the rules, especially at the high school.

Not this time.

His entire insides rattled with panic and the need to find Derek. Get him the help he needed. Do something so he wasn't another lost kid.

"Thanks, Manny. Would you let me know if you hear from him?"

"Sure."

Ryder locked up the center and headed to the gas station. He just needed to know. Hope burned hot and bright that the kid was just working weird shifts, attending GED classes, and caring for his mom. He'd fallen off the grid. Made sense.

He parked the car and went inside. Not spotting Derek, he asked the cashier, who referred him to the manager.

The older man looked gruff and pissed off to be bothered. "You checking on Derek?" he asked in a voice that showed he used many of the packs of cigarettes he sold.

"Yeah, has he been working? Changed any of his shifts?"

The guy flashed a sneer, showing off yellow teeth. "Nah, he hasn't worked here in weeks. Just stopped showing up. Lousy kids these days are entitled. Not like when I was growing up and a job meant something. You know—"

"Appreciate the info," Ryder said, cutting him off. He went back to his car and sat there for a long time.

Derek had lied to him. The truth was always there; he'd just refused to see it. He wanted the money for drugs, not paying an electric bill. It was the oldest con in the book from any user, and Ryder had fallen for it, just as Ford had predicted.

He clutched trembling hands around the steering wheel. The kid could be anywhere. Ryder could get his mom's number and call, but that was crossing hard lines. If Manny or the other kids knew specific info, Ryder was sure they'd keep it from him. He had an idea they didn't want to disappoint him.

Sickness swirled in his gut, but it was the shame that truly defeated him. He couldn't help anyone. He'd been stupid to think he could be some sort of savior. And if he couldn't even help here, how was he going to be as a father? If his own kid ran into a big issue, would he fail? Would he do and say all the wrong things?

The thoughts spun out of control and ripped at his mind. Eventually, he managed to drive home and lose himself in a few glasses of whiskey.

He didn't want to feel anything. Not tonight.

~

It was the storm of the century.

And dammit, she needed ice cream.

Chiara stared morosely into her freezer, which contained a nice amount of vegetables, some pierogies, fruit for smoothies, and a variety of meats. But no Ben & Jerry's Netflix flavor. What was she going to do?

The rain beat mercilessly against the window. The wind roared. Even now, safely encased in his special ThunderShirt to keep him calm, Dex whined softly, sensing Mother Nature was pissed and there would be casualties. "It's okay, baby," she murmured. His gaze clung to hers for reassurance. "Your shirt keeps you safe, remember?"

Her poor dog had a history of storm fear. Before she discovered the weighted vest that calmed him, he'd cry during thunderstorms and try to hide in the bathtub, his entire body quaking. Now, she got notifications of severe weather and immediately strapped him in so when the crack of lightning and boom of thunder emitted from the sky, Dex felt safe.

Slowly, he seemed to relax again and snuggled into his bed, next to his favorite Scooby-Doo stuffed toy.

But her ice cream problem wasn't solved.

She shut the freezer and trudged back to bed. Propping her laptop back up, she rested against the headboard and tried to work. Everyone from Quench was working at home today, not wanting anyone to risk traveling in the hurricane winds. She'd just ignore the craving. Tomorrow was her ultrasound, and she needed to get some work done.

After the fourth error and mounting frustration, Chiara realized if she didn't get ice cream, she'd die.

Screw it.

The store was down the block. She'd be gone only five minutes and then could settle in safely for the rest of the night.

She hopped off the bed, slipped on socks, and heard her phone beep. She swiped it. "Hey."

"Hey, wanted to check in. How are you? How's Dex?"

She smiled at Sebastian's concern. "His shirt is on and he's calm. I'm doing some work in bed—too lazy to even make it to the table."

"It's that kind of day. School had an early release to get the kids home before the storm hit full force."

"Good thinking. Listen, can I call you back? I'm heading out quick."

Silence settled over the line. "Chiara, the roads are a mess. You can't go out there, it's dangerous."

She bit her lip and debated. "I'm not going far. The store is right down the road."

"You can do without milk or bread or whatever it is until the morning. I just heard a report to stay off the roads unless it's an emergency. The store is probably closed."

"No, it's a gas station, they're open twenty-four hours. This is a very mild emergency. I swear I'll be right back. It's literally less than five minutes, round trip."

"You'd risk your and Peanut's safety over groceries?" he growled, obviously trying to hold his temper. "What could possibly be so important it can't wait until tomorrow?"

She blew out a breath, pissed as hell at his bossiness and that he was probably right. "I need ice cream, okay? Not any type of ice cream but

Ben & Jerry's Netflix flavor, and the place down the road has it. I can't concentrate on work without it. I tried." Chiara steeled herself for his derision or temper and swore she'd hang up on him.

"Netflix?"

She sighed at his obvious confusion. "It's a particular flavor called Netflix & Chilll'd. Peanut butter ice cream with pretzels and brownies."

"Got it. I'm on my way—have it to you soon. Just stay put."

"Sebastian! Absolutely not, I'm going to—"

The phone clicked.

She stared at it, half-annoyed and half-charmed. No one had ever done stuff like this for her. She'd been taking care of herself for so long, Sebastian's consistent attention gave her a feeling of warmth and security she'd never experienced before.

Of course, it was for the baby, not Chiara. Still, it was a heartwarming gesture.

Dex cocked his head with inquiry. "He's getting us ice cream," she said. She usually shared some with him after removing the fudge pieces.

The dog's tail wagged, and he trotted over to wait by the front door. Chiara took the time to get decent. She wriggled back into her bra and changed her yoga pants—she'd finally succumbed and hated to admit she loved the comfort—but that was the extent of her prep. After all, he wasn't coming over for seduction.

Her skin prickled at the thought. They'd managed to keep their relationship celibate since their talk, but their explosive night together haunted her. Even worse? Her body was completely hormonal—she'd read that being pregnant can jack up a female's sex drive to crazy heights. If she eventually jumped him, she'd claim temporary hormonal insanity.

The knock interrupted her thoughts. Dex barked, and she flung open the door, blinking in shock at the sight of him.

Sebastian was soaking wet. The wind roared in fury and practically pushed him over the edge of the doorway. She yanked him in the rest of the way and slammed the door closed. "Oh my God, you're drenched."

He blinked through spiky, wet eyelashes while rivulets of water streamed down and formed a puddle at his feet. Black strands of hair clung to his forehead. His clothes were plastered to his body, and he moved a few steps in on squeaking sneakers. "It's a nightmare out there. I got to the store right before they lost power and closed."

"I'll get some towels." She retrieved them from the closet and handed one to him, noticing the two bags he held to the side. "What else did you get?"

He frowned, which looked adorable on his still-wet face. "Please tell me you didn't want anything else, because I'm not going back out there." He kicked his shoes off, stripped off his jacket, and rubbed his head dry.

Chiara dropped the other towel on the ground to soak up the puddle. "You have two bags."

"Oh, I bought all the ice cream in the case. That way you don't have to worry about running out for a bit. Unless you're indulging in Netflix and Ben & Jerry's on a nightly basis. If so, I'll need to find another inventory supplier."

In shock, she watched as he gave Dex his usual affectionate greeting, then stocked her freezer with the goods. Something inside her uncurled and let loose. She tried to drag in a shaky breath and fight it, but God help her, it was like trying to battle the storm that raged outside, reminding her she was helpless under such power.

Chiara burst into tears.

Sebastian froze and stared at her. Gray eyes were wide and a bit wild, like he didn't know what to do, and then he bolted over and pulled her against him. "Sweetheart, what's the matter? Are you in pain? Do you want another flavor? I'll go get it!"

His shirt was damp against her cheek, but smelled of cotton and ocean and the scent that was distinctly his. Her arms came around him to accept the embrace, needing his closeness as she began to shake. "No, I'm fine. It's just . . ."

"What? You can tell me."

"You're being so nice!"

He let out a whoosh of air and eased her closer. Every soft curve of her body fit against his hardness like a puzzle piece sliding into place. His fingers buried into her hair and he murmured her name, pressing his lips against her temple. "Of course I'm nice. Do you think I'd be mean to you?"

She gave a strangled laugh, ducking her head to hide her embarrassment. "No, but you went out in a storm and bought all of the ice cream and you're not even acting cranky. Oh, I hate this. My emotions are all over the place and I'm not acting normal anymore. This sucks."

She waited for him to move away, but instead, in one graceful motion, he scooped her up and brought her to the couch. Laying her in his lap, he pulled her close and held her.

Chiara cried harder.

"There's a lot going on, and the weather is strange today. I find storms bring up stuff we have locked inside." He stroked her hair gently. "Just let it go. I promise I won't tell a soul."

She did. And finally, when she was drained, her emotions calm again, she sank into his heat and strength, not wanting to move. Horror should have been her primary reaction to the breakdown. After all, she'd been responsible for herself for a long time and proud of her independence. Crying jags, pity parties, and whining were foreign and distasteful. That she cracked open like an egg over nothing and exposed herself to Sebastian showed she was changing, and she wondered if it was bigger than the physical pregnancy.

She wondered if something was changing in her heart.

Chiara didn't know what to say, so she remained silent. He didn't seem in a rush to move, so she kept still, soaking in the last of his comfort. Though she took pride in her ability to handle everything on her own, right now, in his arms, it felt good to have someone to lean on.

He began to speak, his voice like misty smoke, filling up all the empty corners of the room. "I used to hate storms. My dad left on a night like this when I was six years old. He had a fight with my mom, slapped her around a bit, then came after me. I wanted to hide under the bed because I was scared of him, but I needed to protect Mom. I needed to show him I wouldn't let him do that."

She held her breath, imagining a small, scared boy facing down his father. Her heart shifted and broke in her chest.

"I remember I was wearing these superhero pj's with Batman on them. God, I loved Batman. He took care of people, but he was also human—he didn't have any special powers from another planet. I stood in my room and told my dad I was going to make him stop hurting us. And he laughed. God, he was pissed and drunk, but he looked down at me with a smirk and just kept laughing. I hated him then. I hated who he was and how I couldn't help but still love him."

"You were so brave," she murmured.

"I didn't feel brave. I felt like crap. Most of my life, I felt responsible for his leaving, thinking it was what I'd said to him. I never told my mom, though. I kept it inside until I was talking to one of my kids at the youth center, and he told me a similar story. I shared mine and had this breakthrough as I was listening to him. I realized I was just like him—I had no responsibility for anything my dad did. I was just a kid doing the best I could. And my father was an asshole who didn't deserve a family."

This time, she was the one who did the comforting. Chiara lifted her gaze to his, needing him to see her face. "You didn't need your father, Sebastian. You became an amazing man all on your own. That's why you're going to be the best dad Peanut can ever imagine."

Shock filled his charcoal eyes, along with a flare of such raw pain, she lost her breath. He stared at her for a while, as if wanting to share more, something that was bothering him. Chiara waited, craving to be the one to listen and comfort, as he always did for her.

But then the pain turned to blistering heat, and her body immediately softened, melting into his, craving more. Slowly, he cupped her cheek with his hand, and she leaned into his rough, warm palm.

His voice was like a low scrape of gravel, giving her goose bumps. "I love when you say my first name. No one else does. Only you." His thumb slid over her lower lip, pressing in the center, coaxing her to part her lips to sip breath. "Why has it always been you?"

She trembled. Lifted her arms to grasp his shoulders for balance, because she was falling and he was the only one to stop her, but instead his mouth lowered, and she met him halfway and fell into his kiss.

Those soft lips mastered hers as if she'd always been his. The taste of him swamped her senses, and she opened for the hot surge of his tongue, her body softening and breaking apart under those firm, sweet strokes. There was no pulling away, no rationale or conversation. There was only an ache that throbbed and demanded release, a need to be covered and claimed by him in every way possible.

He groaned, deepening the kiss, and picked her up to carry her into the bedroom. Never breaking contact, he lay her down on the bed, his hands roaming and exploring over her clothes, until in a rush of gripping need, she raised up and stripped off her shirt and bra, bringing his hands to her breasts without apology.

His hungry gaze roved over her nakedness in a way that was raw and all male. "You take my breath away."

Sebastian tugged off his shirt, and now it was her turn to look at the mass of lean muscle covered by dark, swirling hair. She reached out tentatively and traced her fingers over every hard ridge, each rib, over his flat belly, until his breath hissed and he pressed her back into the pillow, removing the rest of their clothes.

His fingers tugged on her hard nipples while he nuzzled her neck, sinking his teeth into the vulnerable curve until she cried out. She cupped his hard ass, digging her nails in to mete out her own punishment, relishing his matching groan. The delicious scent of him filled her nostrils, while her hands roved to cup his throbbing shaft, then squeezed tight.

"Chiara. God, that feels good."

"Good. Let me give you more."

He shuddered as she hooked her leg over and crawled on top of his chest. Chiara propped herself up, looking at him with a ravenous hunger she didn't want to hide. God, how she wanted to give up and give him everything—the way he seemed to do with her every single day. Showing up for her. Listening. Letting her cry. Offering comfort.

Offering his heart.

She wasn't ready. She couldn't say the words yet.

But she could show him.

Chiara dropped kisses over his shoulders, testing his hard muscle with her teeth. Her hands explored every hot, muscled inch of him, while he gripped her hips, seemingly helpless under her sensual assault. A thrill coursed through her at the feminine power pumping through her veins. She inched her way down, her hair spilling over his stomach, then cupped his erection with both hands. She looked up his gorgeous body and met his scorching gaze. Smiled real slow.

Then took him fully into her mouth.

A blistering curse exploded in the air. She ignored it while she took her time, slowly retreating back and forth, exploring, tasting, licking with delicate swipes of her tongue before pushing him in completely to the wet cave of her mouth.

She sucked.

He exploded underneath her like a wild cat pushed to the edge. With one quick motion, he grabbed her, lifted up, and guided her onto his shaft.

Oh God.

She wriggled madly, but he held her still, forcing her to accept the stretching invasion with no walls between them, no excuses of dreams or fantasies, just the shattering truth of want and need for each other.

"Sebastian." She panted, her heart beating wildly. "It's too much."

"The baby?" he asked in a guttural voice, stilling instantly.

She blinked away the hot sting of tears. "No. I feel too much."

His gaze softened, and in those charcoal eyes, she found an understanding that met the empty place inside and filled it. "Me, too. But I want it, Chiara. I want you."

A shudder racked her body. He waited, and she knew it was still her call. He'd back off if she told him no, but Chiara knew she'd rather die than stop, no matter what the consequences.

She opened to him, her body softening and gripping him tightly inside her.

Home.

It was the same word she'd heard in her mind before—an echo of rightness she'd never experienced before him. She threw her head back. He growled her name. She shimmied her hips. He cupped the full curve of her breasts, watching from slitted eyes as she moved on top of him. Before long, she reached the edge and paused, trying to stretch out the delicious, agonizing moment. He reached down between her legs and stroked.

She fell over.

Body quaking, she rode out the convulsions of pleasure, memorizing his face as he followed, jerking wildly underneath her. A fierce possessiveness took her off guard, and one thought flickered through her mind.

She wanted this man to be hers.

Chiara curled up beside him, not wanting to break contact. His arm moved her close. Her legs tangled with his. The musky scent of lovemaking filled the air. Their breath rose and fell in choppy pants, finally settling in matched movements. His heart beat against her ear.

Chiara closed her eyes, torn apart by needing him to stay. Torn apart by needing him to go because he could never truly belong to her.

But it was too late.

She was in love with Sebastian Ryder.

As if he sensed her turmoil, he whispered in her ear. "Let me stay. Until the storm has passed."

She swallowed past the lump in her throat and nodded. Then held him tight and slept.

~

Ryder stared out into the darkness. She lay curled in his arms, hair spilling over his naked chest. Wisps of breath rushed against his cheek. He tightened his grip, as if by physically chaining her, he'd be able to keep her with him forever.

His chest filled with a fierce longing and pain that reminded him of when Rory had passed. The long, lonely nights aching for her. The guilt and anger at her loss. The shame of his actions that had brought everything full circle.

Now he had a second chance to be with a woman he loved. A woman who carried his baby. Who could give him a shot at a new future, one with love and laughter and family, instead of self-imposed agony and isolation due to his own choices.

Ryder cursed under his breath. Perhaps he'd always known if he loosened his restraints, he could fall easily in love with Chiara. She'd never strayed far from his mind since that night they shared so many years ago. But it was different now. They weren't young and dewy with stars in their eyes. They'd both experienced pain and loss and growth. In a way, he was glad to reconnect with her now, after she'd followed the path to a life she was passionate about. It may have never worked back then since they wanted different things.

And he'd loved his wife. Deeply. Chiara had been a dream from the past he'd easily locked down and refused to regret. But now, she was back in his life, having his baby.

And now, he loved Chiara Kennedy. He wanted a future with her that had nothing to do with Peanut. He wanted her for the woman she was, but he had to convince her it was worth taking a shot on a real future. She belonged in his arms. In his bed. In his heart.

Yet, there were still doubts. Doubts he'd be the father Ryder expected of himself and what Chiara needed. Doubts he could be the best partner to a woman who'd always wonder if he was thinking about Rory. Doubts that if he'd lost Carl and Derek so easily, could he lose more? Maybe he needed to begin pulling back. Leave more of himself safe to be a better father.

Maybe he needed to stop going to the youth center.

His father's voice echoed in his brain, though it'd been a long time since he'd listened. *"You're a failure. You'll always be a failure. Just. Like. Me."*

Ryder had proved to himself over and over that his dad was wrong— he was a man who lived in the light and refused the shadow. But not knowing what was coming with Chiara or Peanut or Derek scared the crap out of him, and for the first time, he questioned all his choices.

Tomorrow, the ultrasound would be the next step in bringing them closer as a family. Chiara had opened up to him tonight in a way that offered her vulnerability and trust. This was beyond lovemaking—this was an emotional connection he intended to fight for. He only wished he knew what the ending was, and if this time, he wouldn't fail.

Ryder closed his eyes and tried to sleep, but dawn came too fast.

Chapter Twenty-Four

Chiara lay back on the table, waiting for the sonologist. Sebastian stood beside her. His presence was comforting and a reminder of how important he'd become in her life.

This morning, there'd been no time to talk since they had a 9:00 a.m. appointment. They'd grabbed their tea and coffee to go, took care of Dex, and headed out. But Chiara knew last night had changed everything. No matter how much she wanted to deny it, Sebastian had gotten into her heart. Pushing him away wasn't helping anymore.

It may be time to let him in.

A woman entered the room with a bright smile and warm, dark eyes. "Hi, I'm Rachel, and I'm here today so we can take a look at your baby." She began to set up, looking at charts and pulling on gloves. "Chiara, can you tell me your date of birth, please?"

She recited the date and began to answer a variety of questions.

"Great. Is this the father?"

Sebastian cleared his throat. "Yes, Sebastian Ryder."

"Nice to meet you. It's always wonderful to have the father here to share in the experience. Now, let's get started."

She explained the procedure, rubbing the cold gel over Chiara's belly. The screen was tilted to give them both full access, and Rachel's fingers flew across her keyboard before taking the transducer and placing it on the full bump of her stomach.

"Ready to hear your baby?" she asked.

Sebastian reached over and took Chiara's hand, squeezing. "Yes."

Rachel moved the round head of the transducer around while Chiara's gaze was glued to the screen. After a few passes she paused, and the swishing sound of the baby's heartbeat rose to Chiara's ears as sweet as a lingering opera aria. "There it is. Healthy and strong. Everything looking great—we have all fingers and toes and limbs."

Relief washed through her.

Rachel took a while explaining what was on the screen, outlining the curl of the baby's spine with her finger, pointing out the position and what she saw as she looked at Peanut. "Looks like everything is developing normally. Now, the big question is, do you want to know the sex?"

Chiara dragged in a deep breath. Her heart beat like a mad drum. "Yes, please."

"Both are in agreement?" Rachel glanced between them. "I can tell one of you and not the other, if you prefer."

"I want to know, too," Sebastian said.

Rachel nodded. "Got it. Well, congratulations are in order. You're having . . . a girl."

The declaration washed over Chiara in waves. Peanut was a girl.

She was having a girl.

She burst into tears. Sebastian laughed and put his head next to hers, kissing her temple.

Rachel grinned and plucked a tissue from the table, handing it over. "She was extremely agreeable with her position. Sometimes we can't say for certain even at nineteen weeks. But I can clearly see the labia and clitoris right here. Has she been active?"

"Not very. I mean, I feel her moving, but no strong kicks yet or keeping me up at night."

"Good, but that may change in your next trimester. Unless she's a chill one."

Chiara couldn't stop looking at the screen.

Rachel hit a few buttons, and the machine spit out a few pictures. She handed them over. "Here you go. For your refrigerator."

Sebastian bent his head, staring at the pictures in rapt attention. "We're having a girl," he whispered, eyes filled with wonder.

"I know. Now we can choose a name and stop calling her Peanut," she said, still a bit weepy.

"I like Peanut for now."

They finished up and drove home together, both of them settled into a silence that was comfortable and reflective. Chiara's mind kept spinning in different directions about all the implications of having a girl. And the reality crashed through her.

Her life was truly going to be changed forever.

When they got to her house, Sebastian followed her inside, automatically taking care of Dex while she collapsed into the chair. *Lord, how do women just go back to work after such a discovery?* She felt as if she couldn't focus on anything but this human growing inside of her who now had an identity. It was so odd. For years, work had defined her and she was happy about it, never feeling the need for something more. She'd been prideful about the fact, feeling freer than her friends who'd craved husbands and families.

Now? It was different. A shift had occurred, and suddenly, Peanut was becoming more central to her awareness. She liked the burgeoning changes in her body. Enjoyed feeling as if she was no longer alone, even though the responsibility still scared her. Her life was suddenly bursting at the seams with so many things she once believed she'd resent for limiting her freedom.

But she had found more freedom in the past months than ever before.

Especially with Sebastian.

He walked in with a cup of tea, and she took it gratefully. His face, which had been lit up in excitement, was now creased with worry. Unease twisted inside of her.

Something was wrong.

Maybe he was unhappy it was a girl after all. Maybe he'd thought about it and was becoming doubtful if this whole thing could work. Just because he spent the night didn't mean he wanted more. Sex was sex. Yes, she knew he cared, but it was because she carried his baby.

A baby he'd wanted with Rory.

Chiara set down her tea and clasped her clammy hands together. "Are you okay?"

He jerked back like he'd been in a fog. "Yes, of course. I'm more than okay."

She nibbled her lip. "Did you want a boy instead?"

"God, no! I'm freaking out that it's a girl. In a good way. It's just . . ."

Her heartbeat felt like it had slammed into overdrive. "Just . . . ?"

He stared at her for a while. Chiara had the sense he was about to say something important; something was about to change both of them forever. But then he forced a smile and shook his head. "It's just I feel bad I have to go. I was only able to take the morning off."

Doubt slithered through her, but she nodded. "Sure, I understand. Go."

"Do you need anything else?"

"No, I'm great. Thanks for coming with me."

He headed toward the door. With every step, her dread increased. Because Chiara knew he was lying. Something was horribly wrong, and he didn't want to tell her.

His hand paused on the knob. "Chiara?"

"Yeah?"

He didn't look back. "I hope you know that ultrasound was one of the greatest moments of my life."

Then he left.

Oh God, it was over. He regretted sleeping with her and just wanted to partner with her as a single parent. He just didn't want to tell her today, after the ultrasound. Silly tears burned her lids. She'd been so wrong. As she was opening up her heart, Sebastian had begun closing up his. The ultrasound probably made him realize he'd never be able to love her like Rory. Somehow, she had to accept the truth.

Sebastian would never be hers.

Chiara sat on the sofa for a while, trying to process the amazing gift of knowing she carried a girl, and the grief of losing the man she'd fallen in love with.

~

Ryder was staring sightlessly at the TV when the pounding began.

He groaned, sensing who it was since he hadn't answered his phone. He'd known this confrontation was coming. He just didn't feel like dealing with it. "I have a hangover," he called out, not moving. "Let's catch up later!"

"Open the damn door, asshole. Now."

Crap. Ford wasn't going away.

Mumbling under his breath, Ryder got up from his sacred position and unlocked the door, then sat back down.

Ford lumbered in, kicked it closed, and glared. "What the hell is going on with you?"

It was the essential question he kept asking himself this past week. Ever since the ultrasound, he'd been haunted by doubts and insecurities he thought he'd beaten years ago. Images of his baby girl pounded his brain. She was so innocent and helpless. How would he protect her from the cruelties of the world? How would he explain to Chiara he was afraid he'd never be enough? It was a question a young man should struggle with. But he was thirty-five years old, and all of his demons were rushing in.

When he'd found out the baby was a girl, so many emotions hit him all at once. Elation. Gratitude. Anxiety. Fear. The noises and other images roared in his mind and ears and attacked his vision. Of Rory's face, and the kids he counseled, and the mistakes he'd made along the way. He needed space from all of it, so he'd backed off a bit. Stopped consistently texting Chiara and dropping by. He figured it was for the best.

"Nothing's going on. Why are you yelling? I'm sitting here watching some damn television after a long day at work."

Ford shook his head with disgust. "You haven't shown up at the youth center. Why?"

He tried to pick his words carefully. "I'm taking a break. The kids have you, and I know Jenny wanted to take on a few more sessions. I'm thinking it may be better to back off for a bit. Want a beer?"

He felt his friend's probing gaze on his face, but Ryder kept looking at the TV. "Is this about Derek?"

He winced. Frustration and anger tangled together, but those types of emotions got him nowhere. Better to stick with the simple truth. "You were right, Ford. About everything."

"How'd you find out?"

"I checked at his job and found out he hadn't been at work. Then I crossed the final line and went to his mom's house. She was never sick, and there was no electric bill." A humorless laugh escaped his lips. "His mom said he's using again. Just like you told me."

Ryder had still been hopeful. But after the ultrasound, he'd decided to show up at Derek's home to try and get answers. The look on his mother's face had punched him straight through the gut.

Ford gave a long sigh and sat on the edge of the sofa. "Yeah, I figured. He'd been distracted and quiet for a while. But he has a sponsor and a mother who cares. I have hope for him, Ryder. You should, too."

He snarled. "That's bullshit, and we both know it. The odds are stacked against him. And I can't do this anymore. I have to think about myself, and Chiara, and the baby. I can't be chasing lost kids all the time or expending my energy on hopeless cases."

Ford's brow shot up. "Oh, so you're taking that defense? Clever. This way, you get to pretend it wasn't your fault you walked out. It's easy to ignore the ones that you do help, isn't it, dude?"

"I'm not ignoring them."

"Yes you are! They're all asking for you! Everyone's worried because you haven't checked in or even sent a message. How do you think that feels to them?"

"Don't give me that guilt trip. You're the one who's always telling me not to get attached!"

"It's not about attachment!" Ford roared back. "It's about your need to save the ones you can't! When you fail, you not only beat yourself up, you retreat and forget about all the kids who still need you. It happened with Carl, and now it's happening with Derek. You get fucked up in the head, channel your asshole father, and blow up your life. Have you told Chiara about it?"

Ryder got up from the couch and paced, the restless, fierce energy pumping from him in a need to escape. "Chiara has nothing to do with this. I was pushing too hard, so I backed off there, too."

Ford groaned and shoved his fingers through his overgrown, messy hair. "God, I wish I could just punch you in the face so you'd get clarity, but we're a generation that needs to use our words. So here we go. Listen up."

Ryder glared.

"Do you remember the fight you had with Rory after Carl? How you changed and pulled back? She threatened you at one point and said that if you kept it up, there'd be serious consequences."

Ryder remembered. He'd retreated and told Rory he wanted to delay the fertility appointments. Suddenly, the thought of having a baby had been overwhelming, and he didn't want to deal with it. "Yeah, I remember."

"Rory and I finally got you to the other side."

He blinked at the memory. "Yeah. But then she died."

Ford nodded. "And then she died. You went to a dark place for a long time, Ryder. But now you have the chance to be happy again. With a baby, and a woman who's in love with you, whether she says it or not. I saw it that day at the center, the way she looked at you." He seemed to swallow hard. "It was something to watch. I wanted it so badly for myself."

He watched his friend's face, and his heart squeezed. "You think so?"

"I know so. But you have to let her in, dude. Tell her what happened and how you got fucked up. Then you need to get your ass back to the center and show up for the kids who are there. Because that's the job. It's fine to try and help the lost ones, but what we do every day is be there for anyone who needs us. Jeremiah, Manny, Maria, and Pru need us. Do you understand?"

Slowly, his friend's words trickled through the cracks in his defenses. Ford was right. God, how had he gotten so entangled with saving Derek, he'd forgotten his true purpose? He'd built a trust with all those kids, and now it was shattered. He'd promised he'd show up, but he'd abandoned them the moment things got hard. Just. Like. His. Dad.

But he wasn't his dad, dammit. And he wasn't giving up because of one bad mistake. "Have the kids been asking about me?"

"Yeah. I covered for you for a while, but they're smart. They know something's up, and that Derek isn't there anymore."

Ryder blew out a breath. "I just wanted to help. Got caught up in my own stuff."

Ford's expression softened. "I know, dude. We all want to help, but we can only offer it. Can't force them to take it."

He'd lost his way, but it wasn't too late. "I gotta deal with this."

Ford nodded. "I'll go with you to talk to the director. I don't think the consequences will be bad. You'll probably get a well-deserved lecture, though."

He rubbed his scratchy jaw. "I have to go see Chiara first. I have to tell her why I disappeared."

"She's going to be pissed. But you owe her the truth."

"Yeah." They stayed together in silence, letting the moment settle. "You want that beer?"

"Sure. You watching the Mets game?"

"Yep. Did you schedule the kids to see you at the station?"

"On the calendar."

Ryder retrieved his friend's beer, and they sat down on the couch together, watching the game. He took the time to process what he needed to do to get back on track, grateful for Ford's friendship. "Ford?"

"Yeah?"

"Thanks for kicking my ass."

Ford grunted. "I enjoy it."

They laughed and Ryder finally felt his chest ease. Maybe it was all going to be okay after all.

Chapter Twenty-Five

When Sebastian texted her to ask if he could stop by, Chiara was ready.

The past week had torn her apart. He'd gone from daily check-ins and bringing her dinner to stony silence. Sure, he'd shot her an occasional text inquiring about her health and work, but they seeped with an awful distance and lacked the intimate warmth his other interactions used to have. The few times she'd initiated contact, she felt uncomfortable when he cited excuses like too much work. So she'd stopped reaching out.

And it had all changed after the ultrasound.

But she had her lecture ready now. She'd be calm, poised, and understanding. Though humiliation had crawled over her like ants on a picnic lunch, eventually she accepted that Sebastian wanted to have "the talk."

When he stepped inside, he immediately knelt to give Dex all the love he'd been lacking. Dex moaned and pushed his nose against him, as if asking why he'd been forgotten. Chiara knew exactly how the dog felt.

"Good to see you," Sebastian finally said, standing up.

"You, too. We've both been so busy!" she said with a false happiness, as if she hadn't been sitting around waiting for him to make contact. "Do you want some seltzer?"

"No, thanks. Listen, Chiara, I wanted to talk to you about something—something you have a right to know."

She swallowed past the lump in her throat and swore she wouldn't cry. "Of course! But first, I'd just like to share something with you I think is important." She tilted her chin up. "That night of the storm? It was amazing. I've never felt so much pleasure."

His shoulders relaxed. "Me, either. I'm glad you feel the same."

"But it doesn't mean anything."

He frowned. "What do you mean?"

"I just mean I don't want you to put pressure on yourself by thinking I want more than you can give. I'm pregnant, Sebastian, and it makes my hormones crazy. It was great, we satisfied each other, but please don't worry that I'm looking for a repeat or a relationship separate from being parents. We've both gone through a lot of changes. It's a lot of pressure. But I've got it handled completely."

Relieved she'd gotten it all out, she dragged in a breath, grateful she hadn't acted needy. She waited for the relief to cross his face, but he only blinked, then shook his head slowly. A burning anger simmered in his eyes, which threw her off. "Is that how you see this? It was just a tumble to release some of your hormones? Wow. I had no idea it was so basic. Excuse me for feeling used."

Her jaw dropped. "I wasn't using you! I'm giving you permission not to worry about me and my needs or demands. I got this," she said again.

"That's how it's always been, right? You on your own, against the world. But that's a crock of shit, Chiara. You let Malia and Tessa and Mike in all the time. They're part of your world. Am I not good enough to accept, too?"

She felt like she was losing her mind. How did this conversation go so wonky? "You're twisting my words. Isn't that what you were going to say to me, what you were worried about—me getting too attached since we've slept together? I'm just trying to ease your mind by telling you not to worry."

"No. We slept together before and never had this conversation."

The breath punched out of her. He was right, but the night of the storm had been different. More raw. And sharing the ultrasound together had been the culmination. "It was different this time," she said, voice torn. "We can ease back from all this . . . intensity."

"What if I want to worry?" Sebastian paced back and forth, jamming his fingers through his hair and mussing up the strands. "What if I want to be the man in your life who has the right to care about you? To actually demand stuff like intimacy and letting you cry in my arms and being able to make you smile? Is that something you'd hate to hear?"

Stunned, Chiara stared at him, his jagged masculine energy emanating from his figure. He walked back and forth like a caged animal. "You don't need to say these things, Sebastian. You will always be Peanut's father, and I will never try to cut you out of her life. There's no need to pretend or force emotions between us. We can go back to the way things were with no problem. I won't be resentful."

He spit out a vicious curse. Dex stared at him from the corner of the room, just as confused. It was as if he were breaking apart in front of them and showing them a man who had none of his shit together. A man who was slowly unraveling and they had no idea why.

"Chiara, all this time, haven't you known what I really wanted? What I've been slowly pushing for as I spent more time with you?"

A trembling began deep inside. She'd begun to think he wanted more, but after the ultrasound, he'd changed. This conversation was getting out of control, and she didn't even know how to respond. "A relationship based on trust and respect in order to raise Peanut?"

He stopped short and turned. "You. I want you. As my partner. As my lover." His fists clenched, and a wild, primitive energy surged between them. "Eventually, hopefully, as my wife."

Chiara stuttered over the words, feeling slow and clumsy. "Yes, but it's because I got pregnant."

He half closed his eyes and violently shook his head. "This isn't about the pregnancy. Yes, that's what brought us back together, but I've always had feelings for you. I know you needed time to get used to it, but I can't go back to the way things were. I don't want to unless you don't feel the same way as me, but dammit to hell, I know you do. No one can fake this type of connection."

Chiara wanted to scream with frustration. "Wait, I don't understand. This past week, you've been completely avoiding me! We spent the night together, had the ultrasound, and you checked out. I figured you needed distance to figure out if this is what you really want."

Regret carved out the lines of his face. "I know. And that's why I'm here, because I owe you an explanation. I screwed up, and I'm sorry I made you doubt my feelings for you."

She studied him for a while, taking in his clenched fists and fiery gaze. This wasn't a man who wanted to walk away. Something had happened to change him, and Chiara needed to find out what it was. "Tell me, Sebastian. What happened?"

"You met the kids at the youth center. Do you remember Derek?"

She nodded. "He was the quiet one."

"Yes, but that's not his usual MO. I've known him to be almost the leader—a vivacious, funny kid who had a rough go of it with an asshole father and drug-addicted past. But he was battling after rehab and coming out on top, with a job and chance to get his GED."

She kept silent, sensing he needed to focus. Sebastian began to pace back and forth. Dex decided to accompany him.

"He came to me first about driving him to work. He was struggling because he has no license—it was revoked for driving under the influence—so I helped him out a bit. I noticed him changing and got worried, so when I asked him if something was going on, he told me his mom was sick and they were going to lose power in the house. Derek explained he didn't have enough money to pay the electric bill. I wanted to help, so I gave him the money."

Chiara wasn't surprised. Sebastian would do anything to help someone he cared about. "That must've been a relief for him. Is his mom okay?"

A grim smile twisted his lips. "She was never sick. Derek lied to me, and I should've known better than to give him the money."

She frowned. "But wasn't it the right thing to do?"

"No, Chiara, it was the wrong thing. Giving money to the kids is a big rule breaker. We're supposed to be there for company and a listening ear. For support. But we're not trained therapists or drug rehabilitators. When Derek stopped showing up at the center, I went to his job and found out he'd left weeks ago. Then I went to see his mother, and she confirmed my worst fears: he's using again."

She pressed her hand to her mouth. The obvious anguish in Ryder's gaze made her want to comfort and soothe, but she stayed still and let him finish.

"I fell apart. Blamed myself for giving him the money and not being able to help. Something similar had happened with another kid years ago, and he ended up back on the streets. We'd gotten close, and it was a big blow. Took me a while to process."

"Sebastian, I can't imagine how much that hurts. I know how you give everything to the kids and how important they are to you. I'm so sorry."

He gave a jerky nod. "Yeah, both kids had crappy fathers and single moms, just like I did. And because of that, helping and then failing them . . . it became more. I began to doubt my own abilities. As a mentor. As a father."

The realization suddenly swept through her. "You thought you'd fail Peanut."

A self-conscious smile quirked his lips. "I guess I got in my head. When I saw her on the sonogram, all I could hear was my father's voice saying I was a failure."

Emotion choked her throat. She ached for the right words to take away his doubts and pain. Chiara closed the distance between them and laid a palm to his cheek, gazing into his troubled eyes. "You're not a failure, Sebastian. Nowhere close. I can't promise you perfect. No one can. I'm terrified of messing up, too, but you've taught me something that's given me courage: all you have to do is love and show up, every damn day, even when it's not convenient or wanted. Even when it's hard. That's why you couldn't be a shred of what your father was, even if you tried. You simply give too much, and I never want you to change."

His forehead dropped to press against hers. The heat and strength of his body surrounded her with a deep comfort and joy she embraced. Wrapping her arms around his shoulders, she drew him close. He whispered against her ear. "Do you think it's enough?"

She kissed his brow, smoothed back his messy hair. "Yes. It's more than enough."

Their lips met, and she fell into a deep, drugging kiss. Time softened, blurred. Suddenly, they were in the bedroom, and they were making love, coming together with a shattering tenderness and care that went beyond the physical. He claimed her, and she saved him. He loved her, and she let him.

Afterward, she was the one to hold him. "You will always be enough," she whispered again.

And she hoped he believed.

~

The Nyack summer street festival was one of the biggest local events of the year.

Chiara took in the endless lines of vendors on Main Street offering goods from the community. Handcrafted soy candles, crocheted and lace goods, carved wooden furniture, and gorgeous landscape art were some of the highlights. The local animal shelters gated off areas to introduce potential adopters to the world of pet rabbits, dogs, cats, and a few pigs. The dog bakery had pampered pets spoiled, and there was a pet café just to enjoy the snacks. Food trucks tempted pedestrians to sample an array of treats, including Greek gyros, cheesesteaks,

BBQ pulled-pork sliders, and the traditional hamburgers and hot dogs. Cupcake stands were plentiful, and Mike always ran a booth. The line twisted long and far for his famous root beer floats on such a hot day.

"You're not going to eat the rum cake, right?" Sebastian asked, obviously trying not to police her but concerned about the heavy dose of rum in the dessert she'd just stocked up on.

She smiled and linked her hand with his. "I'm freezing them and will celebrate after Peanut is born." The screech of kids hit her ears as they neared the bouncy houses. "That's going to be us one day, isn't it?"

He stared at the hyper group of toddlers running around. Some cried, some whined, others took off barefoot after their turn, with weary mothers chasing after. He winced. "Um, I guess?"

"We'll worry about that later."

He laughed. "Agreed."

Her heart did a flip-flop, and this time she didn't question it. Since the day Sebastian had told her the truth about his fears, they'd been constantly together. He'd ripped the last of her barriers away, and she didn't want to fight her feelings any longer.

She'd never met a man like him before. Years ago, she'd chosen to give up the chance to be with him, sensing it wasn't right. But this time, she couldn't walk away again. Knowing how he'd blamed himself for Derek when it wasn't his fault showed her how hard he loved. How responsible he felt for the people in his life. She didn't know how it was going to end, but they took it day by day, getting closer with each moment.

Chiara had no regrets.

She spotted her friends heading toward them and waved them over. "Hey, guys. Did you check on Mike? Does he need help?"

"He's got it under control," Malia said. "We'll meet him later on his break. Where's Dex?"

"Poor thing stepped on a rock and hurt his paw. He's fine, but needs to keep still for a while."

"We're going to bring him home some special bakery treats," Sebastian added.

Tessa grinned. "Okay, I can't help it, but you guys are too cute. How's Peanut?"

Chiara rubbed her belly. "Kicking up a storm. We both feel great except for one tiny problem."

Sebastian frowned. "What? Is it too hot? Need more water?"

She winked. "Churros. Peanut needs churros with chocolate sauce."

They all laughed until a high-pitched scream suddenly cut through the air. Tessa wrinkled her nose. "How about a change of scenery? Preferably one without shrieking kids attacking one another in hot boxes of hell? Let's grab some churros and head over to the beer tent. They're serving sparkling cider, too."

"Done," Sebastian said.

The day unfolded in slow summer glory. Chiara watched the families pushing strollers with a new appreciation and a burgeoning excitement. The body she'd been afraid would change to unrecognizable now fascinated her. She was growing into ripe curves, and her daughter was sharing her most intimate space, occasionally causing a strange stretching inside of her, as if her skin were trying to fit over her bones to accommodate a new person.

It was scary. It was overwhelming.

It was pure magic.

They picked up doggy cannolis and a meaty bone that would keep Dex occupied for hours, stopping along the way to talk to shop owners, friends, and various neighbors. Now that she was showing, the questions poured in. Chiara was honest but offered little detail. She liked keeping Peanut and Sebastian in her own safe world for a little while longer.t

They grabbed a table outside the beer tent.

"Okay, guys, I made a big decision," Malia said. "I'm going to freeze my eggs and stop looking for *the one*. I'll just use men for sex from now on."

Sebastian lifted a brow. "Ladies, I see an amazing beer waiting for me over there. I'm going to excuse myself and meet you later."

Chiara laughed as he hurried away.

Malia winced. "Sorry, didn't mean to scare him off."

"He can handle it; he just wanted to give us some privacy. Now, tell us what brought on this decision."

"My family. My cousin is pregnant with her second child. And you know Cara, my twenty-one-year-old niece? She's pregnant, too! Can you believe this?"

Tessa winced. "That's so young. I could barely keep myself alive at that age, let alone a baby."

Malia moaned. "Yeah, but she's happy, and my mother is driving me crazy. I think it's time to take fate and chance out of my life and go with hard facts. My eggs are getting old, and marriage is not in my near future. So if I freeze them, I know I'll have options."

"I think it's a great idea, babe," Chiara said, giving her a quick hug. "You're in charge of your life, remember? Not your mom."

Malia shuddered. "She still scares the crap out of me."

"Me, too," Tessa said. "Maybe because she has a million kids all over the place, and she's the matriarch?"

Malia had four sisters who were all happily settled with kids, and now her nieces were beginning their families. As the baby, Malia had been overlooked, to her delight, but now her mother was really turning up the heat. Chiara figured that's why her friend had been getting more and more upset over each bad date.

"Don't you ever get discouraged, Tessa?" Malia asked.

Tessa shrugged. "Sure, but I move on. I'm picky and a hard-ass. I don't like wasting my time if I know immediately it won't work. But the cliché is true, and don't forget it: there are plenty of fish in the sea."

"I don't want to keep swimming," Malia said a bit grouchily. "I'm tired. I want to tread water and be happy."

Chiara laughed. "Well, we're here for you with full support."

"Thanks. At least you look happy. Things still going well with Ryder?" Malia asked.

She tried not to beam. "Yeah, we're both happy. Focused on the baby. He has the summer off and is going to do more hours at the youth center."

"Did you tell him what we're working on?" Tessa asked.

Chiara shook her head. "Not yet. It's a surprise. I can't wait until he sees the check and our plans."

"We still have a long way to go, but by the end of summer, I think our accountants and finance people will have everything set," Malia said. Suddenly, her full lips thinned and annoyance sparked in her dark eyes. "And then I can't wait to drop a certain account."

"Oh no. Not Mr. Hot Billionaire?" Chiara asked.

Malia rolled her eyes. "He's not hot, he's a pain in the ass. Who cares if he contributes so much to our advertising profit?"

"Um, I do," Tessa said. "We need him more than ever with this new endeavor. He's already invested, and there's probably a lot more he'll do."

"I don't think dealing with him is worth it," Malia grumbled. "Sure, he's increased his investment stream regularly, but I don't like him. He's arrogant, demanding, bossy, and thinks everyone works for him. Even me."

"You do work for him," Tessa reminded her.

Malia snapped back. "No, I don't! I work for Quench, and if I don't want to sell him ads or beg for money, I won't. And you'll both back me because we do that for each other. Right?"

"Right," Chiara said.

"Not if he's bringing in over a million dollars!" Tessa squeaked. "He runs a wedding empire. Whether you like someone doesn't matter in business—didn't you always tell me that?"

Malia fumed but managed to keep her voice level. "We'll talk about it later. I don't want him to ruin a beautiful day."

Wow, no one seems to be able to rouse Malia's temper except this client. She was such an even, easy person to work with, which was another reason she sold so much advertising. But Mr. Hot Billionaire had been yanking her chain for a while.

A shadow fell over Chiara. She looked up as Sebastian handed her a glass of sparkling cider and the two girls pints of beer. "Figured you could use a cocktail while you're steeped in gossip. Do you need sunscreen? You're not too hot, are you?"

Sebastian looked down at her with concern, and a sudden surge of love hit her hard. This was a man who cared about her; who showed up; who allowed her to be herself without trying to change her. He was a man she was happy to be with, and right now, she needed him to know it.

So she went up on tiptoes, yanked his head down, and kissed him full on the lips in public.

He kissed her back immediately, cupping her cheeks. She enjoyed the warm slide of his lips over hers, the sun beating on her back, the teasing whistles of Malia and Tessa beside them.

He eased away and grinned. "What was that for?"

"I'll show you later."

Malia pointed her finger at them. "That's what I want!"

They all laughed. Tessa patted Malia's shoulder. "You'll get it, babe. Eventually. But for now, it's nice to know it's out there."

Chiara sighed with happiness and finally felt everything was perfect.

Chapter Twenty-Six

Chiara walked into Quench and was immediately stopped by Tessa and Malia.

"We have a problem," Malia said in a low voice. "Come into the conference room."

She followed her friends and tried to keep calm. There was occasionally an issue with an article they posted, or social pushback if one of their products or influencers didn't hit the right mark. Managing a multimedia corporation was a challenge, and she'd learned to remain calm, especially in the role of editor in chief.

But even Chiara realized this had to be pretty bad if both of them looked worried.

"What is it? Just tell me, it's always easier that way," Chiara said.

They shared a pointed look that annoyed her because she was the only one out of the loop. "We need you to remain calm when you see this, okay?" Tessa asked.

"We spoke with the PR team already, but we need you to see this before we can make a decision," Malia said.

"If you don't show me now, I'm going to freak out."

Malia hit her laptop and clicked on the feature flashing on the MSN home page.

The picture smashed the breath from her lungs.

It was her and Sebastian in an embrace. They were kissing, her head tipped back, caught up in the moment and obviously crazy for each other. The swell of her belly was evident underneath her T-shirt. She recognized from the background that it was taken at the Nyack street fair, but the headline was the real problem.

Quench Founder Pregnant by Best Friend's Husband?
Secret Affair Exposed!

"Oh my God," she murmured, immediately sliding into the chair. Her fingers trembled as she scrolled down and read the post, written by none other than Wynter Davis.

Quench co-founder Chiara Kennedy was spotted at the Nyack street fair Sunday with a surprising new love interest: Sebastian Ryder, the widower of previous Quench editor in chief Rory Ryder. The women were well known to be close friends, creating the famous multimedia company together from the ground up. But were Chiara and Sebastian already having a secret affair before Rory's death?

A close source noted Chiara and Ryder had met years before at Remy's Nightclub. "I saw them together one night and they were obviously hooking up," the bartender confided. With Chiara clearly pregnant, insiders want to know: Is her best friend's husband the baby daddy? Looks like the successful entrepreneur is taking over more than Rory Ryder's role in the company. She's taking over her life!

The words assaulted her vision. She jerked back and stared at the screen in growing horror, realizing she would soon be under siege by a bunch of reporters and social media looking to feast on a juicy story.

Even worse? It was twisted with the truth. She'd known Sebastian before Rory introduced them.

She was going to be sick.

"Chiara, look at me," Malia said forcefully. "It doesn't matter. We suspected this could happen, so maybe it's good it's out in the open now."

"We know the truth, and that's all that matters," Tessa said. "Your family, friends, and coworkers have your back."

Chiara bent her head between her knees and breathed. "I can't believe this is happening."

"I'm not sure why this reporter seems out to get you, but it's all lies. You never met Ryder before, and it's just a way to exploit gossip and get clicks. In forty-eight hours, it'll be old news. Just like the last ridiculous story," Tessa said.

Guilt blew up inside her. A painful moan rose to her lips as she looked at her two best friends and realized she had to tell them. There was no way to hide it any longer. Not telling them was completely different from outright lying.

She pressed shaky fingers to her forehead. "I have to tell you something."

"It can wait. Your job is to calm down and let us handle it," Malia said firmly.

"No, you don't understand." Her voice came out choppy, but she couldn't wait any longer. They had to know. "Not all of it is lies."

Tessa frowned. "What do you mean?"

"I met Sebastian before he was with Rory. At that club."

Stunned silence filled the room. Chiara met their shock-filled gazes head-on, knowing it was the only way to do it. Rip off the Band-Aid.

"I don't understand," Malia said slowly. "That's impossible. You would have said something."

The words came out in a rush. "I should have, but I panicked and didn't. I met Sebastian about five years ago, before he started dating Rory. Nothing happened, not even a kiss. We hung out, talked, and made a connection. But I knew even then we were different—he wanted things I didn't. So at the end of the evening, I left. I figured we'd never see each other again. When Rory introduced him to me as her boyfriend, I freaked out. I thought things would be weird if I said we'd known each other. I also knew they'd be perfect together, so I didn't give Sebastian a choice to tell the truth. I pretended we were meeting for the first time and never said a word to anyone."

Her friends stared, obviously trying to process the bombshell. "Why wouldn't you tell us later, after Rory got married? Or even after her funeral?" Tessa asked.

Chiara dragged in a breath. "It seemed too late! And I figured it didn't matter any longer. I swear to God, guys, we never even kissed."

Suddenly, they were both hugging her. "It's okay, it's all going to be okay. I understand why you didn't say anything," Malia soothed.

"I might have done the same thing," Tessa admitted. "Rory could have been weird about it, or even pushed Ryder away. Now I understand why it seemed you two never got along. You were trying to keep your distance and not let anyone know you'd met before."

She nodded miserably. "Oh God, and now Mike's going to know!"

"He'll understand. Just tell him the truth—nothing happened between you and Ryder then," Malia said.

Chiara groaned. All she could think of was how the story was spun, and the world would be judging and picking apart her life. "How do the Kardashians deal with this?"

Tessa grinned and rubbed her back. "Craftily. As we will. It may be bad at first, but eventually, this will die down and they'll be on to juicier stories."

Malia nodded. "We'll get Xio here and stay firm on no comment. It's no one's damn business what your private life entails."

But the article had made it the public's focus. It questioned Rory's marriage and past. It dredged up painful memories for Mike. It made it look like a hot affair had been going on behind the scenes, and it put Quench into the spotlight in a bad way. Sebastian would be judged and questioned by the kids and his coworkers. Even worse? It announced her pregnancy in a tawdry way that made her sick.

Suddenly, she knew ignoring it was the wrong move. The news and social media fed on speculation. It'd be easier to present a strong front and stick as close as possible to the truth. If the press smelled any type of denial, avoidance, or lie, she'd have them crawling all over her—especially competitors.

Chiara made her decision. "No. That won't make it go away. We're going to craft a response and feed it out on our channels."

Malia gasped. "No! You don't need the world in your private space, especially now with the baby. And we can't forcefully deny you and Ryder didn't meet before. I'm sure he'd agree."

Sebastian. She had to tell him and see if he'd back her decision. It would be messier, but her gut told her to meet this collision head-on with no fear.

Slowly, a strange calm settled over her. She rubbed her belly, a fierce protectiveness shuddering through her. "Call the team in. I'll contact Sebastian, and we'll go over the statement. I'm not running from this, guys. I won't let my baby be dragged into a gossip-drenched lie fest about Sebastian and me carrying on a secret affair. Are you with me?"

A few seconds passed. Tessa and Malia finally nodded, moving close and bringing her into a tight circle. "You're such a badass mom," Tessa said, squeezing her hand. "We'll go hard and hit back fast."

Malia agreed. "I'll send an email to my advertisers and reach out to all my contacts." She paused, giving Chiara a worried look. "Just one thing we need to be prepared for. Some of our investors may want to pull out of the foundation. The skittish, cowardly ones, of course. The ones we wouldn't want anyway."

Chiara wanted to duck her head in shame, but that wouldn't help anyone right now. She needed to fight back and hold her position. It was about time she began practicing to be a badass mama bear. "I know. I'm sorry, guys. But hopefully we can manage the damage control."

"We will," Tessa said. "Malia's right—if they fold for a bit of gossip and discomfort, we don't want them as investors anyway."

Chiara nodded, feeling the support of her friends. "Let's do this."

~

When Chiara opened the door, Sebastian embraced her. "Been thinking about you all day. How are you holding up?"

Normally, she'd lean into his strength and accept the comfort. He'd taught her expecting care and support was her right and that she didn't need to do things alone. Not anymore.

But this time, she stepped back, needing the space. "I'm fine. Just making some tea. Want coffee?"

"Nah, seltzer is better. I'm already wired. Now, tell me what happened. I thought the statement was perfect."

She busied herself in the kitchen while he rubbed Dex behind the ears. "Me, too. I think we spun it well and got the focus off the speculative crap about us having an affair. The PR team has it all handled, so now we just step back and keep to the statement." She handed him a seltzer. "How about you? I was worried about Dream On and how it looks."

"I met with the director and told her what was going on. I'm not worried about the kids—Manny and Jeremiah wanted to take selfies with me because I was going viral." He grinned. "Guess they look at things differently than us."

She let out a sigh of relief. "Good."

"How was Mike? I wanted to go with you when you told him."

"I know, but as soon as we had our meeting, I drove straight to the café. I explained it all, and damn, he was pissed."

"At us?"

"No, at the reporter. Took me a while to calm him down. He hated the idea of Rory and me being dragged through the muck, but he agreed with our statement and actions."

"Just like I knew he would," Sebastian said.

She sipped her tea. "Yeah, but it still must've been hard for him. It's another reminder Rory won't be the one living the life she was meant to have."

He cocked his head. "What do you mean?"

Chiara forced a smile. "Never mind. I'm so tired, my brain isn't functioning anymore."

"I have an idea. I'll cook tonight. Give you a foot rub. We can watch a movie—your choice. And we'll just decompress."

Emotion hit hard. He was so sweet. Even now, her entire body throbbed for his touch, to be close, to cuddle in and run her fingers through his crisp hair and let herself go. He'd given her a gift she'd never experienced, and now she'd gotten greedy. She craved him all the time now. Depended on him for things she'd always done herself. She'd let him so deep into her life, they were now intertangled, and it was beyond Peanut. It was about how she wanted him all for herself—man to woman, lover to lover.

But she couldn't. There were too many dark thoughts and doubts slithering through her mind like venomous snakes. She needed some time.

"Is it okay if I take a rain check? I just want to go to bed. I had some soup before, so I'm not hungry."

Sebastian frowned, staring at her with a slightly troubled gaze. "You sure? I can take care of Dex or just be here to help."

"I appreciate it, but I'd like to have some time alone."

She hated the flash of hurt in those smoky eyes. But he nodded. "Of course. Text me if you need anything."

"I will."

She walked him to the door. He hugged her and she hugged him back. He left with a quick searching glance, but she shut the door and locked it before she could change her mind.

Dex whined softly. She petted his head. "I know. But he's not ours, baby. He never was."

Somehow, Chiara sensed today was a sign. The article had slammed her with a truth she'd been desperately avoiding: Sebastian was on borrow. He was the father of Peanut, and they'd formed a tight relationship together. But she was a shadow. A fraud. She'd never be Rory, and a part of her regretted she'd stolen her friend's life, just like she'd been accused of. Sure, her friends and Mike and her work team supported her, but underneath, were they all suspicious she'd craved Rory's life all along? Did they secretly blame her for falling in love with Sebastian now that Rory was gone? And with their secret finally exposed, was it simply more proof they were right?

Sebastian had stolen a piece of her heart that night so many years ago, even with no physical contact. They'd had to become ruthless with their distance in order to keep the secret. But had she cursed them in some weird way? Wished Rory hadn't been in the picture so Chiara could have him instead? She hadn't thought so, but the story opened up the dam, and she couldn't handle the overflow of emotion.

Swallowing back the lump in her throat, she did exactly what she'd told Sebastian—she climbed into bed and pulled the covers to her chin. Maybe this was just temporary. Maybe in a few days, things would get back to normal, and she wouldn't feel like a cheat.

Chiara closed her eyes and tried to sleep.

Chapter Twenty-Seven

Ryder pulled up to the house and stared out the window. Usually, his gut stirred with anticipation and a teenage excitement that thrilled him. Anytime he saw Chiara, her belly full with his child, he was hit again by the realization he'd gotten a second chance at life. At love.

The gift she'd given him was more precious than anything he'd ever received. Chiara made him believe in himself again. Through her, he was finally able to give himself a break. He'd gone back to the Dream On center as a regular, and though Derek's continued absence weighed on his heart, he focused on the kids who were there.

But Chiara was changing. And he was terrified he was losing her.

Ryder let out a breath and rubbed his face. Ever since that damn article hit, she'd been distant. At first, he figured she needed time to wrestle with the feeling of being exposed to the world. God knows he'd experienced the same thing, like his life had suddenly been ripped open for strangers to pick apart and judge.

He told himself when she pulled away from his embrace, or excused herself to go to bed, that she was processing. As she pushed toward her third trimester of pregnancy, Ryder tried to give her space to be moody or spend more time alone. He tried to be available for support without hovering. But it had now been a few weeks, and he sensed the problem was bigger than space, or time, or processing.

It was as if she didn't want him in her life any longer.

Ryder pushed down the mounting fear and swore he'd be patient. Maybe he'd talk to her tonight. They hadn't seen each other most of the week. She cited being busy with work, and he'd decided to back off.

He knocked on the door and balanced the pizza in his hand. Dex barked in welcome, but the flash in her amber eyes gave him the immediate truth.

She wasn't happy to see him.

Ryder forced a smile and ignored the hurt. "Hey, guys. Figured I'd bring a treat for you both. How are you doing?"

She smiled, but there was an obvious strain around her mouth. "We're good. That's so nice of you, but you should've texted first so I'd be more presentable."

Stung, but not wanting her to see, he told the truth. "I wanted to surprise you. And you always look beautiful."

"Thank you." Her answer was pure politeness, and reinforced the horrible distance between them.

He glanced away and set the box down on the counter, then gave Dex the love she wouldn't take. "I know you've been working hard. How's the new article coming?"

Chiara shifted on her feet, looking adorably mussed. Hair twisted in a knot above her head, T-shirt stretched over her growing belly, black yoga pants and bare feet completing the weekend look. Normally, he'd greet her with a kiss, which would lead to deeper caresses, laughter, and maybe a tumble in bed. Now he sensed only the growing distance, a slight chill in the air as she tried to avoid getting close. Frustration flared. He had to address the problem but had no clue how to approach the conversation.

"Good. I just finished and was going to take Dex for a walk."

"I need some fresh air myself. I'll join you, and then we can eat."

She turned from him and fumbled in the refrigerator. "Normally, I'd love that, but I was going to stop at the candle shop and do some business with Ebony. Maybe I can take a rain check?"

Another rain check? His insides shriveled, and ice shattered his heart.

She didn't want him there.

Ryder's fake enthusiasm faded away, and he was left with only the truth. "Chiara, what's going on?"

She avoided his gaze, her shoulders stiff. "Nothing. I just don't want you to be bored. Another time will be better."

"Bullshit. You don't want to be with me."

She turned and finally looked straight at him. Hope surged when he spotted the agony there, the regret along with a guilt he couldn't understand. "Sebastian—"

"No. I need to voice a few things I've been afraid to say." His jaw clenched, and he barreled forward. "Ever since that article came out, you've pulled away. I thought you needed space to process, but it's not helping. You look at me different, and there's a wall between us I thought we'd smashed down. Tell me, baby. What's the matter? What's bothering you?"

Her skin grew paler, and she hugged herself tight. "Do we have to talk about this now? Why is it so wrong to take a break from all the . . . intensity?" Her voice rose like a lash, and he had to brace himself against her words.

Ryder kept his expression neutral. "I didn't know the intensity bothered you."

"Well, it does! Yes, I know this is your baby, but we're not married, and I'm not Rory! I can't give you the perfect little life you expected, and I'm tired of trying. I just want a break from the pressure. God, is that too much to ask?"

The accusation washed over him, and he took it. It was the first time he questioned the way she felt. Sure, they hadn't admitted they loved each other, but every time he held her, kissed her, surged deep inside her, Ryder was telling her she was the one. Each time she arched underneath him or laughed or touched his cheek, her heart was reflected in her gaze.

But now? He didn't know anymore. And he wasn't about to guilt her into being with him for the baby. "What are you saying?" he asked, his voice roughly breaking. "That you don't want to be with me anymore? I wasn't trying to push, Chiara. I thought you wanted this, too. Being with you makes me feel complete."

She let out a breath and backed away, face twisted into an expression he couldn't recognize. "Stop. Please, don't say any more. We got confused because of the baby, and began to think it was us. But it's not. It never was."

Fear burrowed into his heart, and everything stilled. She couldn't have meant what she said. "What are you saying?"

"I need you to leave."

He stared at her in shock. The floor tilted beneath him. "What?"

"Please. You need to go. I don't want to do this anymore, and if you care about Peanut, and me, you'll accept my decision."

He wanted to yell and demand she tell him what was really going on. Instinct told him to push harder, but he was afraid of upsetting her and the baby. She was standing in front of him, yet she'd never felt farther away. But there was one thing left. One thing he'd kept locked up inside that she deserved to know.

"Chiara, I love you."

The silence shattered. He waited, standing before her, vulnerable, hoping she'd take the leap with him.

Her hand mashed against her mouth, and he caught a low moan. He began to move toward her, but she shook her head wildly. "I'm sorry, but this can't work between us anymore. Not like this."

"Chiara—"

"Please! I need to be alone."

His fists clenched by his sides, but he had no choice. "Okay, I'll go. But you need to answer one question. Do you still have feelings for me?"

Her voice was dead and cold. "My feelings for you are because of the baby. Not anything more."

Ryder heard the words, but it was too much to process, like bullets tearing him apart. He stumbled toward the door.

Dex whined softly, glancing back and forth between them, and trotted over to try and block Ryder's exit. It was as if the canine knew leaving wasn't the right thing—that they needed to talk—but there was no other option.

He drove home and wondered why he'd opened himself up for this type of pain a second time. Unfortunately, it was too late. Chiara had thawed the numbness, and now there was nothing to do but feel all of it.

~

Mike opened the door and stared at her in surprise. "Chiara? How are you, honey? Everything okay?"

She nodded, even though she knew lines of exhaustion were carved into her face. She hadn't slept well for days. Between Peanut's nighttime activities and her aching heart, she didn't know what to do anymore. She hadn't even spoken to Malia and Tessa, who she knew would completely support whatever decision she made. But this was something bigger haunting her—the ghost of a woman she'd loved with her heart and soul. The lingering guilt and worry ate at her. And there was only one person who she felt could help.

Mike.

"Yeah, I was wondering if we can talk?"

"Of course, come in." He immediately fussed like a father hen, fetching her favorite seltzer and clearing off the papers from the chair so she could sit. "Baby keeping you up?"

She pulled a face. "How'd you know?"

"Rory's mom had a time of it. Should have known our baby girl was going to be a fighter. And so will yours." A smile wreathed his face. "I'm looking forward to being an honorary grandpa."

"Nothing honorary about it. You were there for me growing up when I needed it. You were the one who showed me what a father should be."

He cleared his throat. "That's a nice thing to say."

"It's the truth, and that's why I need to talk to you. I don't know where to start or how to even explain it. And I'm afraid to upset you."

He tilted his head and regarded her. Then sat down beside her, propping his hands on his knees. "You just start talking and I'll eventually follow. The only thing that will upset me is you not coming clean with what's bothering you."

She nodded. "You know that article they wrote about Sebastian and me?"

Mike gave a disgusted snort. "Trash. I told you not to even think about it. That stuff can't hurt me because it's a load of garbage."

"But what if it isn't?" Her voice trembled. "What if it's the truth after all?"

A frown creased his brow. "What's the truth?"

"I'm afraid I unconsciously stole Rory's life. I did meet Sebastian before her. I'm having the baby with him she dreamed of. I'm the editor in chief of Quench." Tears stung her eyes. "And I've fallen in love with Sebastian. It's not just about the baby anymore. I love him." The emotions washed through her, and she began to cry.

Mike leaned over and hugged her, patting her back in comfort. "Honey, it's okay."

"No, it's not! Every role Rory held in this life I've stolen from her. I feel like an impostor, especially since I'm just a shadow of who Rory was to all of us. I'm just so sorry. Sorry Rory's not here having all this like she deserved."

"All right, that's enough." Mike's voice deepened into a fatherly command, and she raised her head, blinking at him. "Listen up, buttercup. I will not have you talking like that. You've stolen nothing from my daughter and never did. You stepped in so Quench would be successful because you knew how much the company meant to her. You did it to honor her legacy. You were with Ryder out of extraordinary circumstances, but I believe fate brought you both together to give you a second chance. And the reason you denied meeting Ryder first was to protect Rory because you loved her so damn much. Don't you see, Chiara? You haven't taken anything away from me or Rory. You've given it back."

She gulped back a sob and tried to focus on his words.

"Ryder came back into my life because of you and this baby. And I've always known you loved each other, silly girl."

"You did?"

"Watching the two of you together gives me hope for the future. Rory was like a firecracker—she burned bright and bold and beautiful for the time she was here. She'd hate the idea of us spending our precious time unhappy."

"But what if I'm just a stand-in for Sebastian? I keep thinking how badly he wanted a family. Maybe he's mixing up those feelings he had with Rory and transferring them to me because of the baby."

Mike sighed. "The baby is a blessing, but that's not the reason you both love each other." A flicker of pain crossed over his features. "You know, after I lost my wife, I swore there'd never be another woman for me. I figured you could only have love like that once in life. But lately, I've been questioning if it's more of a choice *not* to love someone. That maybe we all get second chances but have to be brave enough to take them."

He shook his head slowly and held her gaze. "Have you ever thought that Rory brought you both together in some universal way? I believe in fate, and when I see the two of you together, it feels right.

You have to let these ideas go, Chiara, or you will lose something really precious and worth fighting for."

Mike's speech hit her in the core, and the truth shattered through her. She kept pushing Sebastian away because of her own insecurities and fears. "I thought maybe it was best to break up with Sebastian and keep our relationship strictly as co-parents."

He snorted. "Yeah, how's that working out for you? I can't imagine it went over well with Ryder."

The memory of his ravaged face when she denied she loved him haunted her. "I hurt him terribly. But I didn't know how to explain these things I was feeling."

"If you're too afraid to speak the truth, you don't get a chance to fight for what you want," Mike said. "Tell Ryder how you feel, no matter how bad it sounds. You deserve happiness, too, Chiara. It's time you believe it."

She hugged Mike and eventually left, mulling over his words. The afternoon was warm and full of sunshine, so she drove to the park and walked a bit before stopping at a bench. There were so many emotions buzzing inside of her.

Maybe, just maybe, she needed to be brave enough to claim love. She'd been pushing it away her whole life, believing it was for everyone else but her. Now, with Peanut growing in her belly, and her heart connected to Sebastian, she was beginning to see how wrong she'd been.

If only Rory could give her a sign. Some type of indication that she forgave Chiara for not telling the truth about that night they'd met. For falling in love with Sebastian. For wanting to have a family with him.

She half closed her eyes and reached out to the universe. The wind stirred. Birds chirped. A butterfly floated by, and she wondered if that was a sign. Rory liked butterflies.

Oh Lord, she was losing her mind.

An older woman sat on the bench close to her. Her gray hair was in a tight perm. She wore polyester pants, comfortable loafers, and, even in the heat, a green sweater stretched over her frail body.

Chiara smothered the trickle of irritation that the woman was interrupting a sacred moment and there were plenty of other benches free. Oh, there was a robin. Rory liked birds a lot, right? Would she send a bird to land on her maybe? She hoped it wasn't bird poop; that could be a sign of anger. Unless—

"Oh, congratulations, dear! You're having a baby!"

"Yes, thank you." Chiara spotted some wildflowers across from her. Rory adored daisies. Maybe a daisy would be dropped in her lap by some child or something? That would definitely be a sign.

"When are you due?"

Chiara held back a sigh. "November."

"Do you know if it's a boy or a girl? Or did you want it to be a surprise?"

Okay, the woman was definitely a chatterer. Chiara forced a smile and tried to be patient. Maybe she'd make an excuse and find another bench, and Rory would visit her there. "It's a girl."

The woman clapped her hands together. "I have a daughter myself! She's a bigwig now in Manhattan. Runs a company and is all sorts of fancy. She took me to a Broadway play last weekend. *The Lion King*. Have you seen it? The costumes and music were beautiful."

Chiara tried to be nice. The woman was probably lonely. "That's lovely. You must be proud of her."

"I am. She's always been good at math, even when she was little. She used to say she was going to run a company one day. Isn't that funny? Most girls dream of marrying princes or being movie stars, and here she was telling anyone who listened she was going to be a leader." The woman laughed with delight. "No one believed her, of course, even after she studied business in college and got her MBA. But she proved them all wrong."

"She sounds amazing," Chiara commented. Was that a ladybug on the bench? That could be a sign—weren't ladybugs supposed to be symbolic of rebirth? Or was that another creature? The ladybug crawled away, and the lady was still talking.

"She truly is. Always told me that following your dreams was the most important thing you can do in life, no matter how big. Said to never apologize for going after something you love—no matter what the obstacles. It wasn't easy for her, either. Her heart was broken many times before she found the right man—most of them couldn't handle her level of success. Guess who she ended up with in the long run?"

"Who?"

"Her high school sweetheart! They'd broken up, lost touch, but when he came back in her life, she said to me, 'Mom, I think he's the one.' Meant to be, I guess. I'm so glad she was brave enough to try again. Now she has everything she wants—love, a great career, and money so she can take me to all the Broadway plays I want!"

Chiara smiled. The woman went on about her daughter, who truly sounded like a special person. She probably would've enjoyed the conversation if she weren't so intent on communicating with Rory.

Finally, Chiara stood up. "Well, it was lovely chatting with you, but I better get going."

"Of course! Good luck with the baby."

"Thank you." She began walking and almost missed the woman's parting words, but the name drifted in the wind and whispered in her ear.

"Thank you for spending time with me, dear. I do love a good talk, but Rory always tells me I'm a bit of a chatterbox."

Chiara stilled, then slowly looked back. "What did you say your daughter's name was?"

The woman smiled with a secret joy that comes only from being a mother. "Rory. Isn't that a beautiful name? She hates it, but I told her it's unique like her. Feel free to borrow it for your own!"

It took a while for her words to process.

And then suddenly, Chiara was laughing.

She tipped her face up to the sun and sky and laughed with her whole heart and soul, because of course, Rory would never give her a subtle sign that could be easily missed.

"Thank you, my friend," she whispered, throat tight with tears. "Thank you."

She began to quicken her pace.

She had to see Sebastian.

Chapter Twenty-Eight

Sebastian opened the door immediately.

Chiara was shocked by his appearance. Old sweatpants hung low on his hips. The ripped white T-shirt he was wearing was stained with chocolate. His hair looked like it hadn't seen a comb for days, and a rough beard had grown in, making him look like a bit of a bad boy. Bare feet picked their way across a carpet littered with papers, books, and some empty water bottles. At least he wasn't on a bender, she thought.

"Did you come to talk?" he asked. His voice was like gravel. Charcoal eyes looked hooded as he gazed back at her, almost like he was trying to protect himself from what he thought she'd say.

Guilt overwhelmed her. She'd hurt him by pushing him away and having him believe he wasn't deserving of love. But her best friend had pretty much smacked some reality into her, and now she was ready.

She just had to convince him.

"I'd like to. I'm calmer now. I'm sorry I said those things to you."

He rubbed his chin. "Me, too. I didn't believe you at first. I thought you were afraid."

Her heart beat fast. "And now?"

"Now I'm afraid you were telling the truth."

She moved closer but stopped at the look on his face. She'd never seen Sebastian so guarded. The old coolness seemed to have overtaken him. Even his mouth was back into that thin-lipped line that used to annoy her. But now she knew better. He was the warmest, kindest, sexiest man she'd ever met, and it was time she showed her own vulnerability to give them a real chance. "I was about some things. But not others. You're right—after that article broke, I began questioning everything between us. Because what I read seemed like the truth. That I had pretty much stolen my best friend's life."

He shook his head. "It was slanted to gain readers. The people in our circle know the truth."

"I know that, but I'm trying to explain how I felt. Suddenly, we're in this relationship together that made me happier than I've ever been. But you were hers first. Every time I turned around, there was something else I felt like I stole from Rory. Her job, her baby, her husband, even her father! It hit me all at once, and I couldn't take it anymore."

"We never planned for it to happen this way," he said roughly.

"I know, but the outcome was the same." Her hands automatically rested on her belly. "I've been afraid, Sebastian."

"Afraid of what?"

She took a breath and took a leap. "That I'll never be enough. For either of you."

A muscle worked in his jaw. He muttered a curse and faced her. Frustration and male anger pumped at her and filled the room. Her heart hammered in her chest from the chemistry and connection leaping to life between them, reminding her of the unconscious pull that was always there, simmering in the air. He stared at her with an implacable gaze. "I can give you all the reassuring words in the world, but it won't help if you don't believe me. Or yourself."

"I know. That's what I finally realized." She walked slowly forward until she was inches away. "I don't want to be afraid any longer. That night you left? I lied." A sob rose in her throat. "I could never feel nothing for you."

Understanding gleamed in charcoal eyes. An array of emotions flickered across his face, and his mouth suddenly softened. "Chiara, don't you see? I love you. If I admit it to myself, I've been a little in love with you since that night when we watched the sunrise. You took a piece of my heart, and yeah, maybe that's wrong. I loved Rory and the life we built together. But she's gone. And I'm here, standing before you, begging for a real chance. I want a life with you, and our baby, not because you're some type of backup plan, but because I love you." He reached out to touch her, then dropped his hand. "But you need to forgive yourself for loving me, too."

"I know."

"What's different now? How do I know you won't run again when things get tough and you compare yourself to Rory? How do I know you finally believe I love you and it's not just about Peanut?"

Chiara stepped close and cupped his cheeks. Her voice was a husky whisper, her defenses completely down. "Because I love you, Sebastian Ryder. Heart and soul. And though I'm giddy to raise this baby girl with you, it's not because of her that I love you. It's because of the man you are inside and out. I intend to spend every day from now on proving it to you, so you'll never doubt me again. Because I'm yours." A joyous smile curved her lips. "Because we were meant to be."

He blinked and raw emotion flickered across his hard features, settling into a fierce satisfaction that made her eyes sting with unshed tears.

His mouth came down on hers.

She kissed him back, the wild thrust of his tongue and burning need to be close creating an intimate chaos that she couldn't fight. Her body came alive under his fingers, his tongue delving deep into her mouth, plundering with a raw hunger that ripped the breath from her body. She hung on, digging her nails into his shoulders, murmuring his name like a mantra. Wild hunger tore at her insides, but he needed to hear everything. "Forgive me for hurting you, my love," she said.

His kiss gentled, nibbling on her lower lip, stroking with his tongue. "I do."

They fell into each other, clothes melting off until they were skin to skin, and took the slow, steady ride of pleasure, breaking apart together, clinging madly as the final barriers lay shattered at their feet.

"I'm glad you came back to me," he whispered, weaving his fingers with hers.

Chiara turned over and looked into his beloved face. "Rory sent me," she said.

And then she kissed him.

Epilogue

Ryder walked into the facility and signed in. He waited awhile, scrolling through his phone, and then his name was finally called. He was escorted into a room that housed bookshelves, some watercolor paintings, and several tables and chairs with space in between them.

He spotted him instantly and walked over with a big smile. "Derek. How are you doing?"

The kid smiled back, and Ryder was happy to see it was the kind that lit up his eyes. "Pretty good. It's nice to finally be able to get some visitors. I appreciate you coming."

Ryder nodded. "It's a strict program for a reason. You okay?"

"I am. How's everyone doing? Did Jeremiah get into the college he wanted?"

"Yep. Unfortunately, him and Tracey broke up again."

Derek rolled his eyes. "Shocker."

"You cut your hair. It looks great."

"You think?" He ran his fingers through the short strands that now hit above his shoulders. "I don't know, I'll have to see. My long hair made me feel secure. Hid me from things."

"Makes sense." The honesty in Derek's voice told Ryder he was doing the work. A few weeks after his disappearance, he'd shown up at his mom's and asked for help. He'd gone back into rehab and was doing well. Ryder was lucky his mom kept in touch with updates.

They chatted about random things. "I'm sorry about that shit I pulled on you," Derek finally said. The shame on his face was hard to take, but he held Ryder's gaze and didn't flinch. "I lied, and you didn't deserve it. Not after everything you've done for me. I just . . . lost my way."

"Apology accepted. It was my fault for giving you the money. I lost my way a bit, too."

Derek smiled gratefully. "It means a lot that you came."

"Anytime."

"Do you think I could ask you for a favor?"

Ryder cocked his head and waited.

"Would you play a game of chess with me? It's funny, when things got dark here, I remembered the game and I began to practice. Now I love it. Something about it makes sense and soothes me. Is that stupid?"

A flowing lightness coursed through Ryder's body, and suddenly, he was laughing. "No, not at all. And hell yeah, I'd love to play a game. Is the rook still your favorite piece?"

"Not anymore. I like the pawn."

Ryder arched a brow.

"They're truly the most underestimated piece in the game."

"How so?"

"They need to cross the entire board in order to trade up. But there's a lot of shit and obstacles in their way. Most don't make it. But the ones that keep moving forward and do?" The kid shot him a mischievous grin. "Well, they turn into a queen."

Ryder laughed and gave him a high five. "That's the best chess analysis I've ever heard."

Derek got the board, and they sat for a long time with the sun streaming through the window and played.

~

"I have a present for you."

They were crowded in the café, smooshed into their regular booth. But their group had expanded, so Mike dragged chairs over to fit everyone.

Sebastian looked at Chiara with surprise. "Me? Aren't I the one who's supposed to be giving you something?"

Tessa snorted. "Damn right. And you'd better or you'll hear from me."

Sebastian grinned. "Warning taken." He looked down at the plain white envelope Chiara had slid across the table. "Should I open it now?"

"Yes, please. I'd like to know what it is," Emma said.

He opened the flap and slid out the check. Stared at it for a few moments. Then turned to Chiara in shock. "This is a check for the Dream On Youth Center."

"Mike, why don't you show Sebastian what we've been up to at Quench," Chiara urged.

Mike unveiled the manila folder and whipped out the letter. It still gave her a thrill every time she saw the name written on the documents. Finally, they'd accomplished their goal after months with the lawyers and deciding the best way to funnel their profits as donations to various charities. The Quench Foundation was finally legal, and the check Sebastian held was the first official remittance.

Sebastian read through the letter, then shook his head. "I can't believe it. This is amazing."

"We wanted the youth center to be the first official recipient," Chiara said quietly.

Sebastian glanced over at Ford. "Did you know about this?"

Ford grinned. "I was just told this week. Do you realize how this can change things? I can't wait to tell the kids."

"That's not all of it," Malia said. "Tessa's internship program is launching. And Pru enrolled! She'll be a part of our growing team after school and be assigned a mentor. We'd like to help people figure out what their passion is so they don't have to be trapped in jobs they hate."

"They'll be so lucky to have you," Emma said, patting Tessa's hand. "I know I am."

Tessa smiled. "Ditto."

"Well, there's no way I'm going to beat this one," Sebastian finally said.

Tessa quirked a brow. "Don't be such a defeatist. I have a few ideas on exactly how to up your game. Ever heard of Tiffany's?"

Chiara laughed and waved her hand in the air. "I don't need a present, silly. I already have everything I ever wanted and needed—right at this table."

"Me, too. But there's one more thing I really want that I don't have," Sebastian said.

She frowned. "What?"

Slowly, he got up from the booth and knelt down on one knee. Chiara stared at him, heart beating madly in her chest, as the man she loved reached out and presented her with a gorgeous diamond ring. But it was his face that held her attention. He looked at her with such tenderness and love, every part inside her melted.

"Chiara Kennedy, would you do me the honor of becoming my wife?"

Tears filled her eyes, and she gave a shaky nod. "Yes."

The crowd gave a whoop, and Sebastian slid the ring over her finger. She took in this perfect moment and told herself to hold it close in her memory.

Then it happened.

A mad shriek split the air, a sound that struck fear into the hardest of hearts. Chiara leaned over and looked down as their daughter scrunched up her face in a temper, mouth pursed, and let out another demanding cry.

"Oh, sweetheart, Mommy's sorry," she cooed, unstrapping her from the car seat and sliding her expertly into Sebastian's arms. "Are you hungry again?"

"I brought the bottle," Sebastian said, running a gentle finger down the baby's smooth, rounded cheek. "We're going to celebrate. Mama and I are getting married!"

Mike stood up, a proud look on his face. "I'll open up some champagne and warm up the bottle." He'd been amazingly hands-on with diaper changing, feeding, and babysitting.

Emma watched him go. Things had seemed to shift between them. Mike now stared at her moodily when he thought no one was looking. And Tessa was slowly getting Emma to be more confident, which was starting to show up in her appearance.

Chiara hoped maybe they still had a love story to follow.

"You can have a glass of champagne, right, babe?" Tessa asked.

"Definitely. I knew we'd be celebrating the foundation, so I pumped forever to be able to indulge. I just didn't know we'd also be celebrating our engagement."

She looked at her daughter, in Sebastian's arms, her daddy gazing at her with such adoration it filled her up. Sebastian looked up and gave a wink, and she laughed with joy over this new life she never dreamed possible.

Lifting her gaze up, Chiara gave silent thanks to her best friend for helping to guide the way.

"Okay, my turn. Hand Veronica over," Tessa announced, squirting some sanitizer into her hands.

Malia frowned. "No, it's my turn. I'm her godmother."

Tessa rolled her eyes. "So am I, idiot. We're co, remember?"

Sebastian gave over the baby, and Chiara's friends shared the embrace, cooing and making funny faces until her cries turned into laughs.

Veronica Ryder was going to have a beautiful life filled with family, love, and friendship.

And so was she.

ACKNOWLEDGMENTS

I'm thrilled to launch this new series with so many talented people.

Big thanks to the amazing Maria Gomez and the Montlake team for supporting my work through the years, from cover design to amazing copyedits and all the details that make a book successful. Thanks to Kristi Yanta for her hard work editing this book to make it shine. I'm grateful to Kevan Lyon, my talented agent, and my team behind the scenes: Nina Grinstead from Valentine PR, and my assistant, Mandy Lawler, who keeps things running as I write.

Thank you to the amazing readers, bloggers, and bookstagrammers for sharing and supporting my work. There are no words for how much I appreciate all of you.

ABOUT THE AUTHOR

Photo © 2012 Matt Simpkins

Jennifer Probst is the *New York Times* and *USA Today* bestselling author of eight series, including The Sunshine Sisters, Stay, The Billionaire Builders, Searching For . . . , Marriage to a Billionaire, The Steele Brothers, Sex on the Beach, and Twist of Fate. Like some of her characters, Probst, along with her husband and two sons, calls New York's Hudson Valley home. When she isn't traveling to meet readers, she enjoys reading, watching "shameful reality television," and visiting a local animal shelter. For more information, visit www.jenniferprobst.com.